CYNTHIA ST. AUBIN   CINDY STARK
KERRIGAN BYRNE   TIFFINIE HELMER

❀ Created with Vellum

*To sisters, born or conjured.
And to our readers, who make every day of our lives magical.*

"*What the hell are you doing?*"

Tierra de Moray jumped with the knife poised over her palm. Ah, crap. She'd been found out. Now there would be hell to pay.

"Aunt Justine, *don't* sneak up on me like that!" She'd have to start the chant over now. Everything had to be precise or the spell wouldn't work, and it *had* to work. She couldn't go on like this any longer without going crazy.

"You don't know what you're dealing with," Justine said, her fingers curling at her sides. Her face lost its mask of youth and she looked more her true age of sixty than the glamour of forty. "You're dabbling in things you don't understand."

It wasn't like she hadn't asked over the years. "It's a simple finding spell." With a lot of summoning added in.

"Tierra, listen to me. Some things are lost for a reason and should never be found." Panic rose in her voice, causing it to shrill and stir the wind in warning.

"Are you ready to share those reasons with me?" Tierra demanded.

Justine had raised her after her mother had died in

childbirth. Whoever her father had been still remained a mystery as the de Moray women didn't keep their men. There wasn't a man alive who had what it took to live with a de Moray witch. One of the many things Justine had refused to speak of, and Tierra had asked, begged, and wheedled over the years to no avail.

She waited with bated breath one last time to see if Justine would finally answer her questions. The tightening of Justine's lips was loud enough.

"I thought so," Tierra muttered, ignoring the hurt that came with her aunt's continued silence. "I need to find out. Part of *me* is missing. Once and for all, I'm putting an end to this." Either she'd finally know what had been taken from her, or she'd lose this void that echoed in her soul for good.

It was a two-part spell. She didn't waste energy if she could help it. Her movements were sure, confident as the earth whispered to her of ancient things, and directed her in the pathways of witches who'd practiced before her. Her bare toes curled into the lush grasses and rich soil underneath her feet.

She was an earth witch and while she rocked on the spring equinox—and the solstices—it was the autumn equinox that was really her night to rule the world. She couldn't wait that long. The circle was closed. The elements of air, water, fire, and earth all present at four directions within the circle representing north, south, east, and west.

Tierra untied the soft cotton shift and it drifted like mist to the ground. She stood naked under the tree limbs, having previously bathed with essential oils in preparation. The Pacific Northwest's old-growth forest of spruce, hemlock, fir, juniper, and bristlecone pines hovered over her in protection, their branches curved as though cradling a child. The air stirred and teased the long strands of her hair, the color of burgundy wine, in a dance around her torso. The scent of burning sage, lavender, and thistle wafted in the crisp night air.

"This is nonsense, Tierra. Don't make me put an end to this." Justine tried to break into the circle and was repelled back a few steps. It spoke to her aunt's level of power that the push hadn't sent her all the way home.

Justine could try, but she wouldn't be able to enter the circle. Tierra had planned to perform this spell tonight, on the spring equinox, with its blood moon, making sure she'd be more powerful. More powerful than her aunt.

For as long as Tierra could remember, she felt as if a significant part of her had been ripped from her soul. The only thing that made sense was an article she'd read about soldiers who'd lost limbs in battle, and the phantom pain that never left them. She had all her arms and legs, fingers and toes, but on another level something just as important had been severed from her.

Justine wasn't talking, and neither was the coven.

The earth would reveal her secrets.

"*Stop this, Tierra.*" There was a threat in her voice now as Justine tried to tear into the circle, her fingers shaped like claws. This time the circle tossed her back a few yards. The next attempt would knock her on her ass.

Tierra restarted the spell her aunt had interrupted and raised the knife until the light of the blood moon glinted crimson off the blade.

"*Keeper of secrets, release what was taken, Hear me now—answer in three*

> *Return to me what has been forsaken,*
> *By earth, air, fire, and sea...*"

She continued to chant as power infused her body and the air charged with energy. Her aunt's yelling and repeated attempts to break into the circle disappeared as Tierra lost herself in the spell. Her lungs expanded, and her heart raced. New spring flowers swirled in a tunnel of frenzy as vapor in the air caught fire and rained sparks. She drew the blade across her palm and blood flowed into the copper bowl, mixing with the dandelion, myrrh, sage, and wormwood.

Something tore free from her, stealing her breath, and the contents of the bowl burst into flame. Silvery, iridescent smoke twirled like ribbons into the starry, midnight sky, splitting and then shooting three different directions. An implosion shook the circle and the resulting percussion sealed the spell.

Tierra was thrown backward. The soft meadow grasses reached up to cushion her fall. She lay there, catching her breath as her mind raced.

The earth sighed and a truth she was never supposed to know manifested itself.

Her spell had broken another. A banishing spell as old as she was.

Whatever had been taken from her had also been banished never to be reunited. The acrid taste of pine was sharp on Tierra's tongue.

"What have you done?" Justine whispered, though the words sounded like a scream inside Tierra's head.

Justine's jade eyes were wide and scared, and her cherry-red hair had been teased into a chaos of twists and coils around her ashen face. Her aunt's mop of hair was always restrained, her clothes perfectly neat. Nothing about her was restrained right now. She looked wild and desperate.

Just how hard did Justine try to break into the circle?

A skittering of fear shivered over Tierra's skin. Shaking, she climbed to her feet, breathing like she'd hiked to the top of the Olympic Mountains.

"Would you quit overreacting?" she said, reaching for the shift to cover her nakedness as the cold needled in. "It's not like I just brought about the end of the world."

"You insolent witch." Justine slowly got to her feet, her face a mask of anger and terror. "That's exactly what you've done."

I

MOIRA

By Cynthia St. Aubin

❧ I ❧

"What in the Sam Hill you doing, girl?"

Moira Malveaux shooed the teacup pig out of her suitcase and tossed in a handful of silky black panties. "Hog-tying a catfish. *Packing*. What's it look like I'm doing?"

Uncle Sal shifted his wad of snuff from one stubbled cheek to the other and adjusted the straps on his waders. Silver-black hair swooped from his orange trucker cap like wings. His lanky form invaded her small doorway with the slouching angles of a scarecrow. "What for?"

Moira twisted her wavy mass of dark auburn hair into a bun which she secured with the well-gnawed pencil from her night stand. A breeze whispered across her damp neck like a lover's sigh. "Don't know yet."

"Packin' a bag for nowhere. Well, that sounds like a fool thing to do." Sal reached down to Moira's pillow and tried to pet the little pig. It gave an indignant squeal and climbed back into the suitcase.

"Oh, I don't think so, mister." Moira scooped up her pet with one hand and kissed the downy spot between his ears before setting him in her sock drawer. The lack of fur gave his pink skin an almost human warmth.

"Momma's trying to pack, Cheeto. Besides, you know you're coming with me."

"He's coming with you *where?*" The brown gob of Sal's spit sailed through the open window by Moira's bed and married with the mossy sludge below.

"Already told you. I don't know yet." A stack of tank tops and tight T-shirts joined the panties. Several pairs of worn cut-offs kept them company.

"You ain't gonna get very far with a plan like that."

Moira snorted. "Last I heard, you and *plans* were scarcely acquainted."

"Now that ain't true a'tall. I was *plannin'* on taking the General Custer out on the water this afternoon. I was *plannin'* on taking my favorite niece with me. And I was *plannin'* on heading to the HooDoo Shack to sink a few when I got back."

"You were *plannin'* on making me stir you up a net full of crawfish so you have money to get shit-faced with Red, Mookey, and Little Earl." Moira squelched the bubble of affection that rose at the mention of her unofficial uncles. *Unofficial* kin was the only kind Moira had.

"Still a plan," Sal protested. His self-conscious smile failed to soften the ice crystallizing around Moira's heart.

"'Fraid you're gonna have to figure out how to catch them fair and square," Moira said. "My crawdad whispering days are over."

"Aww come on, Moira Jo! Ain't no one can talk them out of the water like you can. My business will go belly up quicker than a whore in the bog if you take off."

Moira dropped her well-seasoned cast iron skillet into the suitcase and wheeled on her uncle. "It's Moira *Joule* goddammit, and don't you *Moira Jo* me! I'm about damn tired of you feeding me bullshit so I can keep you flush in booze and chew. I want to know *what* I am, and I want to know *now.*"

"What do you mean *what you are*? You're my niece."

As ever, Uncle Sal was as slippery as a corn snake when it came to any discussions of her past. Moira herself tended to crash through the underbrush like a wild hog, her arrival announced through commotion, her legacy—the destruction left in her wake.

"You know any other *nieces* that can talk fish onto a line, or crawdads into a net?" she asked.

Sal regarded the unfinished wood floor of the small bedroom where Moira had grown up the only student of his unconventional tutelage. "Not directly."

"Not at *all*. You know more than you're telling me. I don't know where I'm going, but I know there'll be answers when I get there."

"What makes you so sure?"

The answer to this came easily, but not in a form Sal would understand.

Words on the wind.

Moira had awoken in the sweaty depths of the night to see the Spanish moss outside the window reaching for her like witches' hair. Branches spread their fingers in slow motion. The world reorganized its spin around her—a new axis. Moonlight thickened the air to pale silk that slid across her skin, and her every movement unfolded through space as dense as seawater.

And then, she'd heard it.

Syllables spoken not to her ears, but to her soul.

"Return to me what has been forsaken,
By earth, air, fire, and sea..."

The ground had been warm as she padded out of their small, tin-roofed fishing shack and walked to the bayou's edge. Mud anointed her feet like a poultice, sending a tingling through her ankles and up her legs, clear to the space around her heart. Strange that such a sensation should be borne of earth and water alone.

Animal voices added a haunting refrain to the incantation. The darkness alive with collective hums, chirps, and croaks of a thousand creatures, calling to her.

Calling her *home*.

Morning had found her naked as a jaybird beneath the cypress trees, feet on the bank and half-covered in moss. She'd pulled her negligee back over her head and walked into the house, knowing only that she needed to pack.

Well, shower, eat some cold fried chicken, and *then* pack.

A girl had to have priorities.

"Well?" Uncle Sal's expectant question reeled her back into the present.

"You wouldn't understand." Moira leaned across the scarred leather suitcase so she could zip it closed.

A foreign expression clouded the weathered brown skin of Sal's face.

Hurt.

He sank down on the edge of her bed. Moira looked at the denim quilt dipping beneath him, already missing the weight of all those faded scraps cocooning her in at night. No way to pack it. Just another thing she'd have to leave behind.

Moira sat next to him, their combined weight causing her mattress to groan in protest. *Good thing she never brought her work home.*

"I'm sorry, Uncle Sal. I just..." Moira consulted the backs of her hands for an answer she knew wouldn't come. "I just can't be here anymore."

Uncle Sal shifted, his weight pulling her off kilter just enough so she had to lean the opposite direction to keep from sinking toward him. He had ceased to be a bigger object in her universe in any capacity save size. Was this realization a burden to her? Or a comfort? On this day, she couldn't yet say.

The little pig pushed his way out of the wallow he'd

constructed in her pillow to scoot into her now available lap. His hooves pressed indentations into the length of her tanned thighs as he turned his habitual two-and-one-quarter circles before settling himself in the trough where her legs met. His warm belly against her skin brought a small measure of comfort.

"If I told you where you come from, would you stay?" Sal ventured a sideways glance at her from beneath his dark brows.

Moira let the look slide off into the ether, where all missed communications gathered.

"I don't know." Moira felt the lie burn its way down her throat like the moonshine Uncle Mookey cooked up in a still he'd rigged from stolen car parts. The taste of dishonesty was twice as oily and half as pleasant.

She *did* know.

She knew that no matter what left Uncle Sal's lips, she would be leaving Stump Bayou today. Yet the prospect of having this question answered proved too seductive to resist. There wasn't another question on earth that could scoop out room beneath her roots, make her vulnerable to this kind of bargain.

"Was twenty-something years ago," Sal began, pulling his ball cap off to mop the sweat from a liver-spotted brow with a wadded bandana from the pocket of his overalls. "Me, Red, and Mookey was out on the bayou but hadn't caught more than heat rash and a chapped ass. It was hell for everyone that summer. Like the whole damn parish was cursed."

Something broke loose inside of Moira and skittered away into the shadows to avoid direct scrutiny. *A curse.*

"It was almost sundown," he continued, "and we'd just about give up and decided to come back when Mookey starts haulin' in the net. Next thing I know, we was ankle-deep in crawfish and Mookey's hollerin', 'We done caught a baby!'"

Wind stirred the red-black tendril that brushed Moira's cheek. "You pulled me from the bayou in a *net?*"

"Sure enough did. And a helluva lotta other critters too. Seems they was keeping you company. You shoulda seen Red just about water his britches when he tried to pick you up and a snapping turtle damn near made sure that fool could only count to seven."

Moira fought a smile as the scene played itself out in her mind. In addition to running the town's only car repair shop, Uncle Red periodically provided entertainment as a part-time gator wrestler—a hobby which had cost him his left thumb and his right pinky.

She saw Red as he must have been in those days— short and stocky with muscles earned by manual labor, blasted with freckles, clad in worn jeans and white tank top, his orange hair bright as molten glass in the dying sunlight. Uncle Sal always looked like pulled taffy next to Red. Moira could practically see Sal falling backwards, off the rickety three-legged stool he perched on when gutting fish. His hooting laughter would have set the blue light flashing off his raven-black hair.

All of this she could have conjured easily to memory. It was herself she couldn't see. Couldn't fathom the baby she might have been wriggling among the muddy creatures pulled from the bayou's bottom.

"I was alive?" she asked.

"Alive and wailing like you's being skinned," Sal said. "I flipped the snapping turtle over the side and scooped you up. You's so muddy we couldn't hardly tell if you were a he or she at first. Mookey motored us back toward the dock while Red and me got you cleaned up as best we could. You didn't think much of your first bath, I'll tell you that right here and now. I s'pose I wouldn't have neither, with the ice and all."

"Ice?" Moira asked, the gears in her brain grinding. "What ice..." The image came to her at once and complete: the battered green beer cooler that stored both beverage and bait on her uncles' fishing excursions. "You cleaned me off in the *beer cooler*?"

Sal's bony shoulders jerked toward his ears. "Was the best option at the time."

"So, you pulled me out of the bayou in a crawdad net and cleaned me up in the beer cooler. Then what?"

"We figured you might be upset on account of bein' nekkid and cold, so Red stripped off his shirt and we made you some britches, and I wrapped you up tight in a gunnysack like I seen ladies do sometimes. When that didn't quiet you down, we figured maybe you was hungry."

Or maybe I wasn't thrilled with a sweat-stained diaper and a onesie made of burlap, Moira thought. A pent-up breath hissed out between her teeth. "Please tell me you didn't feed me night-crawlers."

Sal managed to look shocked. "Of course not! What kinda fool you take me for, girl?"

Several answers suggested themselves, but Moira kept her mouth closed around them.

"We gave you a beer," Sal continued.

"You gave beer to a *baby*?"

Cheeto squeaked in protest at Moira's raised voice. She laid a hand on his back to quiet him.

"Well we was out of grape Nehi," Sal answered. "And we didn't think you could manage the pickled pigs' feet Mookey'd brought, since you didn't have any teeth."

Moira saw Cheeto's eyes narrow, and she gave his curly tail a little tug. The pig returned his gaze to the window.

"What happened when you got me back to town?" Moira asked.

"We took ya home of course. Gave you a proper bathin'. Made you some grits. Red's little girl had just growed out of her baby clothes, so he had Mavis run some over."

"But you didn't take me to a doctor? Or call the law?"

"We thought about it," Sal said.

Moira knew protracted silence marked the coming of something he didn't want to say.

"Moira, if you's kidnapped, or missing, we'd have heard about it. People don't come pleasure cruisin' through this neck of the woods. You know that better than anyone. Best we could figure, whoever..." Sal paused, the effort to find better words digging creases into his face. "It wasn't an accident, you being in that swamp. Whoever put you there done so on purpose. We figured it was best if they went on thinkin' they'd finished the job."

They didn't come back and try again. The unspoken sentiment fluttered through Moira's mind like a dropped handkerchief.

"That, and we's afraid of what might happen if folks found out about your..."

"My *what*?"

Sal pushed himself up from the bed, the floorboards releasing a chorus of groans as he paced the small length of her room. "We were all over the bayou that day, you see? We was alone. If someone had left you, we'd have seen it. By the looks of you, you'd been in that water for *days*. You shoulda been dead."

Truth stabbed as deep as any blade, and Moira felt it slide between her ribs, her breath escaping from the puncture.

Sal knelt before her and wrapped one of her hands in his leathery grip. "You know how *funny* people round here can be about anyone who's different."

Moira knew all too well. She had daily felt the barbed stares, the suspicious glances scalding her skin like acid, the disapproving huffs and whispered words that trailed in her wake.

The familiar empty ache found her.

"You should have left me." Her tears were warm as they fell on her thighs. "Saving me was a mistake."

Sal's bony hands tightened around her own. "Don't you never say that," he insisted. "You wasn't a mistake. You was a *miracle*."

Bitterness hardened around the edges of Moira's words. "Different names for the same thing."

"They're not either. But you are right about one thing," Sal said.

"What's that?"

Sal's eyes were bright with a sheen of tears when Moira finally found them. "Good can come from both."

A sob closed Moira's throat as she flung her arms around her uncle's neck and squeezed him to her. The scent of salt, tobacco, and cheap aftershave bloomed from the leathery neck she wet with her tears.

"It's all right, girl," Sal soothed. "You go on and do what you need to. You just don't forget us."

Moira felt Sal's bones beneath his slackening skin as she hugged him tight. Each year sanded a little more of him away. His shape in the world, in her life, became less precise with each passing day. How much of him would be left when—*if*—she found her way back? "I won't forget, Uncle Sal," she promised, scrubbing away her morbid thoughts. "Never could."

"Good," he said. "You about packed? S'pose I can help you get your things out to the Badger."

The Badger seemed as good a name as any for the 1969 Plymouth Barracuda parked beneath the cypress tree beside their shanty. Low, growly, and densely built, the Badger had mowed over more than a few ditches chasing down a soused Uncle Sal. Some nights, Sal's phantom butt cheeks jiggled above the shifting mist as she motored home from the HooDoo Shack after a long shift of slapping away the patrons' unwelcome pinches and gropes.

Sal found britches a sight too confining after a night on the bottle.

A fresh wave of grief assailed Moira as she peeked out the window at the Badger. Leaves stuck to the glossy black hood from the night's mixture of wicked wind and strange omens.

As a child, she had walked these roads until the soles of her feet were tougher than leather. The thought of not blowing down them in a cloud of dust was as disjointing as waking up to a different face in the mirror. They were as much part of her spiritual topography as the veins that carried blood to heart. "I'm gonna have to leave her here, I'm afraid," Moira said.

"Leave her here? Why?"

Sal looked properly shocked. In previous days, Moira would have sooner left her beloved pig for the buzzards before parting with the predatory machine she powered down the tangled back roads of Terrebonne Parish.

"I'm headed to the airport," Moira explained. "And I can't leave her settin' in the lot till Judgment Day. Lord knows what I'd owe for parking by the time I got back. I'll pole Skip over to Little Earl's dock and have him run me into St. Bernard. I can catch a ride into New Orleans from there."

"So, you know at least that much about where you're headed." A wary shine waxed Sal's eyes. "What are you gonna do when you get there?"

Moira shrugged and scratched beneath Cheeto's chin with her index finger as the little pig leaned into her hand. "I'll know." Of this, she had total confidence. Some unseen anchor had sunk deep into her middle, binding her to a larger force whose trajectory she could either follow willingly or be dragged behind. The longer she sat talking here on the bed with Sal, the tighter the rope pulled, the more unbearable the pressure to take flight became.

"You got money?" Sal asked.

"Enough," Moira answered. The lie clung to her throat as she swallowed it down. But she found she was glad she had spent her last wad of tip money stocking the fridge and cupboards now she knew Sal and the boys would be on their own for a while.

"Well," Sal said, rising from the mattress, "I guess you better get on your way then. Light's best on the water with the sun overhead."

Moira knew. Knew the way she had always known when it came to the water. She could look at its surface and read it as clearly as the expression on a beloved's face. She reached for the oversized shoulder bag she had stitched together from the worn-out camouflage pants Red always picked up from the Army Surplus. More than four decades out of Vietnam, he'd still wear nothing but.

Lifting the flap on the compartment she'd sewn especially for the purpose, she tucked Cheeto inside, sliding his collapsible water and food bowls into additional pockets.

Last of all, she slid her feet into the worn flip-flops by the door, already hating the thought of keeping them on until she reached whatever destination was in store for her. The stairs sang their familiar lullaby of squeaks and groans as she and Sal made their way down and out the screen door.

Moira paused at the patch of dead grass by the Badger's tail pipe, grass daily blown flat when she'd light out for wherever she was going.

She laid a hand against the car's rear spoiler, already warm from the spring sun. "You be good," she instructed.

The dock shifted beneath their feet like a funhouse hallway as they made their way out to Skip, the old pontoon lashed to a metal peg by a length of slimy rope. Moira hopped down first and waited for the boat to settle before reaching up to take her duffle bag from Sal. "Promise me you'll get Bunky out to look at the dock."

Sal snorted and spat another brown glob into the already murky water. "Bunky Robichaud's got a pecker for a head and brain small enough to fit."

Moira bit her bottom lip to keep from smiling. If Uncle Sal had actually *seen* Bunky's junk, he'd know that was more compliment than insult. "That may be," she admitted. "But he's a decent carpenter and he's already agreed to fix the dock. Ordered in the new poles an' everything." *After I rode him to glory and back*, came her mind's unwanted addendum. "Promise me?"

"Oh, all right," Sal grumbled. "But I'm hidin' the beer before he comes over."

"I told you," Moira said. "You ain't got to worry about that no more. He and Layla are back together. He's not drinkin'."

"You never did tell me how you managed that," Sal said, that familiar suspicion creeping back into the creases of his face.

"Never told Layla neither," Moira winked. "And it's better that way." A brief flash of borrowed anger welled up inside her, shaking her enough to sit her down hard. She covered it up by reaching for the rope, which Sal unlooped in three practiced swings.

Sal paused at the top of his motion, holding the last line tying her to the life she knew. His eyes filled with unshed tears as he reached across the distance to put one leathery hand on her cheek. "You be careful, Moira Jo. Okay?"

Moira laid her hand atop his before pulling it to her lips to kiss his bony knuckles. "Only if you are."

Sal gave her his customary nod and hooked his thumbs into the straps on his waders as she slid out the pole she would use to push her clear of the weed and swamp grass at the end of the dock. The can opener-sized motor bogged down if a duck so much as farted near the blades.

Uncle Sal shrank into a slim shadow on the horizon as Moira was pushed farther away from home by time and tide, disappearing entirely as she rounded a lazy bend toward the mainland.

As soon as she was out of sight, Moira cut the motor and waited for the water to still before looking over the side of the boat. Her own image stared back at her on the shifting surface, her wide aquamarine eyes taking on a greenish cast from the surrounding moss. The hair she unbound from its penciled pin-up spilled well past her shoulders in dark, unruly waves. Her full lips whispered words upon the water's face as she dipped a single finger into the bayou.

The familiar surge of warmth flooded her, swimming in her blood, dancing between her cells, rippling out from this one point of contact. Perfect silence descended. A stillness beyond thought and being.

She submerged her hand to the wrist, turning it palm up like a cup, waiting for the silken slide of the body she beckoned. The briefest flash of gray announced the arrival of one of the swamp's own elder statesmen—a catfish she had named Methuselah, who had long since grown too large to comfortably rest in one hand.

The simple stream of his thoughts wound through her anxious mind like a cool ribbon. A pure distillation of life at its core: the search for food, mate, and progeny.

Words were not needed, but Moira spoke them anyway. As much a prayer to soothe her soul as a supplication to the fish. "I'm not going to be here for a while. You think you could see that Sal and the boys do well enough to eat? Not too good, mind. You know where the extra goes."

Moira had fished enough beer cans out of the bog

under Methuselah's watchful eye to know he took her meaning. The return message arrived in the sensation of ripples pushing through Moira's mind.

He would do so.

"Thanks." She stroked her thumb between his wide-set alien eyes, but only once. Catfish were more like cats in this respect than most people would guess. His departure sent a spray of droplets flying, jewels that caught the sunlight just in time to disappear back into the swamp.

Hand still in the water, Moira drew to mind her destination, and asked the bayou to comply.

And it did.

It always had.

❦ 2 ❦

"Awful lot of young men around here going to be disappointed," Little Earl teased. A crooked grin occupied only the half of his mouth facing Moira. The side nearest the driver's window of his '78 Ford F-150 had been largely uncooperative since the stroke that felled him from a barstool at the HooDoo Shack a couple summers past.

Times like those were an unwelcome reminder that those closest to her were the ones she could help the least. The kind of healing she had a knack for required a *hands-on* approach Moira just couldn't bring herself to apply to her uncles, unofficial or no.

She been in fist fights on more than one occasion at the suggestion that her relationship with Sal, Mookey, Red and Little Earl had been anything but avuncular. Doc Fontenot, St. Bernard's dentist, had gotten awfully good at bridgework thanks to her. Without his efforts, she'd wager half the parish's female population could suck sweet tea through a straw without opening their teeth.

"And an awful lot of women going to be pleased as punch," Moira retorted.

"That's the truth," Earl agreed. "You never been too popular with the womenfolk around here."

"Don't I know it?" Moira reached into the camou-flaged bag on her lap to offer Cheeto a bite of potato chip, which he eagerly snaffled up. "Hell, Edna as good as ran me down at the Piggly Wiggly the other night."

Earl's ruddy face tightened at the mention of the steel-haired battle-axe who presided over his home with an iron fist and a rolling-pin used more often for thumping skulls than making biscuits. "She's just got the wrong idea about you. That's all."

"I don't care if she is your wife," Moira replied. "She's two parts hen and one part gator. All beak and a big bite."

"It's just that not everyone understands how you..." He paused to scratch the back of his neck, hork, and spit into one of the many discarded wrap-pers littering cab before continuing. "How you *help* folks."

"When she caught you in Earl Jr.'s hospital room that night—"

"He woulda died," Moira insisted. "He was more tore up than a trailer park in tornado season." The memory of Earl Jr.—Little Earl's son—jacked into a multitude of tubes and machines surged back to her. Big Earl—Earl Jr.'s granddaddy—had only nodded as he cleared the room, knowing of Moira's *abilities* firsthand. At least, it had been her *hand* that pulled the Earls' el-dest statesmen back from a heart attack he'd suffered on her porch one sticky evening.

"*I* know that," Little Earl assured her. "But seeing as he'd just rolled his truck and was in the intensive care waiting for surgery you bein' on top of him like you was just didn't set well with his momma."

"Surgery," Moira pointed out, "that he didn't end up needing after all, if you'll remember."

"Oh, I remember." Earl's easy laugh filled the truck like a floodlight. "That doctor did get mighty fetched up at you, though. I think he was actually looking forward to doin' something other than sewing up a bar fight for once."

Sudden exhaustion crept over Moira like a fog as the sensory memory of Edna's disgust and rage filled her head with broken glass. Lord, was she tired of other people's psychic backwash. The trees on either side of the road seemed to sag with it as well, their hanging Spanish moss making them look like mourners at a procession of which she was always the deceased. "I don't like the means any better than Edna does."

"Neither would your Uncle Sal," Earl said.

They were coming to ruts they had already worn in the road now. A conversation as at home in this old truck as the chain of beer tabs hanging from the rearview mirror.

The cracked ridge around the old truck's bench seat pinched the back of Moira's thighs. She readjusted the coarse saddle blanket that doubled as a seat cover. "You swore you wouldn't tell him."

"And I won't. I'm just sayin' you might oughta think about what helpin' folks has cost you. That's all."

"Would you rather Earl Jr. had died?" Moira asked.

A rim of white appeared around Earl's thin lips as he pressed them together. He squeezed the steering wheel like it might give back some reassurance in return. "No, Moira Jo. I'm glad of what you did. I'd be lyin' if I said otherwise."

He paused, but Moira knew better than to speak into the silence.

"Earl Jr. was the fool who drank a twelve pack with his buddies and thought it'd be a good idea to drive home in the dark." Earl's eyes fixed on hers for as long as the road would allow. "You understand?"

Cheeto's small hooves folded down the edge of the bag closest to Moira as his wet, pink nose twitched in the direction of the chips she held at her side. "No more," she said. "You've been eatin' like a—" she paused, looking down into his shining black eyes. "Well, you haven't been eatin' very good."

"Moira?" Earl pressed.

"No," she said finally. "I don't understand. I don't understand why I can do these things if I'm not supposed to help people. I don't understand why helpin' people brings nothing but trouble to my door. I don't understand one goddamn thing."

The truck bumped along in silence for the space of a few moments.

"It ain't your job to save everyone, Moira. Sometimes folks need to experience what they've got comin' to them. Sometimes that's what it takes to learn."

"And if they won't learn? You're just supposed to sit back and watch them hurt?"

"Pain ain't the problem for most people" Earl answered. "Pain is just the booby prize for dancin' with their demons."

Moira shivered despite the oppressive wall of body-temperature humidity beginning to kick up from the marshes. "Or for dancin' with me."

"You can't think like that, girl. You was made the way you was for a reason. I believe that." Engine grease hid in the creases of the thick finger Earl brushed by his eye. "We all do."

"Thanks, Uncle Earl," Moira said.

Little Earl's uneven smile hitched up further in her direction, a sure sign she was in for some ribbing. "You keep talkin' that nonsense, we're going to have to fix you up with Beau Enos once you come back."

Taken together, Bucephelus Enos's nickname sounded to Moira like a part of the body that ought to be kept out of the sunlight. Which, when she thought about it, could be pretty well applied to the rest of Beau as well. He'd spent most of their childhood peeking up skirts and dangling from trees, pretending to be a possum.

He also wore his underwear outside his pants on occasion.

"You been threatenin' me with Bucephelus since kindergarten," Moira snorted.

"And he's still willin'. Why, ever since you healed him up after them kids got aholt of him—"

"We are *not* fixin' to talk about that," Moira interrupted. She took a breath against the memory as it rose, trying not to recall the taste of fear on Beau's split and bleeding lip, nor the shocking size of what she'd found beneath his patched overalls.

"Well," Earl said at last. "You keep talkin' like a fool—"

"I might as well marry one," Moira finished for him. "You know, that never did make any sense."

"Don't have to make sense." Earl straightened in his seat and raised his chin in mock pride. "I'm an old bastard from *Looziana*. So long as I'm colorful, I'm doin' my job."

"Then you're due for a raise, by my estimation," Moira laughed.

"Been tellin' management that for years." Earl winked.

Moira's breath caught at the sight of the New Orleans airport rising from the flat flood plain stretched out before them. "Thanks for bringing me all this way," she said, slipping her feet back into the sandals she had discarded when she folded up cross-legged in the passenger's seat.

"'Course," Earl answered. "Was the least I could do. You fixed okay for money?"

Moira jerked a hasty nod. She'd resort to other means of acquiring cash long before she would let Little Earl give her a dime. A worm of dread already gnawed at her gut, thinking of him spending the gas money to drive back to Terrebonne. "Will you check in on Uncle Sal for me?"

"Often as I can," Earl agreed.

"And don't let him drive the Badger," she said, depositing the keys in the dusty cup holder between them. "Last time he tried, he just about tested if it's amphibious."

Earl picked up the keys and dropped them into the front pocket of his worn work shirt as he pulled up to a curb in front of the wide terminal doors. "She's safe with me. You got a plane ticket?"

"Not yet," Moira admitted. "But I will."

"They let you buy them things with cash? I didn't think you had any cards."

"I'm sure I'll be able to work something out," Moira said, gathering straps and adjusting pockets.

"So long as it's some*thing* and not some*one*. Promise me that?"

Moira flashed him a disarming smile and planted a quick peck on his cheek before scooting out the passenger's door. "No."

❅   3   ❆

Y*es.*
    First she would say it. Then she would scream it.

Only fair for taking *his* window seat.

Nicholas Kingswood allowed himself a leisurely glance down the length of the interloper's long, tanned legs, ending in bare feet propped up against the seat in front of her. The slut-red lacquer on her shapely toes brought to mind candy apples. His mouth watered in anticipation. He'd suck them until she cried. Until she *begged.*

Millennia on this planet had left him with precious little tolerance for small annoyances. After a few thousand years, they tended to add up. Here, the window seat he'd paid for and specifically requested was now occupied by a woman who displayed no intention of vacating it.

Head tipped against the window, dark eyelashes feathered against her cheeks, the woman appeared to have nodded off waiting for other passengers to board.

It had been a couple weeks since he fucked in an airplane bathroom. Those legs would look marvelous braced against a wall on either side of his hips.

But then, her delicate fingers would be equally attractive wrapped around his cock, though the best view would have to be obstructed beneath a blanket. In his opinion, a quick jerk was the only acceptable use for those cheap-ass scraps of fabric in the overhead bin.

He might even make her come as a reward.

Right after she got the fuck out of his seat.

He followed the line of her legs back toward the seat in question, and was delighted to find the view just as promising. Denim cut-offs and a skin-tight black tank top dipping low across breasts rising in time with her measured breaths. Wherever the *HooDoo* Shack was, he would have to make a pilgrimage simply to thank them for splashing their name across those tits. He had every intention of tracing the graphic with his tongue. But first— "They're real."

Nick looked around, but saw only the flight attendants scuttling around in the galley. Which is precisely how he had arranged it, save for one detail: her.

"You stand there with your mouth hanging open much longer, some critter is like to set up house in there."

This time, he saw her lips move—the sole sign indicating she had said anything at all. Her head remained against the window, her eyes closed, her arms crossed against her flat stomach.

"I'm sorry?" Nick forewent an accent, though anything British typically spread legs the quickest. His Yorkshire would have been nice for her. A taste of the crude gamekeeper, Oliver Mellors, in *Lady Chatterley's Lover*. It drew out the hard "U" in any word to a guttural grunt. His cock twitched at the thought of spitting filthy words into her ear while he pounded her against the aluminum sink. But with her smoky, honeyed southern drawl, any accent off the continent ran the risk making her feel uneducated. It wouldn't do.

Her lids lifted, revealing aquamarine eyes twice as cold and hard as the gems they resembled. "What for?

Staring at my tits ain't a crime. Hell, it's practically a pastime where I come from."

Nick treated her to a rueful laugh as he ducked under the overhead bin and slid into the roomy first-class aisle seat with a practiced ease. At six foot three, performing this maneuver gracefully had taken the better part of a century to master. But master it he had, like so many other pursuits.

His leather attaché case stashed beneath the seat in front of him, he turned toward her to shrug out of his suit coat, watching for the telltale flick of her icy eyes assessing his broad shoulders. It didn't come.

She only chewed her full lower lip and slid an uneasy glance at the bag by her feet as passengers began to shuffle in like livestock through a chute.

Had the bag moved just now? He had been too distracted by her white teeth sinking into the red pillow of her lip to give the matter his full attention.

"I hope you're not too hard on them," Nick answered at last. "I imagine even the most cultured academic could be quickly rendered witless in your presence."

The woman rolled her eyes and snorted. "If they had any wits to speak of in the first place. Most men don't, in my experience."

Nick made a show of rolling the cuffs of his tailored dress shirt back to reveal powerfully sculpted forearms, always a trump card in his favorite game. "I'm not most men." He reached a hand across the empty seat separating them. "Nicholas Kingswood."

She looked at his hand from beneath dark lashes. Only a split second, but her hesitation told him things she herself would not.

"Moira J—" she paused, rearranging her thoughts before grasping his hand with surprising force. "Moira Malveaux." The name rolled from her tongue like a bolt of silk, but the palm she pressed into his was as rough

as any laborer's. God, but that friction would be delicious when she—

Pain seared through Nick's fingers, shooting up his
veins like white-hot fire on its way to his heart. In its
wake came a rush of pleasure so fierce and dark, it
threatened to steal his consciousness.

A witch.

Nick read the fear plain and pale on her face as she
released his hand with a sudden, horrified gasp. *Had she
recognized him?*

They stared at each other in stunned silence, neither of them capable of summoning words to circum-
scribe what had just happened.

Until hers came in a jet that would shame a fire
hose.

"Oh God!"—a word that in her pronunciation
sounded more like *gaw-uhd*—"Did I smush your lil'
hand? I'm so sorry! I forget sometimes that not all folks
are used to physical work and all. Here you are in your
nice suit and your soft hands, and I go grabbin' and
shakin' it like a coyote with a rat."

The swell of defensive anger had Nick volleying
reckless words in reply. "Soft? You think power comes
from jerking off a fishing rope? I could show you—"

"Would you like me to hang up your coat, Mr.
Kingswood?" The flight attendant's arrival dragged him
back into the present moment, the slideshow of gore
and torment that marked his long life evaporating
under fluorescent cabin lights.

He could feel himself collecting, gathering once
again into something solid and stable. "Would you?"

"Certainly." The smile she gave barely scraped the
bounds of propriety. "Can I get you something to
drink?"

"Scotch, neat." He turned to Moira, who had begun
to fiddle with her bag, apparently unaffected by his

words. "Anything for you?" She shook her head no, but didn't look up.

When he returned his gaze to the flight attendant, he discovered her glaring at Moira with undisguised loathing. "Nothing for the lady," he said, by way of dismissal.

"Let me know when you find one," the attendant muttered, turning on her heel and shoving her way through the passengers.

"She don't like me." Moira had ceased worrying over her bag and was now sitting with her arms wrapped around her knees, her heels pressed close to the frayed edge of her denim shorts.

"Why is that?" Nick asked.

Moira looked beyond him to something in the aisle. "Same reason he *does*."

Nick glanced in the direction of her focus to find a paunchy, middle-aged pilot leaning against the bathroom door, his face bearing a hazy expression of the "I just got fucked good and hard" variety. The pilot winked at Moira and sauntered toward the cockpit.

Nick didn't recognize the feeling at first—this immediate need to wipe the smile from the pilot's face with his knuckles and relieve the bastard of his teeth with the heel of his leather loafer. *Jealousy?*

Impossible. He understood it in theory. Jealousy implied someone *else* had something he wanted. In actual practice, he'd never been presented with such a scenario.

When Nicholas Kingswood wanted something, it was his.

"You!" Nick barked at the pilot.

The asshole could hardly manage a facial expression with muscles so thoroughly sex-slackened. "Yeah?"

"Zip your *fucking* pants," he growled.

Several gasps and whispers rose from the seats surrounding them as the pilot looked down and jerked his zipper up.

The flight attendant scurried over, depositing the scotch on Nick's armrest. He took the first silky swallow and turned back to Moira, who was twining a long, thick auburn lock of hair around her finger.

"So is that how you acquired my seat?" The look she gave him made it clear she expected a lecture. Nick had other plans. "Very resourceful of you."

She shrugged, the gesture somehow childlike and innocent in contrast to the revelation he had just received. "He needed it anyway."

Aspirated scotch burned up Nick's nose and choked off the air to his lungs. The offending liquid found its way back up in a cough that sent a spray onto the seat back in front of him. "He—" Nick had to fight off another spasm "—what?"

"He needed it anyway," Moira repeated. "Sometime folks have problems. Sometimes I can...help."

Nick took a moment to appreciate the way Moira's breasts bounced when the airplane started to back away from the jet bridge. A small flicker of pleasure warmed his chest. This would be so much easier than he had thought. "So you're a *healer*? That's remarkable."

"Of a kind." The bag in front of her seat squeaked. She nudged it with her foot.

Nick shot the rest of his scotch and waved his glass at the flight attendant, who unbuckled herself from the jump seat despite the squawks of her neighbor about takeoff. She hurried through fastened bins to pour and deliver the second drink, returning to her seat just as the plane powered into an abrupt acceleration.

"And what would a healer be hiding in there?" Nick asked, nodding toward Moira's bag.

"Nothin'." Moira picked at a string on her edge of her shorts, pulling it until it snapped.

The sound slid through Nick's center, taking root

behind his cock. When she plucked another, recognition registered. The small snaps were a perfect replica of the slapping sound their flesh would make as he pounded her. He caught her hand when she reached for a third. "Don't," he ordered.

"Sheesh." Her arms resumed their crossed position beneath her breasts. "Someone's awful jumpy. I wouldn't think a big man like you'd be scared of a little plane ride."

His ardor quickly mutated into irritation. "I'm not scared of a plane ride. I just don't think you can stand to lose anything off those shorts."

Moira's dark brow inched toward her hairline as a sly smile twisted her lips. "I'd have thought you'd like that, seeing as how you were gawkin' earlier."

The engine's roar swallowed his denial as the plane lifted from the earth in a breathless lurch.

Nick felt the blood pounding in his throat, his temples. "I was *not* gawking. I was wondering what you were doing in my seat."

"Gawkin'." She settled back against the headrest with a self-satisfied smirk and let her eyes fall closed like the conversation was over.

"I was not—"

An unexpected sensation brought his words to a screeching halt— the smooth length of her finger pressed against his lips.

"Shh," she yawned. "I'm fixin' to nod off."

Rage rattled through Nick, mixing with the simmering irritation like a volatile cocktail. This insolent witch had *shooshed* him? *Him*? The one before whom warlords groveled and kings bowed? The one who measured time not in minutes, but in the shrieks of the defeated? The one who had made rivers from the blood of his enemies and built mountains from the bodies of the conquered dead?

No. She hadn't recognized him. He doubted if she

even recognized herself or had any clue as to the power pulsing just beneath her skin.

She *would* know him. She would submit. She would surrender, or he'd be damned.

They both would.

�֍   4   ✺

She'd be damned if this puffed-up, self-important peckerwood was going to ruin her first airplane ride. Even if he did look like the devil's own lawyer. Hair the color of a dark roux, eyes like sunlight through Jack Daniels, and body like a college linebacker—or at least the college linebackers of her *acquaintance*—Nicholas Kingswood had *predator* written all over him.

She'd seen more genuine smiles on a rat snake, and she had no intention of being another notch in his probably-imported belt.

True, she could have just moved, but he was awful fun to look at.

Even now, she stole a glance at the man fuming in her peripheral vision. He was remarkably big. She had seen enough of men that clothes didn't hide much from her anymore. If her estimations were correct, it was a wonder Mr. Kingswood could bring his knees to touch at all. Poor Bucephelus would be jealous as hell.

Moira allowed herself to imagine what a man that size would look like hard. In the absence of the sleep that fled from her like a thief, it helped keep the tidal wave of borrowed emotions at bay.

So many people, so little space.

Their combined sorrows, joys, and resentments

swirled around her, seeking a path into her mind like electricity trying to ground itself.

"No one smirks like that in their sleep." His voice—deep, dark, and buttery as pork ribs left overnight in a smoker—punctured the thin film of her vivid visualization.

She opened one eye and tilted her head toward him. "You the nap police or somethin'?"

"If you're not sleeping, the least you can do is finish our conversation."

"No," she sighed. "The least I can do is nothin'. Which I'd like to do, if you'd quit pesterin' me for five minutes."

The muscles bunched beneath the shadow of stubble on his strong jaw.

Goddamn, but he was fun to annoy.

"Pestering *you*? You take the seat *I* paid thousands of dollars for, and *I'm* pesterin' *you*?"

Moira ignored the perfectly mimicked rendition of her own twangy patois. "Yup."

"Unbelievable." He reached down to his attaché case, withdrew a sheaf of papers and began leafing through them.

"I don't see what you're all bunched up about. You still got a seat. And a pair of tits to stare at besides. You oughta be happier than a pig in slop."

A grunt from the bag at her feet sent a burst of fear skittering down her spine. *Quiet*, she willed Cheeto.

Nick's unnerving amber eyes fixed in the direction of the sound.

"What's in that bag?"

Moira swung a protective leg in front of it. "None of your business."

His lips, and the sultry smile they formed, could have been stolen from one of the wicked satyr statues Moira had seen in a book at the St. Bernard library.

"Yes," he said. "Please put your legs in front of the

bag. I'll split them to get to it and enjoy the effort twice as much."

The threat lodged further south of the Mason Dixon line than Moira was comfortable with. "You reach one finger toward that bag and I'll break it quicker than you can shake your dick."

"You mean the dick you were *gawkin'* at while you were pretending to sleep?"

Blood burned into Moira's cheeks. "I wasn't either."

"You were. And judging by the grin on your face, you liked what you saw."

"Please." Moira rolled her eyes in feigned disinterest. "I seen enough of them things to choke a humpback whale."

"So why not see one that can do the job on its own?" Nick scooted down in his seat, arms folded behind his head, knees splayed in the most brazen invitation Moira had ever witnessed, and after working Saturday night at the HooDoo Shack during Mardi Gras, that was saying something.

Don't look at his junk. Don't look at his—goddammit! Moira's eyes moved of their own accord, focusing in on the long shape now traversing a good distance down Nick's thigh. "Sufferin' savior!" she gasped. "You got a license for that thing?" Up until now, she'd thought *too big for your britches* was just an expression.

She swung her gaze toward the window, and her legs followed out of habit. The next moments unfolded at a speed both too fast and too slow for Moira to follow. Her foot connected with the bag. The bag toppled over. A blur of pink shot out.

All the frames of action slammed into one another as time resumed its normal speed. The little pig's frightened squeal knifed through Moira. She reached for him, but too late.

Nick scooped the pig from the floor in one large hand and brought him to eye level.

Cheeto's hooves pedaled in the air, his snout twitching, his tail flicking. Moira could see he was working up to a shriek that would alert passengers both alive and dead to his presence, which would be followed by something infinitely worse.

"Give him here!" she ordered. "Right this second."

"You poor bastard," Nick said to the pig, ignoring Moira entirely. "Stuffed in that tiny bag all day."

Moira made a desperate grasp for Nick's elbow, but he jerked it away before she could pull Cheeto back to her. "Mister, you best hand over my pig before you get yourself hurt."

Nick's laugh was cut short by Cheeto's ear-piercing shriek, and Moira snatched her hands away just in time.

Whumph.

A puff of bright orange flame blotted out everything as it engulfed Nick's head.

Brief, intense heat rolled over Moira's bare arm and licked its way down her thigh. It was over as quickly as it had come. Moira scanned the aisles to see if anyone had noticed. Luckily, the bright flash of light had failed to rouse the passenger in the opposite row, whose eyes were sealed behind a black sleep mask, just as his ears were sealed behind a pair of those fancy noise-canceling headphones.

Satisfied no immediate damage control was required, she glanced over at Nick, who still held Cheeto at eye level. His face was frozen in a mask of disbelief, his eyebrows singed and smoking.

"Thanks," she said, leaning over to grab her pig while he was rendered motionless. "Mind if I borrow this?" She filched the rolled up blanket he had tucked next to his armrest and wrapped Cheeto in it before snuggling him down in her lap.

Nick's hands dropped onto the armrest. His head ratcheted slowly in her direction.

"What. The *fuck*. Was that?" Fine filaments of burned hair fluttered down to his shirt as he spoke.

Moira stroked an idle hand over Cheeto's fuzzy head. He tended to get a little wound up after these run-ins. "What was what?"

Nick glared at her in disbelief. His voice skated over low, dangerous gullies of anger. "You know damn well *what*."

Leaning forward, Moira retrieved a paper sack she'd squirreled away in her bag before leaving home that morning. Her stomach rumbled in anticipation when she saw the patches of grease dotting the brown paper like X's on a treasure map. She reached in and pulled out a still-crispy leg. "Chicken?" she offered.

The same lips that had earlier worn that luxurious smirk were now turning white around the edges. Moira half expected foam to start spilling from between them.

"Your fucking pig just shot a fireball at my face!"

"I'm guessin' that's a no on the chicken," Moira said. "More for us, Cheeto." She flaked off some of the brown, crumbly coating and sprinkled it in a little dip in the blanket for easy access.

"You're going to sit there and pretend that didn't just happen? I demand—"

"General Custer on a three-legged mule! Did I get a good scald on that or what?" Even at room temperature, the salty-sweet crunch of the chicken's crust gave Moira a rush of pride. At least that was *one* thing she could do right. She'd only made the mistake of entering her cooking into the county fair the one time. The way the other ladies reacted to her winning first, second, and third place had her expecting to be lynched behind the Tilt-a-Whirl.

Nick gripped the armrest with whitening knuckles. "For *Christ's* sake, no one cares about your chicken! And stop interrupting—"

"I care," Moira argued. "And Cheeto cares, which by

my count makes two out of three people in this aisle that care about my chicken. You're overruled." She paused to savor the expression of abject shock on his face. His mouth opened and closed, trying to summon words the way a fish out of water tries to summon air. "Also, you might want to do somethin' about your eyebrows on account of they're mostly sprinkled down the front of your shirt."

Moira reached out a helpful hand to brush away some of the ashes and couldn't stifle her gasp when Nick seized it with surprising speed and force.

Mixed hungers warred in his golden gaze. Moira reached for what she saw, let her mind feel him out, stretching tendrils of thought like vines.

But he wasn't a tree, nor anything else she could wrap her senses around.

What she could see, what she could feel, were only the smallest fraction of what he was. Older than the world, more changeable than the melted rock beneath its surface. Deeper than the ocean, more inconstant than the wind.

It was what she *didn't* find that scared her most of all.

Need.

"Another drink, Mr. Kingswood?" The overpaid peanut-pusher had returned, only now she had a cart and an equally prissy friend.

Nick released Moira's hand, but not her gaze. "Yes. Another scotch. And a whiskey on the rocks for my friend."

"No!" Moira knew at once she had said it too loud. Panic welled up in her chest as she saw the woman's narrowed gaze come to rest on the bundled pig in her lap.

"I'm afraid we'll have to reseat you," the flight attendant said.

"There are no *animals* in first class."

"Then how come they let you wander up and down the aisle all the time?" Moira spat back.

Nick made a sound somewhere between dismay and stifled laughter. After he had regained his composure, he beamed a smile at the flight attendant that snagged Moira's stomach like a fishhook. "You'll make an exception," he said. "Get us our drinks."

"Forget the drinks." Moira tucked Cheeto under her arm, grabbed her bag, and stood as tall as the bin overhead would allow. "What y'all can do is get the hell outta my way."

"Where do you think you're going?" Nick asked, making no sign whatsoever of withdrawing the long legs he'd stretched out in front of him.

"Away from you. And Miss Twisted Britches," Moira said.

"You don't need to go." Nick glanced over his shoulder at the woman shoveling ice into glasses. "Isn't that right, Cheryl?"

Moira wasn't about to wait for an answer. "You gonna move? Or am I goin' over you?"

"Please." The word might has well have been a porcupine for all the trouble Nick had working it up his throat. "I would like you to stay."

"Don't much care *what* you'd like. Y'all can keep your drinks, your seats, and all the asses that ever creased them, while you're at it." She took a step forward, but found her progress arrested by Nick's arm barring her at waist level.

"Stay." It wasn't a request this time. It was an order. A decree. An edict.

She looked down into those fathomless eyes again, felt herself losing ground in their insistent, relentless will.

"Oops," she said, seconds before the open bottled water lurched from the cart and fell into Nick's unguarded lap.

Nick doubled up on a grunt, hands flying to his now wet crotch.

Moira secretly congratulated herself on her aim as she shoved her way past the cart and bolted down the aisle toward the back of the plane. She'd only meant to create a distraction. Catching Nick Kingswood in his king-sized spunk bunkers turned out to be a much more satisfying solution.

She found an empty row by the bathroom and scooted into the seat nearest the window. He wouldn't come back here.

Placing the still-bundled pig on her chest, she bent down to plant a kiss between his velvety ears. "Sorry about all that," she whispered.

Cheeto's quiet grunt was as much of an acknowledgement as she needed.

"You wanna see?" Moira pushed up the shade and held her pig as close to the window as she could without pressing his nose against the cold glass. "Look at all them clouds."

The sun had begun to sink into the horizon, melting away like a lemon drop into the endless sea of feathery white, drawing darkness over an azure blue like Moira had never seen.

For one unfiltered moment, Moira thought about scooping up some of that sky in a mason jar before it went away altogether. She had learned early and well not to count on things that beautiful stickin' around.

"Gonna be dark by the time we hit Port Townsend," Moira said, nestling the bundle back in her lap.

Port Townsend.

Moira had ducked into one of the gift shops at the airport soon after she'd arrived. Right after she'd eaten a cinnamon roll that nearly restored her faith in Jesus. Leafing through the pages of an Atlas with still-sticky fingers, she'd gotten a nasty paper cut on the Washington Coast.

One single drop of blood fell, and Moira watched in horrified fascination as it dripped *up* the page, and with jerky strokes, circled Port Townsend.

Startled, stunned, and weak-kneed, Moira had spent half of all she had left in the world to satisfy the pencil-eyebrowed clerk behind the counter. But for her insistence that Moira ought not touch what she couldn't afford, she might have torn the page out and walked away.

It would be a couple hours before they landed in Seattle, and there would be a couple more that would need driven after that.

And then there was a driver to consider. Mostly, that she'd need one.

Exhaustion settled over Moira, draining what little reserve she had left. She couldn't think about that just now. She couldn't think about anything.

Especially not about Nick.

$\maltese$ 5 $\maltese$

"I'd rather suck off a truck driver." And so she had.

Moira's parting words to Nick circled her brain as she stood out in the street in front of a building that looked less like a house and more like a layer cake.

Three stories, each painted a different color, the ornate woodwork so delicate in contrast to the tin-roofed shacks of her hometown, they looked as fragile as spun sugar. Even the windows, glowing golden like butterscotch candy from lamps within, looked like something right out of a storybook.

Things didn't end well for kids who ran across candy houses, the way Moira remembered it.

The strap of her duffel bag dug into her shoulder, a reminder of what had coaxed those flippant words from her lips in the first place.

Nick had waited for her. Had pulled down her battered old duffel bag from the compartment where she'd left it when she stormed off. The man stood there with it slung over his shoulder like a soldier going off to war.

"I'll carry this out to my car for you. My driver will take you where you need to go."

Spoken in anyone else's voice, it would have sounded like an offer.

Coming from him it was an order.

She wasn't in the habit of taking them.

And riding the Ray Dean Express wasn't a purely opportunistic move on her part. Poor Ray, the Seattle truck driver who had picked her up just outside the airport, hadn't ever grieved the murder of his mother. Two hours and fifty-six miles later, he'd finished grieving for momma, a handful of dead pets, and a high school sweetheart who'd run off with his best friend.

Moira took another breath of air heavy with salt and sea. Just as dense as what she was accustomed to, but cool and clammy. They were practically a hound's sneeze from the ocean. She could feel it in her bones.

Just as she could feel whatever was in that house, pulling her like the moon pulled the tides.

And yet, here she stood. Frozen.

She had gone as far as to imagine walking up those tidy steps, standing on the wrap-around porch, and knocking on the door when she stopped.

She'd grown up on the other side of those kinds of doors. Had them slammed in her face. Been thrown out of more of them than she cared to remember.

What if she had come all this way just to have another one closed on her?

The thought stirred up a hollow ache that brought her attention to the chill creeping into her skin. Her cut-offs, tank top, and flip-flops were keeping the cold out about as well as fishing net kept away gnats.

A small sneeze from her shoulder bag finally set her feet to moving. It was one thing for her to set out in the cold. Another thing altogether for her baby to suffer.

"All right," she said at last. "Let's get this over with."

Out of the street, across the sidewalk, and up the steps she marched, pausing only for a moment to snort at the wreath of dried weeds affixed to the front door. She'd seen them used for a lot of things in her day, but never for decoration. Uncle Sal and the boys would laugh themselves stupid about this.

"Here we go," she whispered to Cheeto.

The old brass knocker retreated from her just as her fingertips had brushed it. The door flung wide open, and Moira's heart tripped into a panicked hum when the silhouette of a woman appeared inside its frame.

She had scarcely mapped out the best path for a hasty retreat when the porch light blinked on, and what it revealed stunned Moira like a whack over the head with a skillet.

Staring back at her from the woman in the doorway...was her own face.

ॐ

NEITHER OF THEM SPOKE FOR WHAT FELT TO MOIRA like an eternity. Or at least the average duration of a Sunday sermon with old Reverend Dupuis spittin' brimstone behind the pulpit.

In the silence, Moira found herself doing just what had been done to her time and time again: staring like a wide-eyed carp.

The face was where any similarity ended.

Well, maybe the hair, but Moira found it hard to tell on account of all the flowers, clips, bobby pins and what not keeping the burgundy mass loosely piled atop the woman's head. Several dark locks escaped their confines despite her best efforts, winding alongside that familiar face like kudzu.

A body roughly the same shape and size as her own hid inside loose, gauzy layers of scarves and skirts. Bangles and beads climbed her wrists and dangled from her neck and ears.

When their eyes finally met, Moira couldn't shake the sensation of staring into a mirror, though the eyes looking back at her were not bright blue, but glass green.

The return appraisal was quicker than Moira had

expected, with the woman's studying gaze skimming over all the spots where ladies at home usually set to scowlin'.

When that face broke out into a triumphant grin, Moira nearly flinched. She'd been prepared for just about anything but that.

"Oh my hell!" the woman said, grabbing Moira by the shoulders. "I knew it!"

Moira's body tensed beneath her grasp. She could still duck, drop her bags, turn around quick and have her knee in this granola girl's back quicker than she could say *sprouted wheat*. "What?" Moira asked. "You knew what?"

"Oh my goddess!" Her cheeks flushed pink with girlish enthusiasm as she stepped back, but kept her grip on Moira. "Say that again! Where are you from? How did you get here? You have to tell me everything! Wait! No, come inside."

And with that, she turned on one bare foot and disappeared inside with a swish of skirts.

Moira stood on the porch and glanced at the swing swaying in the breeze. The night was empty of the evening chorus of chirps, squawks and croaks that would have settled into the bayou by now. The chime of a distant clock tower and a nearby harbor's creaks and sways were too foreign to yet be comforting. With no trees providing a canopy overhead and the silent sky bearing down on her, she felt as exposed as a cockroach on a coffee table.

"Come on!"

Gooseflesh rose on Moira's arms at the sound of being beckoned by her own voice in a foreign accent. Herself, as she might have been, with a little more schoolin' and a little less fishin'.

"I guess we're goin' inside," she mumbled to Cheeto.

Once over the threshold, Moira kicked her sandals

off and set her duffle bag by the door where it would be easy to snatch up if she had to make a hasty exit.

Scarcely had the door closed behind her when she ran face-first into a wall of scent that damn near ripped the hairs right from her nose. And it was no wonder.

The inside of the house looked like someone had knocked over a florist's shop. Pots of foliage crowded every horizontal surface, jostled for space on the mantel over an antique fireplace, leap-frogged over one another up the old wooden staircase. Flowers, herbs, and ferns were literally *everywhere*.

Areas not overrun by plants were cluttered, but clean. Ornately carved tables, shelves, and credenzas piled with books, vases, knickknacks, and assorted lamps gave the foyer and sitting room the elegant claustrophobia of the antiques stores Moira wandered through on occasion. At least the couches looked well worn.

Moira ran a hand over the satiny dark wood bordering the burgundy damask fabric of the settee. How many hands had stroked it smooth over the years? Throw pillows of all patterns, sizes and colors congregated on the matching couch across the coffee table and marched the length of a bay window nook overlooking the street. Moira found herself looking at it with longing. She wouldn't mind curling up in a spot like that for a spell, even if she had to fight a few plants for legroom.

The walls, painted in hues of deepening shades of freshly dug earth, golden tobacco, and warm sand dragged Moira's eyes up to crown molding abutting ceilings higher than even the churches back home had.

Somehow, they made her feel smaller and bigger all at the same time.

"*Goddamn*," she heard herself whisper.

"I think you mean *goddess*," the woman corrected, stopping to pick a dead leaf off a drooping plant on the ornate credenza. "Everyone knows who *really* wears the pants in that relationship. Speaking of which…" She turned and called up the stairs. "Aunt Justine! We have company!"

"Tierra de Moray, I'm already in my dressing gown," came the testy reply. "Who in the goddess's name is it?"

Moira placed the voice at about the age where women stopped plucking their eyebrows and started waxing their upper lips.

"It's—" Surprise widened Tierra's eyes.

"Moira. My name is Moira."

Moira hadn't intended to finish the sentence. Just the opposite. She'd almost wanted *Tierra* to flounder for not even having asked. And maybe a little for having grabbed her like a ragdoll and trotted her in to show off to some crusty old aunt.

They blinked at each other.

It had just *happened*. As easy as breathing and just as natural. "Moira," Tierra repeated.

An ominous creaking sounded at the top of the stairs, followed by a shallow pool of light creeping across the landing. The shadow crept down the hall like something out of the slasher movies Moira had always covered her eyes for in the beds of pickup trucks at the drive-in.

In this moment of doubt, it was Uncle Sal's voice she heard in her head. "You be just as scared as you want, Moira Jo. But don't you give nobody else the satisfaction of seein' it."

Taking a deep breath, Moira straightened her spine and pointed her chin toward the stairs just as she saw the slippered feet begin to descend it.

A crushed velvet housecoat gradually took shape then, but halted abruptly when Aunt Justine's face came into view.

Moira wouldn't have thought it possible, but the long, thin face blanched a paler shade of porcelain when those eyes—a harder hue of Tierra's—fixed on her. The pale ghost of a hand fluttered up to finger the dark red braid laced with silver strands resting over her shoulder.

The housecoat concealed a body that looked more like a bundle of branches to Moira than it did a woman. Sharp shoulders, protruding elbows, a bony nose, and more knots than a forest of redwoods.

Moira's head itched just looking at the severe line of scalp pulled hard enough to tighten Aunt Justine's slackening features.

Some of those features were hers.

And Tierra's.

"It worked! The spell worked!" Tierra announced into the deafening silence. "I have a sister!"

"I can see that." Justine descended the remaining stairs with slow, deliberate steps that barely set the old wood creaking.

Moira didn't trust a person who didn't make any noise when they moved about. She'd have to keep an eye on that one. "Sister? Would someone mind tellin' me what the hell y'all are talkin' about?"

Justine turned to Moira, pinning her with a gaze so pale green it bordered on gray. "You shouldn't have come."

The pain of those words was intense, but brief—only the needle's first sting. Once it got past her skin, Moira found the dull ache mostly bearable. Especially when her blood and bile came rushing to meet it. Her face felt hot. She could hear her own pulse like the ticking of a pocket watch.

"Aunt Justine," Tierra began. "Moira—"

"Shouldn't?" Moira's hand found her hip, and she leaned into the welcome comfort of the gesture. "So long as we're talking about *shouldn'ts*, you shouldn't wear dark colors on account of your complexion lookin' like the inside of a clamshell. That about covers *shouldn'ts* for the moment?"

Aunt Justine flinched like she'd been slapped.

"Moira!" Tierra scolded.

"Well 'scuse me all the way to hell's waitin' room. It's not like I just rolled outta bed this morning thinkin', 'Gee, you know what'd be more fun than skinning a wet cat? Lightin' outta here for someplace I've never been, leavin' damn near everything I own, gettin' harassed all goddamn day by everyone and their ass mites just so some pinched-face old bat can as good as spit on me for my trouble.'"

"You—" Justine's gnarled finger stabbed at Moira despite Tierra's attempt to wedge herself between them "—have *no* idea what you've done by coming here."

"How in the hell could I?" Moira asked. "I barely know where *here* is."

"Port Townsend," Tierra said. "You're in Port Townsend. You're going to love it here. I have the cutest shop just downtown where I sell organic teas and handmade pottery and—"

"I got the Port Townsend part, thanks. I *can* read, it might shock you to know. What I don't know is *why* I'm here. And why *here* is important. And where in the hell I got a twin sister!"

"Why don't you come into the kitchen and I'll brew you a nice cup of lavender and milk-thistle tea to calm your nerves," Tierra offered.

"I'll explain everything."

"I'll take the explanation, but you can keep your weeds." Moira folded her arms across her chest to prevent Tierra from grasping them.

"You see how impossible this is?" Justine's red-rimmed eyes were growing more frantic by the second. "What you're hoping for is worse than a foolish fantasy. There is a reason you were separated. Did you never think of that?"

Tierra's hands tightened into fists at her sides, the chunky rings adorning each finger making them look like medieval weapons. "Maybe if you had been willing to tell me the truth, I wouldn't have had to cast a spell to find out."

The wood floor vibrated beneath Moira's feet. All around her, plants nodded and bobbed, their leaves shaking as if caught up in some ghostly gale.

"Tierra!" Justine barked. "Stop."

All the energy rushed out of Tierra along with the breath she had been holding. Her chest rose in rapid bursts, but the eyes she turned to her aunt were wide and full of an emotion Moira was well acquainted with, pain. "How could you keep this from me?"

Justine's hand found the high lace collar of her nightgown and clenched it at her throat. "You're no more ready to know than you were to cast the spell that brought *her* to our doorstep."

Side by side, they watched Aunt Justine stomp up the stairs and disappear back into the darkness where she seemed most at home.

"Well, that could have gone better," Tierra said, brushing a stray lock of hair away from her face. "Let's go to the kitchen. I think better there."

Moira stood rooted to the spot, her gaze flicking between the kitchen door and an easy exit. "I ain't sure I should be anywhere in this house with ol' pickle-puss skulkin' around upstairs."

"Oh, she's more bark than bite." Tierra waved a dismissive hand. "Anyway, this house is as much yours as it is hers."

"How's that?" Like it or not, the casual announcement had her like a hook through the gills, and she wasn't about to let Tierra wander into the kitchen unfollowed.

Compared to the kitchen in Uncle Sal's fishing shack—little more than a galley with a couple electric burners that worked only when they felt like it—this space, with its stained glass accents, tiled backsplash, and dark wooden cabinets, might have been dropped right out of a palace.

It was the kind of cozy, clean hub Moira had imagined herself having heartfelt chats in with the mother she'd never known. They would sit at that island with steaming mugs of something-or-other, the shiny copper pots winking overhead like a chandelier, her gentle hands untangling the snarls that daily plagued Moira's hair.

Tierra breezed over to the cabinet and slipped on an apron embroidered with the words *Kitchen Witch*. "This house has been in our family for ages. It's yours now too."

Moira looked around at the neat stacks of dishes, the lovely old table and chairs, the cookbooks and linens. *Hers?*

"Sit down," Tierra urged. "Take a load off. Tell me everything. Don't leave anything out."

Moira eased onto a stool at the kitchen island and watched as Tierra sifted through cabinets and drawers with a kind of dancing, unstudied ease. Pulling down mugs, hip-checking drawers closed while snipping bits from various plants and tossing them into a gleaming copper kettle.

"Well," Moira began.

"Turmeric," Tierra pronounced, pausing to consult a gleaming array of glass bottles. "Definitely."

"'Scuse me?"

Tierra unburdened her long, slim arms of their bottles and vegetation. "Turmeric. It's for your liver. From the looks of things, you could use a cleanse."

Moira looked down into her bag as an excuse to give herself a subtle sniff. Seemed all right. "I clean myself just fine, thanks."

"It's not your outsides I'm worried about," Tierra said. "It's your insides. I can only imagine the kind of things you've been eating. Not to mention *drinking*."

"Speaking of," Moira said, eyeing the fridge. "I'd love a Coke if you've got one."

Tierra's eyes widened in horror as she tore the greens from a sugar beet and tossed them in the kettle. "Do you have any idea how many toxins and preservatives are in that stuff? You might as well drink formaldehyde."

"If they sold it in cans labeled 'Coke,' I just might." Moira reached into her bag and stroked Cheeto's snout. He'd been out cold since they shared a bag of dill pickle sunflower seeds in Ray Dean's truck.

Tierra opened the fridge and snagged an earthenware pitcher, which she set in front of Moira along with a glass. "When is the last time you ate something green?"

Moira chewed on her lower lip as she thought. "I made a bunch of fried okra the other night."

Tierra sighed. "Oh, Moira. You have so much to learn."

"I don't mean to be rude or nothin'," Moira said, knowing she didn't entirely mean it, "but the only thing I'm real keen on learnin' at the moment doesn't have to do with greens. You follow me?"

The blade chopping dark magenta flesh from the beet slowed on its downstroke. "Let's start with the basics. Which kind of witch are you?"

"Pardon?" Moira had heard the word hurled at her many times, but usually while someone's husband or boyfriend was pulling on his clothing and ducking other projectiles.

"Witch," Tierra repeated. "You're a witch. I'm a witch. Aunt Justine is a witch."

Moira looked up at the ceiling. She could easily imagine that stuffy old biddy with her ear hovering over a heating vent, hoping to catch snatches of their conversation. "That I'd believe."

Tierra shook her head and tucked a tendril of hair

behind her ear only to have it fall across her forehead again. "She hasn't always been like that. When I was younger, we would go for walks in the woods, gathering herbs, roots, flowers."

"She raised you? Y'all lived here all your life?"

"Right here in this house," Tierra confirmed. "What about you?"

"Uncle Sal brought me up on Stump Bayou in Terrebonne Parish, Louisiana. He caught me when I's just a baby."

"*Caught* you?" Tierra tumbled the cut beets into the kettle and started stripping herbs from their stems. "You make it sound like he snagged you on a fishing line."

"Hell no," Moira snorted. "It was a net."

Tierra looked up from her thick wooden cutting board. The mixture of pity and disgust written on her face made cold sweat bloom on the back of Moira's neck. "He found you *in* the water?"

"Yup."

"But how on earth did you get there?"

"That's exactly what I's hoping you could tell me."

❧ 6 ❧

Nick watched the fine mist settle on the windshield of his Corvette Stingray—a considerable step down from the Ferrari 458 Italia he liked tooling around town in for daily errands. The 'Vette's copious safety features robbed him of the chance to dominate a truly dangerous machine but saw him to his destination in decent time.

The lights in the house across the street glowed yellow like a jack-o'-lantern's grin. Cozy, he supposed some people might find it. For him, it was little more than a prison with better bars.

She was in there. Moira.

He could smell her on the damp night air, an intoxicating mix of rain and wild muscadines. Her curving silhouette sashayed across the backs of his eyelids every time he blinked. Over and over, she marched away from him, her ass winding a lazy sideways figure eight.

The symbol of eternity, and rightly so, for he could hold her in his memory this way for as long as he wished.

An ache in his groin reminded him that memory was not the only place where he wanted to keep her. He wanted her skewered on the cockstand he had endured ever since she had turned her back to him and sauntered off in search of other means of transportation.

And find it she had.

He had watched her step up into the stranger's truck, admired the way she gripped the handle and propelled herself into the cab with one powerful jerk. The length of her leg disappearing under the streetlights.

They had been easy to catch. Once he dismissed the driver arranged for him and took the wheel in his own hands, he was ghosting their taillights in the space of ten minutes.

He hadn't killed Ray Dean. That was a first.

Hadn't forced him off the road, gutted him like livestock, and left him in a ditch bath of his own blood and offal. Hadn't dragged her out of the cab and made her beg forgiveness on her knees around a mouthful of his cock.

No.

What he'd wanted was to watch Moira linger in the street, looking like she was stepping off a cliff rather than a curb.

Again and again he scraped the night, searching for her thoughts. What was she doing here?

A vibration within his coat pocket had him searching for his cell phone, and bringing it to his ear, answering it without looking. No one who had his number dared call without reason.

"What?"

"You've been malingering for over an hour now. What *are* you doing?"

Julian Roarke's voice always felt like a silver stiletto sliding into Nick's ear. Sharp, cool, smooth, and deadly accurate in its aim.

"Jules," Nick said, both acknowledgement and greeting.

"The last unfortunate who called me Jules died horribly of a syphilitic esophagus."

Nick shifted to loosen his slacks from the place where his pulse throbbed. "I remember. Crusades, wasn't it?"

"Constantinople. 14th century."

"Right. The beginning of that plague business in Europe. How could I have forgotten? Some of your best work to date, if I may say so."

"You have done," Julian replied. "On several occasions. But flattery was never your strong suit, brother."

"And tact isn't yours. Remind me why you called me again?"

Nick could practically hear the kid-gloved hand find the spot where Julian's silver-black hair met his pale temple. "That dreadful brooding of yours is giving me a migraine. You haven't been this preoccupied since you toppled Wall Street in 1929. What exactly is it you traveled to Port Townsend to do?"

"Just a simple operation. Buy out the entire town and devastate the local economy by shutting down the timber operations in the name of a green energy government grant thereby delivering them into my complete control."

Julian's sigh was as soft and restless as autumn leaves. "How you love your droll little dramas. Couldn't you just find a widow to put out in the street instead? Conquer a convenience store or something?"

"It's not the operation that's the problem."

"Oh?"

Nick drew in a deep breath to force out words he didn't want to speak. "It's a witch."

"Which witch?" Only Julian's highborn, crisp accent could make this seem a valid question.

"Don't be cute," Nick grunted.

"I think we could both agree that *cute* is the last adjective that could accurately be applied to me."

"True." In days long past, Nick had resented his brother's cultivated suavity, his ability to incite in any woman that longing for drawing rooms and stormy gothic ruins to be rescued from. With his fine features and romantically tormented air, Julian Roarke promised Mr. Darcy...but delivered Vlad the Impaler.

"I fail to see how one witch represents a challenge. I've seen you take on as many as five when the mood suits you."

The memory did little to help cool the ache radiating through Nick's core. "This isn't a simple Greek orgy, Jules."

"So, dominate her. Humiliate her. Chain her to something and torture her. I hear that's all the rage these days." These words possessed no more interest in Julian's voice than would announcing an upcoming dentist appointment.

"Whatever you do," he continued, "just bloody fuck her and get it over with so I can have some peace and quiet."

"I plan to," Nick said.

"Do I hear an implied *but* in that statement?"

The silence mocked Nick more than any of Julian's barbs could have. None of the declarations he could devise carried the brute force of truth, the only answer his canny brother would accept.

"Don't tell me—" a dry, rasping rattle only Nick would recognize as a laugh danced through the phone "—she turned *you* down. Oh, how *delicious*!"

"She didn't turn me down," Nick insisted. Throwing water at him and singeing his face via a fire-breathing pig didn't constitute an official refusal by his account. Just a temporary delay of the inevitable.

"Could it be that the great Nicholas Kingswood has finally met his match?"

Fine hairs rose on the back of Nick's neck. "There's no such thing."

"Not according to the prophecy," Julian teased. "How does it go?

By the blood moon's light, one of four will by sacrifice rite—"

"You need to spend less time fondling your books, brother."

"That, you may rely on. The world is due another pandemic. The bottom rungs have grown swollen once again. A good culling will set things to rights. Let's hope, for my sake, the lapse in your gifts isn't *contagious*."

"I see what you did there." Nick couldn't suppress a laugh, though it came more out of a kind of twisted affection for Julian's erudite brand of humor than actual hilarity caused by it.

"Go forth and conquer, and all that," Julian said.

"By this time tomorrow," Nick vowed, "this entire city will be at my mercy."

"Pity you don't have any."

"A damn shame," Nick agreed.

❧ 7 ❧

"Here," Tierra said. "Put this in your bra."

Moira looked dubiously at the flat, smooth red stone pooling like blood in her sister's palm. "What's that for?"

"It's red jasper," Tierra explained. "It will re-anchor you to the earth's energy and detoxify your root chakra."

Moira blinked at her. "My *what*?"

They stood behind the counter of Tierra's shop—Ambrosia's Brews and Charms—after hours of conversation and one restless night's sleep behind them. Whatever revelations Moira had expected to anchor her in this town failed to materialize. She felt more out of place than a gopher in the gumbo.

Walking down the hill toward Water Street only half an hour earlier, they had passed more storybook homes tucked between thick stands of trees just beginning to shake out their glossy leaves beneath the spring sun. Buildings of colorful brick bunched up on either side of the road, their shingles swinging in the breeze like flags, inviting tourists to carry their recycled coffee cups in for a peek at artisan wares.

Moira hadn't minded the walk.

It was the lecture she could do without. Already,

she'd learned that the Badger, her car, likely caused the deaths of countless sweatshop orphans and created a hole in the ozone layer big enough for Saturn to stumble through.

And all before breakfast.

Tierra's dark brows drew toward each other. An expression Moira was quickly learning to dread.

"Your root chakra. Look, I don't have time to explain everything right now. Just put this in your bra. We need to get the herbal teas brewing before the customers start wandering in."

"Never wear one." Moira's shudder of revulsion at the mere mention of those wire-rimmed devil's bear traps brought a heightened awareness to the way her breasts swayed with the movement.

"Moira Joule de Moray," Tierra huffed. "You left the house this morning without a bra?"

Moira was sure regretting telling her sister her full name, all right. "It's Malveaux," she corrected. "And I sure did. Believe it or not, I made it all the way across the country without a single lick of help from a brassiere."

"You can't walk around my store looking like that." Tierra's beringed fingers drew a hasty circle around Moira from knees to knockers. "I run a respectable business. It's bad enough you're dressed like a—"

"Like a what?" Moira interrupted. She stood there with her hand on her hip, challenging Tierra to give her a reason to turn tail and run. Since learning that Tierra had no idea who their father was and their mother died during childbirth, she was feeling less and less motivated to stick around. Particularly with that squinty aunt shooting her the stink-eye around every corner.

"Forget it," Tierra muttered, whisking behind a closet door. "But you're putting on this apron."

Moira looked at the sage-colored fabric covered in purple paisley swirls. It was easily a full foot longer than the jean skirt that brushed her upper thigh, and looked like something the quilting bee biddies back home might wear. "Sure, I'll wear that apron. Right after you build that stepladder to the moon."

Tierra held her gaze and the apron both, unflinching. "Everyone who works here wears one."

Moira folded her arms beneath—not over—her breasts. "Good thing I work at the HooDoo Shack, then."

The eyes Tierra narrowed at her looked wider than her own, accentuated by soft, shimmery eye shadow very different from Moira's application of sultry charcoals and raven-black mascara. "The *what?*"

"The HooDoo Shack. It's a bar just on the edge of St. Bernard. They don't make me wear an apron, and I serve the customers just fine."

"I'll bet you do," Tierra snorted.

"And what's that s'posed to mean?"

The jingling of a brass bell announced the front door's opening as a petite sprite with pink dreadlocks piled atop her head strode a practiced path through the café tables and groups of armchairs. "Hey, T," she called, not pausing to look up as she gathered books piled on the many tables and started re-shelving them on the wooden bookcases against the far wall.

Layered tank tops in gray and white revealed arms covered in a swirling mural of tattoos reaching down to her delicate wrists. Jewelry of the kind on display near the store's entrance encircled her wrists and neck. Her tight black leggings were tucked into knee-high leather boots Moira had to concede were pretty damned kickass, though she'd never owned anything of the kind. Silver studs traced the curve of her ear, the upper part skewered by a long metal post that pierced her in two places.

Moira wondered how those body-scanning boxes at the airport would react to so much metal in one person.

Tierra cleared her throat. "Sunny, there's someone I'd like you to meet."

Sunny glanced up, and the armful of books clattered to the wood floor at her feet. She looked from Tierra to Moira and back again.

"What the hell?"

"Sunny Brooks, this is my sister, Moira de Mor—"

"Malveaux," Moira found herself interrupting. "Moira Malveaux."

"Sister? You never told me you had a *sister*." Sunny stood with her back to the bookshelf, pale behind the black rims of her glasses like she had seen a ghost. And a ghost was just about what Moira felt like in this place —a strange echo of someone else's life, a shade in a world she didn't belong to.

"I sort of didn't know," Tierra said.

Moira heard a lingering trace of resentment in Tierra's words and felt her aunt's shadowy presence behind it.

"How do you not know you have a *twin*?" Sunny stooped to pick up the books piled at her feet.

"Long story," Tierra sighed.

"Oh." Sunny nodded knowingly. "One of those super-weird separated at birth sort of things?"

"Something like that," Tierra said. "I'll catch you up later."

"Let me help you with that," Moira offered, wanting any task that could reasonably be done without the apron still clutched in Tierra's hand. She felt Sunny's sharp-eyed gaze trace her profile as she bent to help pick up the books.

"Where you from, anyway?" Sunny asked.

"Louisiana," Moira said, stacking books on her arm. "Terrebonne Parish."

"Dig your accent." A bright pink rhinestone flashed at the corner of Sunny's nose when she smiled.

"Thanks." The self-conscious tightness lodged at the base of Moira's throat eased off a bit.

"Sunny, could you get the teas going? And check to make sure we have enough taro root for today? We're running a little behind this morning."

If there was a reproach loaded into Tierra's statement, Moira chose not to hear it.

"Sure thing, T." Sunny slid the last of her books onto the shelf and grinned down at Moira. "Nice meeting you, long-lost sibling."

"Likewise."

"Apron," Tierra called, dangling the fabric over the counter.

Sunny paused on her way to the small kitchen. "Don't bother fighting her on this one," she said. "Trust me. I've been trying for years."

"See?" Tierra's smile was brighter than it had been all morning.

"She knows."

Moira took a deep breath and let it out in a rush. "Fine."

It was the first concession of many she would make that day.

❧ 8 ❧

Twelve.

The precise number of women in this incense-choked bohemian boutique Nick could fuck if he so chose. They gathered in groups of twos and threes, sipping flowery tea, flipping through tarot cards, and playing at divination.

But of all the mood-ring wearers, crystal consulters, and part-time tourists, his eyes followed only one.

Moira.

She hadn't seen him yet—and wouldn't. Subverting the awareness of those around him was so easy, it couldn't even be considered a game any longer. Not when he could move among them, turning their attentions elsewhere until he decided to be noticeable.

Which wasn't just yet. Watching her weave through the tables while balancing a tray loaded with heavy, hand-thrown ceramics was a little like observing a canary in the coal mine. A bright, beautiful thing amongst all that shifting gray, the harbinger and oracle of destruction she knew nothing about.

Destruction he would bring.

He swept the crowd once again, dividing them in the ways he found most amusing.

Thirteen.

The number of men he could kill in the space of time it required for Moira to draw a breath and release it again. The number of men who had slid their eyes up the length of her legs not obscured by the apron that he would be burning at the first opportunity. The number of men who had traced the curve of her breasts and tested their weight with phantom hands.

Times like this, he regretted the efficiency of modern weaponry. Hearing their bones yield to the honed edge of an axe would have been far more melodic than the racket oozing out of the speakers to assault his ears. Some kind of wind chime battle someone had slapped with the appellation "new age" and sent out into the world to rob people of their natural inclinations toward violence.

On him, it had precisely the opposite effect.

Like the excess energy gnawing the fraying edges of his awareness, the sounds and smells of this place slipped a red filter of rage over his vision. Conflict would bloom around him like the pots of flowers and herbs mobbing every surface if he didn't quit this place, and soon.

Moira swung by a table and leaned in just enough to flash the crescent shadow below one shapely ass cheek. His cock twitched at the sight.

In less than a minute, he could dismember every person in this place and have Moira on the counter, legs spread, his face up that excuse for a skirt.

He would taste her through her panties first. Force her to endure the maddening sensation of his tongue working through the thin layer of cloth. Though she didn't wear a bra, she would be wearing a thong. He knew it as surely as he knew she would fight the pleasure. He might slide the fabric aside for her second orgasm so he could shove his tongue inside her when she came. By the third, he would have torn the scrap of silk away with his teeth for better access while he learned the curvature of the wet, wanting ache inside her with his fingers.

He would fuck her raw, exploiting every angle to create the frenzied, frenetic state he needed.

And then he would *own* her.

Make her beg for—

"Jesus Christ on a Ferris wheel. What the hell are *you* doin' here?"

Nick spun around to find Moira not only in close proximity, but *behind* him. His back had been to the corner. He had known it. Made certain of it. When had he moved? How had she *seen* him?

"Moira *Jo* Malveaux," Nick said, tweaking her name into a twangy rhyme. "Imagine running into you here of all places."

She propped her tray of used mugs against the curve of her hip. "Well, if it ain't Mister Slicker'n Owl Shit Hisself. Why do I get the feeling that you don't *run into* anyone?"

"Because you know as well as I do that there's really no such thing as chance," Nick answered.

"That," Moira snorted, "or you didn't get your fill yesterday and decided to follow me home like a hang-dog."

"I'm afraid I'm here on business." The edges of Nick's vision bled a deeper shade of crimson. "Can you fetch your *boss* for me?"

Moira's dark head rose an inch in his vision as her spine straightened. "My *boss* is back in Louisiana. You plannin' on hopping back on a plane?"

"Forgive the error," Nick said. "I just saw that tray and apron and reasoned that you might work here."

"Probably you oughta spend less time reasoning," Moira suggested. "You're not all that good at it."

Nick worked against the muscles in his jaw threatening to grind his teeth to powder. "So you stop into random establishments and volunteer your services, then?"

"Naw," Moira said. "I'm just helpin' out my sister."

"Ahh. Your sister wouldn't happen to be Tierra de Moray, would she?"

He guessed by the stricken look on Moira's face that he had hit his mark.

"Thanks for your help." Nick clunked his empty coffee cup down on Moira's tray with more force than was necessary and brushed past her on the way to the counter where a tattooed minx with a bird's nest of pink dreadlocks on her head coaxed coffee and steamed milk from a hissing copper behemoth.

He knew Moira would be at his elbow before he could so much as catch the barista's attention.

"What do you want with my sister?" she demanded.

"None of your concern, as you don't work here. Excuse me," Nick said, flagging down the barista.

"What else can I get for you? Another double espresso?" the petite woman asked. Koi fish jumped and slithered down her toned biceps as she tamped espresso into a filter with a stainless steel press.

"Tierra de Moray, to begin with," Nick answered.

Pain rolled through Nick's head like the shockwaves of a nuclear explosion as the familiar face leaned into the doorway.

Moira. But *not* Moira.

The features were the same. The expression they wore was not. Wide-set eyes, high, smooth cheekbones, pillowed lips and a halo of that strange red-black hair. In Moira, the combination was a feral as cloudburst, the kind of intense, accidental beauty that sent people running for safer ground.

In Tierra, they were the unfolding of a season—relentless in their loveliness and supremely confident of their right to exist. "Who wants me?" she asked.

Twins. Julian's mocking, lyrical voice looped through Nick's mind. *By blood moon's light...* Nick shoved the thoughts away, drawing his focus back to the task at hand.

"I do," Nick said.

So strange to see that face slide easily into a smile. Tierra wiped her hands on her apron and pushed a stray lock of hair away from her face with the back of her wrist. "And who might you be?"

"A pain in the ass, mostly," Moira commented, depositing the mugs from her tray in the deep sink behind the counter.

"Moira!" Tierra's voice held a mix of motherly rebuke and embarrassment.

"It's all right," Nick said. He waved a casual hand in Moira's direction. "We've met. I'm acquainted with your sister's native...*wit*. Nick Kingswood."

The hand she offered was shaken with a grasp as warm as a sundrenched rock, and lacked the accompanying jolt of pain and promise. But she *was* a witch. He had felt the low-level hum crackling like the air before a lightning strike.

"Tierra de Moray," she announced. "What can I do for you?"

Nick hesitated. He wanted a few extra seconds to drink in the expression on her face. This moment, the space between a contented existence and the end of life as she knew it was his foreplay. His Christmas Eve. He returned her confident smile as an appetizer to the killing blow. "You can be out of here in three days."

Yes. There it was. Her smile slid from its moorings, buffeted by confusion and disbelief.

"Out of where?" Tierra asked. "What do you mean?"

"Here." Nick swept a hand over the crowded cafe. "This store. My building."

A spontaneous burst of laughter set Tierra's eyes dancing. "Yeah, right. *Your* building. I've been renting this space from Mrs. Cavendish forever!"

"Which explains why your lease hasn't been updated recently. It seems the last one you signed ended about eighteen months ago." Nick set his leather briefcase on the counter and popped the lid, withdrawing a manila folder. "Here we are."

"Let me see that." Tierra snatched the yellowing, dog-eared document away from him and flipped through the pages. Moira had taken to cleaning the same patch of counter over and over again as she leaned over her sister's shoulder for a peek.

"That can't be right," Tierra said, worry creasing her face.

"Mrs. Cavendish was so eager to sell when she learned I was buying the rest of the block. Did you know she's wanted to retire in Boca for years?" Genuine pleasure touched his heart at the memory. It had taken less than five minutes for Nick to secure her signature on the document now quaking in Tierra's hands.

"Now I *know* you're lying," she accused. "There's no way Port Townsend would sell an entire block of historic Water Street to a private citizen."

"I suppose that depends on whether the *citizen* had acquired a renewable energy grant. You would be amazed at how much revenue those bring to a city. Not to mention the jobs."

"*Jobs?*" Tierra repeated. "And what do you suppose will happen to the jobs of all the people here? All the businesses?"

"Sometimes sacrifices must be made in the name of the greater good. I'm sure you can understand that. We're talking about renewable energy here, Miss de Moray. Or are you so arrogant as to think your presence here justifies environmental damage on a global scale?"

"*My presence?*" Tierra sputtered. "*Environmental damage?*"

If Nick cared for popcorn, now was when he would have sat back to indulge. The color rushing to the witch's cheeks, her glass-green eyes standing out against them like shining marbles.

The coffee cups rattled on the shelves, clinking against their saucers. For a split second, Nick felt the ground beneath him submitting to a will other than his own.

"Don't pay him no mind, Tierra," Moira said, coming up behind her sister. The cups went quiet as she laid a hand on her shoulder. "Just cause he's got enough money to burn a wet mule doesn't mean he can push you out of your store."

"Actually, Moira *Jo*," Nick said, "that's exactly what it means. And your sister knows it. Don't you, Miss de Moray?"

Tierra shoved the papers at his chest with surprising force. "Get out of my store."

"I think you mean *my* store. Or should I say, Crown Industries' store?"

The haughty toss of her head reminded Nick of dark warhorses of days past. "Not for the next three days, it isn't."

Nick leaned across the counter, drawing close enough to make sure Moira could also hear his whispered words. "Don't come between me and what I want, Miss de Moray. I would take great pleasure in showing you how much you have to lose."

He looked straight at Moira and winked.

One last splendid sip of their defeat was all he allowed himself before walking out into an afternoon bruised with storm clouds.

Now, for the others.

❅ 9 ❅

"**W**hat an *ass*!"

From her vantage point, Moira had a hard time knowing exactly how Tierra meant it.

Nick Kingswood's hindquarters in a pair of tailored trousers did as much to recommend him as his mouth did to damn him. Well, not his mouth really. That was pretty okay to look at too. He had more mastery over every movement of his face than most men had over their fishing boats.

It was his *words* that were the trouble.

She watched him until he slid behind the wheel of a Corvette Stingray, a car Moira had seen in a magazine down at Red's shop. March's centerfold. She'd damn near torn it out to hang on her ceiling until she thought of the Badger and felt a pang of guilt.

"What are you going to do?" Sunny asked, sliding a steaming latte across the counter to one of the few remaining men who hadn't fled the shop when Nick stood.

"He is *not* getting Ambrosia's," Tierra said, running an affectionate hand over the scarred wooden counter. "I don't care if I have to chain myself to the radiator."

"Somehow I don't think that'd stop him from bull-dozin' it with you inside."

Tierra and Sunny turned in unison to look at her.

"He said you had met." Tierra raised an eyebrow at Moira. "How?" It had been phrased like a question, but felt more like an accusation.

Moira picked up her damp dishcloth and resumed mopping down the counter. "On the plane over here."

"Ugh," Tierra grunted. "You had to share space with that man for five hours?"

"Naw. I got up and left after a while. One of them stuck-up cart monkeys wouldn't let me sit in first class on account of Cheeto."

"Whoa," Sunny marveled. "You flew first class from New Orleans. That had to have been uber pricey."

"Yeah," Tierra agreed. "How did you swing that last minute?"

Moira frantically scanned her bleary memories of last night's lengthy conversation. She had avoided questions of money like a drunk dodges church, but Tierra had been unwilling to let it go.

"Oh, it was one of those last-minute discount things. I was just in the right place at the right time."

"That's lucky," Sunny laughed.

"How much?" The unfiltered weight of Tierra's full attention came to bear on Moira. She could feel it pricking the back of her neck like push pins.

"Well, I—"

"Psst."

Moira looked up from the counter to find Tierra face-to-face with Ray Dean. Judging from the way he leaned toward the counter, he'd found a few bottles on his way to the store.

Moira tried to get his attention behind Tierra's back, but found herself under Sunny's careful eye.

"Can I help you?" Tierra asked.

"You sure can, darlin'." His grin fell into a lopsided leer that had Tierra backing away from the counter. "How 'bout a lil' of what you did for me last night?"

Tierra crossed her arms over her chest. "Excuse me?"

"Now don't pretend you don't remember. I gave you a ride right up to that purty house on—"

"Oh boy!" Moira interrupted, tugging Tierra away. "I think someone's had a snootful. Sunny, would you mind getting our friend some coffee?"

"You!" Ray Dean bellowed, one leathery finger pointing toward Moira. "It wasn't her. It was you!"

"What was *you?*" Tierra asked.

"Nothin'." Moira ducked away from Dean's stare and busied herself refilling the container of half and half.

"Pffft." Ray Dean gave a loose-lipped snort. "What you done for me wasn't nothin'. Ain't no one ever sucked the—"

Hot coffee erupted from the cup Sunny carried to the counter and soaked the front of Ray Dean's shirt. He yelped and scrambled backward, pulling the sodden garment away from his body.

"Oh no," Sunny apologized. "I am so sorry. I don't know how that happened."

"I do." Tierra's green gaze went a shade of gray closer to her aunt's as she grabbed Moira by the upper arm and dragged her through the swinging door to the kitchen.

"Turn me loose!" Moira jerked her arm free, still feeling her sister's steely grip in her flesh after she released her hold.

"You're loose enough already!"

The words hit Moira's chest like a brick. She could feel herself shrinking. That familiar sensation of folding in on herself, knowing that one day, she might just disappear entirely.

"Tell me you didn't sleep with that truck driver for a ride."

"I didn't sleep with that truck driver for a ride."

Technically true. They hadn't done any sleeping. The sexual part of what she'd given him was the least of it, and yet, as always, it was all folks cared to see.

"So he's lying?"

"Look, it's not as simple as you're tryin' to make it," Moira explained.

"Did you have sex with him? Yes or no?"

"Yes," Moira. "But it wasn't—"

"And the pilot? Is that how you got that first class seat?"

"Yes. No. If you'd just listen—" Words tripped over themselves to get to the tip of Moira's tongue, mixing with tears at the back of her throat to become a paste she could neither swallow nor spit out.

Tierra's eyes flew open wide with shock. "The men! All the men winking at me in the shop today. All those times you disappeared. Oh, Moira. No. Tell me you didn't." *That look.*

Pity. Disgust. Fear. Revulsion.

All her life, she had seen it on the faces of women, the only consolation that they couldn't know her. Didn't want to know her. She had grown used to seeing it on the faces of strangers.

But now, it was on her own.

Her own face staring back at her like the mirror capable of showing her to herself.

The world had gone to all this trouble to show her exactly what she had always feared. That old hurt. That loathing for everything she was. Everything she wasn't. The truth she ran from at every turn. She was someone's idea of a sick joke. Given powers to heal others but damn herself.

She came, and trouble followed.

Well, that part she could fix.

"Your aunt was right. I shouldn't have come." She bolted then as she had so many times before. Wasn't a body in all of Terrebonne Parish that could catch her, and she guessed her sister wouldn't be able to either. Not in those lace-up sandals, anyway.

"Moira!" Tierra's cry was nearly swallowed up by the cozy hum of the crowd. "Come back!"

The brass bell clanked in protest at her hasty departure, and she was vaguely aware of knocking tourists away like bowling pins as she tore up the sidewalk.

Rain pelted her face, and the bruised sky overhead rumbled promises of a real downpour. When her wet flip flops slid off her feet, she left them behind. She was faster without them anyhow.

That's right. Get the hell out of my way.

A clap of thunder punctuated the thought, rattling the windows of buildings sliding by in her peripheral vision.

The streets were clearing, people shaking off their umbrellas at the doorways to cozy restaurants and bars.

She cut a sharp left at what Tierra had told her was the Hastings Building, easily one of Port Townsend's most venerated landmarks. Its sky-blue paint had darkened with the rain, drops tracing the nooks and crannies of the façade's cream-colored columns and scalloped windows.

Tires squealed in some distant reality. The scent of burnt rubber mingled with salt air and wet asphalt invaded Moira's lungs.

"Moira!" *Nick.*

She could have picked his voice out even over the howl of hurricane sirens. It pierced her in the same way the loon's call always did. That otherworldly melancholy beyond human understanding.

If she looked back now, she would stop. The world would catch up with her, and so would he.

Run. All thought concentrated itself around this one word. Cement gave way to wet wooden planks beneath her feet. She could see the ocean beyond and imagined how cool and heavy the water would be in her lungs.

Sinking to the bottom like a wrecked ship, she could yield to its siren call of soundless space. Back where she came from. The endless deep pressing quiet hands against her temples to blot out all the pain— her own, and others'.

"Moira, stop!"

Nick's footfalls echoed behind her like a horse's galloping gait.

Gaining on her. He would overtake her before she could get to the edge.

She spurred herself on, muscles screaming, chest threatening to burst. If she could only make one last...

An abrupt, painful force burst around Moira's middle, and she was jerked backward, her motion arrested so effectively, she wondered if she had run into an unseen guardrail.

Moira's gaze whipped back over her shoulder to find Nick with a handful of apron ties.

That piece of shit apron.

A fresh wave of rage sent a stream of obscenities cascading from her tongue.

Nick's hand closed over her arm almost exactly where Tierra's had and spun her around. "What the fuck do you think you're doing?"

Lord, but the man was huge. Not folded into an airline seat, not separated by a counter or some span of distance, he towered over her, his broad shoulders blocking out a stretch of blackened sky. His rain-soaked dress shirt stuck to every slope of muscle on his arms, glued itself to the plains of his chest and ridged stomach.

Dark hair hung in dripping locks over eyes of burning amber. She stared into them with every shred of self-hatred boiling up inside her.

"Let me go!" She pulled against his hold with all the strength she had left, lurching toward the dock's edge.

"No." His grip tightened on her arms, giving her something solid to thrash against.

And she did.

Like a wild cat, like an alligator, like every untamed beast she had ever witnessed meeting its end in the hands of a predator against whom there was no victory. She knew her own fight to be just as futile, but didn't care. Maybe the end would come quicker. Maybe she could bring the curtain down upon them all.

Another clap of thunder stole the end of a throaty growl that served as her only warning. Nick bared his teeth and propelled her backward until the wooden railing sent pain rattling up her spine. The length of his body came flush with hers, pinning her in place. He caught her wrists and forced them away from her chest. They hit the wood with bone-jarring force.

"You can't win." Stinging stubble from his jaw rasped against her ear. "Not against me."

"Don't bet on it," she snarled. "You have no idea what I'm capable of."

"It's *you* who have no idea what you're capable of, Moira. Which is why you will keep destroying every life you touch."

"What would you know about it?"

"More than you are capable of comprehending."

"Just let me go. Let me be." She could hear the strength ebbing from her words the same way it was ebbing from her body. Joining with the raindrops to slide down into the sea.

"So you can *run*? So you can *hide*? You think power like yours will be satisfied with that end? You think you know misery *now*. Wait until what lives inside you has no outlet."

Moira met Nick's eyes for the first time since he'd laid hands on her. She searched his face hoping to find the truth promised in his words. "What am I supposed to do?" Her throat closed over the sob she had been strangling her whole life long. "I didn't ask to be made like this. I didn't ask for this...this *curse*. All I ever wanted is to help. But all I ever do is...hurt."

When the tears leaked from the corners of her eyes, they were as warm on her cheeks as the driving rain was cold.

"What you have is a *gift*. But it will act like a curse as long as you treat it like one. You force it to help others time and again. Have you ever, even once, taken pleasure in it? Have you ever taken *anything*? Just for yourself. Just because you wanted it? You want your gift to stop devouring everything in its path? Feed it."

The thunderclap could have been the sound of her ribs cracking open, her heart naked to the open air. She was seen. She was known.

Moira looked at him. Looked at the ruthless beauty of this stranger laying her bare. "Who are you?"

Nick leaned close enough for her to feel his words cool the drops running in rivulets down her cheeks. "Reckoning."

Never since the earth's dawning had Nick been surprised.

Until now.

Moira lunged at him with the speed of the lightning that tore the sky above them, and yet she still only made it halfway to him before he crashed into her. The force of their mouths meeting sent searing heat through his lips and into his jaw where it doubled back in a hungry, hollow ache.

She grabbed handfuls of his sodden shirt, her fingers scraping his ribcage through the thin fabric. Her teeth sank into his lower lip and she bit down hard enough to drag a mingled moan of pain and pleasure from his chest. Sharper than a dagger's point, exquisite and clear, coloring the world around him in a palette more vivid than the human eye could see. Abandoning himself to it would see his cock inside her in less time than it would take to shoot a bullet from a gun.

Her tongue swept across his and he answered in kind, drinking in the heady taste of her. She was the sex-saturated air of sultry spring. The answering call of a mate in the darkness. The end and beginning of a cycle older than time itself.

Her exploration had become a teasing torment, the

small, wet tip of her tongue tracing the indentation her teeth had left in his swollen lower lip. Raindrops in the mouth of a man dying of thirst.

His fingers dove into the wet tangle of her hair to cup her head against retreat. He held her to the force of his passion the way others held torture victims to a flame. He would extract everything he wanted, and more, from her.

What she wanted, she would have to fight him for.

Nick yanked her hair downward, forcing her mouth open to him. He searched the velvet darkness for the words she spat at him in that husky, honeyed voice, but found only a whimper of pleasure. One hand released its hold in her hair to dip downward past her waist to palm the curve of her ass.

Fingers flexed, he ground her hips against him, and brought her to judgment before the hot, hard length she had wrought.

Her low, guttural groan of appreciation sent a sympathetic shiver through the muscles of his back.

She wound her slim arms around his neck and rocked her pelvis against his with a violence that nearly unmanned him. His hands were on her apron then, each grabbing a side and rending the fabric in twain with one brief rip of protest.

He felt her grin against his lips as he shoved his hand beneath the wet fabric of her tank top and found her naked breast. The flesh was moist and cold to the touch, her nipple as cool and hard as a pearl. He rolled the aching bud until it was heated with blood and then caught it between his thumb and forefinger.

He drank her gasp, filling his lungs with her exhaled pleasure. Their breath came in abbreviated pants, unable as they were to inhale with mouths fused in an angry, devouring embrace.

Delicate fingers trailed down his chest and pulled the wadded fabric of his shirt free of his pants. He jumped at the contact of her hand on his bare skin, pulling away from the intensity of the sensation her fingertips created as they played over each taut abdominal muscle.

One quick, silky flick and her cold fingers slid against his hot, pulsing flesh. Breath caught in his throat when her palm grazed the head of his cock.

Power leeched into the rain-slicked fingers wrapping around him, gliding all the way to his root, tightening as they pulled upward with infuriating leisure.

The building roar burst from him, and he broke their kiss to stare into eyes as feral as blue flame. Her eyelids were heavy, half-open and dazed.

Savage pleasure rampaged through him at the sight of her kiss-swollen mouth, more satisfying than blood on a battlefield. She had been branded by him, rubbed raw and pink by the stubble of his jaw. Marked by his teeth, his lips. Lust pounded a primal drumbeat through his veins as he imagined scraping similar patches on her stomach, her breasts, the insides of her thighs. A victory sweeter than any he had ever known.

And he had known many.

He stripped her hand away from him and grabbed her beneath both slippery thighs, hooking her knees over his hips. Her ass came to rest on the guardrail, the ocean below her surging as if in response to her proximity. The panties tore far more easily than the apron had. The red scrap darkened to crimson before the waves swallowed it entirely.

His fingers skimmed up her thigh until they found the dark curls beneath her skirt.

He claimed her mouth and her sex simultaneously. Both hot. Both wet. Both wanting for his cock. He wanted to bury himself in her until kingdom come. Fill every space. Own every want. Coax every sigh. Wring from her every scream of pleasure.

Parting the folds of her flesh, he drew the ample

moisture upward with long, luxurious strokes, grazing the tight bud with his thumb much the same way he had her nipple. His tongue mirrored the fluid flicks, plundering her mouth with no less abandon.

Protracted moans shortened into mewls of pleasure. Her hips bucked against his hand. Her eyes squeezed tight as if against waking from a dream. Her pulse quickened beneath his fingertips. He could taste the building orgasm mingling with rainwater on her lips.

Shock descended upon him for the second time in his life when she grabbed his wrist and pulled his hand away, pushing him back by the shoulders at the same time. A wicked smile creased her face as she slowly, deliberately reached for his belt and unfastened it, followed by the button and zipper.

He watched in breathless silence as she brought her hand to her face and languidly licked her palm, then stroked it up the length of him.

Using knees and thighs, she drew him back into her until he rested not inside her, but *against* her.

She moved. Sliding her swollen clit against him. *Using* him for her own pleasure.

He would have killed to be inside her then. Would have crushed throats with his bare hands just to split her in two and punish her with relentless, brutal thrusts.

But one look at the wild, worshipful expression on her face robbed him of all such thoughts. Only one remained.

He wanted to watch her come.

His fingers dug into her hips, angling her so the blunt head of his cock stroked her again and again, the heat between them building like kindling for a fire the jealous heavens sought to douse.

Lightning scorched the clouds with brief, blinding light. Thunder startled the water spreading out around them into roiling white-capped waves.

They moved together against this drama of sky and sea. Or maybe because of it.

Moira clawed at his back, bit his ear, whispered curses and blessings into the wind as it whipped her hair against his face.

Her scream was shattered by thunder, carried away in the ceaseless roar of waters. Her body folded up against him as her legs shook. Dark lashes resting against her cheek, her forehead furrowed like she studied the internal sensations. Like she—

It couldn't be. Not her—

"First."

As had been their pattern, Nick wasn't sure she had spoken until she spoke again.

"Yup." She nodded. "Never had one before. Truth to tell, I'd always wondered what made folks' eyes roll back in their head."

Nick's own need still pulsed between his legs, throbbing against the insult of words when only fucking would do. "You mean, out of all those men, you never—"

"Nope."

"Oh, Moira." His temporary irritation was banished by the thoughts of hours they would spend sweaty and naked as he introduced her to every single pleasure his long life had brought him. "We have some serious catching up to do."

She hopped down off the guardrail and shimmed her skirt back down her hips. "'Fraid we can't."

"Can't?" Nick turned the word over like the mystery it was. Words like *can't* and *won't* didn't exist in his vocabulary. "Why not?"

"'Cause of that." She looked at something in the distance. Something over his shoulder.

He turned just in time to greet the oncoming wall of water. "Oh, fuck," were the last words he managed.

❧ 11 ❧

"Well, that was impressive."

Moira whipped around to find Tierra standing a few yards down the dock. Rain dripped from her umbrella and puddled at her sandaled feet. The hem of her long peasant skirt was soaked and soiled. Her eyes shone from the shadow a deeper shade of green, like leaves washed vibrant by a storm.

How much had she seen? A pang of guilt stabbed Moira between the ribs.

The downpour ceased abruptly, disappearing like some faucet in the sky had been shut off, which Moira supposed was as good an image as any for what had transpired. The sudden silence left in its wake was broken only by the ocean's steady hush. "It was an accident." She slid Tierra a small, sly smile. "Mostly."

They stared out at the shifting green-gray seascape. The squall had all but disappeared, and taken Nick along with it.

"What you just did..." Tierra shook the umbrella and folded it at her side. "That wasn't because of what happened at the shop, was it?"

"What I did?" Unable to decipher what all Tierra had seen, answering a question with a question seemed the safest route.

"Blasting Nick Kingswood off the dock, for starters."

"Naw. Though he had it comin' about eight ways from Sunday."

Tierra didn't seem inclined to argue. "What about what happened before that?"

"What about it?"

"You weren't...trying to get him not to..." Tierra trailed off.

Moira raised an eyebrow at her sister, confident she could wait out a silence much longer than the woman fairly bustin' at the seams from the effort of *not* saying something.

A frustrated exhale came seconds later. "You didn't try to hump him out of evicting Ambrosia's, did you?"

"Nope." Moira wrapped her arms around her own goose-pimpled flesh. "It don't work like that."

"How does it work?"

Moira looked at her sister, trying to read her expression like some women back home did tealeaves. Never before had anyone asked her this question. Not once. Not ever. "You really wanna know?"

Tierra nodded. "You tried to tell me earlier, and I cut you off. I'm sorry for that."

"What I done today at the shop, it's how I *help* folks." She waited a beat to see how these words would sit with Tierra.

"What kind of help?"

"All kinds. Hurt feelins', broken bones. I can bring around most anybody. Lots of times it's just somethin' needs drawin' off. I take it from them, and then they're better."

"So how long have you known you could help people like that?"

"'Bout the same time I started my period and all that. Before that it was just takin' care of my uncles. Talkin' fish into the boat and keepin' everyone fed."

Moira watched Tierra wrestle with this information, struggling to form words that were neither bossy nor harsh.

"Moira," she said at last. "You've spent your whole life taking care of other people. Healing them. Giving to them."

"I 'spose." Moira shrugged.

"Listen to me," Tierra insisted, dropping the umbrella and taking Moira's cold hands in her warm ones. "I know you do what you do out of kindness. Out of love for the people around you. But you're more than just what you can do for other people. Do you know that?"

A gull's call in the distance sounded exactly as displaced as Moira felt. "I don't know if there's much left, once you take away the helpin'."

"*I* do," Tierra said.

"No offense," Moira snorted. "But you don't know an awful lot about me besides what I told ya."

"I know the only thing that matters."

"What's that?"

Tierra's hands tightened over hers. "You're my *sister*. Nothing you could ever do or say is going to change that."

"You didn't seem all that thrilled with what I was doin' *or* sayin' earlier," Moira reminded her.

"I know." Tierra's gaze floated out over the water, mining the depths of some unseen past. "I've spent my whole life feeling like something was missing. Like *someone* was missing. Then suddenly you're here. But it's nothing like I thought it would be."

"Tell me about it. In the course of twenty-four hours, I found out I was separated at birth from my twin sister, dumped in a bayou, and raised by a bunch of drunks that pulled me out in a catfish net. Not to mention, I got an aunt that hates me more n' whores hate church."

"Aunt Justine doesn't hate you. She's just scared." Tierra exhaled and dropped her sister's hands. "I guess I was too."

"What for?"

"I saw the way everyone in the shop was with you. The way the men watched your every move. The way the women judged you. You let them take whatever they wanted from you without so much as a word of protest."

Moira made no attempt to deny this. Such had it always been.

"You're better than that, Moira," Tierra continued. "I just wanted you to see it."

"I don't know if I can."

"Say you'll try." The pleading note in her sister's voice left Moira's heart feeling bloody and bruised. It was so raw. So vulnerable. So *not* Tierra. "Say you'll stay."

Moira shivered. "I guess I wouldn't mind a bubble bath in that clawfoot tub upstairs."

"Yay!" Tierra hugged her with such force that the air was knocked clean out of Moira's lungs. Whatever chance she might have of recovering was compromised by the bone-crushing squeeze of her sister's arms around her shoulders.

This is what it was like to be hugged by another female. Such a strange combination of softness and strength.

"I ain't wearin' a bra though," Moira said.

"Will you at least wear this?" Tierra slid out of her shawl and wrapped the still-warm garment around Moira's shivering shoulders. "You're soaked to the skin and cold as death."

The simple kindness of this gesture set Moira's bottom lip to quivering. She pulled the fabric tighter around her, not wanting to lose even a trace of warmth from her sister's skin. "Thanks."

They turned together and angled back toward town.

"Just out of curiosity," Tierra probed. "What kind of *help* were you giving Mr. Kingswood just now?"

"Not a lick." *Lick*. Moira felt regret stir up like silt from a river bottom. She'd have liked to lick Nick Kingswood a little. Probably there was a lot on him that would taste pretty good, if that wicked mouth of his was any indication.

Tierra's eyes narrowed a fraction. "So if you weren't trying to help him and you weren't trying to help me, why exactly were you examining his tonsils?"

Heat flooded Moira's cheeks at the fresh memory. "On account of he's more fun to ride than a rodeo bull. He told me to take what I wanted. So, I did."

"That's great," Tierra said. "I mean, he's a cocky sonovabitch and he's definitely going down in a big way —if he's not already drowned. Still, if he managed to get you to take something for yourself, I might just consider calling the Coast Guard so he can have a proper burial. Ooh! Then I would have a tombstone to spit on."

"Don't think you need to worry about the Coast Guard," Moira said. "Nick Kingswood ain't dead."

"How can you be so sure?" Tierra asked.

"Cause he ain't..." Even as the words left her lips, Moira felt their truth echo in her soul. She could feel him. As surely as she could feel the air she breathed, and with no less insistence. "He ain't human."

"I'll say," Tierra snorted.

"I mean it. He's somethin' else. Somethin'...more."

"Well, that sucks. Any ideas what he might be?"

"Other than a giant pain in the ass? Not a clue. But I have a feelin' it might be in our best interest to find out."

"I think you're right. But first we need to get you dry and warmed up," Tierra said, dropping an arm around Moira. "Let's go home."

"Home," Moira repeated. "I sure do like the way that sounds."

❄   I 2   ❄

"Somethin' ain't right." Moira froze on the porch. A few lone candles flickered in the windows like eyes in the shadows.

"Damn straight," Tierra said holding up the shredded fabric she had retrieved from the dock. "That bastard ripped my apron."

The first wave washed over Moira—as thick and hot as tar. Hate. Fear. "No. Somethin's in there. I can feel it."

Tierra clasped Moira's hand, freezing them both in place. "I feel it too. Whatever's in there is with Aunt Justine." *Unless it is Aunt Justine.*

The front door sighed open without their help. "Ugh," Tierra grumbled, pocketing her keys. "I hate it when that happens in the movies."

"This ain't a movie," Moira pointed out. Though it certainly looked like one. Candles played hide and seek among the plants on the living room's many surfaces, sending shadows dancing up the dim walls. Wax dripped down the slim tapers and pooled on polished wooden surfaces.

"Aunt Justine!" Tierra called down the hallway. "Are you home?" An indignant squeak echoed through the eerily silent house.

"Cheeto!" Moira cried. Still barefoot, she took the stairs two a time, racing toward the bathroom where she had left him with bowls full of food and water earlier that morning. Scarcely had her hands closed around Cheeto's warm body, when her own was pinned to the wall by an unseen force.

It was the stuff of nightmares.

She fought to move her limbs, but the air might as well have been concrete. Even the scream in her throat remained frozen in place. Cries built up behind it until she was choking on her own panicked breath.

Had Tierra met a similar fate in the kitchen?

Aunt Justine's gnarled fingers clawed out of the oily darkness. The hand she held at throat level preceded her like a flashlight in the darkness. Behind it, the pale moon of her face and wild corona of fading red hair floated into focus. Shadows seeped into the hallway after her, additional faces coming into view, their chants a low, threatening hum.

Pain shook Moira's body. She had never before considered screaming a luxury, but she would have given anything in that moment to send her agony vibrating through the night.

Justine was close now. Close enough that Moira could smell dried herbs, incense, and spices that announced her presence. Something else lurked below the surface. Something metallic. *Blood?*

"You," Justine whispered. "You should be dead. As long as you were dead, we were safe."

The thin skin of hope Moira had grown over the course of this afternoon was stripped away as easy as that, leaving her stinging and sore.

"I should have done it myself," Justine continued. "She was my *sister*. She was my responsibility. But I wasn't strong enough. I'm paying for that now. I'm paying dearly, as will we all."

A gentle *pat, pat, pat* drew Moira's gaze to the floor

where a small, dark stain spread at Justine's feet. The curved, wicked blade of a dagger slid out of the robe's pocket. The fingers grasping the ornately carved handle were slicked with blood. Dark rivulets branched down her arms like veins on the wrong side of her pale skin.

"I will do now what I should have done then. I will bleed that others may live. And so will you."

The chant redoubled in power and speed, driven perhaps by the smell of blood thick in Moira's nostrils. Fresh anguish ripped through her and the dagger's curve ceased to be a threat. A silvery smile. The promise of an end. She willed the cool, sharp weapon to find a home inside her troublesome shell.

Her dark thoughts were burned away by a flash of bright orange reflected in the blade before it engulfed Justine completely. It wreathed her in a flaming halo before licking up the robes of the women surrounding her. Their sudden, startled shrieks of pain made Moira realize her own had vanished.

She could breathe. She could move. And she had Cheeto to thank.

"*Tierra!*" The scream had been loud enough to scrape her throat. She tucked her porcine savior to her chest, tripping and sliding down the stairs.

Chanting echoed down the hallway from the kitchen. Moira flattened herself against a wall and set Cheeto down on the wood floor.

"Make momma proud."

The sound of his little hooves clicking was quickly swallowed up as he turned and scooted through a gap in the kitchen door.

Moira didn't realize she had been holding her breath until it filled her lungs in a hot, dizzying rush when shrieks broke out in the kitchen.

Cheeto came flying out of the kitchen with Tierra on his cloven heels.

Words tumbled from Moira's lips in a configuration

that resembled shrapnel more than sentences. "Blood—Aunt Justine—tried to kill me."

"I know," Tierra panted. "It's the coven."

"The what?"

"The coven," Tierra repeated. "Oh, shit!"

Shadowy figures were now oozing toward them from two directions.

Tierra's hand slid into Moira's with the ease that breath found her lungs. A vibration rocked the house on its foundations when their palms met. Plaster dust fell from the ceiling like snow.

"Stop!" Aunt Justine hissed, her charred edges making her all the more frightening. "You don't know what you're doing."

"But I sure as hell know what you were tryin' to do," Moira accused. "I ain't fixin' to die today, if it's all the same to you."

"It must be done," Justine said. Her face bore the zealot's shine Moira had seen on folks wandering out of those five-day tent revivals where wrestling snakes was as common as singing hymns. "There is no other way."

"You're not taking my sister from me." Tierra's grip on her hand tightened.

"She must die." The phrase spoken by Justine rolled through the still-approaching crowd in a whisper. "Or everyone will."

"What the hell kind of nonsense you talkin'?"

"Just give her to us, and everything can go back to the way it was," Justine pleaded.

"So help me goddess," Tierra vowed, "you come any closer and we will bring this house down upon all your heads."

An enraged growl tore from Justine's throat as she brought her hands up, ready to strike.

Power the likes of which Moira had never felt crackled between their clasped hands. A perfect, silent stillness fell around them while the world beyond began to shatter. The house shook, the ground bucked all but Moira and Tierra off their feet. Glass blew inward as golf ball-sized hail tore through house like tissue paper. Vases exploded, paintings leapt from the walls.

Moira watched Justine fight her way to her feet, clinging on to the arm of the sofa for support. "Tierra de Moray! Enough!"

Their bubble of stillness burst outward, and everything ceased as abruptly as it had begun. The black-clad witches looked more like startled women to Moira now, gazing up at them with a mixture of horror and awe.

For the space of several moments, there was only the sound of their ragged breathing.

"They have combined." Justine's announcement was pronounced with a flat, dead calm that sent chills racing over Moira's scalp. "It cannot be undone. On our heads be it." Justine's head bowed as if burdened from above. The women around her rose to their feet and followed suit.

"What can't be undone?" Tierra demanded.

Justine's face was a twisted mask of fear and regret. "The end," she said.

"The end of what?" Moira asked.

"Everything," the voices spoke in unison.

❧ 13 ❧

"The First Seal's been opened, then?" Somehow the statement lacked its proper gravity when yawned in Julian's perpetually-bored aristocratic dialect.

It was the kind of tone he adopted after having spent the entire day indoors in his smoking jacket, mooning over melancholic tomes in his library and exploring every possible iteration of the word *angst*.

"We don't know that," Nick answered. "You'll remember how many false alarms we've had in the past."

"10,873," Julian drawled. "But who's counting?"

Once again parked across the street from the house Moira shared with Tierra and their aunt, Nick watched a procession of black-cloaked figures file out of the house and into the night. "Speaking of counting, there are only two of them," Nick pointed out. "The prophecy calls for four."

"You say it like it's a bloody recipe," Julian sighed. *"Crack four spawn of Satan into a large mixing bowl and beat until frothy or the Apocalypse descends upon the earth."*

"I just don't see any reason to do something hasty until we're certain this time."

"This coming from the man who single-handedly brought about the Siege of Tyre with one off-handed comment to Alexander the Great about the *unconquerable* city?"

"That wasn't hasty. It was strategic."

"Buying a woman a drink so you can bed her later is strategic. Tempting the Earth's most notorious warmonger to tumble a city just because you're reticent to share the appellation *unconquerable* is willful and impetuous."

"You say that like it's a bad thing," Nick quipped. "Anyway, I would have done it myself, but I was occupied else—"

Agony robbed Nick of the capacity of for speech. He clawed at his back, certain it had been set aflame by some new devilry Moira and her earth witch sister had devised.

In his long years, he had been shot, stabbed, drowned, branded and even burned at the stake—an unfortunate afternoon of the Spanish Inquisition he just as soon as forget. And yet, never had he felt anything comparable to this.

It moved across the skin of his back, deliberately tracing a shape his mind couldn't assemble through its haze of anguish.

The pain evaporated as quickly as it had arrived. Nick remained bent with his forehead pressed to the cool leather steering wheel.

"Well that was a ghastly aural assault," Julian sighed. "Not the aftereffects of one of your curry benders, I hope?"

Nick looked behind him at the shape of a bow and notched arrow scorched into the Vette's leather seat—a mirror image of the one now seared into his back. This would be an awkward conversation with the rental car company.

"The bow," Nick whispered. "I have the bow."

The sound of ice clinking in Julian's glass reminded Nick how bone-weary and wrung out he was. Swimming back to shore had taken him the better part of an hour. Returning to the hotel to shower and change had cost him precious time he would have rather spent making Moira pay for leaving him high and dry.

Well, *high* anyway.

"In that case, it's time for you to do what you do best."

"It's not that simple."

"Oh, but it is." The ease with which Julian pronounced these words almost made Nick believe them. "Your water witch has set off a chain of events that will end human civilization. It's only a matter of time before she discovers what she can do if she uses those powers for her own gain. When that happens, the Biblical plagues will look like a children's fairy story."

Nick's own words ricocheted through his head. Thanks to him, she was well on her way. And for her first experiment, she had conquered Conquest himself.

"You know what needs to happen, Nicholas," Julian said. Silence stretched between them long enough for Nick to hear his own heart slow.

"Moira de Moray needs to die."

❦ II ❦
CLAIRE

By Cindy Stark

❈   14   ❈

"What the hell are you doing to me?"

Smoldering orange incense filled the bedroom with a sultry scent as the thick scattering of candles cast flickering shadows on the darkened walls. Sinclaire Brenton inhaled as her incredibly attractive lover ripped her panties from her body, leaving her bare to his gaze as she anticipated the sensual pleasures of the night ahead. His reputation as a notorious player didn't deter her in the slightest.

He claimed her mouth with a possessiveness that sent a delicious thrill racing through her. Strong arms held her against him, his body a chiseled piece of granite that did everything for her physically, but would never touch her heart. He backed her until her thighs bumped the bed, and then he lifted her and tossed her onto the red silk sheets.

She savored his kisses, let him talk sweetly to her as he positioned himself to steal her love. He had no idea they would have ended up in her bedroom with half the drinks he'd bought her and only a third of the sexy flirtations.

She'd given him enough time to think he controlled this seduction. Enough time to settle between her legs and act as though she wasn't another of his many conquests he'd use and discard when dawn broke over Bali the next morning.

Enough time for her power to begin to bend him to her will.

"Let's do this my way," Claire whispered into his ear.

He grinned and complied as she pushed against his massive shoulders and rolled them over. His body was beautiful. Young and strong, the best kind of lover. Tall with muscles earned by surfing the sparkling turquoise waters only feet outside her back door. His sun-kissed blond hair and brilliant blue eyes made him stand out like a red umbrella on a rainy day among the dark-haired, dark-skinned inhabitants of their island. His smile promised so much more than a one-night stand.

His smile lied.

He gripped her hips, his expression already growing hazy. *"Fuck me, Claire."*

"Shh...don't talk. I promise this will be a night you'll never forget."

She leaned forward, her dark hair dropping like a final curtain around his head as she gave him her breast. Greedy lips tugged on her nipple, contracting muscles inside her. Dormant needs ignited like a fire stirred, reminding her of the delicious night they had in store. In his petty little mind, he believed he was the predator, but in the end, she'd walk away with his dark power.

She'd leave the goodness inside him for the next woman he loved and take the destructive need to own women and use them. He'd be a better man, and she'd feed that phantom pain inside her. If only for a while.

She pulled from him, her breasts tingling, begging for more as she positioned him at her entry.

Already his eyes failed to focus. But she didn't need him to see her. Didn't need to wonder any longer if a man could truly love her. She'd known for years now that would not be in the cards for her.

She encircled his hard length as it pulsed, begging

for her to release him from the overwhelming ache he must be enduring by this point. The nameless dark desire she carried inside her burned her as well.

She inhaled as though it would be some time before she could breathe again and impaled herself on him.

They both cried out in ecstasy.

Heated sensations overtook her, removing her from the cruel existence of her world. She danced in the flames of desire, taking from her lover a power that could fuel her for days. His passion filled her soul, igniting the orange ball of light that seemed to dim so easily.

She could sense her body, sense the friction his rock-hard shaft created inside her as her breasts bounced in the sultry heat of the night. But she was not with him in that tangled mass of silk. She'd moved beyond their atmosphere, flying toward the sun burning bright somewhere in the heavens.

A shifting of the earth beneath her physical body knocked her from flight, like the unexpected splash of a chilled ocean wave. A silent voice whispered to her, but she couldn't make sense of the words through the haze and shock surrounding her.

The power she feasted on ceased, and she was sucked back to her room. An invisible hand extinguished all but one flickering candle, leaving the space much darker than before. Her lover still lay beneath her, his face contorted in extreme pleasure.

"Was that an earthquake?" she whispered, hoping for a logical explanation.

"Don't stop," he panted and moved beneath her.

A terrible fear whipped through her, leaving disbelief trailing behind. *She'd lost the one-way current running between them.* If she failed to use her ability to take, she'd surely die. If not from lack of strength, then certainly from loneliness.

He gripped her tighter. "Please."

She started to move, unwilling to let her lover suffer as she did. There was nothing between them now, no exchange of power, at least not for her. Worse, everything she'd taken from him had vanished.

When her lover finished convulsing beneath her, she climbed from him, distraught that she'd been cheated when he'd found his release.

"I love you, Claire," he said, staring at her as if she was a goddess.

"No, not me," she said, the brief flash of expected pain ripping through her. This was always the hardest part, ignoring the look of devotion radiating from their faces. She'd believed it the first time she'd taken a man, and it had cost her precious love his mind.

She'd reacted by plowing her way through several men until she realized there was no man who could survive her love for long.

He stood and walked toward her, taking her by the shoulders. "But I need you. I want to make you as happy as you've made me."

"Then leave whatever cash you have on the table by the door as you leave." She'd decided a long time ago that it wasn't wrong to ask for something in return. After all, she'd given him a new life. The least he could do was buy her dinner for a few days.

He dressed and paused by the door as he emptied his wallet. "Can I see you tomorrow?"

"We'll see. Right now, you should go," she said softly, knowing she could fall in love with the resurrected man gazing at her with adoration. "I know there's someone who waits for you."

There always was. If she made him leave now, he'd go on to have a happy life. He'd be the husband every woman craved.

She'd be alone again, looking for her next fix.

Except even that wasn't a guarantee any longer.

The moment he left, she relit the candles, hoping to

draw some warmth back into her empty soul. When that didn't work, she placed kindling and logs in the fireplace she'd had installed and lit it. She curled on the black fuzzy rug in front of the hearth like she'd done many times before in an effort to be close to the one thing that made her feel alive.

The hypnotic fire popped and spit as it consumed wood, much like she consumed men.

The whispering came again then, as though it had circled around, intent on delivering its message. The words were foreign and yet as familiar as the haunted eyes reflected at her in the mirror every morning.

> *"Keeper of secrets, release what was taken,*
> *Hear me now—answer in three*
> *Return to me what has been forsaken,*
> *By earth, air, fire, and sea..."*

A lone shiver raced over her bare skin as realization dawned. She needed to return home.

Home.

A word that had been a foreign idea for as long as she could remember. There had been a time once when she'd had a home, had a mother. She could still remember her blonde hair and the floral scent that had accompanied her soft touch. But Claire had ruined that when she'd grown angry at being forced to go to bed one night. She couldn't have been more than three or four, but the scent of acrid smoke and the fear on her mother's face remained burned in her memory as if it had been yesterday.

She shook the painful thoughts away as she stood and headed into her bedroom to pack. They didn't matter. The woman hadn't been her real mother anyway. After Claire had turned eighteen and escaped the years of cold foster homes, she'd searched for her true family. But it seemed no one could tell her anything. The mother she remembered hadn't legally adopted her, so when she left Claire at a metropolitan supermarket, there had been no one to contact to pick her up. The authorities had wondered if she'd been kidnapped. If so, no one had stepped forward to claim her. Ever.

So she'd claimed herself. Damn it.

Now...now something somewhere called to her, compelling her to return. She didn't doubt the validity of the summons. It spoke to part of her that no one else had ever understood, the part that spoke truth, even with the dark power always simmering beneath the surface.

She slipped into her orange silk wrapper before she lugged two large suitcases from the back of her closet. She'd pack the necessities, like her collection of rare and exotic daggers along with her well-worn copy of Pride and Prejudice. Anything else she couldn't stuff into her suitcases, she'd pay movers to pack and ship to...

She paused as an image formed in her mind. Fishing boats on a little bay...lots of trees...old buildings and Victorian homes.

Washington...the state, not DC.

Her home was somewhere in Washington?

She'd never been to the Pacific Northwest. But even as she considered the possibility, an affirmation struck in her heart, returning some of the energy she'd lost earlier.

She'd travel to Washington. Tomorrow. She'd catch the first available flight back to the states, any state, and she'd head out from there.

She had no idea who or what waited for her, but damn it, she was going home.

❀ 15 ❀

The airline information screen above Dru Geddes's head updated, indicating the plane from Bali via Tokyo had landed. He paused a moment to savor the spike in his pulse as he embarked on a new mission. So few things continued to bring him pleasure. Knowing he was on the brink of a new war happened to be one of them.

His phone buzzed, and he slipped it from his pocket. "She just landed," he said as a way of greeting. "I'll remove her from the premises and then eliminate the threat as planned."

He'd informed Bane of his planned methods to prevent the end of days, and Death had agreed. Annihilate one necessary piece of the threat, and he would eliminate the whole. Much the way he'd cut off the head of a certain general back in the sixteen-hundreds and, in effect, decimated the entire army.

The battle looming on his current horizon, the one that justified his entire existence, was the most important one of all. He'd spent many lifetimes honing his body to be as powerful as the mystical sword he wielded. His time had come. Not that he cared for the whining, entitled people he encountered daily, but he was a man of honor, and he'd fulfill this commitment to protect their world or die trying.

"I could kill her for you. Death is my specialty," Bane offered.

"No. This one is mine." He'd relish completing his duty. "My sword will cut through any protective spells she's wrought. I'll succeed where Nick failed. When you hear from me again, our fears for the future of mankind will be extinct."

"Good luck, then, friend."

Dru pocketed his phone and set out to locate the luggage carousel where she'd arrive to claim her bags. He'd seen pictures of Moira, the witch Nick had failed to conquer. He would not make the same mistake with her sister.

Four born of one. If Gwen's divinations were correct, the witch headed his way would open the Second Seal, his Seal, and he intended to stop her. No problem. The way he figured it, he only needed to eliminate one of the four to eradicate the prophecy outlining the end of time.

He'd concede Nick had no idea who he'd been dealing with when he'd met Moira. None of them realized their time had come and that Moira would be capable of breaking the First Seal. Still, once discovered, he would have killed her, put the mission before his own personal feelings instead of allowing her power over him to sway his actions.

Now the torch had passed to him, and he would succeed. He'd stop the travesty. He'd be the one to save the world. It was a heavy weight to bear, but he was an excellent soldier, a cunning warrior, born specifically for this monumental task.

OVERHEAD CLOUDS GREETED CLAIRE AS THE PLANE landed in Seattle. She would have preferred a brilliant sun heating the afternoon, but something soft and welcoming hovered in the air despite the gray day.

"I hate flying," said the older woman sitting in the seat next to her. "It's always a relief when we're back on the ground."

Claire smiled. She'd been cool when the plump grandmotherly-type had squeezed into the seat next to her back in Chicago, meaning to exchange pleasantries and then promptly tune her out with a pair of headphones. Social graces were not her forte. But Mrs. Sandra Howington kept right on talking until Claire realized they were halfway to Seattle. The sweet, older lady was on her way home to her loving husband after visiting her daughter and newest grandchild.

"Flying doesn't bother me," she said to Sandy. She'd never thought much about dying. There would be no family or friends to mourn her. In some aspects, it might be a relief to be released from the solitary life that had been forced upon her.

"You're lucky then. It terrifies me."

Claire stood along with the other passengers. "I'd say you're the lucky one, finding a man like Dennis."

Sandy followed her off the plane, and they walked together to retrieve their luggage. "You know, we have never had a serious fight in the forty years we've been married," she said as she struggled to pull a tapestry suitcase from the conveyor belt.

Claire couldn't imagine loving someone that long, let alone never having an argument. "That's amazing," she said as she helped the woman wrangle her suitcase to an upright position.

As Claire straightened, her inner alarm fired, sending a tremble racing through her. She glanced across the carousel to find a man with intense, midnight eyes watching her as though he expected her to make a sudden, lethal move. Her pulse leapt as a feeling of un-ease washed over her. She was used to men looking at her with lust-filled eyes, but their gazes never left her feeling this naked.

Dark, military-short hair covered his head, and a hint of a beard outlined his hard, chiseled face. A long-sleeved black t-shirt stretched across his massive chest and displayed biceps the size of her thighs. Olive green khakis covered the rest of his impressive body. The blood from many battles tainted the air around him, and only a fool would mistake his ferocity.

A soldier returning from the Middle East perhaps?

He didn't break eye contact as he retrieved a long, slender case and a camouflage duffel bag from the carousel in front of him, and she wondered how he could possibly know what he'd grabbed without looking.

"Dennis will be waiting for me outside," Sandy said, forcing Claire to break the connection. "I wish we were headed toward Port Townsend, and we could give you a ride."

"No. Don't even think about it. I'll rent a car and be there in no time."

"I bet your family will be surprised to see you." Sandy's smile beamed.

"I'm sure they will." Whoever they were. Claire only hoped Sandy had been correct when she'd showed her the drawing she'd created from the images in her mind of a little Victorian seaport. Otherwise, she'd come all this way only to find herself lost again.

Sandy gave her an awkward hug and then waved as she headed outside where her dear husband awaited. Claire turned back and gave the area a quick scan, looking for the man who'd somehow chilled and heated her blood at the same time, but he'd disappeared.

She grabbed her suitcases from the few that re-mained and moved toward the exit where she'd catch a shuttle to the car rental facility. Thick emissions from noisy cars assaulted her as she stepped into the humid air. Shouting from a short distance away drew her attention, and she was shocked to find a scrawny, older man standing next to a white sedan screaming up a storm at the sweet lady she'd just befriended.

"I don't have all goddamn day to sit and wait for you to get your fat ass outside." He lifted her suitcase toward the trunk, but before he completed his mission, the top burst open, spilling underwear and toiletries to the pavement.

"You did that on purpose." Anger contorted her kind face. "I can't believe I've been married to you all these years and never realized you're such a jackass."

Claire put a hand to her mouth as sadness and disbelief cascaded through her. She'd only met Sandy on the plane, but she hadn't sensed any dishonesty when Sandy had talked about her lovely husband. People wandered closer to watch the spectacle, the hum of their energy growing louder.

She stepped forward to intervene, if only to help pick up Sandy's belongings. As she moved closer to them, a powerful current of energy slammed her from behind, and she glanced over her shoulder to find the soldier watching the scene with a smirk on his engaging face.

She sensed he had a part in the spectacle playing out before them, and that enraged her more than she'd expected. She swiveled on her heels and marched in his direction.

The second his dark gaze met hers, the soldier picked up his bags and strode away. The fact that he'd turned his back on her made her even angrier, and she quickened her stride. A quick glance behind her proved her assumptions were correct. The older couple was no longer fighting, but hugging instead.

"Hey!" Her heels clipped on the sidewalk as she

tried to catch him, but his legs were long, and he moved with the ease of a predator. "Come back here! I want to talk to you."

A shuttle bus pulled up just as he reached the stop, and he stepped onto it without missing a stride. If he thought that would stop her, he had another thing coming. All he'd done was manage to corner himself. That he was a dangerous man wouldn't deter her. She'd held her own on more than one occasion.

She hurried inside the bus, lugging her awkward suitcases with her. He sat in the back corner, using the crowd of people for cover, hiding like a sniper on the hillside.

"Please stow your bags in the luggage area, ma'am," the driver called to her.

She lowered the handles and stuffed them with the rest of the passengers' bags as the bus began to move forward. Instead of choosing the closest seat, she walked to the back of the bus, heading straight for the soldier.

❧ 16 ❧

An unsettling current of attraction curled around Claire as she walked toward the soldier, forming a sultry haze around her thoughts. He watched her with dark, lust-filled eyes that reached into her soul. She took a deep breath, taking a second to savor the feeling before she shoved her way through it and claimed the seat next to him. "I saw what you did back there."

The soldier didn't answer. Instead, he dropped his dark gaze to her mouth, then her breasts, and finally to her legs. He only looked, but the sensation of him *touching* her was very real. Worse, her body responded. Hot blood pulsated through her veins as her breaths came faster. Tingles spiked in her breasts, and her core contracted in response.

"Stop it," she hissed, knowing if he continued, she'd embarrass herself in front of a bus full of people.

More than that, he needed to answer for what he'd done. "I saw what you did to Sandy and her husband."

"Really? And what was that?" His voice rumbled when he spoke, a deep, coarse sound that vibrated her senses, making her want to scoot closer.

She glanced at the people now watching them with expectant eyes, waiting for some sort of juicy response. Before she could reply, the bus jerked to a stop as an automated voice announced they were now at the first station.

He arched a sexy brow as one side of his mouth lifted in a grin. "My stop." He stood, his muscular thighs brushing her bare legs as he pushed past her.

Oh, hell no. She stood as people around them began to whisper.

He was off the bus and halfway down an aisle of cars when she dragged her suitcases down the steps and hurried after him. She'd have an answer before she let him leave.

He stopped next to a shiny red Hummer, his well-defined pecs flexing as he tossed his duffel bag in the back, stealing her focus. If she wasn't so angry, she'd relish the time she might spend fixing him, stealing some of that formidable energy. Luckily, her cab driver in Bali had proven she hadn't forever lost her capability to take from others.

Claire parked her suitcases behind his SUV as he placed the long case in next. Maddening irritation swirled through her veins like fiery acid from chasing him down. "You're not leaving until you tell me what you did to Sandy and her husband."

He gave her a sideways glance, his lips turning into a self-satisfied smirk. Without hesitating, he grabbed both of her suitcases and tossed them in after his, slamming the back closed.

His actions stunned her. "*What the hell do you think you're doing?*" She stepped forward, meaning to open the hatch again, but he caught her hands. Rage ignited inside her, and she jerked free, pushing against his chest.

The jolt of energy that shot from her into him surprised them both. He stumbled back, but quickly regained his footing, grabbing her by the shoulders and turning her until he had her pinned against the back of his Hummer.

Her breath came in gasps.

His dark eyes bored into her like minions of the devil himself. "I didn't expect you to be so pretty."

His reply caught her off guard, setting off all kinds of internal alarms. "What do you mean? You don't know me, don't know anything about me." She pushed against him again, but he didn't budge.

"But I do." His voice was a low whisper, and there was no mistaking the threat behind it. "I know exactly who you are and where you're going."

She gasped. "How? Who are you?" The vibes radiating off him proved he was beyond ordinary, and she was well aware that he came equipped with more power than his heated good looks and overwhelming physical presence. That didn't mean she was without her own defenses.

He lifted a finger and drew it down her cheek, leaving a warm frisson in his wake. "Let's just say I know who called you home."

Home? The word plucked at the tenuous ties drawing her to Port Townsend. "Tell me who."

He studied her, the cocky look in his gaze filled with self-assured domination. "No. The only way to find out is to hop into my truck and allow me to drive you there."

The condescending way he spoke raised her ire. She lifted a perfectly-sculpted brow, ignoring the way her breaths grew deeper the longer she looked into his eyes. "*Excuse me?* I don't *hop* for any man."

"There's always a first time, sweetheart." Her irritation didn't seem to affect him in the least, leaving her scrambling for another tactic.

She settled for something familiar and let her smile turn sultry as she inhaled a deep breath, pressing her breasts against his chest. His lips curved in a similar grin, as though he was certain he'd won this battle. The man certainly had no self-esteem issues. "I bet you have women fighting for a chance to climb on up into that big ol' Hummer with you."

He gave an almost imperceptible shrug, a satisfied look gleaming in his ever-attractive eyes. "It's happened a time or two."

"Then this might come as a shock to you, but...no."

Her answer flipped his annoying smile, revealing the darker side of him she'd sensed all along. "I don't want to force you."

"As if you could."

His smile returned. "Trust me. I can and will."

"I don't think so." Using the anger he ignited inside her, she lifted her knee with a swift, spiteful force, landing it squarely in his groin. A thick grunt echoed from his massive chest as he bent forward, and she used the opportunity to slip from his grasp.

"Goddamn," he whispered before he sucked in a large breath and straightened, not giving her enough time to reclaim her suitcases. Dark, angry eyes met hers, speaking to the fire burning inside her. His instinct would be to retaliate, she realized, but he'd kept it in check. For now. "Do you really want to do this the hard way?" he asked.

☙❧

CLAIRE'S LEATHER JACKET SCRUNCHED AS SHE FOLDED her arms beneath her breasts, sizing up the mountain of molten steel standing between her and her suitcases. She had two choices. First, she could leave. Let the prick keep her belongings. He'd probably get off sniffing through her panties and bras. It might mean running, but he wasn't the only one in top form.

Second, she could concede to his threats, but she'd never been one to back down from a fight. And the man seriously pissed her off. He might know who had called her to this place, but she was positive he hadn't been sent to collect her.

Her summons had come from a familiar energy, something warm and earthy, not this hulking man who reeked of power and violence as old as time. Even if something inside her responded to his force, he wasn't to be trusted.

She toed off her stilettos, knowing she'd miss them. She couldn't consider the precious daggers waiting inside her luggage, or she'd cry. Too bad she didn't have one in her hand now.

He sent her a warning look, obviously well aware of her intentions. That was okay. He might be upright once again, but she'd nailed him hard. She only needed a slight advantage to make it to a more open area where others would see if he tried to take her. Even if he caught her, he'd have to drag her back to his Hummer, and she'd go kicking and screaming the whole way. Certainly, someone would intervene.

"You know what?" She turned her red lips into her own version of a smug smile. "Fuck you."

She was off, her bare feet hitting the rough asphalt surface as she raced back toward the shuttle station. She smiled when she realized two businessmen waited at the stop. Eyewitnesses whose presence would protect her. The soldier had picked the wrong girl to mess with.

Both of the men grinned as she approached, the usual reaction she received when she went looking for it. "Evening," she said when she'd joined them. Neither of them seemed to notice her lack of footwear or suitcases.

"How long until the next shuttle? I'm late for a flight." She glanced behind her, searching for, and panicking slightly when she couldn't see her powerful assailant.

The balding man in a blue suit checked his watch.

"Should be here in a couple of minutes. What time does your flight leave?"

"What the fuck do you care?" the other man asked, his bushy salt and pepper brows coming together in an angry clash on his forehead. "Do you seriously think this hot piece of ass needs your consideration?"

Claire widened her eyes and took a step back, avoiding the sudden flood of testosterone.

"Oh yeah?" the first guy responded. "How about I show you some special consideration?" He dropped his briefcase and lunged at his companion, knocking him to the ground.

The older man tried to push off his attacker, but failed as numerous blows landed on his jaw and temples.

"Stop it!" Claire screamed, more than a little frightened by the scene unfolding in front of her. She'd seen a similar display of emotions less than thirty minutes ago, and she couldn't help but wonder if the same jerk fostered their brutality.

If the fighting men heard her exclamation, it didn't register with them. She turned, searching for the lethal source of energy. The dark-haired military hotshot had to be close.

A movement to her left startled her, but it was only a young couple exiting their silver sedan. As they walked toward the shuttle stop, they grew wary of the men tussling on the ground. The man pushed his wife behind him as he approached.

"Hey!" He grabbed the bald-headed man's fist before he could strike again. "You've done enough damage."

The bald-headed man stopped his attack, seeming stunned and then genuinely shocked as he looked between the man who'd intervened and his victim. "My God. I didn't...."

"We need to call for help," Claire said, even as two more men and an elderly woman also approached the group. If nothing else, the increased number gave her more security. If hotshot had expected the fighting men to leave her vulnerable, his plan had certainly backfired.

The young woman pulled out her phone as others crowded around trying to help the beaten man.

"Claire?"

Claire turned at the sound of her name, surprised to see Sandy and her husband sitting in their car, stopped only feet from the scene. "*What are you doing here, Sandy?*" They should have been well on their way home.

"Dennis took the wrong turn, and we ended up in long-term parking. We were just circling around when we saw you. What's going on? Why are you out here? I thought you were renting a car."

Warm relief rushed through her. "I was. I am. It's a long story. Could I catch a ride back to the terminal with you?" That would get her out of harm's way faster than anything would.

"Sure, honey." Sandy exited the car and opened the door to the back seat for her. "Maybe you could help me with something on the short drive around."

"Of course." Claire sat in the backseat as Sandy dropped a massive tangle of red yarn on her lap. Claire frowned at the mess, uncertain of her friend's intentions.

"My eyesight isn't the best anymore. If you could dig around in there and try to find an end, I'm sure I can get it untangled."

"Uh, okay." Claire started picking through layers, not comfortable manipulating something so...homey.

"Yes, like that." Sandy reached in and pulled several strings up over Claire's wrists. "You really have to dig in there."

The tangled strands seemed to take on a life of their own, growing more twisted as they wrapped around her hands. She tried to pull free of the mess, but the yarn held tight.

"That'll work," a man's voice replied instead.

Claire jerked her gaze up in time to see the hardened soldier close the door, trapping her inside. She no longer sat in Sandy's car, but in the luxurious leather, front seat of his Hummer. Cold fear hardened her veins, and she yanked her hands, trying to free them. Her bindings were no longer soft red yarn, but rough twine tied expertly around her. The more she struggled, the deeper the fibers cut into her skin.

He opened the driver's door and climbed in, bringing with him the tantalizing sent of gunpowder and leather. He studied her with careful, calculating eyes. "Fighting will only make this worse for you. Already, you're bleeding."

Several crimson smudges marred her wrists, and she wished desperately that she could strike out and hurt him in return. "You bastard. Let me go." The illusion he'd created had been so real. She'd never had a chance against him. Her assumption that they'd been on an even playing field had been a costly mistake.

"I told you we could do this the easy way or the hard way. You chose hard." He jammed the Hummer into gear as though her pain angered him, before he sped off into the chilly evening.

❋ 17 ❋

Claire watched through the windshield as misty miles slipped away, leaving cars and her chance for rescue on the darkened roads behind them. Warm city lights gave way to cool, forested wilderness, and the time between passing vehicles grew longer and longer.

She wasn't sure how or why, but she knew without a doubt this man was a danger to the very fabric of her soul. If he could, he'd keep her from reaching her destination. If he succeeded, there would be no reason to keep breathing. She needed to get home, much the way salmon needed to return upriver in order to secure the survival of their species. Someone waited for her. Someone who needed her as much as she needed him... her...whoever. She yanked again and struggled against the seatbelt that held her in place until the wounds on her wrists began to sting again.

Damn him.

She glared at the arrogant soldier, sending a multitude of hateful thoughts in his direction. Dim lights from the dash illuminated the hard planes of his face, enhancing his formidable, yet attractive appearance. Who was this warrior who'd waylaid her from her destiny? "What's your name?"

He remained silent.

"The least you can do after kidnapping me is tell me your name. If you don't want to tell me your real name for fear of retaliation, then make one up."

"I fear nothing." His deep voice rumbled with certainty, and she envied his position. She wished she could say the same. She had in the past, but the thought of never learning the truth left her distraught and willing to take desperate chances.

She twisted in her seat until she'd made room to maneuver, and then aimed her bare foot at his midsection. He caught her calf with an iron grip before she ever made contact, but his swift action made him jerk the wheel of the Hummer, sending them screeching across the road.

The vehicle swayed as he overcorrected, leading them back into their lane and off into the small ravine at the side of the road.

The Hummer jerked to a stop, dust flying up around them. He turned to her with a deadly gaze that stunned her. Without saying a word, he exited the truck and strode to her side. Frantic, she tried to climb into his seat as he opened her door, but her bound hands made it difficult. With a snarl, he gripped her thighs and hauled her out, her feet smacking against the hard ground.

Her heart pounded fiercely as she struggled to be free. "You're going to regret it if you don't let me go."

He gripped her bindings with one hand, stopping her blows, and caught her face with the other, holding her as he stared into her eyes. "I'll tell you once again, this will be better for you if you don't fight me. I'm not going to hurt you until you make me, and I can't let you go."

She sagged against him, forcing him to hold her entire weight, hoping he'd drop her and she could run. It was a futile attempt at best, but she'd gone far past the point of desperation.

Unfortunately, he lifted her and tossed her over his shoulder while he opened the backdoor. With seemingly very little effort, he dumped her on the seat and once again secured the seatbelt around her. He returned to the front seat and removed something from the glove compartment before he shut the door. She struggled to release the seatbelt.

He pulled her abraded hands back onto her lap. "Don't forget you asked for this. I gave you the opportunity for compliance, and you declined." He lifted a black cotton bag with a drawstring closure and widened the opening. It wasn't until he moved it toward her face that she realized his intent.

She shook her head violently, trying to escape his grasp. "No!"

He captured her head between his hands, smoothing her hair away from her face. "It's for your protection and mine. Your stunt a moment ago could have ended tragically."

"I hate you," she said. Frustrated tears welled in her eyes as she tried to fight him off with her tied hands.

"That was bound to happen," he said as he wiped the moisture from her cheeks. "This will be easier if you remain calm. Deep breaths."

Darkness descended over her, and she tried to breathe through the suffocating blackness.

"Deep breaths," he reminded her.

She tried to still her panic, knowing it was to her advantage not to let him confuse her senses with his military tactics. No doubt, he intended the hood to do more than subdue her. He might have her tied up, but she still owned her thoughts. She needed to stay alert and wait for an opportunity for escape. If it came, she'd be ready.

The unexpected feel of him securing her feet startled her. She kicked at him, making things as difficult as possible. One of her attempts, quite possibly a knee to his face, left him cussing and her smiling. His hands grew rougher as he bound her ankles, but satisfaction warmed her spirit and encouraged her to keep fighting.

When he'd finished, he shoved her squarely against her seat. "You haven't heeded my warnings so far, but I'll give you one last opportunity. Sit here and be quiet. Anymore attempts at escape, and I'll put you in back with the suitcases. Don't think I won't."

Her door slammed shut, and she flinched at the sound.

She remained quiet as he entered the vehicle and closed his door with equal force, not doubting he'd do exactly what he promised. The engine fired with a growl, and they were soon moving down the road again, the bumps all the more obvious now that he'd removed her sense of sight.

"Taking me is a mistake," she said after several minutes. She might not be able to use physical force to get away, but she still had psychological opportunities. "Someone will be looking for me."

"Quiet."

"You know I'm right, and these are people you don't want to piss off." Honestly, she had no idea what waited for her, but whoever had beckoned her must have some kind of power to get a message from Port Townsend, Washington all the way to her in Bali. His continued silence seemed to corroborate the fact. "There's no way I can be that valuable to you."

No response.

"If you let me go now, I'll convince them not to retaliate. I won't even mention all the nasty things you've done since I first laid eyes on you."

He tapped on the brakes, making her stiffen in response. "One more word and you'll be in the back with tape across your mouth."

She pressed her lips together, imprisoning the curses simmering on her tongue. As much as she'd like to release them, she had no desire to have him stuff her into an oxygen-deprived space. She wished she'd turned away the moment she'd noticed him at the luggage carousel. If she had, she'd be well on her way to Port Townsend right now.

Even as she thought it, she knew it wasn't true. Whoever this man was, whatever he wanted from her, she couldn't deny the powerful link between them. He knew far more about her, and she had no doubt he would have found her and taken her one way or the other.

Her only hope was to be patient, watch for opportunities, and wait for him to reveal his intentions. Until then, she was at his mercy.

☙❧

DRU CURSED THE SILENCE SCREAMING FROM THE backseat. She'd finally shut that beautiful mouth full of taunts and questions he couldn't answer. He'd thought he'd be relieved. It wasn't until she'd quieted that he realized the sound of her voice was preferable to the condemnation echoing in his thoughts.

Why *hadn't* he dispensed with her already?

Why *hadn't* he taken one of the isolated dirt roads leading off the main highway, pulled her from the vehicle, and slit her throat? A soldier did not question his mission. He took aim and squeezed the trigger without a second thought.

Yet, here she was still in his backseat as he drew closer to his cabin outside Port Townsend, one of the many places he'd collected over time.

A seasoned warrior like him shouldn't pause to explore his curiosity, to wonder what ticked behind compelling eyes the color of amber ale. Hell, he was one of the big dogs, not a tender pup. He'd schooled others in the most vicious warfare tactics. In days past, he'd wielded his mighty sword with controlled precision, never bothering to look at the carnage in his wake.

Unfortunately, his assignment during the last days of the world was more complicated than he'd originally anticipated. He should have known something this important would be. The sizzling flares of energy that had bored deep inside him the moment he'd captured her gaze had caught him unaware. Surprisingly, red-hot barbs anchored a part of her to some unknown dissident hidden these many, long years in a dark and desolate part of him.

He'd never considered something as dismissive as the sweet honeysuckle scent of her hair or her spicy cinnamon breath to be a threat. Never expected they could deter him from his mission so he could indulge another minute of pleasure. Innocuous tactics at first glance, but torturous nonetheless.

He cursed the gods, past and present, though truly his failure to complete his mission in a swift and certain matter fell on him. A lifetime of war should have taught him never to underestimate his opponent. That he'd thought he could carry out the singularly most important task of his life without a bloody battle had been a mistake on his part. The gods had sent him a formidable adversary, one with unexpected, subtle, yet effective tactics.

A warrior in her own right.

She deserved a better death than a slit throat on the side of an unnamed dirt road. He hated that her life would soon end, and that he'd be the one to dispatch her demise. She was the first soul beyond his immortal buddies who challenged his mind, a feat he couldn't easily ignore.

He would see that she died an honorable death, befitting a samurai or one of the ancient berserker warriors of the past. He was also certain the right to spill her blood would come at a painful price to him. Such a cost was only befitting a battle of this proportion.

So be it.

He was prepared.

For now, he'd take her home and interrogate her so that he might devise a precise plan. Only a fool would proceed without one, and he had no doubt the gods had placed more, as of now, unseen obstacles in his way. He'd need as much detailed information as he could get in order to wage war and emerge victorious.

✿ 18 ✿

Claire jerked when the Hummer suddenly stopped. Bouncing along the roads surrounded by quiet darkness had lulled her into a semiconscious state. She didn't know how long or how far they'd traveled, but apparently, they'd arrived at their destination.

Her captor shut off the engine, and she braced herself for what might come next as he exited the SUV. A few seconds later, chilly air swept in around her when he opened her door. She stiffened, wishing she could catch a glimpse of what waited for her.

A weight suddenly pressed against the top of her thighs, securing her to her seat. She reached out, her fingertips colliding with his solid flesh. She considered lashing out at him with her hands until she realized he'd bent over her, probably to keep her from fighting as he removed the bindings from her ankles. When her feet were free, he released her seatbelt and pulled her from the vehicle.

A thousand needles stabbed her feet as blood freely rushed back into her veins. She stumbled when her bare feet hit the ground, but strong arms captured her before she fell.

She tried not to cling to him as she sucked in a breath, shocked once again by the intense current his proximity generated. "I'm fine. My feet fell asleep because some asshole bound them too tight." She pushed him from her with chaffed hands, and then immediately missed his solid body and the way he'd grounded her. For all she knew, she stood at the edge of a cliff, and she might tumble to her death if she moved.

"Why didn't you say something?" he asked.

She turned her head in the direction of his voice. "You threatened to put me in the back if I did. Numb feet were preferable."

A deep rumble of laughter filled the silence around them, and her heart opened to the sound despite her resistance.

The hood tugged at her hair as he slipped it from her head, and she blinked, quickly taking in the towering trees surrounding them. Pines blocked any light that might have slipped from the slice of moon she glimpsed in the inky sky. Behind her captor, stood a structure, a house, she guessed, but the light from the Hummer's interior didn't reveal many details.

"You could have asked me to loosen them," he said. "I'm not a completely heartless bastard."

"All evidence to the contrary." Once again, his impressive stature thrilled and intimidated her, but she refused to shrink from him. "If I ask you to set me free, will you?"

"No."

She turned from him then and focused on her surroundings instead. One way or the other, she'd find her freedom.

Beyond the house, a small shadow moved, crouching beneath a pine. She stared until she could make out the shape of a dog. It darted again, deeper into the trees, but she didn't miss the longer nose, the fluffy tail.

A fox then. Not a dog after all.

Dru closed the passenger door before taking hold of

her elbow. She purposefully dragged her feet as he guided her toward the house.

"Are you going to continually make this difficult?" Irritation scraped at his words.

"As long as you insist on holding me captive."

He stopped and turned to her. "Aren't you afraid I might decide you're not worth the effort to keep alive?"

A shiver raced through her. "I fear nothing," she said, mimicking his words, the lie coming easier than she expected.

His gaze burned through the darkness as silence claimed the seconds. "Liar," he said after a moment, and then he leaned forward and tossed her over his shoulder again.

She cried out in protest. *"Bastard."*

Each stride bounced her stomach against his rock hard shoulder in an unpleasant way, stealing more of her resolve. He was right. She feared everything. She feared he'd kill or torture her before she could flee. Worse, she feared she'd never escape and find her way home.

The soldier's feet clomped up wooden steps and across a wide porch as he hauled Claire toward the door. He opened it and stepped inside, kicking it shut behind him.

Once again, darkness and silence shrouded her. He moved forward like a lithe predator, her weight and the lack of light not slowing him at all. Unknown objects hulked along the walls, seeming like furniture, but she couldn't be sure. The building smelled of pine and a hint of lemon cleaner. The heavenly scent of freshly burned wood flirted with her senses, making her long for her comforting fire back in Bali. "Who else is here?"

"No one."

But someone had been recently. What she smelled was not a lingering scent, but from a fire that had burned within the last twenty-four hours. If he'd been on the flight from Bali with her, which he must have been since he'd taken his bags from the same carousel as hers, then someone else had been there. "Where are we?"

"An isolated cabin in the woods," he said with a matter-of-fact tone.

He would kill her then. Probably rape her first. The other possible occupant of the cabin might try, too. Why else would he bring her to such a place? Her only hope was, if he tried, he'd become vulnerable to her power. Then, once she controlled him, she'd use him until he was a hollow, useless shell.

Karma would come back to bite him in the ass.

Perhaps she should encourage him and get it over with before anyone else showed up to strengthen his forces.

She wiggled in his grasp, trying to unbalance him, hoping he'd put her down. Instead, he raised a large hand and slapped her on the ass. "Stop," he commanded.

She growled from the sting and from the frustration of him holding her against her will. She bucked and pounded her fists against his back instead. This time, he dropped her, and she landed hard on the floor with no hands available to break her fall.

Before she could right herself, he grabbed her elbow and pulled her to her feet. She faced him again, heat radiating from his solid chest, telling her what she couldn't read in his expression.

"Is this to be the war then?" Aggression vibrated from deep within him as he gripped her shoulders. "Not a fight based on physical strength, but battle of the minds? Did you come to Washington to needle me until I either kill you or you drive me insane?"

The force of his words startled her, and it took her a moment to answer.

"I'm not here to do anything. I've come looking for my family. That's all." She had no desire to be involved in any kind of war. "It's obvious you've kidnapped the wrong woman."

"No." His answer came swift and sure. "I can sense it in you. Tell me you don't feel the magnetic clash between us. That can only be for one reason. Not to mention you look like her."

"*Her?*" His statement put form to the presence that had summoned her, giving her a new piece of information to focus on. "My mother? My sister?"

"Fuck," he whispered harshly before he grasped her bound hands and pulled her forward. She stumbled along, trying to keep up with his long strides as he proceeded through the darkened house.

Then he stopped. "There are thirteen stairs that lead down. If you don't want to fall and break your neck, I suggest you walk down them like a lady."

"Tell me who you were talking about. Who do I look like?"

"Move." His command left no room for question.

She stepped tentatively down, her bare toes searching for the next stair. Her captor held her arm so she wouldn't fall, and as much as she despised him, she hoped he wouldn't let go. "Do we have to do this in the dark? If I could see, it would be easier."

"Easier for you to see where you are. Easier for you to plan an escape. Keep moving."

She took another step and another with him close beside her until no more steps remained. She tried to pretend her heart didn't beat faster each time he touched her, but she couldn't ignore the powerful, pulsing sensations. He was correct. Something propelled her toward him. He'd owned her focus since the moment their gazes had met, the strength of his magnetism unlike anything she'd experienced.

He kept hold of her as he moved her forward again, pausing to open a large, metal door. Once inside, he flipped the light switch.

She blinked, relief flooding her as light washed the room. She'd never been overly fond of the dark.

The spacious room held an ornate bed, the dark wood of the headboard carved with intricate scrolls, reminding her of pictures she'd seen in history books. Luscious red velvet covered the mattress. A bed worthy of a goddess, not this heavily muscled warrior who'd taken her against her will.

The wooden floor cooled her toes as she walked toward the bed, assuming this was where he'd try to force himself on her, where she'd gain her freedom and her revenge, instead.

He caught her arm, shifting her direction to the left as he tugged her forward.

Ahead of her, two shackles bolted to the wall with a pile of chains lying on the floor below warned her of his impending actions and chilled her blood.

Instinct flared, and she shoved against him and ran.

He caught her with an iron grip before she made it through the door.

"No!" she screamed and swung at him with her bounded fists.

"Stop! I'm not going to hurt you." He captured her, wrapping his powerful arms around her and dragged her to the wall. "It's only for a short while. Until I can locate handcuffs. I hadn't planned on bringing you here, so I wasn't prepared to hold you."

She met his gaze with a wild one of her own as she struggled to be free of his grasp. "What was your original plan?" His unblinking gaze told her the truth.

"Oh, my God. You *were* going to kill me." She studied his midnight eyes, learning more than she cared to. "You still *are*."

His conviction wavered, a troubled hesitation swirling in the depths of his eyes. "No. Not if I don't have to."

She couldn't take that chance. She fought him then,

final desperation fueling her. She head-butted him, missing his nose and slamming his mouth instead. He cursed, and she quickly followed with another knee to his groin.

"*Bitch*," he hissed, but he didn't loosen his grip.

"Let me go!" She kicked and tried to free her hands as he shoved her hard against the wall. The force stole her breath long enough for him to shackle one hand.

He stepped back and drew the back of his hand over his mouth, coming away with fresh blood. "Hell, woman. Do you have a death wish?"

She shook her head slowly as she stood before the mighty warrior, fear wrapping its icy fingers around her, her brain unwilling to contemplate what might come next. He'd chained her in his basement where no one could possibly find her. Other than some unknown woman who'd summoned her, there would be no one to look for her. Still, she wouldn't cower.

He cursed again and strode from the room long enough for a tremble to build deep in her gut. When he returned, he carried a sadistically sharp knife, the six-inch blade glinting as though eager to carve its mark on her.

She gave up thoughts of being strong and wanted to scream, to beg for mercy, but all she could do was watch, thinking he was a truly magnificent beast, and he would be the last thing she'd see in this lifetime.

She closed her eyes when he lifted the blade. "Make it swift," she said softly.

He said something in a foreign language that sounded much like cursing, and a sob escaped her lips.

The feel of his hands on her bound wrists startled her, and she opened her eyes as he slipped the blade beneath the twine and jerked it upward. He gathered the cut rope and placed it on the dresser along with the blade.

He approached her again, all massive muscle and

hard edges, an electric current of emotion buzzing beneath the surface. He studied her face, gazed deeply into her eyes, his expression trying to tell her something he would not.

"I'm sorry for this. Neither of us chose this destiny. But it is what it is. As much as it seems wrong to be so, you and I are on opposite sides of humanity. I cannot let you wreak havoc on mankind despite your beauty and your courage."

She stared at him, not understanding his meaning. He seemed sane, but his words and actions cried otherwise. She shook her head. "This makes no sense. I'm not a bad person. I don't want to wreak havoc on anyone."

"It's your fate, your future." He traced his thumb down her cheek, leaving her shivering from first his touch and then the lack of it. "I will find something less medieval to hold you until I can decide what to do. Are you hungry? I'll bring something to eat, too," he said without waiting for her answer.

When he'd gone from the room, she took a moment to breathe. She glanced at the shackle holding her. She jerked it hard, sending pain radiating from her wrist, up her arm. But a speckle of paint fell free from the wall, giving her hope.

Dru returned to the house thirty minutes later in a nasty mood. He'd lifted handcuffs from an incompetent police officer who'd tried to break up a scuffle where Dru had stopped to purchase sandwiches and beer.

On the way back, he'd spoken to Bane on the phone. With a few carefully crafted sentences, Bane had managed to insult his manhood and pride as a warrior, calling him a pussy because he hadn't spilt the fire witch's blood. *Yet*. Dru had tried to explain about honor and a righteous death, but in Bane's eyes, dead was dead.

Fuck it all. Dru understood that better than anyone did. But when all was said and done, it *did* matter how one died. It also matter how one killed a worthy opponent, and he would do this the right way.

He found Claire where he'd left her in the basement, a wild look on her face. Rivulets of blood trickled down her forearm. Pain, fright and anger had mixed into a disquieting concoction in her beautiful amber eyes. He dropped his haul on the bed and strode toward her. "What the hell are you doing?"

She stayed silent, but it was obvious she'd tried to

sacrifice her hand in order to be free and now wore the look of defeat. He should have known he couldn't leave her alone for a minute.

He lifted her shackled hand, observing the damage. She'd worn away the skin in a few places, but she hadn't come anywhere near escaping.

She watched as he surveyed her, her expression reminding him of a struggling fire on a winter's night, trying to stay relevant without extinguishing herself.

He shook his head as he left the room long enough to retrieve a medical kit. He was disappointed she'd hurt herself, but he'd have done the same if someone held him.

When he returned and took her free hand to clean up the scrapes from her initial bindings, she didn't fight. However, she did hiss when he sanitized her abrasions with an alcohol wipe.

"Your other side is going to hurt a lot worse," he said, discarding the wipe and retrieving a soft, rolled bandage.

She didn't respond, and he wondered if she wasn't quite so valiant after all and if the short time in shackles had broken her spirit.

He secured her bandaged wrist with the less-severe handcuffs and hooked it to the second metal ring protruding from the wall so he could tend her wounded hand without fear of her fighting.

It didn't escape his notice that his latest move left her terribly vulnerable to him, with her hands restrained near her head, her body exposed to his whims. If he wanted—and damn it, he did—he could reach out and cup her breast, could strip her bare and see how long she'd fight before she begged for his touch.

A flash of fire lit her eyes, and he smiled. The witch wasn't broken after all.

Disheveled reddish-black curls fell over her shoulders, the ends coming to rest just above hardened-nipples straining against her thin silk top. A short, black skirt made of some flimsy material. Two slices with his razor-sharp knife would leave them in a puddle at her feet without a mark on her. She really had no idea the amount of danger she'd encountered.

He stepped closer, tipped her chin up with his finger so he could look her fully in the face. Live wires sparked between them, emitting a high-voltage energy he couldn't ignore. Her breaths grew deeper the longer he stared at her, and he knew their connection affected her as well.

The gods did not play fair to send him such a lovely creature and then expect him to destroy her.

He lifted a curl, slid the silky softness between his thumb and forefinger until he reached the end of the strand. He purposefully grazed her pebbled nipple with his knuckles as he dropped his hand. She inhaled, and his dick hardened in an instant.

Damn.

If he kept her around for long, he'd be the one in peril.

She arched her back slightly, and he wondered if it was an involuntary reaction to his touch, or if she'd invited him to sample more. She moistened her cinnamon lips, and he followed the sweet trail of her tongue, wishing she'd licked him instead. He leaned closer needing to smell the honeysuckle of her hair if only for a moment.

Unknown forces tugged at him, stroking him with sensual fingers. Gods, it would be so easy to let go, to release the heavy burden he'd carried for so long, to let her burn him with her body.

THE OPPORTUNITY CLAIRE HAD WAITED FOR ARRIVED. The soldier watched her with a pair of eyes darker than the most scorched embers. Powerful excitement flared deep within, her core a volcano on the verge of erupting. Joining with him would be wondrous, but dangerous and deadly as well.

Regardless, she needed to be free. He'd taken her against her will, and he'd have to pay the cost. It would be a shame to waste such a gorgeous piece of flesh, but the mind behind those intense eyes couldn't be trusted.

She dropped her gaze to his lips, took pleasure as she traced the curve of his mouth, wondering what it would feel like to have him claim hers. She inhaled deeply, very aware of the rise and fall of her chest, and the slow, burning ache that ended in tight points at the tips of her breasts.

She followed the thick cords in his neck, down to the strong expanse of his chest. His muscles stretched against the fabric of his black shirt, cotton covering a work of art. She'd always enjoyed molding her fingers and her mouth over well-honed muscles, tasting the power that rested beneath tight skin. His was a body beyond compare, one no other man could make her forget no matter how long she lived.

If her hands were free, she'd press them against his groin, trace the heavy bulge outlined beneath the khakis, and erase any doubt of her intentions.

A low growl rumbled from his chest, and she looked up to find her energies affecting him despite the fact she hadn't physically touched him yet. He stared down at her, his body rigid as though prepared to fight, but heated desire flooded his veins and called to her.

He wanted her. He wouldn't be able to resist.

"I dare you to take a step closer," she whispered, knowing she tempted a beast. "Or are you afraid?"

He held her gaze for an unbearably tense moment. "I told you. I fear nothing." But he didn't move.

"Don't you wonder what I taste like?" Her heartbeat raced in anticipation. It amazed her that she could be so afraid one minute and so turned on the next. Facing one's mortality could do that she supposed. "Don't you want to know how it's going to feel when you put your mouth on me?"

In the span of a blink, he moved, his hard body coming up against hers, trapping her against the wall. She fought to catch a breath, fought to keep the agonizing need from stealing her senses.

An ominous promise shadowed his eyes as he lowered his head. She opened for him the second his lips touched hers, eager to take his power. Energy exploded in her veins, dark and infinitely powerful. She fought to accommodate what he unknowingly offered.

Instead of growing weaker like he should have, he demanded her passion, his tongue dancing against hers, leaving the taste of licorice and of danger in its wake. He fisted his hands in her hair as he dominated her with his potent kiss.

Lust pushed away her worry. It would take longer for her to dominate a warrior like him. That was all.

She sucked in air when he slipped his mouth from hers, moving to the sensitive spot behind her ear. Molten need pooled in her core, stealing her strength. She needed him inside her, needed access to the center of his strength before she lost all sense of time and space.

"Take me," she said, a gasp escaping along with her request.

He stepped back and trapped her gaze, holding her prisoner as his large hands cupped her breasts with a savage touch, molding her to his palms. A delicious shiver rocked her, and she dropped her head back and closed her eyes. The incredible experience of having a man control an encounter for once left her shaking. Excitement and fear swirled through her veins, creating an addictive cocktail.

He would love her. He might kill her. If he didn't, she'd be the end of him.

Regardless of the outcome, she'd never be the same come tomorrow.

❧ 20 ❧

Silk hissed as the soldier gripped her blouse and ripped it open in an effortless motion. Claire shivered and strained against her shackles as he devoured her with his gaze. She wanted to reach out, to touch him. That she couldn't, tormented and teased her.

His roughened hands grazed her skin as he gripped her waist, moved slowly upward over her sensitized breasts until he gripped the top of her red lace bra and exposed her to his view. He captured a nipple, moist heat seeping through her skin. She mentally clung to him as heightened sensations she'd never experienced forced a tortured moan from her lips.

Second by second, her control faded. Primal need battled her previous intentions. His energy still infused her, but it seemed to strengthen him more than it did her.

Somehow, that didn't matter. She no longer wanted to escape.

She only wanted to *feel*.

His mouth on her bare breasts. His hands possessing her ass. The cool rush of air as he lifted her skirt. *God.*

She couldn't remember him removing her panties, but she caught a glimpse of them on the floor behind him when he gripped her thighs and hauled her upward, pinning her against the wall. She swallowed as the hard length of him pressed against her, promising so much heaven.

Her breath came in pants, and he watched like a predator might before he devoured his prey. "I'm going to take you, Claire, and fuck you until you can't remember your name. Until you don't remember why you're here. Until you want nothing more than to make love and make peace for the rest of your life."

"Yes," she whispered, knowing if he walked away now, she'd die. It didn't matter that his words sounded much like her thoughts before she destroyed a man.

She did her best to hold his gaze as he eased inside her. His size matched the rest of his physique, and she tried not to cry out from pleasure as she accommodated him.

Once in, he moved out and then back in with a powerful thrust. From there, everything blurred. Hot desire tightened her muscles, and she closed her eyes, trying to control the friction building inside her.

So powerful, so fast. She clenched, as a shudder erupted deep within.

He drove right through it, catching her descent, insisting she go higher.

She tried to breathe, wishing she could grip something, praying she'd survive him. He pushed her, surrounding her with a red haze punctuated by two thundering hearts. Her thoughts grasped for some sliver of reality, but there was nothing. Only heat. Only friction. Only...

She cried out as a blinding white fire exploded, sending pieces of her flying in every direction.

Moments passed.

The sound of a heartbeat against her ear slowly drew her back to the present. A breath in. A breath out.

She rested against a massive chest covered in black

cotton. The weight of a heavy arm curled over her hip, and her hand lay at the base of his neck. His pulse throbbed against her fingertips as a sated, heavenly feeling floated through her. She had no memory of them moving to the bed, nothing beyond...

The clock on the table proclaimed it morning. But it couldn't be. She swore only minutes had passed. Then again, without windows in the room, she couldn't be sure.

She lifted her head, found hard, searching eyes watching her, waiting for her to make a move. She stared back, uncertain what to say.

Neither of the scenarios she'd expected had happened. She was alive, and he seemed to have retained all of his warrior sensibilities. She'd never planned to have to look him in the eye after what they'd...done.

She couldn't begin to consider where he'd taken her. The heat, the pleasure.

She blinked, trying to focus. Men she'd encountered in the past left in a haze of love, never looking at her with such an intense, determined gaze.

"What?" he finally asked with a sexy rumble.

In the clarity of a single moment, she realized she'd shared her body with a man she didn't know anything about other than he'd kidnapped her and he was some kind of fierce warrior. Not that she hadn't had sex with other men she didn't know well, but that was different. She hadn't *shared* anything with them. She'd *taken*.

This man...not only was there an intangible, undeniable link between them, but *he'd survived her*. He'd tasted and touched her, given his energy, and it hadn't hurt him. In fact, he seemed all the stronger for it. "I don't know your name."

"Drustan." He stared, assessing her with an obscure gaze. "Some call me Dru."

"Drustan." She let his name roll off her tongue, everything even more intimate now that she knew his name. Dru with his dark eyes that seemed older than his years. Dru with a mysterious scar near his left temple. Dru that could chain her to a wall and then hold her tenderly against him.

"Everything okay?" he asked after another long moment.

Her brain struggled to regain control of her body and her thoughts. "It's fine."

Dark eyebrows rose toward his almost-shaved hair. "*Fine?*" It was as though she'd insulted him beyond forgiveness.

"Good?" She seemed to be missing the intent behind his question.

His serious gaze cracked into a disbelieving smile. "In the many days I've been cursed to crawl this earth, I've never been labeled *fine*. Or *good*. Like my performance was barely satisfactory."

"Ohh..." He wanted her to rate him as a lover. It surprised her to find the battle-hardened soldier had a vulnerable side. He moved beneath her, his rock-hard erection evident against her thigh. Vulnerable *and* potent, it seemed.

"However, I'd have to disagree with your assessment if your endless cries of ecstasy were any indication."

"Endless?" A heated blush stole over her. She might have expressed herself vocally a time or two. "I think that's overstating things." She pushed off his chest, needing some distance before he stole her sanity again.

He secured her with solid arms, bringing her back into alignment with him. "Are you afraid you'll fall to my undeniable charms?"

She smiled, not sure how to handle this sexy, flirting side of him. Danger, worse than what she'd encountered the previous night, lurked in his teasing eyes. "There's nothing undeniable or charming about you. You're the one who fell under my spell." She placed her hands on the sides of his face, prepared to give him another demonstration. One that didn't end with her in a melted puddle of exquisite sensations.

Before she could kiss him, he rolled her over and pinned her to the bed. "I don't think so."

She was about to challenge him again when she realized both hands holding his jaw were bandaged when only one had been before. She frowned.

"When did you wrap my other hand?" Unanswered questions flooded her mind, pushing away the lovely, newly-discovered pleasure of basking in the afterglow. "More than that, when did we move to the bed?"

He looked away before rolling to his feet, the antique bed groaning as he robbed it of his weight. Chilled air took his place. "A while ago. You were asleep."

"No." She shook her head and sat up. He might have swept her off her feet, but he hadn't completely incapacitated her. "I would remember something."

"I guess I'm that good after all."

She paused, trying to pinpoint the odd feeling nudging her. She glanced across the room to where the shackles hung from the wall. The handcuffs he'd brought rested on the table next to the bed. Then she focused on him again.

"You're dressed." She glanced down. "I'm dressed."

He shrugged. "It never warms up down here. I didn't want you to get cold."

She narrowed her gaze, vivid memories flashing in her mind. "You ripped my blouse off my body before you held me against the wall and made wild, passionate love to me."

"I did? We did?" He swallowed. "No, I didn't."

She climbed off the bed and fixed him with a heated gaze. "Yes, you did." She jabbed her finger against his solid pecs.

"Don't lie to me. You've already as much as admitted

we had sex. You can't deny it, unless..." Anger exploded inside her. "Unless it wasn't real."

She stepped back from him. "Was that another illusion you conjured? You son of a bitch."

He folded his arms and stared at her with obsidian eyes. "You should thank me."

"For what?"

"For sparing you the humiliation when I rejected your advances. For allowing your fantasy instead of suffering while I tended your wounds.

You obviously enjoyed yourself, so spare me your indignation."

The breath of air she'd held while he spoke slipped from her lungs instead of fueling her response. He'd rejected her. Worse, her powers no longer worked on men. The test kiss with the cabbie must have been a fluke, and she really had lost her ability. The one thing that kept her going.

"You're a cruel-hearted bastard," she whispered. "Just kill me or let me go. I can't stand to look at you anymore." He'd slaughtered her hopes that there might have been someone in the world who could survive her, who could give her more than she took from him...the hope she might one day...

She couldn't bear to consider her broken dreams another moment. She dropped to the bed and turned her gaze from him. She couldn't pretend to guess the motives behind his actions, but he'd get nothing from her from now on.

Minutes ticked by, but he didn't move. Neither did she.

"I'm sorry. I never meant to hurt you." The mattress sank as he sat next to her.

She tucked in her lips. She would not allow him to draw her into conversation again.

"I meant it when I said it wasn't right that we'd been forced to take opposing sides. Unfortunately, it happens with war." From the corner of her eye, she could see him flex his fingers wide and then clench his fist as though acting out his frustrations.

"The gods gave us our destinies when they sent us here. I can't deny mine any more than you can deny yours."

She couldn't hold her words any longer and turned to him, wishing she could access the fire burning in her heart. "*What the hell are you talking about*? Destiny and opposing sides? I'm not fighting whatever imaginary war you have raging in your head. I'll say it again. *Kill me or let me go.*"

A hollow sadness filled his eyes. "I'm sorry. I can't do either." He fell back on the mattress in a show of defeat.

She turned to find him staring at the ceiling. He seemed so vulnerable, so...*real* at the moment. "Why?" she asked, starving for answers.

"You say you don't know, and maybe you don't. Maybe your ignorance is part of the gods' game, but your appearance in Port Townsend will set about events that will bring an end to this world." He paused, meeting her gaze with a foreboding one of his own. "Unless I stop you."

A shiver raced across her skin. She wanted to discount what he said, to argue his craziness. But too many things cast doubt against her certainty. He was obviously no ordinary man, and she knew she had certain powers over people. Or at least she had in the past. Or maybe her powers were only useless against him. Still, she'd never wielded anything strong enough to end the world.

She also had to consider the compelling summons to return home. Whoever had sent that was no ordinary person either.

Dru studied her with midnight eyes. "My task is to

bring about your demise, or face consequences that will bring about the end of humanity."

He couldn't be serious. But she could see that he was. "What are you waiting for?" she asked, not certain she wanted the answer.

He looked at her, his solemn gaze studying her eyes, then her mouth, before he blinked, breaking their connection. "I've spent my life preparing for this moment, preparing to do the job when the time came. But nothing prepared me for the internal battle I'd face when I realized you were my target. I should have taken you out from a distance. I should never have gotten close enough to see the fire burning in your eyes or touch your soft skin."

He sighed. "Perhaps after all this time, I've grown weary of war and long for something more."

Her breaths grew shallow as she considered his words. By all rights, she should be dead. Her blood should be on his hands. "I guess I should beg you to kill me now. I don't want to be responsible for the fate of the world."

He gave a sardonic laugh. "Neither do I."

"I don't want to die, either," she whispered.

He moved like a rattlesnake, one second relaxing on the bed, the next sitting alongside her. "Give me your hand."

She held out the least tender of her hands, and then sputtered when he grabbed the cuffs and secured her to the headboard. "What the hell?" She'd thought she'd made some headway with him just now.

He stood. "I need to talk to someone, figure out a way around this. In the meantime, you'll need to stay down here. I'm not leaving the house, so don't think you can escape." He fired a warning look in her direction. "It will be in your best interest if you remain quiet and don't let anyone know you're here."

G wen knocked on Dru's door precisely at ten. The woman was more punctual than a clock, and the soldier inside him appreciated that. He opened the door and let her probing gaze and invisible fingers caress his face, his biceps. He was certain the witch didn't realize he could sense her touch, and he'd never bothered to impart that knowledge for fear she might stop.

"Good morning." He smiled, enjoying the way her icy blue eyes warmed when he greeted her. By nature, she was a cold person, nothing like the heated, sensual fire witch he had chained in his basement. Still, when Nick had warned him of the impending doom, he'd resumed his residence in Port Townsend and made friendly with some of the locals, including Gwen. He'd enjoyed toying with her, pushing her beyond her comfort zone. "Please come in."

"*Salut*, Dru." She glided past him, her platinum hair and turquoise skirt flowing behind her like an airy breeze, reminding him of the cool, salty ocean. She wasn't two feet into the house when she stopped suddenly and turned to him with an alarmed gaze. "She's here."

"No," he answered quickly as he directed her into

the living room. "She was, but I moved her last night. Please sit."

Gwen searched the area as though looking for something only she could see. "Her power is strong." She settled gently on the couch, watching him as though she anticipated an attack.

"Would you expect her not to be strong?"

"No." She shook her head. "What's she like?"

He slipped on the mask of indifference he'd used so many times when double-crossing allies in order to fuel a battle. "I haven't had enough time to interrogate her to find out. I will later today. But as you said, she's strong. Not stronger than me, however."

She narrowed her eyes. "You have tortured her here, though. I sense her agony."

That knowledge nipped him harder than he'd expected. "I've done what I must."

Gwen smiled, seeming to take perverse pleasure in the fact. "Why haven't you killed her already? Why take the chance?"

He nodded, trying not to give away too much. Gwen belonged to a dangerous coven in town, the same coven to which Claire's mother had once belonged. Unlike Claire's mother, her aunt Justine still lived and participated with the group. The fact that he'd invited Gwen to his home, given her proof Claire was in the area had been a dangerous, yet necessary tactical move. The witches of Port Townsend spread gossip amongst the town like one of his buddy Julian's virulent diseases. His only hope rested on the fact Gwen and the others opposed Claire's two sisters. He'd waged his success on knowing the coven wanted him to succeed as well and would not disclose information to the two women who threatened them.

"She's in a secure place where she can do no harm," Dru said. "She received a summons, but she has no idea why nor who sent it. She knows nothing of your coven or her sisters."

"They must know she's coming. You have to kill her. Do it now before they realize she's here." Panic tightened her features, stealing some of her loveliness. "The coven tried to kill her sisters and failed. *They joined.* Their powers have increased exponentially, making them all the more dangerous. Justine is highly concerned about what they might do. We all are. They're not capable of apocalyptic disaster yet, and we must prevent that. This witch cannot meet them."

"I agree," he said in a voice he hoped would calm her. "You were correct when your visions showed her coming to town. I've interfered as is my destiny, and I will keep her from joining them. I've asked you here for help. I need to know if there's any way to kill her powers instead of her."

The witch studied him with suspicion. "Why would you want this? Why not just kill her?"

He sighed. "It's more complicated than I expected."

She lifted her nose as though the air might provide her with more details. "She has power over you."

"No." He couldn't admit that. "I believe she has information on the fourth sister, something that will help us locate her. We know she exists. Otherwise, one of the witches wouldn't have been able to open the First Seal."

They'd had so many false starts throughout history, but the time had finally come.

"Claire will die," he continued. "But it's imperative we keep the other sister away as well. You've just said the two that have joined are a threat. It would be wise to keep that threat from growing, even if it can't rise to the apocalyptic scale." Intel on the last witch was a secondary reason, but it provided good cover.

"Claire," she repeated with a musical lilt. "You know her name?"

"Of course I do. I'm a master of collecting intelligence on *our* enemies." He purposefully stressed the word *our*, playing up the unconfirmed alliance. "I need to know if there's a way to neutralize her so I can extract further information before I kill her."

She heaved a sigh. "A blood oath will keep her from practicing magic."

"*How?*" He needed the details, and he needed them now.

"If she mixes her blood with yours or whoever she's promising, she will be bound to that promise until she dies."

"There's no way she can break it?"

"Only the person who owns the oath can break it." She gave him a sly look. "If you carry that oath, you do realize you're placing yourself in a dangerous position. If the sisters find out, they will search you out relentlessly until you break it. You could never allow that to happen."

"I'm a warrior, Gwen. I will die before I let anyone break me." Although he doubted anyone on the mortal earth could kill him or one of his brothers.

"Hmm..." She nodded. "I do admire that about you." A soft caress fluttered over his cheek.

He ignored the feeling. "Tell me the exact specifications of this blood oath."

⚜

DRU WAITED ANOTHER TWENTY MINUTES AFTER Gwen had departed the area to be certain he wouldn't give away his secret. One whiff of Claire's presence sailing on the wind, and he'd have the whole damned coven flocking down on him.

He descended the stairs and opened the thick, metal door that had kept her immediate presence a secret. She waited inside, sitting on the mattress, still chained to the bed. He was grateful she hadn't struggled and hurt herself this time.

Her amber eyes reflected a darker hue, her face a mask of anxiety.

"Who was here?"

He strode forward and sat on the bed next to her. "Another witch."

"*Witch*? Is that what I am then?"

"Did you not know?" He couldn't imagine it being so, but her power did hold a raw, untamed edge. Not to mention, other than her trying to seduce him the previous night, he hadn't sensed any particular use of magic.

She shook her head slowly, obviously bewildered by the information. "My mother or sister, the woman you compared me to, she must be a witch then as well. That's how she summoned me."

"Yes." He knew he played a dangerous game, giving her any information, but he'd learned if he allowed a few tidbits, it paved the way to trust, and he'd eventually gain much more.

"Why did she wait so long to find me?" Pain and confusion painted her expression, longing evident on her face.

He took her hand and unlocked the handcuffs, rubbing warmth back into her fingers. "I can tell you this and so much more, but only on one condition."

Her eyes brightened, but still held wariness. "What condition?"

He braced himself for the fatal move, the one that would end the war if he succeeded. "As a witch, you have power. Possibly, more power than you realize. I've already told you of our destinies, and you've denied your intent to do harm." She nodded.

"I've discovered a way that can render you harmless without taking your life. If you agree, I can tell you all you wish to know and more. It requires a blood oath between us, giving up your ability to cast spells, but it will protect you and your family along with the rest of the world."

"*My family?*" She said it with such wistfulness, reviving his long dead heart. "There's more than one person?"

He nodded. Using those words had been a calculating move on his part, another cannonball volleyed in this emotional and intellectual battle. "You've said you don't want to harm anyone. The oath will prevent you from doing so, and it will erase the need for me to take your life. I'll be effectively killing your powers, which will satisfy the prophecy without actually having to kill you."

"Then we would no longer be on opposite sides?" she asked in a soft voice.

"No. We could be friends." Or more. He stared into her beautiful eyes, wondering if there might be a life after destiny. One he might explore and share with her. She would no longer have powers like he did, but she'd still have that beautiful mind, that fighting spirit that called to him.

"I'll do it."

22

The voice in Claire's head screamed in protest as Dru left to collect the necessary items to complete the ritual. She addressed those thoughts, countering with rational explanations of why this would be the best choice. She'd no longer be able to control men with her presence, but who cared? She finally had the opportunity to connect with people. The sexiest man she'd ever encountered could be her *friend*. Another thing she'd never had in her life. The dark fires burning in his eyes when he'd said it suggested there might be more than that.

And she'd have *her family*. She'd be able to discover who'd called her home. She'd find the place she'd always longed for. And better yet, she wouldn't be able to destroy it with her cursed power.

Dru returned a moment later carrying the long case he'd had with him at the airport. He laid the scarred, black leather case on the bed and opened it. An intricately carved, long sword lay gleaming against red satin, quiet in its repose, but lethal nonetheless. A reverence fell over her as she recognized and paid homage to the power the weapon wielded alone, without the warrior holding it. "It's beautiful."

Dru lifted it from the case, sending a sick aversion through her. She blinked and tried to calm her stomach. Instead, her heart raced as moisture coated her skin, leaving her cold and clammy.

He drew his brows together. "Are you okay?"

She wiped a hand across her damp face. "I don't know. I was. It's that..." She blinked again and tried to keep her gaze focused.

"Let's get this done, then. You'll feel better afterwards."

She nodded, glad she hadn't eaten anything that morning.

"Hold out your hand and repeat after me."

Her fingers shook as she lifted them, and she wasn't sure she could hold that stance for long.

"*I wash all power from my soul. Accept its vital gift no more.*" His voice boomed with authority. "*The fire pumping through my veins will cease upon this very day.*"

She repeated his words as her heartbeat thundered in a deafening roar.

"With the blood from my body..."

"*With the blood from my body*," she whispered, her limbs growing weak.

"I pledge this covenant to Drustan Geddes and vow to never break it."

"*I pledge this covenant to Drustan Geddes and vow to never break it.*"

She flinched as he lifted the virulent sword and sliced into his palm. Crimson blood surfaced, repulsion rolling through her like a frigid wave. Violent shivers claimed her as he placed the bloody blade on her hand and drew it across her skin. The sounded of her cry echoed endlessly in her head, an inferno erupting in her soul.

Through blurred vision, she watched as he clasped her hand with his and held her. Her very essence faded from her, and she could do nothing to prevent the feeling of slipping away.

❧

HE'D KILLED HER.

Dru panicked at the sight of Claire lying pale against the vivid red covering on the bed. Remnants of her blood sizzled on his hand as he placed fingers against her neck, feeling for any sign of life.

It never occurred to him that Gwen might have given him a spell that would take Claire's life. She wanted her dead after all.

But she hadn't. A slight pulse tickled his fingers, and he quickly scooped up Claire's frigid form, leaving behind the carnage of the past two days, and carried her upstairs to his bed.

She sighed as he jerked back the covers and carefully set her down before pulling the luxurious, down-filled comforter over her. The healthy, vibrant tone of her skin had paled. When he touched her cheek, she was colder than he and his fellow soldiers had been during the Battle of Chosin Reservoir. Her breath barely moved the black covering up and down.

Helpless frustration pounded at his conscience until it felt like a bleeding, bruised mass inside his head. *He shouldn't care.* He didn't have a conscience. He'd neutralized his target. That's all that should matter.

Still, he couldn't leave her lying there wondering if she'd ever wake. He climbed in beside her, pulling her limp, lifeless body against him. He wrapped his arms and thighs around her softness, praying some of his warmth would seep into her and restore her energy. He knew she wasn't his to keep, knew his destiny bound him to a lifetime of loneliness despite his wish otherwise, but it would give him comfort to know she'd still be among the living. That he hadn't taken the life of the most beautiful soul he'd ever encountered.

Damn the gods.

Minutes crawled into hours as he held her, as he watched flickers of sun burst through the clouds and onto the walls of his bedroom only to disappear again. Her pulse remained steady though weak, and she didn't wake.

There had been many times he'd lain in wait to take out an enemy or for an opportunity to whisper incendiary words into the right ear and then stand back as casualties of war mounted higher. It was his gift and his curse. But never had time threatened to defeat him.

His phone rang, disturbing the deathly quiet house. He reached over Claire and took it from the table near his bed, the jostling not affecting her in the least.

The name Nicholas Kingswood flashed on his phone screen.

"*What?*" he said to Nick.

"Bane said you haven't killed her yet. Why not?"

Damn him. Just because he knew when a soul departed from Earth didn't mean he had to hold it over his head. "I've neutralized the threat she posed." She might possibly die as a result.

"But she lives."

"She has no power. She's barely alive." In an effort to spare him the pain of taking her life, he'd reduced her to nothing. He should have given her the warrior's death she deserved.

"The coven knows she's in Port Townsend."

"It doesn't matter. She freely relinquished her power to me and sealed it with a blood oath. She can't hurt anyone now." Perhaps he should *ask* her sisters to come. They might be able to help her.

"Damn it, Dru. I've come up against her sister, Moira. She knocked me on my ass *before* she linked with

Tierra. They've bonded, making them capable of more than the ordinary witch."

"The only way Claire's powers can be returned is if I give them to her. I've experienced every kind of torture known to man, and there's nothing that will make me change my mind." Even now, the fiery ball of her essence burned deeper through his layers, like hot ash through the pages of a book.

A tremble shook her frail body as she struggled for a breath. God. She *was* dying. He'd wrongly believed her heartbeat meant she'd live.

Instead, it only meant she hadn't died yet.

"I'll meet you later at *Sirens* and tell you everything. Right now, there's something that can't wait." Dru hung up the phone before Nick could reply.

As Claire struggled for another breath, he climbed out of bed and lifted her into his arms. What he offered her wasn't enough. There was only one possible way to save her, and it rested in the hands of others.

The gods were truly devils in disguise. He'd known that forever, known he was a pawn in their cruel plots. He'd never understood why they hadn't brought about the end of the world centuries earlier. Why allow so much pain and suffering to continue? But *this* pain, *this* suffering would be his undoing.

He carried Claire's limp body through the waning evening light to his SUV and placed her on the backseat. With fire burning a hole through his core, he climbed in the driver's seat and started the engine. The tires of his Hummer screeched as he hit asphalt and barreled down the winding, forested road toward town.

He stopped when he reached the home where Claire's family resided. The picturesque Victorian house loomed before him, lights glowing from the windows as unseen eyes surely watched him. No doubt, the occupants would damn him to hell if they could. Hopefully, they'd save Claire first.

Claire weighed next to nothing as he lifted her in his arms. He was steps from the porch when the front door flew open wide. The visage of a woman with Claire's face appeared in the doorway, causing him to pause. Her stature, the shape of her face appeared identical to the woman he held in his arms. The color of her hair reminded him of a rich Bordeaux, and her eyes were the shade of deep emeralds instead of the golden amber he ached to see again.

"*Oh my God.* Moira, come now!" she yelled backward into the house before she marched toward him like one of the many valiant soldiers he'd encountered in his lifetime. "What's happened to her?"

Before he could respond, another image of Claire rushed up behind her sister. This one had her hair pinned up and long legs that led to a very short skirt.

"Great toasted Christ on a cracker, Tierra. There's another one of us?" Her gaze moved from Claire to him, her turquoise eyes condemning him on sight. "*This hunk of meat done killed her.*"

He pushed past them and into the house, stopping to look for somewhere to lay her down. "She's not dead, but she's close. Can you help her?" His heart tripped as the impact of his words and what he'd done slammed him harder than a berserker's mighty axe.

"Upstairs. First door on the right," Tierra said. The anger burning in her eyes had morphed to frantic trepidation.

Dru took the stairs two at a time, entering a darkened bedroom overwhelmed by plants and unlit candles. Claire rasped a breath, and then groaned as he placed her on the bed. As bad as she sounded, he was glad she'd made a noise after being dead silent all morning.

Tierra turned on the light before she shoved him out of the way, her brightly-colored skirts swishing as she took charge. The silver bangles on her arms tinkled as she reached out and placed a hand on Claire's forehead. She closed her eyes and took a deep breath.

No one in the room moved as she made her assessment.

Then her eyes flashed open, and she turned to her sister. "Moira. Downstairs in the kitchen, get the peppermint salve, a cinnamon stick and witch-hazel. Someone's drained her power, and she doesn't have enough energy to recharge herself."

She turned to Dru. "I don't know who you are or how much of this damage lies on your head, though I sense you're anything but innocent. But I need your help, too. Start a fire in the fireplace over there. Get it burning hot. *Now*."

Grateful to have a task that might help, Dru did as she asked, using kindling and wood from a nearby basket. Flames snapped to life, and he added two large logs. Orange fire danced, licking the sides of the wood as they used its energy to sustain themselves.

Softly muttered words came from behind him, and he turned to find Tierra rubbing Claire's hand briskly as she whispered. Then she tucked an orange-colored stone against Claire's palm and closed her fingers around it. He moved closer, thinking some color might have returned to Claire's cheeks.

Moira entered the room in a rush, giving him another sideways glance like she might give to a coiled rattlesnake. "Here, Tierra."

Tierra stopped chanting and took the items. She removed the lid from a small blue ceramic jar and stuck her finger inside, scooping a glob of shimmery paste. She whispered soft words as she rubbed it at Clair's temples, between her breasts, and on her wrists. She took the witch-hazel, whisked it across Claire's lips before she pried open her mouth and forced the cinnamon stick against her cheek.

Claire inhaled sharply once before her breathing

slowed again. Tierra put another cinnamon stick inside her other cheek. Again, Claire took a deep breath and then calmed.

"Give her another," Moira said.

"If I administer too much, it could kill her, too." She placed her hand on her forehead again. "But I think it's helping. Her essence is stronger."

"Will she live?" Dru asked, needing the answer more than oxygen.

Tierra ignored him. "It's strange because I sense her power in the room, but it's like…dormant."

He had perhaps moments before they figured out what he'd done.

Tierra glanced at her conscious sister. "Can you feel it, Moira? I'm not imagining it, am I?"

"Maybe." She tilted her head. "Is it that deep pulse? It reminds me of the pulse in Ricky Wade's trouser snake the first time he groped me in the back of his daddy's Chevelle."

Tierra gave a slight shake of head as though to clear away what Moira had said. "Yes, that's it. It's strong, but she's not."

Dru moved to the other side of the bed and took Claire's hand. Her fingers tightened around his for a second before they relaxed again. He wanted to believe she'd sensed him there, had responded to his touch, but likely her movement was a reaction to stimulus.

"Claire?" He squeezed her hand. "Can you hear me?"

She took another deep breath like she had when Tierra had shoved the cinnamon stick into her mouth. Tierra and Moira both turned to him with a questioning look.

"She responds to you." Tierra said, assessing him with a guarded look. "You called her Claire. Who is she to you? Do you know how she came to be here?"

"She's…a friend." He'd promised her friendship if she'd agree to the oath. The pledge that had stolen her essence and buried it deep inside him. He doubted she'd forgive him if she ever woke. Gwen must have known what this would do to her.

Was this his punishment then if he couldn't complete his task? To watch her slowly fade away like a dying ember?

"A friend, huh?" Moira folded her arms beneath her breasts and fixed a doubting look on her face. "If that's the truth, then I'll be a possum's pooper-scooper."

He met their gazes with a steely one of his own. He couldn't tell them the truth. They wouldn't understand. They'd use any means available to get him to return her power, which would put her in worse jeopardy, if that was possible.

Tierra caught his hand where it twined with Claire's. Their eyes clashed, and she jerked her hand away just as quickly. "*Thief*," she hissed.

Dru took a step back, prepared to fight.

"What'd he steal?" Moira asked.

Tierra held his gaze, hers a condemning mixture of hatred and anger. "*He has Claire's power.*"

The floor began to rumble, and the walls shook. Dru ached to stay long enough to see if they could revive Claire, but time had deserted him and he needed to retreat.

Lights flickered as he strode from the room with both sisters chasing him out of the house.

"Come back here!" Tierra yelled. "You can't take what doesn't belong to you."

"*Do something.*" Moira's voice sounded as desperate as he felt. "Stop him."

Dru jumped into his Hummer and started the engine as the ground bucked beneath him. Asphalt broke, pushed up by the earth beneath it into mounds as rain fell in sheets around him. He put his SUV into gear, the tires gripping the uneven ground, allowing him to go up and over the earth witch's devastation to undamaged pavement. His headlights punched through the wet skies, illuminating a crack in the road as it snaked from beneath his vehicle and began to widen. He stomped the accelerator to the floor, and his Hummer shot forward, away from the chaos expanding around him.

＊　23　＊

Dru thought twice about stopping to meet Nick. *Sirens Pub* sat on Water Street, not far enough from the Victorian house. He had no idea if Claire's sisters could track him by the power that burned through his soul, but if he had a battle on his hands, he'd just as soon wage it with Nick at his side. Neither of them, nor their other two partners in crime, could experience death. Hell, Killian Bane owned the word. But pain? None of them had escaped that enemy.

He ran a thumb over the scar near his eye, remembering the betrayal like it had happened yesterday instead of hundreds of years ago. Death would have been a mercy. Agony was a vile beast that ripped through his entrails until death seemed like a lover's kiss on a warm spring day.

A blade slicing his skin or a witch's concoction burning through his veins was nothing less than torture. Emotional agony was the worst.

Out of the three similarly-cursed men, he worked best with Nick conquering by his side.

Decision made, Dru parked his muddy Hummer on a darkened side road, out of view just in case. He avoided the front door and headed toward the back entrance, climbing the stairs to a deck that hovered over the water, offering an amazing view of Port Townsend Bay during the daytime. Right now, the bay appeared to be a vast expanse of blackness eager to swallow them both.

Nick sat near the railing, alone at his table amidst a crowd of other customers who laughed and talked as they blew off the workweek's steam. His friend stared off into the distance as a cool breeze ruffled his collar.

"See something you like?" Dru said as he stepped into view.

Nick flashed an annoyed gaze in his direction. "No."

"Hoping a water witch will appear and seduce you again?"

Nick met his gaze with serious eyes. "Fuck you."

Dru laughed and dropped into the chair across from him. "That's what you get for thinking with your dick instead of carrying out your mission."

His friend snorted. "You're one to talk."

A blonde waitress approached, interrupting Nick. "Johnny Walker Red?" she said to Dru before her gaze slipped to Nick and then back to him as though she couldn't take her eyes off Nick long enough to get Dru's order.

"As always, Angelica," he said with a smile.

"Did you need another?" she asked Nick.

He arched a sardonic brow, as though chastising her for interrupting them. "You'll know when I do."

She blinked, obviously flustered. Nick had that effect on most women. She hurried off as though the devil sniffed at her tail.

"You're such a jerk," Dru said with a smile. Nick could be a real ass and quite often was, but who could blame him? Too many lifetimes tended to harden a person in one way or the other.

Nick turned to him, a smooth smile crossing his

lips, his cool demeanor ever in place. "As I was saying, you haven't met Moira. She's a little more than...I expected."

Oh, he'd met her and the earth witch, but he wasn't about to admit they'd chased him from their house. "She's a woman, Nick. You've brought down Athens, Rome, and Constantinople... certainly you can handle one female."

Nick leaned back in the wrought iron chair and sipped his whisky. "*Handling* Moira is like calling the Dionysian orgy of 27 B.C. a wet dream. But, enough about me. The biggest threat we're facing at the moment is on *your* playground. Or is the fire witch no longer a concern? All it takes is one dead witch to solve our problems. Moira has bonded with her sister and won't be as easy to conquer as a solitary witch." He lifted a questioning brow, heavy with coercion.

If only it were that easy. "I've already told you Claire no longer has her powers. She's not a threat."

"Because *you* have them." His tone conveyed how little faith he had in Dru's decision.

He met his friend's gaze with a dark one of his own. "That's right."

"Don't be so naïve." Nick leaned forward. "This is the end of the world we're talking about. As long as she and her powers co-exist on this planet, she's a threat."

Behind Nick, a woman stood and slapped her boyfriend's face before she stomped off. Dru barely gave her a glance. "Her power *isn't* on the planet. It's buried deep inside me. There's no way for her to reclaim it. Besides, she gave it up freely. She didn't want it."

Nick chuckled. "You're playing with fire, brother."

"I've eliminated the threat. No further action is required."

Angelica brought his whisky, and Dru knocked it

back with one shot. "I'll take another," he said as the fiery liquid traced the familiar path down his throat. She nodded and left.

"She can't win," Dru continued. "There's nothing stronger than blood magic, and there's no way I'll return her power to her. Problem solved."

"Do you truly believe when she reunites with her sisters, they're not going to convince her she made a mistake?"

Dru sucked in a deep breath, expanding his chest, not letting on that he'd already delivered Claire to her sisters. "Don't question my tactics, Nick. I'm aware of what's at stake, but the threat is dead."

Nick narrowed his eyes. "She has your balls."

An argument broke out behind Dru, one man taunting the other, leaving the second man to threaten to kick his ass.

Dru leveled a heated look at Nick. "No fucking way." Just because he didn't want to kill her didn't mean he wouldn't if necessary.

A mocking laugh erupted from Nick's chest. "She has your fucking balls. All of these centuries you fight like a heartless bastard, but when the time comes to prove you're the ultimate warrior, you let a woman castrate you. A fire witch no less."

Angry shouts multiplied around them, but Dru didn't take his eyes off Nick as his own wrath swirled in his veins. "I have her fucking power burning a fiery hole through my goddamned soul right now, and I'm telling you, she's *never* getting it back." He lifted his hand in time to catch a sailing tankard before it shattered against their table.

"Then you better get the hell out of town because one Seal has already been broken, and I can damn well guarantee those witches aren't going to stop hunting you. They'll get what they want, or they'll die trying."

"I'm not afraid of them. If they come sniffing around me, I'll start a war they won't likely forget. They'll be too busy plucking bloody bodies off the street to fight me."

Dru stood and grabbed a burly fisherman flailing in his direction, shoving him back toward his friend where they both fell in a pile of other fighting bodies. "What the hell's the matter with these people?"

Nick snorted. "This is only the beginning, my friend."

❧

SIZZLING SENSATIONS SEARED CLAIRE'S MOUTH, AND she pushed at the burned areas with her tongue. She met tiny balls of resistance and forced them out between her lips as she coughed and tried to clear her airway. Bright light assaulted her eyes, and she blinked in an effort to regain her bearings.

Turquoise eyes peered intently into hers. "Tierra! Hop your ass in here. I hauled her back from the brink like a ten-pound catfish into the boat!" the woman yelled.

Claire stared at the strange, yet familiar face, wondering if a dream inside a dream held her prisoner. Had she somehow been trapped in a mirror that distorted her image?

Dru had held her prisoner. Was this another of his illusions? She lifted a bandaged wrist, sure she wouldn't have brought that memory along with her into a dream. It must be real.

"Oh my goodness!" Another woman rushed into the room, bangles tinkling as the scent of lavender and roses accompanied her. She gripped Claire's hands, and again, her own face, smiled back at her. They were so alike, and yet so different.

The room, filled with plants and the heavenly scent

of burnt logs, was nothing her imagination could have conjured. She inhaled, letting the ginger and nutmeg smells fortify her. "Dru?" she managed to whisper, thinking he must be there somewhere.

"Not that bastard," the woman who held her hands hissed.

"He's the one who stole your powers and dumped you on our doorstep like a bag of day-old gator gizzards. You don't want *nothing* to do with that skunk-licking bog buzzard. You got your kin now. I'm Moira."

"And, I'm Tierra," said the one with the bangles. "I can't tell you how happy I am to meet you. When I sent out the conjuring spell and Moira showed up, I thought that was it. But now I find I have *two* sisters. I can't imagine anything better."

"'Cept the prick almost killed you 'afore we even knew you was alive." Moira studied her face with excitement shadowed by a hint of hesitation.

"*Sisters?*" Claire tried to sit, but found she didn't have the strength.

"Don't try to get up," Tierra took an orange carnelian and placed it in her palm. "You gave us a nasty scare. We thought for sure you'd wither after that bastard stole your power. Luckily, I found an old potion in Aunt Justine's things that I hoped would work, and it looks like it did."

"That and a shit load of Red Hots," Moira added with a laugh.

Tierra narrowed her eyes in question. "*You gave her what?*"

"Red Hots. You were worried about giving her too many cinnamon sticks, and I remember when Butch Tucker and I ate a whole bag full of Red Hots one night sitting out on the dock when we was just kids. It set our mouths on fire, let me tell you, but it didn't kill no one. So I figured why not? She's a fire witch. They're probably right up her alley. And look, it worked."

The sting of cinnamon still hovered on Claire's tongue, helping to take away the cottony feeling in her mouth. "Sisters?" she said again as tears formed in her eyes. After all this time, after all these years, she had *sisters?*

Tierra gathered her into a hug. "Yes, sisters."

❀ 24 ❀

It took Claire two days, numerous cups of Tierra's special fire potion, and a pound of Red Hots before she had enough strength to shower and dress. Afterward, she made her way downstairs, following the scent of coffee, wearing a deliciously warm brown sweater Tierra had loaned her. She tried to ignore the hollow feeling echoing inside her. It wasn't until she'd woken up without her power that she realized how much of her very being existed inside the gift that she'd so willingly given to Dru.

Dru who'd promised her friendship. Dru who hadn't stopped by *or* called to check on her. Dru who'd dumped her on her sisters' doorstep when she'd needed him the most.

Claire found her sisters sitting at the kitchen table, Tierra staring intently into a teacup while Moira slathered butter on a slice of toast. Her heart melted at the sight. She had sisters. Real live, honest-to-goodness sisters. They were worth the trade.

As she stepped inside the kitchen, she caught sight of her suitcases sitting next to the back door. "Oh my God! My stuff!" She'd been wondering how she'd manage to get new clothes. She no longer had the power to convince men to give her money, and she didn't want to start her new relationship with her sisters by asking for a loan.

"Goddess," Tierra mumbled as she helped herself to a slice of wheat toast.

Claire glanced at Moira, hoping she could decipher Tierra's comment, but Moira just shrugged.

"Did Dru stop by?" Her sisters had cursed his name each time she'd mentioned him, so Claire knew the question wouldn't be well-received, but a small part of her still wanted to believe in him. She longed to see Dru, longed to feel his arms around her, hoping beyond hope that she'd feel her fire once again if he held her. It might be how she'd survive the loss of her element.

She'd tried to get her sisters to discuss the events that brought her to their house, but they refused. They limited conversation topics to sharing their pasts, and anything more would have to wait until she was stronger.

Tierra scowled at her from beneath lowered brows, while Moira rolled her eyes and looked away as though she wasn't about to get in the middle of the forthcoming discussion.

"We need to have a talk, Claire." Tierra stood. "Have a seat, and I'll get you some tea."

She took a spot next to Moira where the sunlight coming through the window would warm her. "Don't you have coffee? I swore I could smell it."

"See?" Moira said to Tierra. "Not everyone likes to slurp that hot water of yours."

Tierra tisked. "We're going to have to fix that along with a few other things."

Claire glanced between the women, jealous of the relationship her two sisters already had with each other.

"Thank you," she said when Tierra placed a steaming mug of black coffee in front of her. Moira pushed the sugar toward her with raised brows that said if she was going to commit a sin such as drinking coffee, she might as well go all the way and add sugar and cream. She gave her rebellious sister a smile as she did exactly that.

"How on earth will you ever realize your true powers if you keep polluting your bodies with those toxins?" Tierra asked, her face a mask of serious concern.

"Slowly," Moira answered. "Plus I think the powers like a challenge, which is why I make a point of givin' them plenty of toxins to fight with on a daily basis. Anyway, you've had your whole life to learn up on this stuff. We'll catch up after a bit." She winked at Claire, letting her know it was a ruse to keep Tierra happy.

"I saw that," Tierra said as she refilled her teacup and settled in.

"You didn't know about your power, either?" Claire asked Moira.

"Nope. I mean, I could get a man to drop his pants just by looking at him."

"You could have done that without your power, Moira," Tierra said with a sarcastic tone.

"I know. But all those men needed my help. I've told you this."

"That doesn't mean they all have a right to..." Tierra shook her head and lifted her teacup.

"She don't like my whoring ways." Moira gave Claire a serious look. "I'm working on it, learning some self-respect and all that happy horse pucky. It helps. Having sisters, ya know?"

Claire drank her coffee, letting the scalding heat soak into her body, giving her a glimmer of warmth. If Tierra didn't approve of what Moira had done, she certainly wouldn't appreciate her own antics, so she'd be keeping that tidbit to herself. "How did you find us, Tierra?"

Tierra took a cleansing breath. "I *knew* you were there. All my life, I've known something was missing.

Aunt Justine kept discouraging me from exploring my better senses. She warned me something bad would happen if I didn't leave things alone. But I couldn't ignore the yearning inside me any longer. I sent out the call to bring you home. Look at us now. How can this be bad?"

"Aunt Justine? Is she here?" More family? Claire glanced about the homey kitchen. And then to the doors beyond.

"She moved out," Tierra started.

"You mean we moved her sorry ass out." Moira turned to Claire. "She didn't like me, and she won't like you. I'm used to women wanting me dead, but I ain't ever had none of them come at me like that coven did. If it wasn't for Cheeto, I'd be deader than the pecker on a corpse."

"Cheeto?" Claire asked.

"My little pig." Moira nodded as though pet pigs were an everyday occurrence. "I'll introduce you when he wakes from his morning nap."

Claire looked to Tierra, and she shrugged. "He's adorable."

"I look forward to it." Her sisters were anything but ordinary, and she suddenly realized she preferred it that way. She'd always been an outcast, but now, finally, she belonged.

Except she didn't. She'd given away the thing that made her different from others, but bonded her to her sisters.

Tierra fixed her with a determined look. "Now that you're stronger, we need to find that son of a bitch and take back what belongs to you. I felt it inside him when he brought you here, and he ran like the devil when we questioned him." Her expression fell into a tangle of worry.

"I'm scared to ask what he did to you to get it."

Claire shook her head as clammy emotion churned

in her hollowed out soul. The feeling was foreign, unwelcome. "I'm all right." Tierra's concern and pity weighed on her, making her feel *less-than*. She'd always been alone, always had her strength if nothing else. She'd always taken what she wanted, even if she couldn't have what she needed.

She didn't have to worry about that anymore, though. She'd made the choice to give her curse away. She had her sisters instead. That would be enough.

"Did he hurt you?" Moira asked with wide eyes. "Like rape you or torture you to get you to give your magic?"

Heated thoughts of their imagined encounter swarmed her, making her ache for his touch. "No."

"But your wrists..." Tierra said in a soft voice.

"That was my fault." She'd struggled when she should have listened.

"How'd he do that, anyway?" Moira watched her with eyes the color of stormy seas. "I can't imagine it's like guttin' a catfish or anything."

"No," Tierra interjected before her gaze strayed to Claire. "She'd have had to give her soul to him."

"I did. I gave him my power." The disappointment in their eyes echoed the grief in her heart and nearly undid her. What if they no longer wanted to claim her?

"*Why?*" Tierra asked with a look of bewilderment that nearly broke Claire's heart.

"So I could find you. So I could have a chance at a real relationship...maybe with him." His explanation had made so much sense at the time.

"*With him?*" Moira asked, her expression turning again to pity. "Why would you ever give up your power to be with a man?"

Claire ventured into new territory. She'd never given up anything for anyone. It had seemed so noble. "He's not like any other man I've met." When she turned to

Tierra, she found her face ashen, like remnants of scorched earth.

"Good goddess. *Do you even know who he is?*"

Claire searched both of their faces, never feeling so powerless in her life. "Dru?"

Moira lifted disappointed brows. "War, Claire. The man is *War.*"

She wrinkled her expression. "War? I don't understand."

Tierra leaned closer. "War, as in one of the Four Horsemen of the Apocalypse. As in heated crusades and bloody battles. *As in, you willingly gave him your power?* What do you think a man like that will do with your fire?"

Claire swallowed as a shadow of her previous essence sparked. "He said it was the only way he could let me go. It was the only way I could find you. It was the only way he and I could be friends."

Tierra scoffed. "Do you really think War has friends?"

"Now don't go getting your britches in a bundle, girls. Claire ain't the first girl to fall for a cheap line." Moira split her focus between her two sisters.

"Cheap line? Neither of you have a clue what I went through to find you. Tierra sends out this cryptic message to return home. I had no warning of danger, no idea who or what I was looking for, no idea who I could trust. He might be War, but there's a man behind that title, and he's not completely heartless." Whatever fire she'd found fizzled. "If he was, he would have killed me like he'd planned."

Moira patted her hand. "Don't feel bad. I had my own demon to fight, too."

Claire gave her a sideways glance. "What did you do?"

She grinned. "I blasted his ass six ways to Sunday with a huge wall of water. That soggy bastard will think twice 'afore messing with me again. Seriously, we have to get your power back. I had no idea the stuff I could do. With Tierra helping me, it's like a Cajun Christmas every day of the week."

Claire couldn't deny she yearned to have her power back as well. Without it, she'd be surviving, not living. "Dru said me having my power would bring about the end of the world. What did he mean?"

"He sounds like Aunt Justine and all her crazy-ass talk." Moira took another bite of toast and licked the stream of butter trailing down her thumb.

"He's wrong, Claire." Tierra met her gaze head-on, sincere belief echoing from her eyes. "Aunt Justine feared the same thing, but they're wrong. Look at us. We're three women. Good women, not spawns of the devil. We're not going to hurt anyone."

"Least not anyone who don't deserve it," Moira added.

Tierra nodded. "Everyone knows it's the Horsemen who bring about the end, not us. War having your power plays into that scenario better than anything does. Fire is *your gift, your heritage*. It doesn't matter if you believe he took it for a good reason or not. It's yours, and you need it. You're lucky you've survived without it."

Claire slowly nodded. Her soul without fire was like the heavens without the sun. She'd die without it. If not now, then soon. Perhaps Dru hadn't known that. If he'd wanted her dead, he could have just killed her. "I need to talk to him. If I explain, maybe he'll give it back."

Tierra choked on her tea. "Oh, Claire. I've lived one of the most sheltered lives, and even I'm not that naïve. It's because your fire is missing. I know you wouldn't talk like that with your energy burning inside you."

"Like I said, you ain't the first person to believe a man's lies," Moira added. "Before I started helping guys on a regular basis, they was telling me all kinds of wild stories."

"Why didn't he just kill me outright, then? Why let me live? Why bring me to your house after he had what he wanted?"

"Can't you see?" Tierra shook her head, emerald earrings dancing at her ears. "This was the only way to take your power. If you die, it dies."

She bit her tongue as she stared at her sisters. Were they right? Had Dru lied to her to get what he wanted, and she'd fallen for it?

There was only one way to know for sure. She needed to look him in the eye. "I'm going to get my power back."

"Damn skippy! Let's light a fire under that boy's ass!"

"How exactly do you plan to do that?" Tierra asked.

"I'm going to his house, and I'll ask for it. If he won't give it to me willingly, I'll figure out a way to take it." She glanced at her sisters. "I might need your help."

"Don't you think we would have done that already if we knew where he was hiding out?" Tierra asked. "Moira and I have been planning a few spells while you recuperated, but we have to wait until we find him...unless you have his address."

"I don't have his address, but I know where to find him." She touched her chest, near the empty, aching spot inside her. "This will lead me. My power wants to come home. I feel it with every breath I take. I hear it sometimes, calling to me. Sometimes, I think I hear him, too."

"It's not going to be easy," Tierra cautioned.

"But it will be funner than mud-wrasslin' a drunk monkey," Moira added. "We should try that spell we found in the book Justine kept under her bed. The one that uses gun powder."

Tierra shook her head. "No. We can only fight blood

magic with blood magic. That's why nothing we've tried so far has worked."

"You've been trying to get my power back?" The thought that someone would fight on her behalf left a warming tingling in her heart.

"Yeah, but all we got was smoke and no fire." Moira frowned.

Tierra took her sisters' hands, a grave expression on her face. "I have to be honest. I have very little experience with most spells. None with blood magic. The coven forbids it even in the smallest circles because it's so dangerous. Aunt Justine always said it could bring hell down on us. If we do this, I can't promise something bad won't happen."

"Like what?" Claire whispered, fear striking deep inside her.

Tierra shrugged. "That's just it. I don't know. Aunt Justine would never discuss it with me. No one would."

"I can't ask you to put your lives on the line for me. I've just found you both, and I don't want to risk losing you again." Her sisters were the reason Claire had given up her power in the first place. She couldn't ask these two women to share the consequences of her decisions. "I'll do this on my own. I'm not afraid."

"Like hell," Tierra said. "We're in this together."

"Together," Moira added. "I'll bring Cheeto just in case."

❈ 25 ❈

"Did you get the prickly ash bark?" Tierra met Claire in the kitchen and then directed her to a covered porch just off the kitchen.

Claire held up the bag of brown wooden crumbles that had been where Tierra had directed her. "Is this it?" The delicious scent of burning wood captured her attention the moment she stepped outdoors.

Fresh flames licked the logs, beginning the first steps in the renewal of life. She inhaled deeply, the smell and heat infusing her lungs, giving her a boost of energy. Being without her power left her exhausted most of the time.

"Excellent." Tierra opened the bag and extracted a pinch, adding it to the miniature cauldron hanging over the fire.

"This is really how you do spells? It seems so fictional."

"It's how we make potions." She gave her a mischievous smile. "You should know better than anyone that fire is one of the most effective ways of combining elements."

"And water," Moira said as she joined them on the porch carrying other ingredients. "Rosemary and ginger. Just like you asked."

"What exactly is this supposed to do?" Claire asked as Tierra added to her concoction.

"It's a compulsion potion. It will make Dru want to give you whatever you ask for."

"Kind of like fire did before?" she said, remembering her long and tainted past.

"What do you mean?" Moira's eyes flashed with interest.

Claire glanced between her sisters. "Nothing." She waved her hand. "Just nothing."

Someday she'd tell them. Moira anyway. She wasn't sure Tierra would understand. Tierra might have grown up without them, but at least she'd known who she was. What she was.

"How is this supposed to trump a blood oath? It doesn't seem like it will be strong enough with just plant extracts." Claire addressed the question to both of her sisters.

"Don't discount Mother Earth's babies," Tierra responded. "Their power might be understated, but they're the ones to rebuild after all of your devastation. Not to mention, belladonna will kill people just as quickly as fire or drowning."

"True. I've seen Tierra in action. Besides, we've already figured out the strength part of this potion." Moira gave them both a sly grin. "Just add our blood to that little pot over there."

Claire lifted a brow and deferred to Tierra who seemed to be the expert on the subject.

"I don't know if it will work," she said, her tone grave. "But I think it's our best option. With the three of us in there together, it should give it a boost of power. In return, it might make us weak for a few days. Or so."

"Or so?" Claire asked. She didn't know if her body could survive another hit, but she had her choices:

wither away or go out fighting. "I don't have my magic any longer, so I don't know how my blood will help."

"Just because you can't access it, doesn't mean it's not there in some form." Tierra gave the pot a stir before she removed a small dagger from her apron. The sharp silver blade glinted in the afternoon light.

"Are you ready?"

A shiver raced through Claire. She knew so little about the gift she'd been given, but something in her recognized what they were about to do was of monumental importance.

"Hell, yeah," Moira said and stuck out her hand.

Claire lifted hers as well.

Tierra made a smooth slice in each of their hands. "I think it's best if we follow the same cut made during the original oath for you," she said to Claire as the sharp blade followed the festering wound on her hand. Crimson blood rushed to the surface as if it was eager to do its part.

"We should all let a few drops fall into the pot, I think," Tierra directed.

As each droplet hit the simmering brew, it sizzled and spit.

Tierra stirred as she peered at the mixture. "Maybe a few extra of yours, Claire, since it's your magic we're trying to recover."

Claire forced a few more droplets of blood into the pot, a small voice in the back of her mind questioning whether they should be playing with such serious magic when even the most knowledgeable of them seemed to be groping in the dark.

"It looks good, has the right consistency," Tierra announced. She closed her eyes and began muttering words beneath her breath.

The ground shook. Cooking pots that hung inside the kitchen clanked against each other. Moira took her hand and squeezed. When Claire met her gaze, she whispered, "Don't worry. I'll help you." Clouds gathered in the once-sunny sky and opened, letting a soft rain fall upon the earth.

"There," Tierra pronounced dramatically, giving Claire a start. She used a pair of tongs to remove a congealed red ball from the pot before slipping it into a plastic bag. It reminded Claire of a hard candy.

"That's it?" she asked, staring at the ball in amazement. "What do we do now?"

"You're going to have to get him to eat it. He only needs a taste." Tierra handed the bag to her, and Claire swore power emanated from it. "But don't touch it. Otherwise, it might affect you, too."

"That don't sound too hard," Moira added. "Make him think it's a breath mint or something. Could even slip it in a drink. Just make sure it's dark so he don't see it."

"And then I'll have my power back?" For a dangerous blood oath, that seemed harmless.

"Sort of," Tierra replied. "After he eats it, then you'll need to ask him to return your powers. If this works and he agrees, then your magic will return."

Claire pondered the scenario for a moment. It didn't seem much different from when she made love to a man and asked him for money, leaving his heart open to love in return. "Will it hurt him?"

"Doesn't matter," Moira said, removing the pencil from her hair before twisting the strands again and weaving it back in.

Claire didn't want to admit to these women the depth of her feelings for Dru. She could barely admit it to herself. On paper, he looked like a complete jackass, kidnapping her and stealing her power. But there was more to him than that. A deeper, darker connection existed between them that mere words could never explain.

"Fine. When do we do this?" she said instead.

"Now," Tierra and Moira said in unison.

DRU FOCUSED ON THE SOUNDS OF CREATURES MOVING through the quiet forest as he sat beneath a large pine, eyes closed. The red fox was close, he knew. Every time he'd stepped outside for the past few days, the woodland animal had stalked him, watching him from a distance with intense eyes. Dru had left bits of meat as an offering, but the fox never approached. Only watched.

He exhaled a deep breath, meditating on the surrounding cool atmosphere, trying to overcome the heat burning inside him. His vessel struggled to carry such a volatile power, and it took all his strength and mind-control not to let it reduce him to a quivering mass.

He could wrestle this force into submission if given enough time, but it would take all his concentration. He could not remember ever facing such a powerful, mental and emotional foe.

He inhaled again, breathing new life into the fire inside him, bringing home once again the sensation of Claire. Her scent, her essence surrounded him, lived inside him, and taunted him with each breath. He wanted her like no other. The fire inside him begged to unite with her, to meld with her, to become one.

His own power seemed to succumb to hers, and he fought to keep them separate. They blended so well, his war and her fire, destined to be one eternal fighting machine. But if he let that happen now, he would lose control.

First, he had to bend it to his will. Then he could command her power.

He leaned forward as a sharp, fiery pain ripped through him once again, adrenaline forcing all his muscles to contract. Her essence proved to be a worthy opponent, grappling for domination.

During moments like this, he could feel her. Every inch of her, more powerful than before.

Fuck. He opened his eyes as realization dawned.

The time had come. Claire drew nearer to him with each breath he took. Her fire sensed her. Wanted her.

Gods. So did his body.

❧ 26 ☙

The rain stopped, and the sun was back full force by the time the three women reached the spot where Claire told Tierra to turn off the main highway that was surprisingly not far from their home.

Tierra slowed and turned onto the narrow dirt road. "Are you sure he's back here? The road looks like it leads to nowhere but a bunch of trees."

Claire couldn't say anything looked familiar about the place. She'd had a hood over her head when she'd arrived, and she had no recollection of leaving. "He's here. I can feel his heartbeat pounding in my chest." She wondered if he could feel her as well.

Her question was answered as they pulled up to a familiar rustic wooden cabin and the front door opened before she exited the car.

"This will be easier if I go in alone." Claire opened the passenger door.

Tierra nodded. "I've got my senses on you. If something goes wrong, I'll know, and we'll be right there."

"I've got Cheeto right here if you need him." Moira petted the sweet, little pig sitting in her lap.

Claire gave them both a confident smile, though it was only surface-deep. If what Tierra said was true and things went awry, who knew what they'd find on the other side. She exhaled a breath. "Thanks."

A swallow lodged in her throat as she advanced toward Dru's home. The small, red ball in her pocket seemed like an inept defense against such a powerful man. Her strength was a shadow of what it used to be, and she'd had a difficult time controlling him when she'd been fully alive.

If it wasn't for the incessant ache to reclaim her fire, she'd turn and leave.

No. That wasn't true. The need to see him one more time, to know if there really had been something between was almost as strong as the need for her power. God help her.

Her boots clomped on the wooden stairs as she moved closer to the open door. She could see furnishings inside the house, but not him.

When she reached the doorway, she peered inside.

"I knew you'd come."

His deep voice reached out from the darkness of the house, startling her. The same voice that had circled in her head the past few days now wrapped around her like lightning. Her body sang with the knowledge that her power was near. Even though she didn't house it, she received a burst of energy.

She took a breath and stepped inside. It took a moment for her eyes to adjust to the dimness.

He stood near the ashen fireplace, heat radiating from him like a furnace. He wore nothing but a pair of black boxer briefs, and she raked her gaze over him like a greedy whore. Images of him holding her, touching her, gripped her as though the experience had been real, and she thirsted for more.

She walked toward him, needing to be closer.

He watched her with dark eyes, his expression neutral, closed.

She wanted to reach out, to place her hands on his

face. But it didn't seem right. They were strangers. And yet, not.

"You knew I would come? Are you happy to see me?" Her sisters had tried to convince her he'd used her for his own gain, but she couldn't dismiss the pounding in her heart that said otherwise.

"You shouldn't have come."

His reply was an arrow piercing her armor, stinging with its sharp point, but not enough for her to give up on him.

"I had to. I need what's mine."

He reached out to her then, drawing a roughened thumb down her cheek, sending a tremble racing through her. "If I give it to you, it will make us enemies again." His voice seemed strained, almost breathless as though he struggled to maintain control.

"We're not enemies now? My sisters disagree." She touched his bicep, closing her eyes for a second as sweet heat saturated her. She sighed with contentment.

"Don't do that." He took a step back.

She left her hand where it was for a moment, hovering in the air, before she let it drop. "I can't resist. You have a part of me that I can't live without." She advanced, placing her hands on his pecs, shivering as delicious heat filled her again.

"Stop, Claire," he said, but he didn't move away this time. "Think carefully about what you're doing."

"I don't know what I'm doing. I just know I need this." She pressed against him as power swirled through her veins in a dangerous rush.

This time, he shoved her away, anger pulsing at his temples and in his eyes. "You need to leave."

A cold rush of emotion drenched her, bringing her back to reality. "I thought you said we could be friends. You told me if I gave my power to you, I could have my family and we'd be friends. But that was a lie, wasn't it? You didn't save me from my evil power that would destroy the world. You seduced me, took what was right-fully mine, and left me with this shell. *Why? To make yourself more powerful?*"

"Do I look more powerful?"

He looked like a god. "Please give me back what's mine," she said, trying a softer approach. She didn't want to hate him. Didn't want to hurt him.

"I can never do that. It's better if you leave and never come back."

Pain welled inside her, and she fought it, resurrecting the fierce shield that had protected her heart from aching loneliness all these years. The truth stood in front of her, slaughtering the pretty words he'd spoken. He'd used her. He'd stolen from her. There would never be anything between them but a battlefield.

If that's how he wanted it, then she'd wage a war against him, the likes of which he'd never experienced. He wanted to play with magic? Play with her heart? Fine. From this point on, there'd be no going back.

She inhaled a deep breath, sucking energy that radiated from him. *Her energy*. "Can you not at least consider my point of view?" She took another step closer.

He moved back, farther into the shadows.

She advanced again until she'd backed him into the corner. He looked down at her, his gaze watchful and calculating. She had no doubt he could escape her if he chose, but for the moment, he let her have her way. A few moments would be all she'd need to execute her freshly formed plan.

She placed a hand on his cheek, reveling in the sensation, watching his gaze grow hazy. She might not have her fire, but she had some kind of power over him. "You need to understand, being here with you is a drug to me. I haven't felt this alive in days. You said you didn't want to kill me, but I'm dying, Dru, growing weaker each day without my energy."

"You look stronger than you did." His voice sounded hopeful.

"Only because my sisters pumped me full of herbs and potions. But it won't last. I can't live like this forever. I need my power. I feel it inside you, and I crave it like an addict. Just touching you..." She closed her eyes as she moved her hand down his throat to where the inferno blasted near his heart. "If you won't give my energy back to me, then don't deny me this."

Hesitation and desire warred in his eyes. She recognized the weakness in his defenses and pressed forward. She slipped her hands behind his neck, but he resisted when she tried to bring his head closer to hers.

"Kiss me, Dru. Let me taste you. Share some of that heat with me."

He groaned and put his hands on her hips as though to push her away.

Before he could, she placed her lips on the smooth span of his heated chest and kissed him there. She traced her tongue over his nipple, absorbing more and more fire energy.

He caught her and turned them in a swift, dominant move pressing her against the wall as he sought her mouth with a vengeance. Fiery passion whipped through her, increasing her strength along with her need.

Yes. He might not care about her, but he still wanted her.

She had to act fast before he consumed her.

She caught his bottom lip between her teeth, nipping it to draw his attention as she slipped a hand into her pocket. She soothed his lip with her tongue before she teased him, drawing his tongue into her mouth. She struggled to open the plastic bag without him noticing. In a desperate move, she pressed her free hand against his erection, caressing the bulge, refusing to release him from their kiss.

Tierra had said not to handle the hard ball they'd created, but Claire had no choice.

Her fingers sizzled when she touched it, but she ignored the pain. She had to get him to taste it, to consume some portion of it, and she was running out of time.

She broke their kiss, gasping for air. "Oh, God, Dru. I need you so much." The worst part of her wicked plan was that she would never be able to experience this again.

"Me, too," he growled as he nuzzled her neck, his hands slipping beneath her shirt.

Shivers raced over her as she sent one last prayer to the gods or goddesses above and popped the fiery ball into her mouth. *"Kiss me."* Hot sparks erupted inside her head, tainting everything with a red haze as Dru claimed her mouth.

The moment his tongue breached her lips, she forced the cursed ball inside his mouth.

He stepped back from her, a stunned look on his face. He spit the ball onto the floor, anger blazing in his eyes. "What the hell was that? Feels like it's burning a hole through my goddamned tongue!"

"Give back what you took from me!" she yelled as adrenaline and fear broke over her, afraid their spell hadn't worked.

"No!"

But even as he said it, she felt it. Delicious power snaked through her as everything around them began to shake. The picture above the fireplace fell to the floor. The sound of glass shattering punctuated the chaos. Books leapt from shelves and a lamp crashed to the ground.

He reached for her, but she moved away, putting the couch between them.

"What have you done, Claire?" he demanded, holding onto the mantle as her power slipped from him.

"It's mine, Dru. It belongs to me."

Then everything quieted like a roaring freight train that had disappeared around a bend.

"I can't let you go. I can't let you have it." He moved slowly toward her.

Fiery energy and anger combusted inside her as the last bit of her essence returned. "Try to take it again, Dru. I dare you."

"It won't be your fire that I'll take next time. It will have to be *your life*."

A sonic boom came out of nowhere and shook the house, knocking Claire harder than a load of dynamite. She lay on the floor stunned for a few seconds before she regained her clarity and searched out Dru. He'd been knocked down as well.

He stared at her, his eyes growing wide as his gaze focused on her mid-section. Afraid of what she'd discover, she looked down. The unearthly sword Dru had used for their blood oath rested next to her.

Her gaze flew back to him. Fury owned his expression, forcing a barrage of panic to rain down on her.

"*Do you know what you've done?* Gods, woman, you've opened the Second Seal."

She had no idea what that meant, but instinct screamed to get the hell out of there. In a fluid motion, she gripped the heavy sword as she got to her feet and ran for the door as a horde of invisible demons chased her.

Thick blood, weighted by magic, coursed through her veins as her boots ate the distance between Dru's porch and Tierra's car. The passenger door opened before she reached it, and she flung herself and the sword inside.

"Go! Go! Go!" she screamed.

She looked back to see Dru only footsteps from the car as Tierra put it into gear. She sped off before he could do anything worse than pound once on the trunk.

"You have your power!" Tierra yelled victoriously as her car raced down the road. "I can feel it."

"Yes!" Hot adrenaline scorched her veins. "The potion worked, just not the way we thought."

"That's a mighty big sword you brought with you," Moira said as she leaned over the seat, eyeing the beautiful piece of workmanship.

"It's *his* sword."

"*What?*" Tierra asked, glancing rapidly between the carved steel and the road.

"It came out of nowhere," Claire said, her heart still racing. "As soon as I had my power back, there was this huge boom, and I found myself on the floor with it beside me. So I took it and ran."

Moira laughed as she fell against the backseat. "Lord Almighty, that is just the most perfect example of karma I've ever heard."

"Right?" Claire said, embracing the revelry, drunk on sweet power. "He'll learn to mess with me."

"Goddesses help us," Tierra hissed, the fearful tone of her voice wiping out their excitement. "This is serious, girls." She placed a hand on Claire's arm. "You do realize you've just stolen War's sword."

Doomed silence encompassed the car, leaving them all to ponder the significance of what they faced.

Then a snicker escaped Tierra's lips, and Claire turned to her, amazed. Tierra laughed again, bringing a smile to Claire's lips. Then Moira joined in, and soon they were all laughing.

"My sisters are some pretty bad-ass witches," Tierra said between breaths. "No one better mess with us."

"That's right," Moira agreed. "Or little Cheeto. He'll fry their asses, too."

Love and sisterhood surrounded Claire, fueling her energy, leaving her feeling invincible.

If it wasn't for the dangerous look she'd left on Dru's face, everything would be perfect.

DRU STUMBLED INTO HIS HOUSE LIKE A MAN WHO'D been castrated against his will. Anger pulsed through his veins and filled the hollow space that had once held Claire's power.

She had his fucking sword.

The fact that he now understood the pain she'd endured increased his fury. The empty ache he must have left inside her when she'd given her gift to him. Afterward, the overwhelming need to retrieve what belonged to him, the sword that had been with him throughout eternity.

The part of his soul that screamed for vengeance.

He tossed down a shot of whisky and found his phone. He scrolled through his contacts and dialed Pestilence.

Julian might well be the only one who could end this.

Dru and Nick had gotten too close to their targets, and that had cost them dearly. That wouldn't be a problem with Julian. In fact, proximity would aid him.

Dru waited until his friend's British accent came across the line, sounding as old as time.

"I failed." That admission was a brutal blow to his ego. "They've broken the Second Seal."

Silence echoed across the distance between them for several seconds. "I see."

"I know you hate to leave your fortress, but your presence is required in Port Townsend."

"These de Moray witches, what makes them so powerful that they could best two of the Horsemen?"

Dru could picture his friend sitting in his study, pondering the question over a glass of the finest wine. In the spirit of the occasion, he poured himself another shot of whisky. "They're subtle enemies, skilled in the art of seduction. I underestimated their abilities and determination along with the power of the prophecy. The end of days is destined to happen and will not be easy to stop."

"Obviously the gods believed we were up to the task. I shall make accommodations, then. Expect me within a few days."

Dru ended their call and set about strategizing his next move. One that ended with his sword in his hand and Claire in his bed. With her sister dead and the crisis averted, there was no reason he couldn't have both.

III

AERIN

By Kerrigan Byrne

❧ 27 ❧

"**W**hat the hell are you doing?" White sheets took a tantalizing journey down Dev Atwal's bronzed, lean torso when he sat up in bed and rubbed sleep from his bleary eyes.

"I'm curing cancer. What does it look like I'm doing?" Aerin Doe shoved her favorite Brunello Cucinelli cashmere sweater next to her favorite Manolo Blahnik pumps and grappled with the zipper on her luggage. Was it against the rules to sit on a Gucci Suitcase?

Fuck the rules, she had a plane to catch.

Turning around, Aerin hopped up and landed ass-first on the top of her suitcase and ground her cheeks into it for good measure, managing to slide the zipper around the rectangle with a victorious breath.

"You smoke too much to cure cancer." Dev's measured East Indian accent irritated the shit out of her at the moment. Also, now she wanted a cigarette.

"I need you to handle the requisition meeting next week," Aerin told him, bustling to the bathroom and dumping her shitload of beauty products and cosmetics into her carryon. She added a curling and straightening iron to her bag, because who knew what the humidity in the Northwest would do to her hair? Anti-frizz gel and curl intensifier followed, along with clips, elastics, pins, bands—was she forgetting something? "The rep from Luxul is going to help with the new wireless and network implementation, so have him work with Stan. They're the best, so make sure they're treated well." She waved a box of tampons at him as she said this, before adding it to her bag.

Dev's marble-black eyes followed her around the bedroom as she opened her slut-red leather tote and organized her wallet, work laptop, e-reader, wireless speaker, and smart phone.

"Also, fire Eric. That gold brick is pissing me off and I want him replaced by the time I get back."

"And when will that be?" Dev queried.

The diamonds on her watch told her she had time for a smoke before her car arrived, and that still afforded her an hour and a half to get from Manhattan to JFK Airport.

"I'm not sure," she evaded. "If there is an emergency, Sandra will be able to get a hold of me."

"What if I need you?"

"Like I told you." She gentled her tone as much as possible. "If you have an emergency, talk to Sandra. But I have complete faith you'll be able to run things while I'm gone. You've done it plenty while I'm away on business. I trust your judgment." Except for his taste in women.

"Is that what you're doing, leaving on business? Can you at least tell me where you are going, or do I need to get that information from your assistant, as well? I'm the VP of Operations, Aerin, it is good if I have information to give should someone ask." The inflection in Dev's voice remained, as it always did, smooth, with a zen-like resonance that matched the cords of blue in his sleek, black hair.

But he was hurt. Aerin could tell.

She'd always been able to tell.

The air vibrated with a lie at a different frequency

than it did with the truth, and each emotion had its own wavelength. She'd never known why she could read those waves, why they brushed at the fine hairs on her body with an undeniable veracity. Some kind of sensory perception disorder maybe? Was she on the spectrum? Psychological overstimulation stemming from her years in the foster care system?

Who knew? Who cared?

She sure as shit didn't.

Her stomach clenched and her hand shook as she reached in her bedside table for her cigarettes. "I'm flying into Seattle where I've scheduled a few meetings with a certain global online marketplace," she lied, placing a hand on the ivory handle of her balcony door.

"You usually take me with you. What if you need me?" Well, shit.

"I won't," she murmured. "I need you here. I also need you to get dressed, as I have to lock up in exactly nine and a half minutes." Was that a bitchy way to tell him it was time to leave?

His eyes told her that it was, so she slipped out onto the balcony to escape the sad-face emoji frequencies that were certain to follow.

She berated herself as she thrust her cigarette between her lips and lit up, taking that first morning drag deep into her lungs and letting the soft wave of nicotine roll through her veins with an addict's bliss. God, she loved smoking.

Aerin waited for the effects to take root as she listened to the teeming mass of humanity down below. The trembling stopped after three pulls. The vibration that had rattled about in her chest quieted at five, and she could again feel her limbs become weighty and normal.

Who needed to taste their food? Better yet, who the fuck had time to eat when there were corporations to conquer and a world to connect? Smoke breaks were... So. Much. Better.

Looking down, she let the spring breeze caress her face, and felt the vertigo that always came with heights. She did this every morning. Her ritual.

Coffee. Smoke. Lean over the balcony. Think about jumping. Decide not to. Go to work.

It wasn't about suicide. That was just it. Something in her blood told her the bagillion story drop wouldn't kill her. Which was proof that she was probably psychotic. But whatever, psychopaths ruled the world and ran corporations all the time.

Sighing out a cloud of white through her nose and mouth, she eyed the little black bundle tucked into the eaves of her loft. Shiny, black wings with fine webs of veins cocooned a fury, ebony body with a comically snouted nose and adorable Mickey Mouse ears.

"Good morning, Doctor Lecter," she quoted her favorite book series between drags. The bat twitched, dragging one clawed wing below its beady eyes to greet her, or to glare at her, she couldn't be sure. She could just imagine him saying, "Hello, Clarice."

What the hell a vampire bat, who was native to the Central and South American climates, was doing in Manhattan beat the hell out of her, but Aerin couldn't say she minded the little bastard hanging around, as it were. When he'd found her earlier this year, she'd been tempted to call a pest control company, but damned if she didn't get attached to his adorable/ugly face and constant presence.

She'd done research on him, instead. Genus: Desmodus rotundus. A social animal, usually roosting in colonies. They tended to have strong family bonds with tendencies toward reciprocal altruism, even adopting parentless babies.

A strong kinship had formed on her part after reading that, and Aerin had spent almost every morning coffee/smoke with Doctor Lecter perched high above Park Avenue. Both of them supposedly part of a huge colony, and yet apart from it.

Alone. But together.

Return to me what has been forsaken,
By earth, air, fire, and sea...

AERIN WAS TEMPTED TO SLAP HER HANDS OVER HER ears, but she knew it wouldn't work. The chant was in her head. Had been for weeks now. Months, maybe. She'd blocked it out at first, but the pull became stronger. Physiological symptoms had manifested. Headaches, tremors, heart palpitations, restlessness, sleeplessness. The constant pull west.

Why west?

Regardless of the direction, last night, or rather, that morning around three am, she'd booked the next flight out of town, as fucking west as she could get in the lower forty-eight.

Amazingly, it had helped.

Dev knocked around in her bedroom, getting dressed, shutting the bathroom door, turning on the water, and muttering curses in that lyrical language of his. It bothered Aerin that she didn't know what he was saying. She'd never learned his language. German, French, Japanese, Spanish, and Mandarin rounded out her repertoire nicely. Maybe she needed to add another to her list.

Tapping out her first smoke, she lit a second and resolved to linger over this one. She probably wouldn't learn any Indian dialects. It wasn't like she was dating Dev. He was her employee. Hell, she didn't even know why he'd slept over. Usually they just fucked somewhere and he left, or she did, depending on where they'd ended up. He only lived a block and a half away. They hadn't had that much to drink last night, had they?

"What if he's getting attached?" she asked Doctor Lecter. "What if he's getting like—feelings?"

Doctor Lecter sneezed. Or, at least, she thought it was a sneeze.

"You're right," she nodded, flicking ash into her crystal tray. "That's what I get for dipping the pen into the company ink. Er—wait—aren't I the ink? Because I don't have a pen—er—penis. But it's my company, so am I technically doing the proverbial dipping?"

The tiny mammal's silence turned distinctly judgy.

"Yeah, fuck the whole metaphor. Point is, I shouldn't be doing it— him," Aerin said, watching a sleek black town car pull up to the front of the building as she tamped out her half-smoked cigarette. "Hang tight, Doctor Lecter. I'll see you when I see you."

When she entered her apartment, she found it empty. Empty of color, decorations, and empty of Dev. He hadn't said goodbye.

Could she blame him?

God she was such an asshole.

Stepping into her power pumps, she reached into the drawer and threw bottles into her tote. One anti-depressant, two anti-anxieties, nicotine gum for the flight, and a metric fuck ton of sleeping pills.

That accomplished, she pulled her tote over one shoulder, her carryon over another, and tugged out the handle of her luggage to roll behind her.

No more thinking about Dev. It was time to get a new vibrator. They were much less messy; emotions weren't a problem, and easier to throw away when she was through with them.

❈ 28 ❧

"**D**ev just hit on me." Even on the phone, Sandra Carvatali's accent may have belonged to the Jersey Shore, but her quick wit and photographic memory made her damn near a MENSA candidate. "Which is just wicked weird, because, like, aren't you two fucking still?"

"No," Aerin clipped as she wound her way through the busy SeaTac Airport's baggage claim with a finger on her blue-tooth earpiece to press it closer and block out noise. "We're not still fucking." At least not as of thirteen hours ago.

Ignoring the censuring look from the elderly woman next to her in a kitty sweater and Q-tip hair, she searched the turnstile for her suitcase and kept being shouldered out by the press of bodies.

Not that she had any claim over Dev, but Aerin would have thought he'd wait a good twenty-four hours before trying to slip it to someone else. Especially her personal assistant. But didn't guys only need twenty-four minutes until they were ready again? So what the hell did she know?

"Okay then," Aerin could almost hear Sandra's shrug. "Do you want me to put Anthrax in his coffee?

Because my second-cousin on my mother's side, Carmine, he knows a guy and I think he takes credit cards."

Buying illegal chemical weapons with your American Express card? Just what would the receipt say? "No, Sandra, that won't be necessary." What if the NSA just heard her assistant say Anthrax? Weren't they listening to everything nowadays?

Aerin looked left to right and behind her, feeling a weird tingle of hairs at the back of her neck, even though they were schpackled into a tidy and professional updo.

"That ass clown should know better than to test my loyalty, boss. Besides, I'm not into sloppy seconds, even if his people wrote the actual book on all the great ways to have sex. I'm too classy for that."

Aerin pictured her assistant's up-to-there hair, eyeliner bills, and closet full of leopard print. At least that closet was on the Upper East Side. So, maybe classy wasn't the apropos descriptive word. But still, the woman was indispensable and very well-paid.

"Though the sentiment is... appreciated. I think. Let's hold off on any terrorist activity, at least until I get back."

"All right." Aerin could also hear Sandra's eye-roll. "But where I come from, it's a sign of weakness if you don't at least slash his tires. You know, show him you care."

"I don't care," Aerin said honestly.

"Oh, that's different then. How's Seattle?"

"Gray and rainy."

"Well, it's spring. It's supposed to be nice in the summer." The click clack of long fake nails on a keyboard punctuated a pregnant silence. "So... you need me to prepare any documents, call meetings, book hotels, a car, buy bribery gifts, put together PowerPoint presentations, you know, the usual?" The vibration of Sandra's anxiety reached through the continent between them. "You left without telling me what you're doing. I'm flying blind, boss, I can't even link the calendar. I haven't made an Excel chart in weeks. My life has no meaning."

Aerin laughed at her assistant's dramatics. "This is more of an informal visit. No worries, just keep your eye on things there. Make sure that Windmark Tech doesn't fold while I'm away." Spotting her luggage, Aerin shouldered through the crowd and pounced, dragging the ginormous bag back through the press of pushy assholes while trying to find a spot big enough to turn around in, regain her bearings, and figure out just where the hell she was going.

"Oh that reminds me," Sandra perked up. "The numbers came in from last year and we're up two billion instead of the one point five we projected, so we're close enough in the rankings to that company that shall remain nameless to give Bill his next prostate exam. Top five, baby!"

"That's great," Aerin said, distracted, as she wrestled with her luggage. You'd think you'd pay two thousand dollars for luggage and the goddamned wheels would work even after six months of heavy usage.

There. A break in the crowd. She'd reach it and then she could breathe. Now where could she smoke? That was the question. Using her sharp elbows, she made her way to the edge of the crowd.

"The internal audit turned up some surprising reports," Sandra droned on. "You were right about those second quarter losses. They were regained in the fourth with no..."

To say that at the sight of the moody prince in front of her Sandra's voice faded into the background would have been one hell of an understatement. It was more like everything just... vanished. The crowds. The walls of windows with their spectacular display of thunderclouds. The drone of planes taking off and landing. The announcements of the loudspeakers. It all disappeared.

When Aerin stepped into the circle of empty floor around the tall, impeccably dressed man, it was as though within that precise circumference a Bermuda triangle effect took hold.

Heh. What would they call this one, the SeaTac circle? What was next? The Montpelier Square? The El Paso dodecahedron? Nah, those were three dimensional, so probably not.

Blinking rapidly, Aerin shut her ridiculous thought digression down. Her brain tended to haywire a bit when the vibrations overwhelmed her. And his were off the charts.

Power.

It was what kept the people at bay. They didn't know what they were doing. They didn't even stare or particularly seem disrupted. They merely packed themselves tighter into their own space to avoid his.

Who could blame them, really? The sheer force of his presence rolled off him in ultrasonic waves equally in all directions. Hence, the circle. And he stood in the middle of it like the tall, straight leg of a geometric compass.

The perfect center to a perfect circle.

His liquid-blue eyes pinned her with a look of mild intrigue that quickly heated into astonishment. Words that had never been part of her MIT educated vocabulary filtered through as her brain tried to process him.

Regal. Elegant. Dark. Lethal. Mysterious. Ancient.

Ancient? Really? Couldn't be. He only looked like thirty-five...ish.

But his eyes. His pale, lovely blue eyes held secrets darker than the underworld. Stories that began with

"Once upon a time," could pour from sensuous lips like his and she would believe every fairytale to be the God's honest truth. Because he'd been there. He'd seen it all.

Though, judging by his appearance, the only role he could play was that of the villain.

God. She could slice her finger on those cheekbones.

"Those will kill you, you know." His British accent melted from that mouth like dark wine and darker transgressions.

"What?" Aerin looked down, shocked to see the pack of her cigarettes clenched in her hand. When had she reached for them? When had she hung up her phone?

His tone had been a bit ironic, as though maybe she wouldn't have the time to wait for smoking to finish her off. Like maybe Death was coming for her sooner rather than later.

"Oh," she breathed, fighting a shiver. "You—don't happen to have a light, do you?"

"But, of course." With one hand he unbuttoned his suit coat, and long fingers disappeared into the pocket of his vest, from which a gold watch chain gleamed. "It's the very least I can do." He nodded toward the exit a few yards away. "Shall we?"

"Don't you have luggage?"

"I posted my things overnight to my destination." A solid gold lighter appeared in his glove. His black Armani leather glove.

Nice.

Aerin couldn't decide why every molecule of her body told her that following this man anywhere could be the last bad decision she ever made. In the end, addiction and attraction won out over common sense. It was just a smoke. What could go wrong? They were in a crowded place with Homeland Security agents on hand for Chrissakes.

Besides, he didn't look like the kind of man who got blood on his own hands—er—gloves. And he was lonely. He was so goddamned lonely it sang through the air with an intensity that would bring her to tears if she was the crying sort. It was an isolated desolation that couldn't be contained in a mere lifetime.

God. Maybe she was losing it. He was perfectly collected. Besides, someone that handsome, rich, and powerful would never want for company.

"Let me," his voice carried a gentle, almost apologetic note as he very deliberately pulled the fingers of his gloves from his hands and put them in his coat pocket before reaching for the handle of her luggage.

Aerin flashed him her most brilliant smile and warmed at the flare of heat in the otherwise solemn depths of his eyes. "And they say chivalry is dead."

"Not yet." His returning smile was genuine, but held a hint of... of what? Regret? Sadness?

Maybe she was seeing things.

Aerin surreptitiously studied his side profile as they walked to the door in companionable silence. He was what her PR manager would call a "tall glass of water." Six-foot-four, at least, maybe taller. And on the thin side of well-built and the sickly side of pale, but he made it work for him. More gothic vampire than cancer patient. This was Seattle, after all. And he was obviously from the UK, which was a notoriously pale area of the world.

Harsh overhead lighting bounced off the silver strands in his otherwise ebony hair in a decidedly romantic way. Aerin couldn't tell how long his pony-tail was, as the turned-up collar of his black wool overcoat hid most of it.

God he was beautiful. Like, runway model beautiful. Like, archangel beautiful. Like every-woman-glared-at-

her-with-more-dislike-than-usual-as-he-held-the-door-
for-her beautiful. He was someone you chanced upon
on the Scottish moors or in a Bronte novel, not at the
Seattle-Tacoma International Airport baggage claim
terminal.

They faced each other beneath the awning, and she
couldn't help but notice how his wide shoulders and
perfect posture contrasted with those dwindling
number of souls who hunched against the moist cold,
protecting the orange glow of their cigarettes.

He declined her offer of one, so she pulled it from
her own pack, transferred it to her left hand and extended her right. "I'm Aerin, by the way, Aerin Doe."

Liquid eyes flicked to her hand for the most imperceptible moment of pause before he opened the hinge
on his antique lighter and flicked the wheel in one fluid
movement. Offering it at a respectful distance, he allowed her the dignity of lowering her unshaken hand to
light up. Someone less observant would have missed the
calculation in that maneuver.

But observant was her middle name.

"Julian Roarke," he murmured.

Of course his name was Julian. Someone with that
face, with those eyes, could never be named "Brian" or
"Dale." It would have to be Julian or Sebastian or Vlad
fucking Tepes.

A breeze threatened the flame, and Julian brought
his palm up to cup it against the wind as he watched
her draw on her cigarette with unprecedented interest.
Aerin could feel the heat from his hand almost as tan-
gibly as if he'd cupped her cheek. The sensation affected her in such a way she jerked back.

"It's a pleasure to make your acquaintance, Ms.
Doe," he said as though he hadn't noticed. "Is that
dough as in pastry, or doe as in female deer?"

Aerin expelled a white stream politely through the
side of her mouth and relished how his courteous conver-

sation belied the white-hot sexual vibrations emanating from him. It was as though he wanted to know her, but didn't want her to know that he wanted to fuck her.

It was bloody weird, and she liked it.

"Doe as in person of unknown origin," she admitted.

"Ah," he nodded tactfully. "I see." His smooth expression said that he really did see, that he *knew*. Speaking of weird.

"Do you live in Seattle, Mr. Roarke, or are you visiting?" she asked with real curiosity.

"Julian, if you please. May I call you Aerin?"

"Sure." With a voice like that, he could call her any damn thing he wanted.

"I'm in town for a summit, of sorts, with a few of my colleagues," he said.

"Oh?" Aerin prodded.

"We're all here at the behest of our...boss."

"Who's your boss, maybe I've heard of him?"

"You undoubtedly have done, but I'm afraid I cannot say."

"That so?" Aerin flicked ash to the pavement. "I was curious before, now I'm intrigued. Let me guess, the Mafia?"

His silent smile caused the finest of lines to branch in his otherwise flawless skin as he shook his head.

"International drug cartel? Private security? Fashion Police? Interpol?" she joked. "The Vatican?"

A dark eyebrow twitched.

Her stomach twisted. "Oh God, don't tell me I've been flirting with a really well-dressed priest."

Julian's dark sound of amusement washed her in goose bumps.

"Not quite."

"Good thing you're not vague," she snarked with a good-natured laugh. "These colleagues of yours. You in charge, or what?" Aerin had been in business a long time, and men such as Julian Roarke were never just middle management.

"We all have our roles," he conceded. "Nicholas is in acquisitions, mergers, and hostile takeovers. And Drustan... he makes cuts where need be. Spends most of his time on the front lines, as it were. And Killian, he's mostly in weights and measurements. Product distribution. Getting everyone where they ultimately need to be."

"And you?" At this point, her relentlessness shut down most men. Not Julian Roarke, he seemed even more amused by her.

"I'm often more of a silent partner, called in only when my expertise is needed."

"Which is..." She rolled her hand in an impatient gesture.

"My specialties are microbiology and bio-chemistry. Though I have been known to dabble in agriculture and the... population density management of certain carbon-based organic colonies."

Aerin grinned. "Cool, I'm in IT." It wasn't hubris to admit that it was hard to find men who could keep up with her intellectually. It seemed that Julian Roarke could not just do that, but also challenge her.

Which was so rare.

And so unbelievably sexy.

His smooth, cool façade warmed another notch, a pale fire glowing bright in his eyes. "So, Aerin Doe, you've been flirting with me?"

"I think I was working my way up to being less subtle." She gave him a look from beneath her lashes, and if she wasn't imagining it, a tinge of color dotted his cheeks.

"What brings you to Seattle?" he dodged the subject. "Business or pleasure?"

The way he said pleasure caused odd warmth to bloom in the region of her panties.

Down girl, she thought.

"I'm still trying to figure it out. I think I have to be on a ferry in the morning." Somehow, she hadn't gone west enough. And someone with her own voice was calling her across the Puget Sound.

"Are you hungry?" she asked him. "Can I buy you dinner?" *And then have you for dessert?*

His brows drew together and his expression turned stormy, as though she'd just asked him to lick the ashtray. "I would rather die than allow a lady to pay for my meal."

She shrugged. "Okay... You haven't caught up to the twenty-first century, but I can deal. I'll let you buy me dinner."

"There isn't time," he whispered with a look of such profound regret, Aerin suddenly felt desperate not to let go of him. What the fuck? Desperate wasn't a word that had ever been in her repertoire before.

"Drinks?" she offered. They could exchange info, and maybe meet up later.

"You're not intimidated by me, are you?" It was a question in the form of a declaration and it intrigued Aerin to no end.

"I could ask you the same thing, Julian Roarke. Are you intimidated by me?"

"You terrify me." The statement was full of truth. And sex.

She put her cigarette out. "I promise to be gentle... the first time." She threw him her most suggestive look.

That sadness was back. That reluctant, ancient loneliness. A yearning...one that went beyond sex, beyond emotion, into a realm she didn't quite understand blasted at her from him, and she had to fight not to take a step back.

"There is something I must do Aerin," he murmured by way of rejection. "I truly wish we'd met under different circumstances."

Aerin had learned to cover her feelings long ago, and it took every last modicum of strength she had to pull her shit together and keep her face as cool and smooth as his. "Yes, well. *C'est la vie*. Thank you for the light, Julian. And good luck with your summit."

She reached for the handle to her suitcase that rested between them, hoping to escape before she really embarrassed herself.

"Aerin, wait..." He reached out, but his hand paused half-way, suspended there as though held by a marionette string. "Meeting you really was an unexpected pleasure... as brief as our time has been."

Then ask for my number, you ass.

"You too. Maybe we'll run into each other again someday," she hinted.

"Perhaps." Though his face said *not bloody likely*.

They both had shit to do, she guessed, and slid her fingers into his big hand for a goodbye shake.

His entire body jolted at the contact. He closed his eyes as though savoring the moment and when he opened them, his nostrils flared with a raw, almost animal hunger.

Okay...weird.

Aerin went to pull back, and for a moment, she thought he wouldn't let her. But he released her hand, finger by finger, and extracted his grip as though fighting some kind of adhesive.

A phone in his pocket rang, and Aerin was glad it broke the moment's intensity.

"Good-bye, Aerin Doe," he said ominously. "I'm sorry."

Aerin nodded, suddenly unable to find her voice, as he fished a phone from his pocket. "Yes?"

Turning away, Aerin let his portentous words follow her back inside.

"It is done."

Whatever. She needed to find a rental car counter, and then some Scotch.

On the tail of that thought, the first sneeze wracked her body.

❧ 29 ❧

Port Townsend was no Hamptons, but as a seaside-port-town-turned-tourist-destination it was damn cute. Charming even. Nestled on the tip of the Olympic Peninsula's Sun Belt, hundred-year-old brick buildings shaded Aerin as blue skies reflected off bluer water on three sides of the isthmus. On the hill, Victorian homes lined the roads like painted ladies, shamelessly baring their bay windows, large porches, gables and spires in a neat, yet colorful array. The whole place bespoke of the genteel opulence of the merchant shipping class in an industrial bygone age.

Aerin passed store windows on the shaded waterfront thoroughfare that had once been bustling with cobblers and co-ops, haberdasheries and milliners. Now, the colorful brick buildings housed art galleries and boutiques, creperies and bistros.

What she needed was some decent fucking coffee. This was Washington, right? This place gave birth to Starbucks. Wasn't there supposed to be a coffee shop on every corner?

She'd be able to use her phone to find a café if she wasn't stuck on a conference call with her Board of Investors, Kai Masashi and his contingent from Japan, and of course, Dev the dick bag.

She could fire him...if she hadn't fucked him. Last thing Windmark Tech needed was a scandal and a sexual harassment lawsuit.

She felt like warmed-over shit, and hid her puffy eyes and raw, runny nose with ginormous Dolce & Gabbana sunglasses and enough makeup to require a grout scrubber to remove. How had she gotten sick? She had the immune system of a Honey Badger.

"We haven't seen market numbers this high since we went public," she assured the board and the insidious misogynist, Mr. Kai Masashi. "That being said, this deal isn't going to make them drop, it'll only drive them higher."

She crossed the street and noted that the vintage clothing boutique, S'Klallam Native Art Gallery, the Good Vibes Yoga Studio, and Raven Song Pottery all had signs in their windows advertising "going out of business" blowout sales.

More casualties of the economic downturn? Damn shame, that.

"We understand, Miss Doe." Masashi put too much emphasis on the word. "But Windmark is still young and untried. It hasn't weathered the storms that it's bigger, older contenders have..." He paused.

There! Two doors away, on the far corner of the block, a purple shingle advertised Ambrosia's Brews and Charms—wicked coffee, spellbinding tea, and magical sundries.

Fuck, yeah.

Aerin rushed for it, almost yanked some hippie's arm out of his socket when she opened the door and dove inside, letting the smell of fresh-ground dark roast envelope her in ecstatic anticipation.

"It is, miss, isn't it? I presume you're not married," the snide twat Masashi was saying.

"It's Ms.," Aerin annunciated very smoothly. They wouldn't be having this conversation if she had different genitals. "And I guess you could say that Windmark Tech is young and untried, but you'd be contradicting opinions with some very powerful dissenters."

"Such as...?"

She pressed the mute button on her blue-tooth. "I'll have your largest shot in the dark, black, no room for cream." She threw a ten-dollar bill on the tray of a pink-haired pixie who pranced past her with the fleet-footed, light-heartedness of the young and irresponsible.

"Keep the change."

Figuring that the kid stared at her with such wide-eyes because she needed time to process all those words that were not in text speak, Aerin waved her off while addressing Mr. Masashi.

"Such as JD Power and Associates, Fortune 500, The Wall Street Journal, Forbes, Fortune, Wired, Fast Company, my fucking Cayman Islands and Swiss bank accounts... need I go on?"

Jesus, it looked like Stevie Nicks took a gypsy shit in here. Fringed shawls acted as café tablecloths weighted by various themed decks of tarot cards. Candles burned everywhere infusing the air with a confusion of scents that, despite their overabundance, were pleasant. It was hard to find a surface not littered by crystals, herbs, pottery, handmade jewelry, knick-knacks and books.

To say the place kinda shimmered would be like saying Larry Page was kinda rich.

Mr. Masashi wasn't through acting like a little bitch. "All I'm saying is that it's troubling to spend this kind of capital—"

"What I find troubling," Aerin bit out an interruption. "Is that you flew all the way to New York to balk at terms you've already agreed to. If you have a problem with the deal, get the fuck out of my building, and I'll call the next person clamoring for this opportunity in your market."

"L-let's not be hasty." The very real worry in Masashi's voice did enough to lower her blood pressure.

"Let's be plenty hasty. Sign the papers or don't, but either way, stop wasting my valuable time." She hung up in time to bury her face in the elbow of her fawn jacket and let the sneeze wrack her bones.

"Sinclaire?" The pink-punk hadn't unglued her silver-buckled combat boots from the floor.

Aerin shook her head. "Sorry, you're mistaking me for someone else." Turning, she took a seat closest to the window.

"Another one?" The barista's bouncy voice matched the tits that her pleather bustier mashed up to her chin. "Are they like, cloning you, or what?"

Apparently, they were cloning morons.

"What nonsense are you talking?"

Fake lashes blinked a few times brushing the glass of her cat-eyes spectacles. "Sorry but... you're definitely not Moira, or Tierra."

"We've never met. I'm not a local, kid."

On such an alternative canvass, the girl's smile held a tinge of youthful innocence that didn't seem to match. "I can tell. You'd have to go to New York or L.A. to get a coat like that."

Aerin scoffed. "Honey, you have to go to Paris or Milan to get a coat like this."

"No doubt. I'm Sunny. Are you here to meet your—"

Aerin's phone pealed loud enough to echo. It was Dev, the douche weed.

"You have an ETA on that coffee, Tacklebox, or do I have to make it myself?" Aerin quipped.

To her surprise, Sunny tossed her pink dreadlocks and grinned. "Tacklebox, because of all this." She motioned to her umpteen face piercings. "That's funny. I like you."

"Great, I can die happy."

Sunny laughed. "Shot in the dark, coming right up."

"Good, and don't spit in it. I'll be able to tell."

They were both smirking when Sunny sauntered off. Aerin liked her too. She reminded her of New York.

"What?" she barked into her phone.

"We Asians are not used to that kind of lack of respect or decorum in our business dealings." Dev also dispensed with niceties.

"Did he sign?" Aerin ignored the reproach in his voice.

The silence told her that the papers were signed.

Goddamn but she was sick of the fragile male ego. "I give respect when it's earned, and when it is given in return. That dildo hasn't shown me one ounce of respect since we started this deal and you don't hear me crying about it, do you?"

Dev paused. "Are you sick?"

"Are you kidding?" Aerin rubbed her aching, stuffy head with one hand to try to alleviate the pressure building behind her eyes. Her hands were freezing, but her forehead felt as hot as the bottom of a badly vented laptop.

"It's only that, I've known you for five years and you've never once been sick."

"There's a first time for everything, I guess."

"And, you're bitchier than usual."

Aerin sighed. He wasn't wrong. "I'm only human," she murmured, gearing up for an apology. She sucked at those, but she cared enough to try.

"You sure about that?" Dev snarked.

Okay. Never mind. Fuck the apology. "Did you need something, or did you call under the mistaken impression that just because you woke up in my bed that gives you the right to censure me? Because last time I checked, this was still my company and I was still your boss."

"Aerin—"

She cut him off. "Oh, and while I'm away, please refrain from trying to grudge-fuck my assistant? It makes her uncomfortable."

"I can explain—"

"Don't bother, just do your job." She cut off the call and silenced her ringer.

"Here ya go, sister." The pleasant southern twang heralded a gigantic recycled coffee cup appearing in front of her.

Aerin's eyes watered with the precursor to another soul-wracking sneeze. She gasped out a "thank you" to whoever wasn't Tacklebox and let loose into a table napkin.

"That's a mighty cold you got there. You been lickin' door handles or something?"

"Excuse me," Aerin said dismissively as she wiped her nose and checked her loaded inbox from her phone. Wrapping her freezing fingers around the blessedly warm cup, she lifted it to her lips and took that first tentative sip.

And promptly spit it out, soiling the glass covering the crimson shawl on her round café table. "What. The shit. Is that?"

She turned in her seat to confront the waitress and shock caused her to leap to her feet, which set her stuffy head to swimming.

"I know, I know," drawled the woman who displayed her Exact. Same. Features. She didn't just look similar, nor did she have a mere resemblance, like a relative. She was wearing Aerin's face. The tall, stunning beauty had her identical black-cherry hair knotted in two braids that teased the nipples visible through her skin-tight t-shirt. The bottom of her pockets peaked below the hem of her barely-there jean shorts, and her legs went on for miles and miles until they ended in a pair of shapely, but well-used feet.

"Drink up," the woman prodded. "It tastes like somethin' that squirted out of the south end of a northbound mud duck, but trust me, it'll scare them nasty critters out of your sinuses."

Holy Christ, she had a hillbilly doppelgänger. One who'd apparently never heard of a pedicure.

"She's here?" An excited cry filtered from the swinging mahogany doors behind the coffee counter. Another incarnation of herself rushed forward. "What took you so long?" the gypsy-woman demanded a bit breathlessly. "I called for you ages ago!"

"Wha-?" Aerin looked down into her coffee mug. Had she just been drugged?

A red motorcycle roared to a stop in front of the shop and a long, shapely woman clad in black and red leather peeled her body from the seat and sauntered through the door. Pulling off a black helmet brushed with flames, she shook down long auburn waves and flashed Aerin's her own fucking smile

"Look at this bad boy I just bought!" The biker called in Aerin's voice.

The room spun. Aerin felt hot. Then cold. Then like she was on fire. "The—Fuck?" she groaned, before the hardwood floor rushed up to meet her and darkness saved her from her hallucinations.

30

I *promise to be gentle...the first time.*
Every time those words stormed, unbidden, through Julian's memory, images of the invitation in Aerin's liquid-silver eyes accompanied it.

The first time. Their first time. His first time. Would she have been gentle?

No, he thought with a bittersweet smile. She was not a woman bred to gentility. They would have fought for supremacy in the bedroom.

He'd have let her win, that first time.

Would have. Past tense...

As his body heated and hardened, his heart froze and shriveled. The agony was so acute, it drove him even deeper into solitude than usual.

The first time that could never be.

Her body, the epitome of desire's own creation, had been clad in a suit like a man. And somehow, it had made her breasts that much more lovely, because they were such a mystery. Wide-legged trousers hid, yet hinted at, what must have been shapely legs, lent height by uncomfortable-looking spike-heeled shoes.

Strange, feminine elements reflecting a wardrobe which bespoke masculine power alongside a great deal of money, and taste. Julian savored a sip of his 1962

Cote d'Or Burgundy wine, closed his eyes against the fire crackling in the stone hearth, and let the melancholy transcendence of Pavarotti's rendition of Una Furtiva Lagrima tear at the furrows of regret in his chest.

He'd picked this vintage because it matched the dark velvet red of her hair. He'd never know the length of the tresses she'd pinned to her nape. Never hear the lush, yet crisp tones of her voice. Never erase the memory of her elegant fingers clasped against his in a shake as decisive and firm as any man's.

Never feel that grip...elsewhere.

Because by now, she was dead.

"Listening to Puccini by firelight and sipping a fifty-year-old wine that is not a sipping wine?" Nicholas Kingswood strode from the entry to the stone manor's library, helped himself to a glass, and joined him at the hearth as though the flames could answer his unspoken questions. When they didn't, he turned his dark head toward Julian. "What is your bereavement this time?"

"This time?"

"Last time you left Le Chateaux Morte and ventured into the world, I found you thus the very next morning. How long ago was that, a hundred years or so?"

Julian took another sip and turned from the fire, preferring the shadows to his comrade's shrewd, calculating gaze. "Nineteen-eighteen," he murmured.

"Ah, yes." Stripping off his charcoal suit coat, Nicholas released the cuffs of his blue silk shirt, and claimed a great deal of the leather couch with his powerful body. "Influenza, a stroke of brilliance on your part."

"A stroke of genocide."

"Buck up, Jules. Genocide is what you do best." Nick raised his glass in salute. "You're a maestro of the massacre. It was your last work that truly went 'viral.'" He chuckled around a sip at his own pun.

"This is no time for levity, Nicholas, a woman is dead."

"As opposed to the seventy-five million casualties in the nineteen-eighteen pandemic?"

Julian grunted his irritation.

"Don't you think maybe a few of those corpses were women?" Nicholas asked.

"And children, and the elderly! Did you come to salt my wounds, or does your visit have a purpose?"

Contrition wasn't a display that lay organically on Nicholas Kingswood's features, but the attempt was appreciated. "I came to check in on you. And to...thank you."

Julian made an ironic sound in his throat. "And to what accomplishment is your gratitude owed?"

"I don't know, Julian, saving the fucking world from the Apocalypse, I guess," Nick spat. "God, a hundred years of solitude makes you a surly dick hole."

Julian joined Conquest, folding into the throne-style chair next to the table of wine. "My apologies," he muttered. "I found the task more...distasteful than was expected." It was an admission he could only make to Nicholas, for the same reason he knew that only Conquest, himself, would venture into the library drawn by good music and better wine.

"Where's Drustan?" he changed the subject.

Nicholas shrugged. "Lurking in the hedges somewhere, practicing the more physical skills of the art of war. You know nunchuck skills, bowhunting skills..."

Julian did crack a smile at Nicholas' perfect rendition of Napoleon Dynamite. But when he looked over, Nicholas was studying the fire through his wine glass, as though only just discovering the intriguing color of the vintage.

"Julian, do you ever wonder... Do you ever question our...purpose?"

"The question being, what is the bloody point?" Julian finished. "Constantly."

He studied Nicholas over another sip from his goblet. Conquest, brilliant as he was, never had been a man prone to brooding. He built empires and toppled civilizations all in a day's work. He was a man of action. Decisive, confident, and damned effective.

So why the sudden cognitive dissonance?

His swarthy, brutal features darkened. "Why would they create the four of us, the billions of them, the prophecy, the Grimoire, the...de Morays?"

Julian had given it a good deal of thought. Not just ponderance, but study, prayer, meditation, et al. "I suppose, this world—this short life of theirs—is only one chapter in the eternal tome that is existence. Perhaps we are an end to the chapter. A cliffhanger of sorts. Even a transitory vehicle to the next phase of being?" It was the best he could come up with thus far.

"Fuck off. I'm no astrophysical, hypothetical transit authority."

Julian chuckled. "That's not precisely what I was alluding to... Though, I often wonder. Why would the gods create creatures of such majesty, power, vitality, beauty and infinite potential only to have us lay in wait for the day we must destroy them?"

Nicholas' eyebrow went up. "You hold the mortals in higher regard than I realized."

Julian maintained his silence. He hadn't been talking about the mortals.

Only one of them.

"I thought you were weak, you know," Julian admitted. "You and Drustan. I didn't understand why you hadn't yet destroyed the de Moray witches while they were still estranged and easily broken. I couldn't comprehend how three of them had found each other and cast magic before you were forced to call me away from Le Chateaux Morte."

Nicholas didn't look at him, but drained his glass in two gulps. "And now?"

"And now I realize just how much power a mere woman can wield."

"And those are just the ones without Druid magic."

They shared a look of amusement, but neither of them could seem to summon so much as a smile. "Once I touched her... I never would have been able to do her violence."

Nicholas poured himself another glass and topped off Julian's as well. "Then it's a damn good thing your touch is so lethal."

The Library door banged against the wall, and the Tiffany glass chandelier overhead blazed to life with a flip of a switch. "That's it!" Drustan's voice boomed over the groans of his comrades. "I'm taking away your Pavarotti. You're bumming me the fuck out."

Julian stood and took a threatening step toward War. "Touch Pavarotti, and I'll give your precious Claire chronic, oozing boils on her unmentionables."

"She'd still have a mouth." Nicholas grinned.

"What crawled up your ass and died?" Drustan shucked his sweat soaked shirt, uncovering a torso marred with the scars of millennia of warfare, and threw it in the fire.

"I have a right to a moment of melancholy," Julian challenged. "I'm the only one who could carry out our task."

Drustan picked up the bottle of Burgundy and made a face. Putting it down, he strode to the sideboard and pulled a local microbrew from the chest of ice. "Think again, *Mon Ami*. Aerin de Moray is alive and kicking. Well, swearing...for a woman, she has the mouth of a sailor, a soldier, and a trucker. Combined."

Nicholas's dark chuckle was one part surprise, two

parts smug superiority. "Is she now?" He stood, draining another glass of wine before turning to Julian. "You were saying?"

It took Julian a full minute to recover. It wasn't humiliation that choked him, nor was it anger at the news. But elation.

"It isn't possible," Julian said slowly.

"I wouldn't have believed it if I hadn't seen it myself," Drustan insisted.

"I touched her suitcase. I shook her hand. She should have been dead within the hour."

"You're sure it was her?" Nicholas asked.

Julian nodded. "I took the photograph of the others you sent me. There was no mistaking that she was one of them."

Aerin was alive. He'd look into her silver eyes again before this was all over. He'd hear the smoky alto of her voice. He'd breathe in her scent that reminded him of thunderstorms and the clean winter wind.

"How did she survive, Julian?" Drustan demanded.

"I—she shouldn't have."

"Is she with them?" Nicholas asked Drustan, standing and punching his arms back into his suit coat.

"Yup." Drustan cast an accusatory glare at Julian.

"Don't you dare look at me in that tone of voice," Julian thrust his finger at War. "If you'd used the proper sword to thrust into Claire, we wouldn't be in this situation."

Dru's eyes flared with his legendary temper. "Hey, fuck you, pansy ass. At least I did more than shake her hand."

"Indeed," Julian said with his signature chill. "You managed to lose both your weapon and your wits to her."

War attacked but ran into Nicholas' bracing shoulder. "We don't have time for this shit. These witches are more powerful than we thought, and we need to come up with a plan."

Drustan growled at Julian but put his hands up in an 'I'll behave' gesture. "We need to put an end to at least one of them before they find the Grimoire and we're all fucked nine ways to Sunday."

Julian acquiesced as he followed his brothers toward the garage door. "Upon that, at least, we agree."

"First things first." Drustan grabbed a clean, black tank on his way out, pulling it down over his belted jeans. "I'm getting my fucking sword back."

"And your man-card along with it." Nicholas laughed.

"I got my man card right here." Drustan cupped himself.

"You may need it," Julian said soberly. "It seems to be one of the only effective weapons against this cadre of witches. If we are to defeat them, it may have to be through one of the oldest and most dissolute means known."

Both Conquest and War gave him almost comical matching stares of suspicion.

"The art of seduction, *mes frères*, is just as lethal and dangerous as the art of war."

31

Someone was working on the inside of Aerin's throat with a belt sander. It was the first pain that returned her to semi-consciousness. The second was a sinus headache. Then neck pain, joint pain, muscle pain...well...everything pain, really. Her stomach clenched with emptiness and nausea, and her lungs struggled against being full.

A gentle hand pressed something cold against her burning forehead, and she wanted to bless whomever it was. She should probably work on opening her aching eyes first.

"She's coming around," said whoever held her head in a rather leathery lap.

"Good," said another in that slow drawl. "I would have tried to catch her, but she dropped faster than a greased hog down a garbage chute. Wouldn't have pegged her for the faintin' type."

Aerin was not the fainting type, and she was going to set that straight just as soon as she woke up all the way.

"She still doesn't look so well," worried the first voice.

"Let's take her to the house, I have a few things that will help her along," said a third.

That galvanized Aerin. No one was taking her any-where without her say so.

"Take me to my hotel room!" she demanded. Well, it was more like she rasped, "Take...me...hotel..." But un-less they were idiots, they'd get the gist.

"Like hell," the gypsy was saying when Aerin finally summoned the courage to open her eyes. "We're taking you home."

"I'm not going anywhere with you," Aerin croaked as she struggled, and failed to sit. "You're strangers with my face." Damn, she was usually more articulate than this.

"We're family," said the gorgeous woman whose face was upside-down as she was the one holding Aerin's head in her lap. Helmet hair somehow looked good on her.

Bitch.

"I don't have family," Aerin insisted, unable to look anyone in the eye for any amount of time. Her brain just couldn't seem to process the three identical, yet in-finitely diverse women all surrounding her.

"Well, you do now," Daisy Duke announced. "Con-gratu-damn-lations."

Aerin squeezed her eyes shut against the pounding in her head; hoping things had changed when she opened them again.

No such luck.

"This isn't real," she breathed, hiding behind her eyelids again. "What the shit did you give me?"

"Weren't nothin' but some healing weeds Tierra put in a brew. I figured you needed it on account that you're sick."

"Laced with what?" Aerin's voice had turned from a rasp to a squawk, but she couldn't exactly say that was progress. "Acid? Mushrooms? LSD?"

"Laced with love," said the gypsy. "Now shut up and help us get you off the floor and into the car."

It took all three of them to peel her off the café's hardwood floor and get her into a semi-upright position.

"Sunny, please watch the café," Gypsy said over her shoulder as she handed Aerin off to the other two and snatched up Aerin's purse and phone.

"Sure thing, boss."

"I'm...not...going..." No matter how Aerin fought it, she lost her protests to the darkness yet again.

⁂

SHE DREAMED OF EYES SO BLUE AND SO FATHOMLESS, the entire planet rotated in their depths. Her sleep was filled with a yawning millennia of loneliness, though cool, strong, and elegant fingers stroked her burning skin with a tenderness that brought tears to her eyes.

"Don't make me do this," Julian's silken baritone held a note of desperation.

Then her dreams became nightmares.

She was lying in a pool of blood, looking into the vacant, lifeless eyes of women who looked like herself. Then she was flying above the earth, over piles—no—mountains of corpses. Men, women, children. Their flesh rotting and stinking of disease. Soldiers missing limbs and weapons strewn about fields and forests scorched bare and littered with ash and death. Armies of creatures unidentifiable terrorized and tortured what few souls were left writhing in grief, pain, and misery.

The sun became a black ball of ash and soot. Even the moon dripped with blood.

Whump.

Aerin woke with a scream stuck in her throat, and sweat dripping from her pores. Her body collapsed down onto a bed made of clouds or some shit and several unrequited addictions screamed through her all at once.

Smoke. Coffee. Water. Bathroom. In that order.

"She really is air," someone murmured. "Did you see that?"

"Wish I could fly in my sleep," snarked someone else.

"Did you guys hear something else fall?" A third asked. "Sounded like it was coming from the table over there."

Alarm dragged Aerin through the fog and into the land of the living. She peeled her lids apart with herculean effort. "My purse," she hissed over a dry, heavy tongue. "Cigarettes."

"You are not smoking in my house," Gypsy said, crossing her bangled arms over her breasts. "It's time you quit, smoking will kill you." *Those will kill you, you know,* Julian had said.

Aerin shook her head to rid it of the memory and winced. "Yes, please," she groaned. "Just let them kill me now." Though she still felt pretty craptastic, the pounding in her head had abated a little, and she no longer felt like she was on death's doorstep. But she was pretty sure she was still in his yard.

"Drink this." The smokey-eyed biker beauty handed her a pottery mug with a disarming smile.

"Nuh-uh." Aerin used the back of her hand to push it away. "I learned that lesson the hard way. I'm not taking anything from any of you until you tell me where the fuck I am, who the fuck you are, and what the fuck is going on."

Her head was swimming again, so she focused on the white lace canopy above her bed, which could have comfortably slept all four of them with wiggle room to spare. From what she gathered in her periphery, the entire bedroom was done in spare black or white arabesque.

She approved.

"You're at Maison de Moray," Gypsy said, spreading

her arms to encompass the room, but losing the effect in bell sleeves and bangles. She looked out of place in this room, her riot of color clashing with the clarity of the decor. "And I'm Tierra de Moray, your sister."

"Moira Joule Malveaux," said Daisy Duke, with what had to be all the twang that could possibly be found south of the Mason/Dixon line.

"Pleased to make your acquaintance."

"de Moray," Tierra corrected. "We're all de Morays."

"Sinclaire D'Ambrose," said the sexy biker with that disarming, genuine smile.

"de Moray," Tierra interjected again. "We're going to have to take you all to get your names changed."

"People call me Claire." The woman didn't skip a beat. "And I'm still trying to figure out what the fuck is going on, so you're not alone, girl."

Aerin liked Claire right away. She had a strength and wit shining from her eyes that instantly drew her.

"We all are." Moira's aqua blue eyes shimmered with an intelligence that many might not look past the tits and accent to find. "These past few weeks have been crazier n' a Klansman at a sheet sale."

Aerin still hadn't been able to get past the word "sisters." Past the fact that this room was filled with undeniable proof that she had a family. Each face a facet of her own, the only variances being eye color and subtle differences in bearing and deportment.

"And your name is?" Claire prodded.

"Aerin. Aerin Doe."

Tierra stomped her sandaled feet, the chimes on her anklet making a cheerful noise that she obviously hadn't intended. "de Moray, goddessdamnit! Are you not all listening to me? We're family. We are part of a legacy as old as humanity. The de Moray women have been witches for as many generations as have been counted. But who we are, the four of us, that is something new. Something so powerful that other witches fear it. Fear us. We have a destiny, a great purpose. Haven't you always been able to feel it?" Her eyes turned watery and her features tightened with a desperate longing. "I called you here because I knew there was a part of me missing. And because...we're sisters. We need each other."

Aerin's throat clogged for a reason other than illness. She couldn't deal with this shit right now. "What I need is a cigarette." She tried to push herself up on arms that felt as weak as cooked spaghetti. "And then some answers that have nothing to do with this nonsense about magic. Like paternity and shit."

"Ain't nonsense." Moira defended. "You can't deny that you were just levitating more'n two feet above that bed in your sleep. Just imagine what you could do awake." Her lovely eyes widened. "Shit on a shingle, can you fly?"

"I don't know, can you count to twenty with your shoes on?"

Hurt immediately darkened to anger on Moira's features, and Aerin did her best to squelch the guilt pooling in her chest. But, what the hell kind of question was that? Of course, she couldn't fly. She was a person, and people didn't fly, they fell. Aerin had had to pick her sorry ass up enough times to know that beyond a shadow of a doubt. It sure would be nice to levitate to the top of the game, but she'd had to climb hand over bleeding hand, sometimes kicking her opponents off the wall to get where she was.

If she'd had any doubts they were sisters, those were shriveled by the narrow-eyed glare boiling through the air at her. It was the same one Aerin, herself, had visited on innumerable adversaries.

"Quicker'n you can strap yourself into that suit you musta mugged a door-to-door salesman for." Her accent lent the acerbic tone a wrathful note.

"You're one to talk about taste." Aerin tried to

swing her wobbly legs off the side of the bed to get closer to her cigarettes.

"That was uncalled for," Claire reproached.

"This whole fucking thing is uncalled for," Aerin bitched. "And can we all just hold off a damn minute until I gain my bearings here?" Bearings meaning cigarettes. She eyed her purse which was now hidden behind a very large, ancient looking book that she could have sworn wasn't there a minute ago.

Oh yeah, come to mama.

Carefully putting her feet on the ground and testing her weight, Aerin tried to ignore the emotions tossed about the room like a chaotic typhoon. Though she could recognize them, she was having a hard time identifying the source, and the barrage became suffocating.

Hurt and disappointment underscored some curiosity, confusion, anger, desperation, and hope. God, she needed to get to her cigarettes. Once she started smoking, it would quiet the fumes of emotion and allow her to think clearly.

Making a desperate grab for her Gucci purse on the sturdy white sideboard beneath the window, she was nearly bruised by the force with which the huge book in front of her bag exploded open, it's thick, yellowed pages flipped by a strong wind.

"Holyratfuck!" Aerin yelped as she jumped back, almost bowling Claire over. "What the shit is that?"

"You mean you're not doing that?" Tierra demanded, wide green eyes fixed on the book.

"How in the ninth level of hell could I be doing that? That's not supposed to be happening! It's... It's..."

"Impossible?" Claire finished, her voice laced with a touch of irony. "Yeah, that too."

As abruptly as the pages began to fly, they stilled, the book cracked open to a gilded page with stanzas no one could read from where they stood. The room filled with the silence of a tomb in the aftermath. Everyone watching. Waiting. Unwilling to step closer.

Moira broke the silence by emitting a loud humph, as she kicked her hip to the side and slid fingers into her tiny short pockets. "Okay," she said evenly. "I'll admit that was rarer than armpits on a snake, but seems to me a book opens on its own, it's just askin' to be read."

Aerin felt woozy again, and this time she wasn't sure illness had much to do with it. That cold void of... something—power?—started to swirl within her, and she had to stop it. Had to shut it down before it consumed her. The only way she knew how to do that was with the cigarettes, but they were on the other side of that possessed book, and she couldn't bring herself to reach for them just yet. The withdrawals screamed through her blood, threatening to set it on fire. The ice and heat somehow clashed like a storm front and sent lightning and thunder reverberating through her in the form of an irate anger the likes of which she'd never encountered.

"You first if you're so eager to touch that thing." She turned and gestured to Moira. "That is if you're literate."

Moira advanced, skimming a narrowed eye over the crumpled fabric of Aerin's creamy suit. "Last time I saw that color was on a secondhand gown at a shotgun weddin'. Bride called me a slut on account of she couldn't keep her man's pecker from pointin' my direction. Seems I recall her blood didn't wash out of it so well," she threatened as the glass of water on the bedside table began to rattle.

Aerin drew herself up to her full height, hoping they couldn't see her weak trembling legs or the cold sweats that the fever gave her. "It's Armani eggshell, bitch, and bring it! I grew up on the streets of New York, you backwater, hillbilly skank. I'll beat you so hard you'll be shitting your own teeth. At least when you return back to that mud hole you crawled out of, you'll fit right in."

Moira lunged, but Claire jumped between them, catching the brunt of the impact. "Stop it, you two!"

"You're too weak to punch the wings off a gnat," Moira snarled. "I could finish you off with one hand."

"Yeah," Aerin smirked. "I've heard you're good at that." She could tell that she'd hit a mark, because the hurt that blasted at her from behind the rage intensified.

"That's enough," Tierra hollered, rushing forward and snatching the open book to her chest. "I didn't call you here to fight. Grow up before you ruin everything. You're acting like a bunch of... like you're..."

"Sisters?" Claire laughed, releasing Moira, but keeping her strong body in between the two.

"Savages is more like it." Tierra glared at them. "Moira's right, this book didn't just show up for no reason." Carefully, she peeled the book away from her chest and looked down at the tattered pages bordered with intricate knots.

"I don't know," Claire cautioned. "Seems like when anyone starts reading out of a creepy old book that shows up out of nowhere in the movies, bad things happen. Things like people getting limbs hacked off, or possessed. Maybe we should be careful."

Aerin wasn't certain the book had just shown up. Though, it did seem out of place in this orderly, black and white room. She'd been too out of it to remember anything that may have been there before. This wasn't her house. "Are you sure that book wasn't there before? Couldn't someone have put it in this room when you weren't home?"

Tierra shook her head, though her eyes were skimming the pages in front of her. "It wasn't here when we brought you into this room only minutes ago, and then it appeared after you woke up."

"Like, out of thin air." Claire nodded.

Aerin narrowed her eyes and crossed her arms over her chest. "I don't fucking believe this." Meaning, she didn't believe *in* this. She was an agnostic tech-scientist with two doctorates and a growing corporation. These women we're talking about impossible things. Fantasy. Make-believe. They were alluding to a word that had always danced with Aerin, and she'd always shoved it aside.

Magic.

"You are all delusional," she said, making a swipe for her bag as it was no longer blocked by the freaky book. "I don't know what you gave me in that coffee shop, but I'm not sticking around to see what happens next."

Tierra whispered a few words and flicked her fingers, locking the bolt on the bedroom door from across the room.

Simultaneously, Claire waved her hand, and a fire flared in the white marble fireplace, fueled by absolutely nothing.

Moira's trick was taking the water from the glass and drenching her with it, but at this point, Aerin was too awe-struck to be pissed off.

Though, as she swiped at the water dripping from her chin, she reminded herself to be pissed off later.

"You aren't going anywhere," Tierra ordered. "I worked that spell to call you all here because I knew we were supposed to be together. That we were not complete until we found each other and fulfilled our purpose, our destiny, as a family. And I was right. This book proves it."

She turned the book to face them, and Aerin could only make out the title, written in the strange scrawls of middle English where the 'S' looked like a cursive 'F' and the 'U' looked like a 'V'. She'd studied all kinds of linguistics in college, and recognized it right away.

The Doomsday Prophecy, it read. *The Second Coming of the Four.*

Tierra settled it back into her palms, facing her. "Now shut up and listen long enough for us to figure out just what the hell is going on."

Aerin felt shaky, and her legs were grateful to be relieved of her weight as she sank to the edge of the bed and was almost simultaneously joined by Claire. Moira remained standing, but leaned against the bedpost with her arms crossed beneath her breasts. All of them stared at Tierra, whose face became more dramatic and animated with every movement of her jade eyes across the pages. "Well," Moira finally broke the silence.

"It's kind of...a letter," Tierra breathed.

"From who?" Claire asked.

"From a man—a king—named Malcolm de Moray. It's dated just about a thousand years ago..." She drifted off.

"Well, hell, woman you gonna tell us what it says?" Moira drawled. "Or at least who it's for?"

Tierra mouthed a few words that Aerin didn't catch, but she could feel the waves of overwhelming disbelief underscored by excitement and anxiety emanating from the gypsy.

"I think..." Her eyes skimmed a little lower, and then she lifted them, touching each of the sisters with her wide, astonished gaze. "I think it's written to us."

32

"How is that possible?" Aerin puzzled, finally summoning the strength to include herself. "How could a man who lived a thousand years ago know that we were going to exist?"

Claire's leather jacket creaked a bit with her sultry shrug. "If it's a prophecy, then it makes sense."

"What are you talking about?" Aerin asked, sweeping her hand through her damp hair. "None of this makes the least bit of sense."

Claire fiddled with a buckle, her long lashes swept down over her cheeks. "Sometimes, when I look deep enough into the flames, I see... things."

"What, like dead people?"

"Maybe? No. I don't know. Like scenes of a movie or a montage. If that ever happens, I know that I'm going to see that exact same thing happen again, or hear about it happening later. Usually it's something awful. Something that terrifies me." Claire finally lifted her head, tucking her thick locks behind an ear in a self-conscious gesture. "If this Malcolm was anything like me, if he had an affinity for fire... who is to say it's not called a prophecy?"

Moira went to Claire and sat on her opposite side, placing a hand on her back in a careful way, as though she didn't expect Claire to accept her gesture. "Sometimes, when the bayou is real still and clear, and no critters have churned the bottom, I've seen things in the water."

Claire's whiskey eyes brightened. "The future?"

"The past." Moira's aquamarine gaze filled with a pain wrought of knowledge that she obviously didn't want to possess. "Things that have already happened, things I can't change. Though one time I did see Uncle Red try to fix his carburetor with a frozen catfish on account of its little mouth was stuck open and he was too drunk to tell the difference. So it weren't all bad." They chuckled.

Aerin's mouth was suddenly dry, but she forced her admission through lips drawn tight with trepidation. "I—feel things."

"You sure about that?" Moira asked sardonically.

"I mean it," Aerin tried to keep the sharpness out of her words, but it didn't work. "I can feel..." She looked for a description that didn't sound too hokey, eschewing words like "energy," "vibrations," and "empathy." She didn't want to sound like she was some kind of bullshit hippy.

Cringing, she threw Tierra an apologetic look, though the woman had yet to look up from the book and Aerin was pretty sure she couldn't read minds.

"I can sense change in electromagnetic wavelengths caused by the alterations in the neurotransmitters or chemicals of the pituitary, amygdala, hypothalamus, and endocrine system. Namely oxytocin, adrenaline, dopamine, serotonin, norepinephrine, peptides, et cetera." Letting a deep rush of breath out of her throat, she realized that she felt lighter. "Feels good to get that off my chest. I've never admitted that out loud before."

Looking up, she met more than one blank stare. "I'm still not sure you've exactly admitted to anything." Tierra wrinkled her forehead.

"Other than the fact you may have violently raped a medical dictionary at some point," Claire snarked.

"She's sayin' that she can feel other people's emotions, ain't that right?" Moira arched an eyebrow.

"Yes. Kind of. Maybe." This was crazy. They all sounded insane.

"You all should have been there the first-time plants and animals started communicating with me." Tierra rolled her eyes. "I thought I was losing my mind, but it was just my earth magic manifesting itself. I suppose I was lucky to be raised by a witch, so she could tell me just what was going on."

Aerin held a hand to her roiling stomach, wishing like hell everyone would stop saying stuff like that. Magic. Witches. It was all too fucking weird.

"Listen to this, guys." Tierra jangled a hand at them. "This Malcolm de Moray writes that he is a Druid and King of the Picts. He wields earth magic, like me!"

"de Moray," Claire repeated the name. "What is he like a million generations back great-grandfather?"

Tierra studied the book, chewing on her lower lip. "Apparently. He says that three de Morays are granted innate elemental and seasonal powers every generation since the evolution of man. His sister, Morgana is a water witch, and his cousin, Kenna, is a fire witch." She looked up to Claire. "She must have the gift of prophecy, like you." Claire gave a low whistle.

"He writes that there's a prophecy in this book, written in the language of the first Celts that is called the Doomsday Prophecy or the Prophecy of Four.

Aerin was almost afraid to ask, which meant she bowled ahead and did it anyway. "What does the prophecy say?"

"He said that he's translated it into English for he knows that's the language we'll speak."

Tierra didn't seem like the kind of woman who

easily rattled, so when she shifted her feet and took a bracing, shaky breath, it unsettled Aerin even more.

"Verily when four elemental Druids are born to one house and cast behind one gate, they will hear thunder, the heavens will weep, the earth will tremble, the air will burn, and the Seals will be broken, one by one. The First will be Conquest, on his white horse given a bow and a crown so he could go forth and conquer. The second horse is red and power is given to him that rides it. Power to take peace from the earth, to slay with his sword, and to bring war."

Claire gasped, and a look of unadulterated shock clashed with the women's gazes that Aerin didn't at all understand.

"The Third Seal is a man on a black horse, his relic a scale and balance, and he shall bring with him pestilence and famine the likes of which the world has never seen. And the Fourth... the Fourth Seal is Death, on his pale horse. And he shall bring with him the might of the Underworld."

A pall of shock permeated the room, and pieces of the past couple of days began to fit together like cogs in a timepiece. Aerin sneezed into her hand and groaned as it set her head to aching again.

Pestilence, eh?

Moira pushed off the bed and went to Tierra, squinting down at the strange volume with a little hope buoyed by skepticism. "I been in the South long enough to recognize a paraphrase of the bible when I hear one. Reverend Dupuis spat that brimstone at me like a double-tongued cobra every blessed day of the week and twice on Sundays. When he wasn't grabassin' his way 'round the Hoodoo Shack, that is. That's the book of Revelations with a few twists."

Claire also stood. "Revelations as in, the Apocalypse?"

"The Four Horsemen of the Apocalypse." Moira

nodded. "And I think I have to call bullpucky at this point. Druids and Christians ain't exactly known to share folktales."

"That's what's so crazy." Tierra closed her eyes, running silver-ringed fingers delicately across the parchment. "This book is older than the bible by a lot."

"How can you tell?" Aerin asked.

"I can feel the elements contained in the book. The ink is iron, sulfate, and sometimes... blood. The parchment is linen, sometimes animal hide, and the cover is —" With a squeak, she dropped it, letting the tome crash to the floor, and wiped her palms on her skirts chanting all different forms of "Ew."

"What?" Claire asked. "What's wrong?"

Tierra shuddered and toed the book closed and they all stared. Blue, runic markings swirled in arcs and spirals around the gilded corners of the book, pointing toward a foreign, beautiful script embossed in the center of the lightly tinted leather.

"That cover is skin." Tierra rubbed her arms as they sprouted goose bumps. "Human skin."

❧ 33 ❧

Aerin couldn't stop staring at the book, drawn to the power emanating from it. She sensed... something pulsing from within. A will, if not sentience. A purpose, if not desire. A need to be opened, to be read, and to be used.

What she couldn't tell was if that particular need was well-meaning or malevolent. The vibe she felt was sort of neutral, ambivalent even. If a book could be such a thing.

What about this Malcolm? Perhaps the book merely contained a residual of his potency, or of his intentions.

"Gross." Claire grimaced. "Anything made of human skin can't be positive, right? I mean, am I the only one getting an *Evil Dead* reference here? *The Ninth Gate? The Mummy? Hocus Pocus...* Anyone?"

Aerin slid off the bed, crouching down and reaching for the tome. "I don't think it means us any harm. In fact, I'm pretty sure it wants us to use it."

"I think her fever's done gone and flared again." Moira managed to sound droll, even with her expressive accent. "It's a thing. It ain't a person."

Gingerly picking it up, Aerin carried it back to the bed trying not to let the warmth of the cover gross her out. The smooth binding was not unlike flesh. "Are you saying you can't...feel it?"

"Maybe," Claire admitted, leaning over to her. "Something like... desire?"

"Or life." Tierra nodded.

Moira looked away, tapping the bedpost with her toe. "Or belonging."

With shaking hands, Aerin pried open the cover, and let the errant drafts leaf through the ancient, heavy pages until it rested open in her lap.

"Do you think Aunt Justine knows about this book?" Claire asked.

"Maybe she's the reason it's here."

Tierra's skeptical look made her words moot. "I don't think so."

"That old bat wouldn't piss on us if we was on fire," Moira spat.

Like actually spat. On the floor.

"Don't say that!" Tierra scolded. "She's family."

"And all she done, far as I can tell, is ignore you for her coven of harpies and try to take our powers. Even my life."

"She's old and afraid." Tierra's words were more convincing than her expression. "She's let me stay here in her home, and raised me as best she could. In a way, what's written in this book sort of proves many of her fears valid."

"But what about us?" Claire asked. "She had to have known there were four."

"Yeah, what made you special enough to keep?" Moira demanded.

Tierra's eyes widened, the edges becoming glassy with the hint of moisture. "I-I don't know. I don't think it had anything to do with me. But... now that we're all together, we should probably ask her some questions."

"Good luck getting the truth out of her," Moira harrumphed. "I'll bet she lies like a no-legged dog."

Their conversation faded into white noise as Aerin ran her manicured fingers over the faded parchment. She might care that she had a hesitant aunt later, but at the moment, she couldn't tear her gaze from the astonishingly well-drawn sketches in front of her.

The stanzas of spells were carefully scrawled in a script so foreign; she couldn't even tell where one word began and another ended. It could have been a recipe of some kind.

But the pictures fascinated, confused, and elated her all at once.

In the upper left corner of the left page, a sapling tree grew from roots already deep in the earth. Separated by words, the picture in the upper right of the page showed a staff, roughly the size of the tree, flayed of bark and branch, the wood green and moist, and alive.

In the lower left of the page, was what appeared to be a bunch of hay or straw lashed together at one end in the shape of a bush. Across from it, the bush had been lashed to the staff making a very rudimentary broom.

If that wasn't self-explanatory, the next page showed the bristles of the broom on fire, or at least, smoking, which lifted the form of a slender woman off the illustrated floor.

That wasn't what caused Aerin to catch her breath, though. It was the robed figure in the bottom right of the right page. Her hair dusted a dark red, and swirly puffs of magic leaving her mouth as she blew the smoking broom into the night sky.

One word, scrawled in bold blue script meant a damn thing to her on the entire page, right beneath the Druid woman.

Aer.

Slamming the book shut, she drew the notice of her sisters.

"What?" Tierra narrowed her eyes. "What did you find?

For a moment, Aerin began to panic. Her limbs twitched with the sensation she'd so feared since her youth. Weightless. Disembodied.

Falling. Falling. Flailing.

Flying?

The ground coming toward her. The earth threatening to break each one of her tiny bones.

"Nothing," Aerin wheezed. Her throat constricted and her lungs struggled as she shoved the book at Claire and pushed herself up on wobbly legs. "I just need—" She swiped for her purse, but Tierra got there first.

"Oh, no you don't! You've been sneezing and hacking since we carried you up here. There's no way I'm letting you smoke."

"You. Don't. Understand." Aerin could feel her capillaries expanding, the oxygen infusing her blood. She couldn't take it. Not right now. "Please," she begged around a bout of coughing brought on by her desperation and whatever bug she was fighting off.

"This is for your own good," Tierra announced, opening her purse and fishing out the pack Aerin so desperately wanted.

A high-pitched squeak echoed through the room, followed by whatever ear-splitting sound Tierra made as a small black body exploded from her tote, and began to chatter and flutter around the woman's unruly curls.

"Butter my ass and call me a biscuit!" Moira grabbed the poker from the fireplace and took a swipe at Doctor Lecter. "It's one of them flying rats."

Where had he come from? How had he—?

"She doesn't look so well." Claire's voice was suddenly far away, like Aerin was listening to it through the thin walls of a shitty New York apartment. The cacophony kept sliding farther and farther away, and suddenly the soft, white rug was rushing up to meet her.

And for the third time that day, Aerin let the darkness claim her.

❧

THE FEVER HAD BROKEN BY THE TIME A BITCH OF A nicotine fit pulled her from the nightmare Aerin had fought since before she could remember.

She fell back to the fluffy white bed with a wild flailing of limbs.

Sleep paralysis. It was just a sensation. Nothing more.

She did not levitate in her sleep.

Problem was, she'd never been too good at self-delusions or denial. Never believed in Santa, the Tooth Fairy, the Easter Bunny, or religion. Magic wasn't even in her sphere of consideration.

Until now.

But the proof, however personally anecdotal, was beginning to mount, whether she wished it to be real or not. So she'd better get on board this crazy train before it left the station without her.

Maybe now was the time to reflect on the fact that she levitated in her sleep. Clutching the sheets beneath her against an insane fear that she'd just go drifting away like an astronaut in zero gravity, she swung her bare feet over the side of the bed and reveled in the feel of the hardwood floor beneath her and the weight of her body resting on her bones.

She was steady on her feet. Stable. She felt... better. Her head still pounded, but her nose was no longer stuffy and running, nor did her throat hurt. The body aches were gone and so were the chills, sweats, and nausea.

She felt healthy. And bitchy. Mostly bitchy.

Time for a much-deserved morning smoke. And coffee.

Surveying the black and white room, she found her luggage tucked between an overstuffed arabesque chair and a glass table. On the table perched a pitcher and a glass of water, aspirin, a decongestant, tea that had gone cold, a few bottles of essential oils, and that son-of-a-bitch brew with a card leaned against it that commanded: Drink this first.

Not bloody likely. But still...

If Aerin had to hazard a guess, each one of the sisters had left her own offering on the table. A curious emotion rose from the middle of her chest and clogged in her throat where she coughed it out before it overwhelmed her. She looked around with an almost spastic sense of disquiet. Someone had taken off her shoes and jacket and tucked her into the bed, covered her with blankets, retrieved her luggage. They'd left her medicine for her comfort.

What the fuck was someone like her supposed to do with that?

Her red purse beckoned like the sultry lips of a high-priced courtesan, and Aerin's mouth watered at the idea of a pack of habit tucked into its regimented place. This bedroom even had a balcony. Imagine the luck.

Tiptoeing to her bag, she reached in and rifled through her wallet, keys, papers, makeup, and other sundries, but came up empty of the one thing her body screamed for.

"Oh no they didn't!" she bitched through gritted teeth, suddenly remembering Tierra fishing her cigarettes out of her purse before she passed out.

Aerin showered, changed, and angrily staked her hair into a bun with a pen in record time. Though her body screamed at her to tear down the stairs and rip into the thieves, she'd learned early on that destruction was all the more devastating when perpetrated by an elegant, well-dressed hand.

Silk off-white palazzo pants and a pearl blouse gave her the look of casual royalty. Slicking a tube of her darkest lipstick onto her full mouth, she blotted and regarded herself in the bathroom mirror. "Someone's about to reap the whirlwind." She informed her reflection, and realized it was good practice, because everyone she was about to confront had a face exactly like hers.

❋ 34 ❋

An inhuman squeal blasted through the elegant silence of the house as Aerin stalked from her bedroom in search of reprisal. She descended the plush green carpets of the grand twisting staircase, interrupting a commotion that conjured the chaos of the Bay of Pigs. Speaking of pigs, a tiny pink body scurried past the landing, his comically small cloven hooves slipping and sliding beneath his chubby body in panicked haste.

"I'm going to yank your ugly, little leather wings off with my bare hands, you disease-ridden varmint!" Moira's unmistakable voice hollered.

To Aerin's dismay, Doctor Lecter sped around the eaves of the cavernous ceilings of the ground floor, and disappeared up the stairs with a hiss just as Moira rounded the door frame sporting the business end of a broom like a billy club.

Without missing a beat, she turned on Aerin. "You keep that flying rat away from Cheeto, you hear?"

Aerin snorted. "I don't think that Doctor Lecter likes Cheetos."

"You sure are slower than cream rising in a vat of buttermilk, even for a Yankee," Moira sneered. "I found that critter of yours sucking on the side of my poor pig's neck."

"Oh, keep your bog waders on, your pig is fine," Aerin snarked. "He probably didn't even feel Doctor Lecter, his saliva has a numbing agent and he barely eats enough blood to matter."

Moira's eyes narrowed and darkened from an aquamarine to a tropical blue. "Well if he comes near Cheeto again, the only thing he'll be eatin' is a face-full of my cast-iron skillet."

The real mystery was, how in the hell Doctor Lecter got from New York to Seattle in the first place. He'd been in her purse a while ago, but he certainly wasn't when she was going through security at the airport. Either way, Aerin felt oddly protective of her little confidant.

"You lay a finger on Doctor Lecter and I'll make bacon out of your little hillbilly pet, and eat it in front of you."

"Try it and I'll—" Another squeal and the smell of something burning broke Moira's threat off mid-breath. "Well, shit," she cussed, jamming a finger at Aerin. "This ain't over."

Aerin tried to summon the strength to care, but all her ire was still directed in the direction of whomever had filched her cigarettes. She'd deal with the Moira/weird pet situation later. After smoking.

Searching the main floor, she became more and more aggravated at every empty room. Each brocaded hallway and bohemian surface bedecked with candles, statues, and new-age litter had stoked a tempest of irritation inside her that she was more than ready to unleash.

"What makes you think you can take my shit?" Aerin demanded, finally finding Tierra bustling about the covered porch out back that apparently doubled as a greenhouse. "Hand them over, you thieving psychotic hippie."

Tierra glanced up from where she was tenderly watering something in a terrarium with a spray bottle. "You're awake." Her smile hid the condescending compassion rolling off of her in infuriating waves. "You look like you're feeling better."

"You tell me where my cigarettes are right now, or I'll rip that smug expression off your face and shove it up your—"

"They're right here." Claire sidled up and handed them to her along with a lighter. "Cool your engine."

Aerin snatched them with all the relish of a starving refugee and hunkered over by an open window.

"You're welcome, by the way." Claire's amber eyes made a full rotation of sarcasm in their sockets before touching Tierra's with a vaguely amused wink.

Aerin would thank her after her first drag. She did have priorities, after all.

Fully expecting Tierra to make a stink about her lighting up inside, Aerin was shocked that the woman didn't even look at her as she flicked the roll with the expertise of a long-time addict, and touched the flame to the edge of her cigarette and breathed in.

A flare warned her the second before a flash nearly singed off her eyebrows, and the remains of the entire cigarette drifted to the wooden slats of the floor like tiny, dirty snowflakes.

"The hell?" Aerin mumbled, shoving another butt into her mouth and lighting it, producing the exact same effect.

From under brows drawn down with puzzled consternation, she noticed Claire hiding a smile behind her hand. Tierra's back was to Aerin, but her shoulders shook with silent mirth.

"What did you do?" Aerin demanded. "Did you fucking curse my cigarettes?"

"No," Tierra snorted. "We did not curse your cigarettes. And do you have to have such a dirty mouth?"

"It was more like a hex," Claire admitted, then dissolved into giggles with Tierra.

Irritation cooled into a chilly rage as Aerin stood, dumbfounded, as her sisters shared a laugh. They thought this was so damned funny, did they, messing with her shit?

As she let go a litany of foul language that only a girl who'd been raised in an orphanage in the Bronx could summon, lightning flashed in the distance, illuminating the gabled skyline of Victorian houses. An old tree scraped against the side of the house as a wind picked up, sounding like it asked to be let in. The temperature inside the balmy porch dropped a good ten degrees, and instantly the two women sobered.

"We are only trying to help you." Tierra's earnest jade eyes somehow pissed her off even more. "We want you to be well."

"You want to help me?" Aerin seethed, tossing the hexed pack into a planter that looked handmade. "Then do me a favor and stay the fuck out of my purse. No. No. Better yet, stay the fuck out of my life." She stalked to the door and grabbed what looked like car keys from a hook that bade her 'Blessed Be.' Enjoying the angry clomp of her expensive pumps on the flagstone pathway, she pushed the electric button and a tiny flash of headlights in the driveway told her which car she was stealing.

Of course, it was a damned hybrid, green, clean, and energy efficient. Tierra's car. Ha!

Ignoring the sound of her name and the jangle of Tierra's feet following her, she slid behind the driver's seat, threw her purse across to the passenger side, started the car, and peeled out of the driveway.

Maybe, after she bought cigarettes, she'd trade the sucker in for a Hummer. Take that, carbon footprint!

Aerin realized the impossibility of doing such a thing, and the likelihood that Tierra was already reporting her car stolen, but still, it felt good to plot something devious.

After securing a pack and a lighter at a gas station on the edge of town, she knew she'd have to go somewhere else to smoke. She should just do it in the car, stink up the sweet-smelling interior. It would serve her meddling sister right. But, regardless of how much the idea tempted her, Aerin couldn't bring herself to do it. She'd have to pull over.

Finding herself in a green hollow of ancient forest, she took a fork in the rural road on a hunch and drove up the tree-canopied path until it dead-ended at a meadow.

Daylight faded fast, alerting Aerin that she must have slept through the afternoon. A large, waxing moon rose above the thick green trees surrounding the meadow, guarding the clouds as they drifted past in lazy herds. Tall grasses whipped back and forth in whatever spring gusts had been conjured, and it threatened the security of her bun as she stepped from the car.

Half of her nicotine fits died at the very feel of the pack and lighter in her hand and she took the time to relish the feel of the sleek tube fitting between her lips. She cupped the lighter with her hand to save the flame from the wind now dying to a breeze.

Another high-pitched scream pierced the wind, interrupting the solace of the moment. This one a thousand times more inhuman than that of the pig. Not just inhuman, in fact.

But unnatural.

The hard-won cigarette dropped from Aerin's lips as her jaw fell open in astounded disbelief.

Her favorite poem from school whispered through her thoughts as the figure astride an impossibly large, black horse broke from the tree line and galloped across the meadow.

The wind was a torrent of darkness among the gusty trees, The moon was a ghostly galleon tossed upon cloudy seas...

Man and beast moved together with astonishing grace, each with a mane as black as midnight tossed about in the whipping currents of salt sea air.

The Highwayman came riding—riding—riding...

There was something timeless and visceral about a man on a horse, racing through space as though the speed could put distance between him and his demons.

But they were always waiting for you, no matter how far or fast you went.

"You can't outrun them," Aerin whispered. But it was beautiful to watch him try.

Her whisper could never have carried through the distance to the horse and rider, but regardless, they changed direction, cantering toward her at a breakneck speed.

As they neared, the details of the man sharpened, and Aerin found herself fighting for breath.

If not for the twentieth century invention of the car hood that caught her butt as she plopped against it, Aerin would have thought she'd wandered back through time. The figure had the body of a warlord and the wardrobe of an English gentleman. A loose, white shirt hung open halfway down his torso, catching the wind and blousing out behind wide shoulders with each of the stallion's impossible strides. The slopes and valleys of stark, lean muscle molded the thin fabric with every hypnotic galloping rhythm. As Aerin's notice lowered to where dark trousers sculpted to incomprehensibly long, powerful legs and stretched over hips thrusting in time against the saddle, all moisture vacated her mouth and simultaneously headed for the region of her panties.

The temptation to hide behind the car for protection as they bore down on her was strong. But backing down was against her nature, so she stood her ground, pushing off the car hood and crossing her arms in front of her as though that would somehow protect her.

Mere feet from her the beast reared and stomped, as eyes bluer than the most tropical ocean drank her in from features now carved into her mind's eye. The broad forehead. The stark bones and defined masculinity of Julian Roarke.

They stared at each other in silent disbelief for what could have been hours, but felt like only seconds. The horse danced impatiently, and Julian did little to cull the behavior, though Aerin had the idea that he could have done so very easily.

"You're alive," he breathed, his voice as rich and smooth as she remembered, caressing the currents of air with a vibration she'd never quite experienced before. "I didn't allow myself to truly believe it until now."

"No thanks to you." Aerin tried to summon all the chill she could into her voice, regardless of what seeing him again did to her self control. Hours ago, he'd been a blindingly handsome man she'd tried to pick up at the airport. She'd learned too much between then and now, about both of them. It seemed they were on separate sides of a strange and implausible destiny.

And that fact just shit all over any chance at a relationship.

"You should run, Aerin de Moray," he warned, the wind catching the ebony locks that teased his broad shoulders and lifted them away from his sharp jaw. "This is too dangerous."

There was no need to clarify his meaning. It was painfully apparent he alluded to the current of pure, passionate awareness flowing between them through the space separating their skin. The way their gazes clashed, blue and silver, like the lightning and sky. Unrepentant. Deadly. Mesmerizing.

"You first," she volleyed. "I don't run away." Not when it would give him the opportunity to chase her.

Nudging his stallion forward, he crowded her against the car and reached a leather-gloved hand down to her. "Then run with me," he dared, his eyes full of challenge.

Aerin had never been impulsive, but a reckless wind drove her to reach for him and slide her manicured hand against his. Once his long fingers closed around hers, she was his prisoner, and he pulled her astride his stallion in a shocking, lithe movement that left her gasping for air.

Too many sensations assaulted Aerin at once. His lean hips pressing into her ass, the swells of his chest against her back as he gathered the reins, and silken rasp of his breath against her ear as his velvet voice resonated through her entire body. "I've got you," he said, and kicked his horse back into a gallop, rendering speech impossible.

They rode at breakneck speed, the ground whizzing by in a green blur. Aerin had never been on a horse before and the sheer height made her more than a little dizzy, but the strength of Julian's arms locked her in place, and the surety of his movements coaxed her into making her own hips follow the stride of the steed beneath her. She didn't take time to think, to consider the consequences of her actions here. Instead, she let the thrill of the moment take her away, the stir of the wind caress her skin, and the warmth of his strong body against hers heat her blood.

When they broke upon a vista of shorter grasses and wildflowers overlooking the water, the last of the day was a weak ribbon of blue against the west. Stars already twinkled in the east, dimmed by the moon's reflection off the black and silver ripples of water lapping against the cliffs below.

Julian slid from the saddle, and turned to encircle her waist with his hands before lifting her down and they stood like that, facing each other, breath mingling, before he turned away and stalked to the edge of the cliff. The turbulent wind had died to a lightly ruffling breeze, and Aerin watched the way the moon threaded strands of silver through his onyx hair as she approached his broad form.

"I take it you know who I am by now." He didn't look at her when he spoke, but kept his eyes trained on the moon, his emotions as tumultuous and confusing as the winds had been not long ago.

Aerin reluctantly stepped next to him, not afraid of his proximity, but terrified of the drop to the rocks below.

"Yeah," she confirmed. "You're the Third Horseman."

He nodded. "Pestilence to some, Famine to others. Death to all of whom I come into contact with."

"I thought Death was the Fourth Horseman."

A sad smile lifted the corner of his mouth, causing an intriguing dimple to appear, incongruous in the rigid plane of his cheek. "The distinction is minute," he explained, as though weary of the clarification. "Dying is something that takes one from this state of being to the next. Death—the man who is called death—he is responsible for everything that happens after."

"Oh," she said lamely. She still hadn't grasped the whole being one of the sister-witches who were going to bring about the Apocalypse thing, so it was still somewhat hard to wrap her head around having these kinds of conversations, let alone know how to respond.

"You've read the prophecy, then," he stated.

"Kind of?" She wrinkled her forehead. "I don't know if we read all the way through before I passed out. I was pretty sick thanks to you, I think."

He studied the moon as though it contained the answers to their predicament, and yet they both knew it didn't. "Yes, you are the first living being to survive my touch."

Well, didn't she feel special? Wait… didn't that mean he'd just tried to kill her?

"Why are you here, Aerin?" he demanded, turning from the incredible view and blasting her with a barrage of emotional strain that nearly knocked her off her feet. Regret, elation, deprivation, lust, and a sense of condemned hope confused and drew her at the same time. "If you read the prophecy, if you know what you're going to force me to do, why remain here and tempt fate?"

"What the hell am I going to force you to do?" she demanded, throwing her arms out to the increasing wind. "I don't really understand any of this, which is saying a lot because I'm a fucking genius. All I know is that I have three sisters I had never met, and a freaky ancient book made of human skin says that I'm from some kind of druid family fated to bring about the end of the world. You think I want that?"

"I don't know you enough to speculate as to what your intentions are." His voice as measured as the ingredients of an explosive charge.

"You're goddamn right you don't. I have a life. I have money. I have one of the most successful, lucrative cloud companies on the planet. Hell, I have untried magical powers. Who has time for the Apocalypse?"

To her surprise, his features relaxed into the ghost of a smile as his eyes, illuminated by the moon, traveled her sophisticated outfit with the languor of an immortal.

Which begged the question. Was he one?

"I believe your intentions are good. But it is impossible to outwit the fates. The prophecy is ironclad, and so is our part in it." Waves of sadness emanated from him as he said this with all the culture and poise of a royal decree.

This time, Aerin had to turn away, and when she looked down at the sea, though admittedly not as far down as her brain likely perceived it, she had to sit before vertigo had her pitching herself off the edge.

"Are you all right?" Julian followed her down.

"I'm fine," she insisted. "I just, don't deal very well with heights."

"I see." He reclined next to her, stretching his long legs to the edge of the cliff, and taking his gloves off, setting them neatly beside him.

Now that she'd caught her bearings, Aerin pressed for answers, trying to ignore the attraction that hung as heavy as the salty air between them, or the way he kept staring at her as though he didn't believe she was real. "Why do you care whether I stay or go? Aren't you all the Four Horsemen of the Apocalypse? Isn't ending the world sort of your job?"

"It is a duty we crave and dread all at once," he replied cryptically. "It is almost impossible to convey what an existence such as ours is like. An eternity of servitude to the purpose for which we've been born. Like Nicholas, the manifestation of the very essence of life on this planet. An endless, ruthless reach for not just survival, but for advancement and supremacy. Because the strongest survive.

"And then there is Drustan. The embodiment of the masculine instinct. Destruction, domination, and vengeance. He and Nicholas work very well together. Some of the greatest human advancement comes from the carnage of war, does it not?"

Aerin nodded, unsure of whether to be entranced, horrified, or impressed. "What are you, exactly? Angels? Demons? Gods? Slaves?"

He looked like the question pleased him. "Our genesis is a mystery, even to us. Sometimes we dream of a life, of a past or a childhood, but whether that's a memory or a wish, none of us can be quite sure. We serve masters who never show their faces. We're all being punished for crimes long forgotten. After tens of thousands of years, we know nothing more than whom we are, and what we're fated to do. We are cursed. Cursed to end the world we call home at the whims of four elemental witches."

"That's…" Aerin groped for a word that could properly convey her sympathy and came up painfully short. "Shitty."

Amusement flared in his eyes, then died like a defective match.

"You don't understand what you will force me to do should the Seals be broken. Unlike Nicholas, who conquers the strongest, or Drustan, who devastates soldiers, but brings their families heroes and glory, I will walk as a scourge through the streets of this town and all cities like it. I will visit the hospital and the orphanage. The weak and the helpless will be the first to die. Then the compassionate, the caretakers, the mothers and the elderly. I will starve the hungry and bring suffering to the vulnerable."

Aerin studied the way the moonlight slashed across his face with all the forgiveness of a silver blade. To say he was bleak would be like saying the sea was deep, or the sun was hot. True, and yet inadequate. Though he reclined, his profile remained powerful. He gave off the impression of a great jungle cat at rest, secure in his badassery enough to truly relax. He looked like someone you'd see stamped on an ancient coin. Hard and imperial.

His eyes met hers again, burning with torment. "That is my curse. That is my power. I may not be death, but I bring death. Not with a sword, not with a conquest, but with inescapable suffering and madness." Each word emerged as though he had to pull it out of him with herculean effort. "You cannot defeat a virus with diplomacy. You cannot reason with famine. Or beg a drought for mercy."

"Um, what about Penicillin?" Aerin countered.

His eyes softened on her, and Aerin was more than a little confused by the way he seemed to find every one of her arguments endearing, or at the very least, amusing. Who did that? Men hated to be contradicted by a woman. If she'd learned anything in this life, it was that fact. So, what the hell was the matter with him?

"Mortals have been very industrious in learning to combat illness. It's a sort of biological warfare. Survival, adaptation, rinse, repeat. However, I know it will all end. There is no cure for the devastation I will bring. It will be swift, and it will be thorough. No antibiotic will touch it. No vaccination will prevent it. What is left of humanity after Conquest and War are done with it will be nothing but starvation and rot. They will suffer unimaginably at my hand. And then Bane will deliver the final blow."

"Bane?" Aerin echoed. "Who is that?"

Tugging at an orange wildflower, Julian held it up in his large palm and they both watched it slowly shrivel as he explained. "You are the fourth de Moray to have arrived here in Port Townsend and are, indeed, very formidable."

"Um, thanks." The unmitigated tender way he delivered each word to her was starting to get under her skin—maybe deeper than that—to the part inside that she'd forgotten she had. Her heart. Her conscience. Whatever section of her gut manufactured pathos and caring. She didn't like it. Not one bit.

"Our Fourth," Julian continued. "Killian, is not merely formidable. He's finality personified."

"Death," Aerin offered, a chill snaking through her as she watched the powdered remains of what had been a living plant only moments ago slip through his elegant fingers.

"To die is an action, one that the three of us facilitate in our own ways. He is everything that happens after. The entire awe-inspiring, terrifying, exquisite experience of what is beyond mortality. They say that you should be afraid to meet your maker. What they mean, is that you should be afraid to meet Killian Bane. The Fourth Horseman. The Final Seal. The line of demarcation for the eight of us. Once his Seal is broken, there is no going back. You are committed to the Apocalypse."

"Yeah well, I have commitment issues," Aerin mumbled. "And I don't buy this destiny bullshit. I believe we make our own way in this world, and we are the masters of our own fate."

Without warning, Julian leaned closer and reached out, pulling the pencil from Aerin's hair away without touching her, causing the long waves to tumble past her shoulders and down her back. It was the most intimate thing any man had ever done to her, and he still hadn't touched her skin.

"You speak so boldly, Aerin de Moray. You are such a strong, intelligent woman. I wonder, in the face of all this, in the aftermath of the prophecy, what is it that you believe?"

"I believe in nothing but myself," she answered honestly. "It's the only belief that's gotten me this far."

"What about your sisters?" he queried carefully.

"What about them?"

"Do you believe in them? Do you have faith in their love for you, and in their abilities? Do you believe that they will bring about the end of the world, or that they will work to stop it?" He was studying her now, less like an interested male, and more like a scientist. The distinction irked her.

"I don't believe that is information I should be

sharing with the opposition." She quirked a pointed eyebrow at him.

"Fair enough." His tender smile returned. "We came for you all last night, Nicholas, Drustan, and me. We were after the sword that Claire has in her possession. It is the sword of War, and belongs with him."

Aerin frowned. "How come we didn't know?"

"The Maison de Moray is warded. Those wards are stronger now that you all are together."

"You could have just knocked," she said. "Maybe we would have been able to come to some kind of compromise a la 'Hey, may I please have my sword? I promise not to end the world with it, and stuff.'"

This finally brought a soft breath of laughter from deep in his chest. "I've lived long enough as who I am to know there is no escaping what is to come. Study the prophecy, Aerin," he cautioned. "Learn what you can from the Grimoire before it's too late. Because we'll be coming for you again."

A whirlwind of irate helplessness swirled about inside of Aerin, and she let out a sound of frustration. "Why is this happening now? What gives? Why would the powers at be, whoever the fuck they are, want us all to die?"

He held her gaze. "If you read any of the holy books written since the beginning of time, followed any of the dogma, you'd see that each of them predict that the worst possible thing that could occur is that mortals lose their faith in the Gods who created them."

"No big disclosure there." Aerin shrugged.

"They couldn't be more wrong, Aerin." His smooth voice took on a note of gravitas that sent shivers through her bones. "What is the worst, is when the Gods lose their faith in humanity."

A cold terror licked at her insides. Such a thing had never entered into the realm of possibility. "Why?" she breathed. "Why would they do that?"

"Look around you," he prompted gently.

Aerin glanced about, taking in the beauty of the sea-kissed evening.

"Figuratively, I mean," he said with a chuckle. "The world is an overpopulated, unmitigated disaster. Your governments are all corrupt, incompetent machines run by money and special interests. Humans in the first world are overfed, entitled, heartless bureaucrats who prefer to be blind to the suffering of others so long as they're entertained by screens and buttons and social diseases. They do nothing for those who are still chained by tyrants or starved and abused by those who call themselves holy men. The feminine divine is lost. Wisdom is falling prey to dogma. And fear, greed, and apathy is keeping everyone subservient while corporations threaten entire ecosystems, fish the oceans to emptiness, and turn the planet into their own rubbish heap. This world was a gift, one you mortals have shat upon. So you tell me, in time, what will be left of this place to save?"

"Well..." Aerin rolled her eyes. "Aren't you a fucking ray of sunshine?"

"That's just it." Julian sat up. "The Gods will scorch the earth and begin again. There will be a war out there for supremacy and power from the top to those who will fight over the dregs. It will be worse than anything you humans could do to yourselves, if you can imagine that."

"Who do you think will win?" she asked.

"It's hard to say. The tyrannical, monotheistic retaliator who claims all the glory for himself? The blood-thirsty ancients of the north? The prolific pantheons of the western worlds? Or the powerful, but mostly archaic pagodas of the east? Most of them have moved on, but when the earth is again a field of limitless potential, ripe to begin again, they'll pick her bones and bring all the wonders and terrors of the Other World with them."

Aerin put a hand to her suddenly throbbing head. "Jesus," she moaned.

"Probably him, too."

"Can't you just—I don't know—stop it?"

His hair gleamed as he shook his head. "Can the sun stop burning? Can the earth just stop in its rotation? Can the moon change its course in the heavens?"

Oh balls, so Pestilence was a freaking metaphorical poet was he?

"Yes!" Aerin exploded, pushing to her feet and wishing that his movements weren't so graceful and fluid as he followed her. "Yes, the sun will eventually run out of hydrogen and expand until it becomes a bloated red dwarf and then explode." She began to pace back from the edge of the cliff, gesturing wildly. "Yes, the earth could be impacted by something at the right speed and angle to stop its rotation, or wait for a few billion years for the tidal forces to slow it's rotation to a standstill, and yes, the moon—"

She bounced off a hard, lean chest as Julian blocked her pacing, and stared up at him, open mouthed.

"You are most certainly a descendant of the Druids," he laughed, a hollow, bemused sound. "They were scientists, you know, bent on advancing technology, just like you. Their disappearance cast this earth into an age so backward, you've never been able, as a people, to climb out of the hole."

Standing this close, Aerin could feel more than just the emotions from within his ancient, extraordinary soul. She could smell his clean, arousing scent, something like almonds and ambergris. Could feel the warmth of his breath on her hair and sense the yearning he had to touch her.

"Things could have been so different," he murmured, his voice filled with millennia of regrets.

Was he still talking about the druids?

"How did they disappear?" she asked, wanting to dispel the intensity of the moment.

His eyes glittered down at her, more black than blue now that he was cast in shadow. "To be honest, that's a story I don't think I can keep my hands from you long enough to tell."

Need slammed into her. His. Hers. She couldn't be sure. "You don't have to," she almost panted.

"Oh, but I do."

"Why?" God, her voice had never sounded so plaintive. So... yearning.

He stepped closer, and then retreated. "You know you're the only living thing that has ever survived my touch?"

"Exactly, so..."

"It made you sick."

His concern touched her, and made her want him all that much more. "I know a thing or two about the symptoms I had. And if I am correct, chances are, I'm immune to you. Like the chicken pox. But sexy."

Amusement haunted his lips. "Impossible."

"If I've learned anything, it's to not use that word in this situation." Aerin took a slow step forward, like she would toward a frightened animal about to bolt. "Touch me," she invited, though it sounded like more of a command.

"No." He retreated one more step, holding up a gloved hand to ward her off.

"Then I'll touch you."

His eyes narrowed. "Don't you dare."

Famous last words, Aerin thought as she lunged for him.

Aerin felt his entire form stiffen as her body surged against his and her mouth latched on to his lips. She made herself a burr, her arms snaking around his torso beneath his biceps, and her hips fitting snugly just below his.

Something else began to stiffen against her belly, and she would have smiled victoriously had her mouth not otherwise been engaged.

She made her lips soft and wet and hot against the stunned hardness of his. She moved rhythmically, nipping and licking at him, driving their senses higher as she drove the curves of her body into the hollows and planes of his.

You're the first woman to survive my touch. His words drifted to her through a haze of lust and need. She was the first woman to taste him. The first to kiss him. The first to run her hands into the thickness of his ebony hair and cup the blade of his pale, strong jaw.

He was uncharted territory, and she had all the possessive drive of a thirteenth century explorer with ships full of Spanish gold.

"Kiss me," she prompted, between wet probes of his tight lips with her tongue. "Taste me, Julian."

With an inhuman sound, his strong arms clamped around her, hauling her tighter against a body taut with strength, muscle, and lust. His mouth was astonishingly different when kissing than when speaking. His cultured accent and flawless prose had ill-prepared her for the raw, primal sin that was being kissed by Julian Roarke.

He didn't just taste her, he devoured. He didn't just kiss her, he claimed her. His lips were full of a promise that he wouldn't merely someday get her naked, but that he would strip her bare. And for the first time in her life, Aerin was truly afraid.

Funny, though, how fear and adrenaline can prelude a savage lust as nothing else can. Instead of running from it, Aerin embraced it, wrapping her legs around Julian's strong body and climbing him like a mooring post in a sea gale.

He secured her to him, one hand beneath her ass, the other around her waist with a strength that was nothing less than superhuman.

It astounded Aerin that a man's kiss could be so supple and yet so full of aggression, of all the unrequited needs of countless lifetimes of desolation. Sure, he was one of the Four Horsemen of the Apocalypse, but he was also just a man.

And men needed to be touched. To be kissed. To be fucked.

And she was ready to do it all. With him. Right now.

❧ 36 ❧

With a groan of distress, Julian ripped his lips from hers as though fighting a powerful adhesive and thrust her away from him. "It's too much," he gasped, turning from her, his hand gripped at his sides. "I'm taking you home."

"What? Why?" Aerin went to him, her knees a little weak, which up until this point she'd thought only happened in sappy romance novels.

"Because you are the most desirable, fascinating woman I've ever come across," he accused.

"Okay," she said evenly. "Not following."

Turning back to her, he loomed like a specter of desire, nostrils flaring and blue eyes darkening with thunderclouds of unspent passion. "Because when I'm near you my skin aches to touch yours, my ears search for your voice, and my—body loses every modicum of control over its impulses. I forget that I am immortal. That you are a delicate female. I could very easily hurt you, and that is why you must go. Now."

Don't look down. Don't look down. Don't look down...

Aerin glanced down and then gasped at the barrel of his arousal pressed against the thin trousers he'd tucked into knee-length riding boots. She shouldn't have done that. Though he was cursed to be Pestilence and Famine, he was certainly blessed in the dick department. More than blessed. That thing was a fucking miracle. The eighth wonder of the world.

Her whole life, she'd never had to ask for sex, never had to do much more than crook a finger and bring a man running. But what Julian Roarke had in his pants had her contemplating begging, or whatever else she had to do on her knees, to get at it.

At him.

"It's a risk I'm willing to take," she breathed, reaching down and running her fingertips vertically against the skin that met his belt. "You know, for science."

Though his hands were graceful, they felt like iron manacles as he gripped her wrists. "I can't."

"Oh, but you must," she purred, lifting herself on her tiptoes, pressing hot lips to his flushed collarbone. "I could teach you how."

This time, he thrust her away violently, causing her to almost lose her balance. "No," he grit from between his clenched teeth, the clouds in his eyes adding a flash of anger. "I'm taking you home."

"Why are you afraid of me?" she demanded.

"It is you who should fear me."

Planting her fists on her hips, Aerin marched right back up to him, not breaking eye contact, though his warning was clear. "Well I don't, so get over yourself."

He was the one who backed down glancing away and reaching for the reins of his docile horse. "You don't understand."

"On that, at least, we agree," she spat. "I want you. You obviously want me. So what the hell is your problem?"

Julian reached his hand out and surprised her by waving it to encompass their romantic surroundings rather than touch her. "This isn't reality," he murmured with a voice full of regret. "When next we meet, it will be as adversaries rather than allies. We Horsemen are determined to put a stop to this, to kill if need be." Slowly he reached for her, feathering gentle fingers across her lips. "I couldn't make love to you only to betray you."

A chill kissed the heat coursing through her as reality permeated the pall of lust clouding her judgment. She hadn't chosen to be one of the women prophesied to bring about the Apocalypse. It wasn't her bloody fault.

The unfairness of it all choked her, cooling the rest of her ardor.

"I don't believe in fate," she bit out at him. "None of us want to bring about the end of the world. And so we won't. Why not work together?"

He caressed her jaw, causing ripples of goose bumps to erupt on her skin, then slowly moved down the column of her neck, and over the thin, sensitive skin of her clavicles. "I truly believe that you mean those words. But the Fates are cruel, and the only way we Horsemen can fight them, is to stop you." He paused, his eyes swimming with regret. "For good." With that, he seized her around the waist and tossed her onto his giant black horse.

Steadying herself on the pommel, Aerin glared down at him.

"There is another way, you know. You could kill yourselves, instead."

"Don't you think we've tried that?" he asked sadly, capturing her hand in his. "Don't you think that if there was any other way, we'd take that route instead? I wish we'd met in any other time. That I could have taken you to see the sands of the Coliseum. That we could have climbed the pyramids or swam naked in the Mediterranean. I would have made love to you in fields of Scottish heather. I would have fed you grapes from

French vineyards. In a perfect world, we could have explored the fjords of the north on a Viking barge, or ridden the moors of the Druid homelands on the back of Archimedes, my stallion, when the air was fragrant and unpolluted."

Aerin let his sadness mingle with hers until she felt like it might be the poison that did her in. "Well, you know what they say," she sighed gustily. "If wishes were horses..."

"Then beggars would ride," he finished, slipping the reins into her hand and shocking her by slapping his big stallion on the rump and sending them speeding into the woods, back in the direction of Tierra's car.

⚜

AFTER A BIT OF GROUND-KISSING ONCE SHE SLID FROM the horse's back, Aerin tottered to the car and pointed it in the direction of the Maison de Moray. She evaded her feelings by calling Sandra and getting an update on how the meeting with Masashi went and returning a few business voicemails. Since Port Townsend was a relatively small town, she was in the driveway of the mansion before she was ready to be.

She stood at the foot of the long stone staircase that led to the porch with ornate, hand-carved porch railings that reminded her of Victorian lace. The windows glowed with golden light, not that glaring white of energy-saver bulbs, but of the specialty kind that went in Tiffany lamps.

She had family in there. Sisters.

Do you believe in them? Julian had asked.

Aerin sighed, running her hands through the hair he'd taken down as she seriously considered the question. The answer was, not really. Not any more than they could believe in her. That needed to change. If they were going to work together, to figure this mess out, they needed to start trusting each other.

Or, at least, getting along.

Baby steps, she told herself as she climbed the stairs and followed the wrap-around porch to the side entry that went to the kitchen rather than go in the front. Suddenly, she was starving.

A pair of bare, unmanicured feet propped up on the round, antique table that was tucked into the breakfast nook stopped Aerin dead in her tracks. Those feet were attached to long legs, covered only by the customary pair of cutoffs.

Moira.

Okay, so idealistically not the first sister she'd hoped to encounter but, as Sandra would always say, Whadayado?

Closing the door behind her, Aerin hung her purse on an antique coat stand and carefully made her way across the creaky kitchen floor toward Moira. Two old-fashioned gas lamps cast her shimmering auburn hair with a halo of precious metals and caused her porcelain skin to glow with an ethereal beauty. Clinking ice cubes danced at the rim of a tumbler of thick, caramel liquid grasped in her hand. An amber bottle stood at attention on the table in front of her, its label obscured in shadow.

"Hey," Aerin began, rather eloquently in her opinion.

Moira eyed her like one would an approaching honey badger. "Hey," she echoed.

Okay, things were going well thus far... kinda. "So, I owe you... an... apology," Aerin said haltingly. Whew. She'd never said that before. Apologies were tougher than they seemed.

Moira snorted, then shrugged. "I don't want to be owed nothing by nobody. Least of all you. So let's just forget it."

"I'd like that." Aerin breathed in relief. "What are you drinking?"

Moira turned the bottle around, revealing Celtic lettering. "Irish whiskey, old enough to buy isself a drink."

Aerin smirked. "I would have pegged you for a bourbon girl."

Moira's half smile eerily mirrored her own. "Which goes to show you know fuck all about me."

Carefully, Aerin reached for one of the three remaining chairs tucked into the table. "I'd like to," she admitted. "Know more about you, I mean."

"All right, then." Moira reached behind her and grabbed another tumbler from the hutch nestled between two bay windows, poured a healthy splash, and slid it across the table where Aerin caught it. "Have yourself a seat."

Aerin lowered herself into the chair and took a sip of the whiskey, letting the fire kiss her parched throat and warm its way down to her belly. "Moira, you have excellent taste," she said with a satisfied sigh.

"And you're a filthy liar."

"Well... in whiskey, anyway," Aerin amended, sharing a smile with her sister that did more to warm her insides than the liquor. "Maybe you're not such a hillbilly."

"You bet your britches, I am," Moira argued with a wink. "And you're still an uppity, mouthy Yankee bitch who's too smart for her own good. But that don't mean we can't be sisters."

"I'll drink to that," Aerin laughed, and they reached across the table to clink their glasses together.

"Me too," Claire said from the doorway. Dressed in form-fitting red tank and short black sleep shorts, she padded into the kitchen and went straight for the fridge. "Pour me something, I'm going to get some soda to mix it with and see what there is to eat. Anyone hungry?"

"Starving," Aerin said.

"I could eat the tits off a warthog," Moira piped in. "But I don't take to you mixin' this precious whiskey with a coke. That's some kind of sacrilege."

"Yeah," Aerin agreed, pulling the bottle into her body as though to protect it.

Clare shrugged, taking some interesting cheeses from the fridge and an artisanal loaf of bread from the breadbox. "We're witches," she reminded them as she joined them with the fare at the table. "Sacrilege is sort of what we do."

"Valid point." Aerin smiled, pushing the whiskey in her direction, and reaching for the bread. "Can I ask you guys something?" she ventured.

The other two gave identical nods that almost had her forgetting her question. "Um, do you remember anything about... about when you were little? Like... babies?"

"You mean like when Uncle Earl got his pecker stuck inside the Shopvac?" Moira offered. "Damn near twenty-five years ago, and I still remember that day. Not that anyone lets him forget it. They used their beer money to buy a new Shopvac that week on account as they didn't want to use one that'd been sodomized. Weren't right with the Lord, Uncle Sal said." Moira chuckled at the memory, taking another drink.

Aerin closed her eyes, deciding to approach things a different way. "I have these dreams," she began, staring down into her glass to evade the eyes of others. "I'm falling from the top of a building. The air is cold, and I'm so small, falling so fast it's hard to breathe. But then —I'm not falling anymore. I'm sort of... floating." She finally summoned the courage to look up, and no one was looking at her like she was crazy, so she said the word she'd been afraid of all these years. "Flying, maybe. That's when I wake up and it feels like I fall back into bed."

"You do." Moira nodded. "We all seen it."

"Strange thing is... I was taken to a hospital in New York by a homeless man as an infant, and he claimed that it was raining babies and he scooped me off the pavement. But I didn't have a scratch on me."

"I was saved from a fire once," Claire said after a long drink of her whiskey and soda. "They said I should have died, and I didn't even smell like smoke."

Their eyes met and held as Moira piped in. "I was fished out of the bayou by four of the sweetest drunks you'd ever meet. They said it seemed like I'd been in there a while. Like maybe days."

"Air, fire, and water," Claire whispered. "Interesting."

"Sounds like someone was trying to get rid of us early on," Aerin said, contemplating the shocking circumstances. "But who would try to kill babies, and in such horrific ways?"

Moira put her feet down and leaned forward intently. "Who's been threatening us lately? Trying to take business from Tierra? Kidnapping Claire, and making you sicker'n a dog?"

We Horsemen are determined to put a stop to this, to kill if need be, Julian had said.

"You're right. It could have been the Horsemen," Aerin agreed. Which meant that they weren't merely adversaries, they were truly enemies.

A sniff sounded from the doorway, and they all turned to see Tierra holding the Grimoire open, her eyes red-rimmed and watery. "You're never going to believe what I found," she said, her voice husky with tears. "It's a letter from our mother... written right before she was murdered."

❦ 37 ❦

"I don't want to read it," Aerin said, taking a gulp of her liquor. "I'm not ready."

"Me neither." Moira mirrored her action with a gulp and then refilled both their glasses.

"We should probably be sober when we do," Claire agreed. "Paraphrase?"

Tierra's skirt swept the floor as she made her way to join them, setting the book gingerly in the middle of the table. "Basically it says she knew someone was after her the moment she realized that she was pregnant with quadruplets. She was afraid that she'd be dead before she had a chance to raise us. Even though she was aware of the prophecy, she couldn't bring herself to terminate the pregnancy, and she felt that we were supposed to live, but knew that we would be separated. So she hid the Grimoire with magic so that it only appeared when we, four, were together in this house so we could use it to save ourselves."

To Aerin's dismay, she found she didn't have to be reading the words for them to affect her. Tears burned in her throat and misted her vision and she blinked rapidly to stop their fall. All her life, she assumed she'd been tossed away like someone's trash. But no, she'd been wanted.

And that changed everything.

"It says here that she didn't believe that we would end the world, at least not with fire and brimstone," Tierra continued. "Then she tells us that she knows everything we're going through as witches. The isolation, the pain, the power, the temptations, and the need for... ew." Tierra made a very girlish face of disgust.

"Ew, what?" Claire demanded, her voice a little suspiciously thicker than before.

"The need for... sex," Tierra whispered that last word as though it was a curse.

Aerin busted up laughing, joined by Moira and Claire.

"I guess it makes sense," Claire postulated thoughtfully. "We all do take power or healing from passion, or emotion, and those are the major things needed for good sex."

"Some of us give power and healing that way, too," Moira reminded them.

"I'm no saint." Aerin raised her glass, beginning to really feel the effects of the whiskey. "But no matter how busy, stressed, or angry I am, I still crave the "D," know what I'm saying?"

"I sure do!" Claire giggled. "Who do you think out of the four of us has slept with the most men?"

They all turned to Aerin, who didn't know whether to be flattered or insulted.

"You have the dirtiest mouth," Tierra accused with a laugh. "And the dirtiest mind."

"Don't look at me." Aerin held up her hands. "I pick a pony to ride and keep him in the stable for a while. You know how it is, takes too long to train them right. You two are the queens of the one-night stand." She gestured to Moira and Claire, who looked at each other with mischief in their eyes.

"We'll go on three," Claire suggested. "Just blurt out the number."

"M'kay," Moira agreed with a sloppy smile.

"There's a number?" Tierra asked, her green eyes wide with astonishment. "Like, you keep count?"

"You don't?" Moira asked.

Aerin slapped the table and pointed at Tierra. "Oh my God!" she exclaimed with a loud laugh. "You don't even have a number? As in you've lost count?"

"Damn girl." Claire nudged her. "Respect."

Moira stood, wavering a little and speared Tierra with a withering look. "You're tellin' me that you've been lecturing me all this time about respecting myself while you've been humping like a two-peckered jackrabbit?

"No." Tierra held her hands up, as though to defend herself, her voice raising a few octaves to a defensive squeak. "You guys! I don't even... There's not a number... It's just..."

"Oh shit!" Aerin interrupted again. "It's worse than we thought!" "How do you get worse than that?" Claire asked.

"She's a virgin!"

"Shut up!" Tierra turned as red as Claire's tank top and hid her embarrassed laughter in her hands as they all erupted into peals of jibes and hilarity.

Still laughing, Moira reached for the bread knife, and sliced into the loaf. She squeaked as it flew out of her hand and embedded itself into the floor, sticking straight up, vibrating with an oddly ominous thwang.

"What happened?" Aerin asked. "Did you cut yourself?"

Moira shook her head, her eyes wide, and held up both hands for inspection. "No, it just... did that."

"Oh man," Tierra whined. "It never ends, does it?" Sighing, she reached over the table and grabbed the salt, throwing it onto a candle flame and then over her left shoulder.

"Want to clue us in?" Aerin prompted.

"Did you know that in medieval Europe it was always considered rude to bring a knife to the table? That's why they broke bread with their hands, instead of cutting it."

"So?" Claire asked.

"It's because, if your knife falls from the table and skewers the floor, it is an omen that means your enemies will invade your land." Tierra jerked the knife from the floorboards and tossed it in the sink.

A pregnant pause was permeated only by the sounds of the house settling in for the night.

"We've certainly made a few enemies lately," Claire sighed.

"What was her name?" Moira's quiet, serious voice cut through the building tension with a jarring change of subject.

"What?" Tierra asked.

"Our mother..." She gestured to the book. "What was her name?"

They all regarded the neat, feminine script on the paper as though it contained the answers to the mysteries of the universe.

"Mirelle," Tierra answered. "Mirelle de Moray."

"Welp." Moira visibly gathered herself before reaching out and sliding the book toward her. "I guess we should do what she says, and figure out just how in the Sam Hill we're going to survive this. Because, in case you ain't noticed, we have three incredibly powerful men out to steal our powers or take our lives."

"Not to mention a coven of local witches," Claire added.

It was enough to sober them all and steal the warm glow their laughter had lent the kitchen.

"I'll make coffee." Tierra began to bang open cupboards and bustle about. "It's going to be a long night."

"There is no time for that." Another voice, frail and female, joined them, and Aerin glanced up at the two foreign women standing in the kitchen doorway. One a slim, brassy blonde with penciled in eyebrows that gave her expression a permanent sardonic cast, and the other a wizened redhead. Like them. Eerily similar to them, actually. Lines of age branched from skin that must have once been as smooth and creamy as theirs were now. Shrewd green eyes offset thinning auburn hair streaked with silver.

The infamous Aunt Justine, perhaps? It almost seemed like Claire's words conjured them out of the night.

Aerin didn't like the fanatical vibrations emanating from the older woman, but what bothered her even more, was the maniacal, calculating disdain she read from the blonde.

"They're coming for you." The matron's ominous warning held a hint of morbid anticipation. "The Horsemen are on their way, and they're out for blood."

"What is she doing here?" Moira growled. "You have a lot of nerve showing your face."

"We have time, Aunt Justine," Tierra said, setting the kettle on and measuring coffee into a French press. "This house is warded against all enemies. You helped me cast them, yourself. As long as we're here, we're safe. Just no one leave until we figure out just what our next step is."

"Except for ya'll." Moira stood and advanced on the older woman, a combination of hurt and wrath swimming in her eyes. "You can git. You're no longer welcome in this house. And take that wannabe Barbie witch with you."

"This has been my home longer than you've been alive." Justine's eyes fell on the book and her emotions became so garbled, Aerin had to keep herself from squirming. "I—we came to make amends for the actions of our coven. We acted hastily out of fear and we may have been—misguided."

"Misguided?" Moira spat the word like she would a foul taste. "You tried to kill me you old, harpy bitch. Misguided don't even begin to cover it. I've heard better apologies from a whore on Sunday Morning."

The blonde stepped forward, putting a hand on Justine's thin shoulder. "In our defense, we thought at the time that we were trying to save humanity from the Apocalypse. Now we're looking for another way...one that doesn't end with more de Moray casualties."

Aerin stood. She may be new at this, but she could read something not altogether honest in the other witch's emotional signature. "And just who the fuck are you?" she demanded. "And why did no one tell me that our aunt tried to kill Moira?"

"It sort of never came up," Tierra said, as though the fact also surprised her.

Aerin kind of understood that, she wasn't at the top of the list of dangerous people after them at the moment.

"My name is Gwen," the blonde was saying. "I'm High Priestess of the Olympic Coven of Thirteen."

"Well ain't you just the tomcat's batter sack." Visibly shaking with anger at this point, Moira made what looked like a weird southern insult with her finger. "And then get the fuck out. Both of you." Clouds began to gather over the calm waters of the bay, blocking the light from the moon.

"Moira, calm down," Tierra murmured. "Last thing we need is a storm right now."

"No, I think she's right." Claire stood and moved next to Moira in a show of solidarity. "They should leave."

"I agree." Aerin crossed her arms and narrowed her eyes. "Didn't the knife thing just predict that enemies would cross our threshold?" God, she couldn't believe she'd just said that.

"A knife fell from the table to the floor?" Justine's

eyes widened as she turned to Tierra, who'd frozen with the kettle in her hand, her eyes bouncing from her aunt to her sisters with indecision.

"Yes." Tierra nodded.

"Then the Horsemen are closer than we thought." Instead of retreating she went to Tierra, searching for the only friend she might have left in her family. "I know I made mistakes, immense ones, but you have to believe me, Tierra, my heart is in the right place, and we came to warn you. To help you."

"That makes about as much sense as a shoeshine in a shit storm," Moira said, clearly unconvinced.

Tierra brought the coffee to the table, biting her lip, conflict heavy on her features.

Gwen stepped forward. "Would I have been able to get past your wards if we meant you harm?"

Aerin only had a second to wonder how the Priestess knew that detail before the splintering of wood and breaking of glass shattered the two windows flanking the table, as chaos and violence erupted.

$$\text{❈ 38 ❈}$$

Two powerhouse men unfurled from the glittering shards of glass, landing on their feet, braced for battle before the remains of the window finished hitting the floor. The one next to Moira was empty-handed and swarthy, clad in black jeans and a tight t-shirt the color of blood. The other, a lighter specter of the first, had eyes and hair more the color of an amber whiskey than the black stout of his companion. The moment he landed, his strong arm reached over his head and produced a bow from an invisible quiver, and an arrow appeared between his fingers as he pulled back the string and trained it on Claire.

Neat trick, conceded the only part of Aerin's brain that wasn't freaking the fuck out. A rather polite knock sounded on the kitchen door, and she whirled to see Julian push it open, ripping the deadbolt through the wood as though it were nothing.

"What the fuck, Julian?" Aerin demanded, trying not to let the regret pooling in his eyes calm the waves of betrayal and anger building within her.

"I warned you we'd be coming," he murmured.

"I didn't know you meant like—right now!" Aerin bitched. He looked so different than the man she'd spent the afternoon with. This was the gentleman she'd met at the airport, calm, cultured, suited, and hiding a cold heart and lethal intent behind a veneer of manners and platitudes.

"I'm taking back what's mine." The red-shirted brute held his hand out and said something in a language that sounded harsh yet lyrical, Gaelic maybe?

From the floor above, a crash then a drag, muffled by heavy rugs and heavier floors, preceded a flash as a blur of silver raced past them all. He caught the heavy sword with one hand as though the monstrous weapon weighed nothing. Then turned and flashed dark eyes at Claire, his features tightening into a sinister smile of victory as he raised the sword above Moira. "Only one of you has to die," he said. "If you cooperate, we'll even let you pick who."

"I vote for that one," Justine crowed, pointing a shaking finger at Moira.

"Don't you touch her," Claire and the man with the bow said in unison. Stunned, Claire looked behind her at the arrow trained at her back.

"No one's going to die today." Tierra held up her hands. "Let's all calm down."

"If you kill Moira, then I skewer your fire witch," The man who Aerin assumed by process of elimination was Nick Kingswood threatened Dru—War—of all people.

"Hey," Claire piped indignantly. "I'm no one's fire witch. I don't even like Dru, he took something from me, and I only returned the favor."

"Orgasms don't count." Dru's silken, dark voice held a note of seduction that didn't fit with the moment.

Claire blanched, then turned red. "Don't you dare tease me when you're here to kill my sisters, you arrogant douche bag."

Aerin had not yet taken her eyes off of Julian, as his presence washed over her like silk flowing in a breeze. Insubstantial, sensual, and yet strong. "You have the sword back," she reasoned. "You all can go without anyone getting hurt."

"We have to end this." Julian's shrewd gaze touched everyone behind her, finally landing on Tierra.

Aerin didn't have time to consider if he sent the appeal to her or to some archaic God because he leapt like a great cat across the island with the sink and stove toward Tierra, his boot crashing into the faucet and ripping it off in his haste.

Water spouted from the sink, but didn't slow him, and as Aerin watched in horrified fascination, she caught simultaneous actions in her periphery.

Dru's sword arced toward Moira's neck.

Nick separated his fingers, freeing the arrow to find its mark in Claire's warm heart.

Justine and Gwen both dove for the ancient book still lying open on the table.

The dynamic instantly became clear. The men couldn't bear to kill their mark for one reason or another. Dru wouldn't harm Claire, Nick couldn't bring himself to kill Moira, and Aerin was immune to Julian's lethal touch.

So he was reaching for Tierra with those deadly fingers of his.

The numb weightlessness that had terrified her for her entire life settled in her limbs and rushed to her core through veins coursing with power and oxygen. It had been more than twenty-four hours since she'd had the chance to suppress it with her cigarettes; reducing the oxygen she had available in her body. She knew now what it was that coursed through her, and exactly what she could do with it.

Magic.

They'd said only one of the witches had to die, but in less than a second, all three of her sisters were in danger of losing their lives.

And Aerin would be left alone in the world.

Again.

"No!" she screamed as she flung her power out of her body in a great circular gust of wind. Everyone lifted off their feet, thrown to their backs as every window in the entire house blew out with a deafening explosion.

The arrow embedded in the window frame with a loud 'thwang,' missing Claire by narrow inches, blown off course by the blast of wind.

It was Moira who recovered first. She reached her hand out toward the fountain, now gushing from the sink and made a fist.

The water congealed into an identical replica of Moira's clenched fist, only twenty times as large, that raced toward Dru with the speed and force of a tidal wave.

The impact sent him flying out the window from which he'd entered.

"Tell me you still have a lighter," Claire called to Aerin over her shoulder.

Aerin fished it out of her pocket and tossed it to Claire who, in one fluid movement, caught it, lit it, and blew an inferno toward Nick, who immediately went up in flames like a tinder box.

To his credit, he leapt out the window and dropped to the soggy ground, rolling his now charred body in the water that pooled beneath Dru's coughing form. By the time he finished his clothes had become nothing more than soot clinging to his severe burns.

They whirled on Julian, who'd gained his feet and was again attempting to reach for Tierra. "Forgive me, Aerin," he said as he lurched forward.

"Forgive this, asshole!" Tierra cried as the ground shook. They all staggered as vines, roots and plants erupted from the cracks of the hardwood beneath the kitchen floor and snaked up Julian's body, lifting him, and hurling him outside, farther than the other two, skewering his torso on the dangerous spikes of the wrought iron gate.

Aerin gasped in alarm, a part of her own chest tearing at the thought of him dead, another part of her knowing that they all did what they must to protect each other.

"Is everyone okay?" Tierra asked as the vines and roots withered and retreated back into their hole in the earth.

"Just glad to still have my head attached to my neck," Moira sighed as she picked up a chair and uselessly tucked it beneath the table, a drop in the bucket of the chaos surrounding them.

Aerin panted, still too shaky to form words as she watched the man to whom she'd given his first kiss groan a bit as he lifted himself from where he'd been impaled in their front yard.

Thank like—whoever—they had trees to hide this from their neighbors. Though the explosion of glass might bring the Police Department any moment now.

Dru also picked his soggy ass up from the ground, his wet shirt and pants sticking to his tantalizingly powerful body as he reached for his barbecued brother.

"We're immortals," Dru informed them as though talking to idiot children.

"You can't stop us," Nick threatened through cracked, blackened lips, retrieving his bow and threading it.

"You can only delay the inevitable." A wet, sickening sound heralded through the night as Julian pulled himself free of the fence and walked between the other two Horsemen.

The men advanced, all semblance of reluctance erased and replaced by pure, lethal intent.

Tierra, still standing closest to Aerin, grabbed her hand and reached out to the other two.

"By the power of four, you may harm us no more,"

she chanted, squeezing Aerin's hand tightly, prompting her to join in.

"By the power of four, you may harm us no more." Aerin whispered along with her, feeling utterly foolish even as her words gathered momentum and volume.

Claire joined in, her voice clear and strong, as she latched onto Tierra's other hand.

Moira lunged for Aerin, her accent lending a lyrical sound to the chant as their powers and voices melded.

> *By the power of four, you may harm us no more.*
> *By the power of four, you may harm us no more.*

Their magic surged, each of them feeling how the other fed and also tempered her.

Fire devoured oxygen to burn, destroyed organic life, and evaporated water.

Earth and all of her sentient life fed on oxygen, smothered fire with dirt, and drank of the water.

Air directed or extinguished a flame, tossed the sand about, and comprised two parts of the molecular structure of water.

Water covered the earth, drowned the fire, and tangled with air, always a part of it.

They needed each other. Balanced the seasons. Were essential to life.

And they would find their way through this. Together.

Love spread along with their combined magic, creating a dome of elemental protection that extended to encompass the kitchen, then the house.

Nick's arrows bounced off of it. Dru's sword failed to puncture it. And all the men were physically repelled backward by its strength, until they stood in the streets gawking like awe-struck victims of war, bloodied, burned, and cast aside.

A flash of lightning forked through the night,

touching down at Julian's feet, but leaving him unscathed.

When the light receded, a set of scales, like the ones held by the Lady of Justice sat at his feet. These were about two feet tall and looked to be made of the purest gold.

He studied it for a moment, they all did, knowing the truth of his words before he skewered Aerin with a hard gaze and spoke them. "The Third Seal has been broken."

"And the fault is yours," Aerin volleyed. "You forced us to protect ourselves."

"We'll return for blood," Dru promised, fading into the darkness.

"Practice your pleas for mercy," Nick threatened, following his brother into the night.

Julian stood at the edge of the dome, as the colors faded, but the magic and protection remained. He looked dejected, conflicted, and still resolved. "Sweet dreams, ladies," he murmured, bending down to retrieve his scales. "Until we meet again."

🕸 39 🕸

To Aerin's surprise, she found herself reluctant to release her sisters' hands, wondering if the protection would fade once they separated.

"We did it," Tierra breathed, though whether it was a breath of victory or defeat, Aerin couldn't tell. "We cast together, and this protection spell is so strong. Can you feel it?"

"We broke the Third Seal, didn't we?" Aerin asked, staring into the shadows that moments ago had swallowed the regal form of Julian Roarke.

"Yeah…" Claire let go and crunched over broken glass toward the table. "Maybe we should stop doing that. It really doesn't lend much credibility to our claim that we don't want to bring about the Apocalypse."

"We wouldn't have had to cast magic together if those sons of bitches hadn't forced us to protect ourselves." Moira pointed out before turning toward the two witches still on the floor where they had been thrown by Aerin's blast. "Like we were saying before, time for you to scat."

Tierra also picked her way through the carnage that had once been a charming kitchen and reached down to help her elderly aunt back to her feet. "Hold on," she argued. "I know that things are tense right now, but Justine is our aunt. The only family we have left. And she's also a witch. Don't you think we should try to stick together for both reasons?"

"Is everyone forgetting she tried to kill us?" Moira put her hand on a thrust out hip, abjuring her aunt.

"Every family has its problems." Tierra patted her aunt on the shoulder. "She was trying to stop the Apocalypse. Plus she said she was sorry."

"We are both terribly sorry." Gwen stepped forward after pulling herself up from the floor. She addressed the sisters, but her gaze never left the Grimoire, which lay open where they'd left it, as though waiting for the chaos to pass so they could get back to business.

"No one asked you." Aerin wobbled a little on her stiletto heels, but crunched over to the table to snatch up the book, glaring at Gwen in mistrust. "This is a family discussion."

"A coven is a sort of family," Gwen argued, tossing her blonde hair over her shoulder. "And Justine has been a part of this one since before my time." She addressed the rest of the room. "And so was your mother."

"Your mother would have wanted me to help you." Justine grabbed onto the subject of their mother with both hands. "Mirelle was my only sister."

"I don't mean to fixate on this insignificant detail, but our mother probably wouldn't have wanted you to try to kill us," Moira bit out.

"That is a good point," Claire conceded. "I don't think we should trust her."

"I'm not asking for your trust." Justine stepped forward. "I'm just begging for a chance. All I can give you is a promise that I'll never make another attempt on your life. And our coven will do what we can to help you. To prove ourselves."

Aerin cast a look at her sisters, who in turn sent silent messages to her and each other. They'd discuss Justine and the coven later, as a family.

"I sort of owe you some windows." Aerin toed the glass sparkling in the moonlight.

Tierra laughed. "I'm sending Nick Kingswood the bill."

"Bastard deserves it," Moira muttered.

"And you owe me nothing." Tierra put her arm around Aerin's waist. "You owe the windows to yourself, to all of us, because this house belongs to the four of us. And that's what our mother would have wanted."

Aerin had to struggle to breathe through a band tightening her ribs and pressing against her lungs. "I don't care what the prophecy says," she admitted through a hoarse throat. "I don't believe in fate. I don't believe in destiny. And I don't believe that being together behind this gate is wrong, because we are family, and we belong here."

Even as she said it, a doubt lingered in the dark places of her mind. What if finding her sisters meant destroying the rest of the world?

❧

"Is it done?" Killian Bane's dark voice crunched like the gravel beneath his favorite pale Chimera custom motorcycle. "I felt... something."

Julian sat back in his favorite library chair, his fingers wrapped around his glass of Glenmorangie as though it could save him. "You felt the Third Seal break," he groaned, staring at the scales displayed on a marble stand. They looked too small to hold the world in balance, but that they did, and always had.

A slew of curses both ancient and modern blasted through the phone line, and Julian held the receiver away from his ear.

"We need you, Killian. These de Moray women are stronger than we anticipated. We'll need all four of us if we are to defeat them."

A deafening silence screamed the Fourth Horsemen's displeasure. "The plan was to kill one of them before they all found each other," he finally said.

"I am aware of the plan," Julian said through clenched teeth. "But I think you'll understand the difficulties we faced once you get here and face them yourself."

Taking another sip, Julian ran his finger over the seam of his own lips, remembering the moist softness of his first and only kiss. She been such a hard woman, the tenderness had been so fully unexpected.

He recalled a conversation with a certain philosopher almost two thousand years ago. The man had been in his cups at the time, but he said that he'd stumbled upon the greatest secret to a successful offense or defense known to civilization. The heart and the mind. Win the hearts and minds of your allies...or your enemies, and you will have won the battle. Or the war.

Never had Plato's words been so indisputable than this moment. Because one feisty air witch had begun to wedge herself into his heart, and she dominated his thoughts as though he were an untried pubescent boy.

"What happened, Julian? I've known you for an eternity. In all that time, you've slaughtered more people, women and children included, than Nick and Dru. Combined." Killian obviously tried, and failed, to keep the irritation out of his voice. "All you had to do was touch one of them, and our problem would be solved without spilling a drop of blood."

"I did touch one of them." That had been the problem, hadn't it? Touching her skin. Feeling her warmth. Caressing her unspeakably lovely face. "She is immune to me. I couldn't have known it at the time. Killian, listen to me. The weavers of fate conspire against us, they always have. And if we are to defeat our enemies, we need to be four strong, as they are."

"Well, shit," Killian agreed with a weary sound. "I'm on my way."

Julian placed the phone on the stand at his elbow and drained his scotch, reaching out for Nicholas to re-fill the glass with the offered decanter as he studied the fire.

"What did Bane say?" Dru asked.

Taking another sip, Julian closed his eyes and ran his finger over his lip again, a ball of anticipation and dread settling in the void where his heart had once been. Taking a deep breath, he tried not to think of lovely silver eyes and moonlight as he turned to his brothers.

"Death is coming." And Hell would follow.

❧ IV ❧

TIERRA

By Tiffinie Helmer

$\maltese$ 40 $\maltese$

"What the hell are you doing?" Tierra asked, catching Moira in the kitchen straining a pot of boiled angel trumpet blossoms.

Moira poured the mixture into a delicate bone china teacup that was decorated with red and pink roses. She set the teacup next to the matching plate with a soft-boiled egg and buttered toast. "Makin' tea."

"You can't use angel trumpets in tea, not unless you're trying to kill someone."

"You don't say." Moira turned and hollered up the backstairs, "*Aunt Justine, your breakfast is ready.*"

"Oh, no, you don't." Tierra took the tea from Moira and poured it down the drain. Smoke hissed out, and she looked at Moira in alarm.

"What *else* did you put in there?"

"A little bit of Cheeto's spit. Call it an attitude adjustment in case the angel trumpets didn't git 'er done." Moira shrugged as though she'd asked a stupid question. "And I didn't pick enough to kill her— probably— only enough to make Aunt Just-for-now want to leave us be. She ain't the woman you believe she is, Tierra."

"She's family."

"Yeah, and I'm the queen of cream cheese," Moira muttered.

"What's with all the yelling?" Claire demanded. "I thought we were being invaded again."

"More like you hoped we were," Aerin said, entering behind her and stepping gingerly over the broken and scarred wood floors with her sky-high, strappy stilettos. "I know you want Dru's...sword back."

"Like you wouldn't want another killer caress from Julian."

Aerin shrugged. "Touché, sister."

The house was in a bad state after last night. They'd done the best they could with sweeping up broken glass and other debris, and covering windows and doors with sheets and tarps. Surprisingly, the stained-glass transoms had survived along with most of the furniture, but not the windows or door jams. The back door was nothing but splinters. There was a lot of work to do to put the old lady to rights again. Another thing that Tierra had to do today. Besides, keep Moira from killing Aunt Justine.

"Moira, you have to forgive Aunt Justine. She's not the villain you seem to think she is," Tierra said.

"You sure you didn't take an arrow to the head last night or somethin'? You seem to be forgettin' that sour-faced ol' bat tried to off me." She unscrewed a bottle of whiskey and poured a glass.

"This is her house too, and she's back to stay. This house is big enough for all of us and probably half the coven. Aunt Justine knows she was wrong. She's scared and...elderly."

"And double-ugly to boot." Moira took a sip of the amber liquid, showing no more reaction than if it have been apple juice. "Anyhows, you're reaching."

"So what if I am? We're her nieces and we need to look out for her." Tierra took the glass of whiskey from Moira. "And *you* can't have hooch for breakfast."

"First you won't let me make tea for Aunt Justine, and now I can't even make my own breakfast? Quit motherin' me, Tierra. Just because you're the oldest doesn't mean you're the boss of me."

"How do we know she's the oldest?" Aerin asked. "For all we know, any one of us could be the first born. Hell, I'd be more inclined to think she's the baby. After all, she's the only one still a virgin."

Claire snickered along with Aerin. "Good one." She held out her hand for a fist bump.

"Hey," Tierra said.

"Maybe if she got her cherry popped she'd be more laid back," Claire said. "Girl is strung way too tight."

"Ha! Laid back. I get it." Aerin poured some coffee and sat at the table, booting up her laptop. "Tierra, you really need to do something about that."

"Ain't natural," Moira said, joining Aerin with another pilfered glass of whiskey.

"There is nothing wrong with being a virgin," Tierra defended.

"There is at our age," Claire said. "You're missing out on so much of life. I know my powers intensified after losing my virginity." Moira and Aerin nodded in agreement that this had happened to them also.

"Do you even know what your sexual power is?" She had a sexual power?

"Tell me you know your sexual power?" Aerin asked. "You've at least experimented with yourself. Oh my God, you've never masturbated?"

Color flared in her face. She couldn't believe they were talking so blasé about this subject.

"Sugar, we've got to talk," Moira said. "Idle hands are the Devil's workshop, or so Reverend Dupuis always said. That's the very reason I made sure mine were always plenty busy."

"I know, let's kill two birds with one stone," Claire added. "There's more than one thing around here that would benefit from a good hammering."

Moira squealed. "Ooh! We need fix-it men with them sleeveless shirts and big ol' tool...belts."

"I do like a man who knows how to nail things home." Aerin fished out her phone and started scrolling through her contacts. "I know just who to call."

"No, wait. I don't want my house—*our house*— overrun with men."

"You hush," Moira said. "We get enough muscle in here and you'll be spreadin' them legs faster than peach jam at a church picnic."

"That's probably her problem," Aerin said. "Growing up in this house with Aunt Justine and only the freaky coven for friends. Not enough men."

"Hey, that's not fair. I don't—I don't need or want—"

"Oh, you want. We all *want*," Claire interrupted with a snicker. Moira and Aerin joined in with more snide remarks.

"That's enough! I'm going to work. Call whoever you want to fix up the place. Just-just make sure Moira doesn't kill Aunt Justine."

"Hey, I don't need no babysitter." *Says the one drinking for breakfast.*

"Don't worry about anything," Aerin said, dialing her phone. "We've got you covered."

"You can bet your ass, we do." Claire winked.

Oh my hell.

She had to get out of here or she was going to cast a spell. One that shut everyone up. She needed to check the Grimoire and see if such a spell existed. That would be handier than any handyman.

Grabbing her crocheted bag, Tierra hung it cross-ways over her top, and wrapped a cream throw around her shoulders. She pushed the tarp aside in place of the busted door. Contractors—minus the sexy and shirtless —were definitely a good idea.

Outside in the cool air, Tierra decided to walk the

distance to Ambrosia's rather than drive. It was a lovely day, with bees buzzing, birds singing, and nature unfurling all around her in her glory. For once it wasn't raining. It seemed since Moira had shown up, it rained more often, definitely more violently. But the vegetation enjoyed the extra moisture.

Why did she think growing up as an only child was lonely? What she wouldn't give for some alone time now. She loved her sisters, even though she didn't know them that well yet and wasn't sure if she liked them. She still loved them.

What difference did it really make that she was still a virgin? It wasn't like she couldn't have changed her status if she'd wanted to. She'd had plenty of opportunities. She was pretty to look at. There were three mirror images of herself at home, and her sisters were beautiful.

Stunning. Captivating each in their own way.

She wondered which way was hers?

Mother hen, Moira would say. That wasn't necessarily a bad thing, Tierra thought, but it wasn't sexy. She didn't think any of her sisters would use sexy to describe her.

She glanced down at what she wore. Today she'd thrown on a billowing floral chiffon skirt in dusty pinks and purples with a lacy lavender top that looked like it could have been worn by her grandmother, or great-grandmother, maybe even great-great-grandmother.

She'd procured most of her clothing from the chests in the attic, after all. But she liked how roomy and comfortable her clothes were. She had updated her look with goddess sandals and glittery painted toenails, adding an ankle bracelet that gave a soft, musical sound each time she moved.

Maybe she wore too many bracelets? Both wrists had multiple crystal and homemade hemp jewelry. An old Celtic moon hung around her neck and rested between her breasts. She'd found that in the chest in the attic too.

Well, hell she even wore a wrap to ward off the chill. Was she eighty?

Aerin didn't have anything hanging off her. She was so well put together, sleek and sexy like a cat. Men took her seriously.

Claire was similar, except instead of the boardroom power suit she'd preferred more leather that befitted a bar room. Moira never had enough clothes on to have any kind of style, while Tierra maybe wore too many.

All of her sisters seemed to have their fair share of sexual experiences. They were completely confident in who they were as women. Until today, Tierra hadn't doubted her confidence as a sexual being.

Did she put men off?

No, men approached her, just not the right man. There was a big difference. She hadn't been tempted to sleep with anyone because she'd wanted her first time to be special, memorable. Maybe even be forever. She wanted that guy. The one in her romance novels. The one who would kill for her, lay down his life for her, love her for eternity. Epic love that sonnets were written about, not a forgettable one-night-stand.

Do you hear yourself, Tierra? Love like that doesn't exist. This is not Wuthering Heights, it's Port Townsend. Men like Heathcliff or Mr. Darcy are stuff of fiction.

If she could, she'd conjure up a man who was part Mr. Darcy and Heathcliff. Now that would be a man worth sleeping with.

You've really lost it now.

Tierra turned on Water Street. The Puget Sound came into view catching her breath like it always did. She loved living by the ocean. While she didn't love being on it, and certainly never in it, the cycle of the ocean and moods she stirred added so much to the nature that whispered around her. It was beautiful.

So unlike the conversation she'd just left. What was it with the word masturbate? It was such an ugly word. She wasn't naïve, and she understood how her body responded, but she didn't talk about such things.

Did that make her a prude?

Ha, an unapproachable prude. She caught her reflection in the storefront windows. A dumpy, unapproachable, prude.

Oh stop. She looked eclectic. No one wore the same clothes she did.

Well, maybe homeless people.

That's enough.

She had no time for this. There was plenty to worry about with Horsemen trying to kill them, Aunt Justine and Moira trying to kill each other, and supposedly the end of the world drawing near.

Did it really matter what she wore or that she was still a virgin?

She liked her clothes, but hated that she was twenty-six and didn't know how it felt to have a man inside her, giving over a little of his soul when he lost himself inside her.

The magic and power that her sisters spoke of, what would it be like? She wanted to experience that.

So what was she waiting for? It was just a hymen for goddess's sake. She was an earth witch. And if the end of the world was coming, no way in hell was she dying a virgin.

❧ 41 ❧

"Morning, T," Sunny greeted when Tierra entered Ambrosia's. "Glad to see you doing well. Heard there was a wicked storm out your way last night. Everyone okay?"

"Everyone's fine, but the house took some damage. The...girls are taking it upon themselves to make calls."

"You don't sound too happy about that."

"No, it isn't that. Well, partly." She took off the wrap and her purse and hung them up, tying an apron over her clothes. "You have sisters. How do you do it?"

"Do what?"

"Get along?"

"Oh, no, hon, sisters don't get along, they get through. The bickering and name-calling is normal. But there is no one I'd rather have at my back when everything goes to hell, than one of my sisters."

"Hmm, I can see that."

"One of them say or do something that bothered you?"

Tierra had known Sunny Brooks for years. With her pink-dyed dreadlocks, and multi-ear and body piercings, she definitely stood out. Today she had on military boots, with fishnet stockings and a blue-plaid mini skirt secured down the sides with safety pins. A bleeding heart t-shirt with a studded dog collar completed the outfit.

She probably didn't care what she wore. Tierra loved Sunny's confidence. She was a walking contradiction with her kick-your-ass outfit yet, a giving and compassionate nature.

"Tierra, you okay?"

Where did she start? "It was just a really stressful night." And morning.

Hell, a bunch of stressful months since Moira first answered the spell she'd cast. Guess there was something to that saying about being careful what you wished for.

Tierra glanced around the teashop. There were a few people at the corner tables and more sitting outside in the garden area, but for all practical purposes she and Sunny were alone. No one was paying them any mind.

"So what's really up?" Sunny asked. "It's not that douchebag Nicholas something-er-other still trying to evict us, is it?"

"No, Aerin sicced her lawyers on him and has him tied up in mountains of paperwork." She motioned that irritating problem away with a wave of her hand. "I need to have sex."

"Don't we all."

Tierra leaned in. "No, I mean, I *need* to have sex. Like for the first time."

"*You're shitting me,*" Sunny whispered. "You mean, you've never...yeah, wait. I actually kinda get that."

"What?"

"Makes a lot of sense, now that I think about it. You've been holding out for Mr. Right haven't you? You're too much of a romantic not to. So why are you not holding out any longer?"

"Curiosity?"

"But you can't give it away to just anyone."

"Not just anyone. He has to be hot." Her hand flew

up to cover her mouth. "Does that make me sound shallow?"

"If you are looking to lose your virginity with a one-time-wham-bam-thank-you-ma'am, you don't go for personality."

"That sounds so...impersonal."

"It can be. Sex can be many things, but one thing you have to know—"

Just then a customer came up and ordered a double latte. Tierra waited impatiently for Sunny to be free to finish.

"What's the one thing I have to know?" she asked as soon as the customer was happily on his way.

"About what?"

"About sex," she whispered.

"Right. So, your first time—"

Another customer entered and stole Sunny away from her again.

You've got to be kidding me. Were the goddesses having a laugh at her expense today or what?

To keep herself from demanding that Sunny answer her question, regardless of the customers who would overhear, Tierra busied herself by making a relaxing brew. If she were going to do this, she would need some help in loosening up. She refused to think of it in the terms Moira has so artlessly used.

"Okay," Sunny said after ringing up the order and wishing the couple a good day. "The first time you have sex, it's dissatisfying nine times out of ten."

"Oh, well, that's...

"Disappointing," they both said together, sharing a laugh.

"The key is to lower your expectations. Go in knowing it's going to suck. Oh, and don't do that the first time."

"Do what?"

"Suck anything of his."

Tierra choked on the mouthful of tea she'd just swallowed.

"Yeah, see that's exactly what I'm talking about. Swallow or not to swallow." Sunny handed Tierra a napkin to wipe her mouth. "Just don't worry about anything like that the first time. Get full penetration over with and then you can experiment. By the way, what are you drinking? It smells delicious."

Tierra set the tea down. "Lemon balm and catnip to help relax me, but I think I'm going to need something stronger to loosen my inhibitions."

"Got just the place. Go to *Sirens*. You won't be too far from here if you get into trouble and my friend Phoebe works there. Always smart to have people you can count on if the guy turns out to be a serial killer or something. No, don't worry about that. This isn't Seattle. Nothing bad like that happens here.

"*Sirens* is perfect," Sunny continued even though Tierra turned ice cold as the blood drained from her face. "Not only will they serve you something to loosen your inhibitions, but looking like you do, fresh meat and all, you'll find your guy. Just stop and pick up some protection first."

"I have my crystals." She held up her arm with the multiple bracelets wrapped around her wrist trying to take in all that Sunny had just said. "Oh, wait you're not talking this kind of protection...are you? Pregnancy. I knew that."

"There are worse things than getting pregnant. Which one is the gonorrhea crystal?"

"Eww. Okay, good point. So...uh...where do I get the other kind of protection?"

"They're called condoms and every grocery or convenience store carries them. You know, never mind." Sunny headed into the back room and retrieved a purse that looked like a saddlebag. She reached inside and pulled out a square box. "This should do. It has a range of sizes to fit any man."

"Sizes?"

"Oh hon, you'll soon learn, all men basically come down to size."

* 42 *

D*eath walks into a bar...in Port Townsend, Washington. Where's the punchline?*

Killian Bane claimed the table in the shadowy corner, his back to the wall, where he could sit and watch. Not much happening in the bar since it was well before happy hour. He checked the clock over the bar.

He was about four hours ahead of schedule.

Guess I'm the punchline.

He stretched out his long legs, clad in black denim and black leather boots, crossing them at the ankles. A sleepy seaside town with an artistic, hippie bent with a population that had no idea Death had arrived.

He was tired of waiting. So fucking tired. He hoped to God or the Devil or the freaking goddesses—since they were apparently dealing with witches this time— that this was finally the actual Apocalypse.

He was supposed to meet up with his brothers later, but he'd made good time and decided a few drinks— maybe a good lay—would put him in the right frame of mind to deal with the Three Horsemen who'd failed in their duty and now required he step in.

How hard was it to kill one witch? There were four to choose from.

Death was inevitable. Everyone, even these prophesized witches, had an expiration date. Didn't matter who you were or how you lived your life, Death came for you at some point.

The amiable waitress came up to him with a loose-hipped walk that seemed effortless. She was petite, with a Cupid's bow mouth that he could put to work. Blonde ringlets were artfully styled and he enjoyed that she didn't oversell her sexuality. In fact, she played up her goodness which was a facade. Clever. He looked deeper into her soul, and evil shivered over him. When her time came, she was headed to Hell.

Never ceased to amaze him. Now the big bald, tattooed and pierced biker mixing drinks behind the bar looked like he'd just graduated from Demon High with honors, and he was headed to Heaven.

"Welcome to Port Townsend," the waitress greeted. "You must be new to town because I haven't seen you around. My name is Angelica–" *Of course it was.*

"–but you can call me Angel. What might I get you...to drink?" Clearly she was up for more if he'd prefer.

"I'll take a Cardinal Sin."

"Which one?" Her pretense slid off like a stripper flashed with a greenback. "I'm a fan of all seven myself, but looking at you all I can think about is lust."

Yeah, she'd do in a pinch, but he was tired of her flavor of the month. He was in the mood for something different. Someone like... *Her.*

In walked a rose, a blue moon rose to be more exact. He swore he could smell her from here. Dressed in shades of lavender with slate blue hues, she brightened and revived the bar with her very presence. He heard a slight jingling in his ears and knew it came from the Bohemian enchantress. It was like someone had opened a window and let the sun shine into a room that had continued to darken, smothering the life out of it.

She *was* life.

"Excuse me." He stood, not taking his eyes off the vision in vintage clothing, her hands clutching the strap of her purse. "My...*woman* has arrived," he growled, the word woman already staking claim.

He strode toward her, radiating vibrations of possession to every heterosexual male in the vicinity. A man who'd set a trajectory toward her changed direction as Killian approached.

Good call.

She smelled like Heaven, and Killian helplessly inhaled the sweet, spicy scent of roses and lavender into his lungs, his nostrils flaring as her fragrance infused his brain, resulting in an instant high.

His hand clamped down on her arm. "Come with me."

Her wide, green eyes met his and he instinctively gazed into her soul. Where was she headed? Heaven or Hell. Not that he really cared overly much as long as she detoured to his bed first.

But something was different here.

Killian drove deeper...and saw nothing, felt nothing, other than an overwhelming desire to know more about her. That had never happened before. He probed further and still nothing. It was like her life hadn't been written yet. He hardened.

"What?" she asked, her voice husky and seductive.

"You're here for me," he stated.

"I am?" Artfully shaped brows rose in surprise.

"You just don't know it yet."

Her hair was that dark bewitching shade of red that strained to burgundy. Rare and rich and thick with waves, it cascaded down to her back. He had the irresistible urge to twist the length around his arm and carry her off by her hair. It had been a long time since he'd embraced his beast, but with her he wanted to roar, mark, and take. Instead, he pressed his hand to her lower back and guided her toward his table, the strands of her silky hair caressing his forearm. He bit back a groan, and needed to know how it felt to have her hair caress other parts of him.

"Is that like some kind of come-on?" she asked, her bee-stung lips lifted in a challenge.

Oh, you are so on.

"Would you rather I say something boring like, 'Can I buy you a drink?'"

"Actually, yes. I would prefer a drink to the manhandling," she said.

"All right. We'll play it your way." *And then we'll play it mine.* He dropped his hand from the curve of her back and immediately missed the connection.

He held out a chair for her to sit. "What would you like to drink?" There was no question. He was buying this woman a drink, and then later he was going to get lost in her.

"Uhm, wine?" She bit the bottom of her lip and seemed surprised that she'd gathered her skirts and sat in the chair he'd offered.

He wasn't surprised. She emanated heat, a ripeness, yet, there was shyness that rode along with the others, making her even more intriguing.

Slowly he folded his tall length in the seat across from her. "You don't sound sure of what you want." He needed her to know exactly what was happening here. A woman like her didn't enter a bar in the middle of the day unless she needed a man. And while he was that man, and planned to do his best to talk her into seeing things his way, he never took what wasn't his to take.

"I don't drink much," she admitted. "I mainly stick to wines that I make at home. I concoct a lovely rose petal infused wine."

"Rose water?" Did that explain how heavenly she smelled? Did she bathe in it?

"No." She gave him a slight husky laugh that quivered over him like the first brushes of a bow stroking the string of a violin. "A rose petal wine," she continued. "It's very smooth and has this amazing floral finish."

"I'd bet you'd have a fucking amazing floral finish." The words were out of his mouth before he could swallow them.

She blinked, her jeweled-green eyes flashing with a mixture of uncertainty and interest. "You're bad, aren't you?" Suddenly her diffidence was gone.

"So bad." He couldn't keep back the predatory smile. "So very bad that I'll be the best you've ever had."

A breath escaped her in a rush and the interest sparking in her eyes flared to fascination. "Promise?"

His heart slammed in his chest and it was his turn to have the air rush out of his lungs.

The waitress chose that moment to return with the drink he'd already forgotten he'd ordered. "Is there anything else I can get you," she asked, her demeanor much cooler than before.

"The lady will have an Orgasm," Killian said.

"Can I have more than one?"

There she went again. He couldn't take his eyes off this enthralling woman who clenched her cream-colored wrap like a virgin, yet said such provocative things.

"Make that a Screaming Orgasm," he ordered.

The waitress—whatever her name was, he'd forgotten already—left with a flounce of her short skirt.

Leaning across the table, he traced the lacy, scalloped edge of her top with his finger, thrilling at the goose bumps that rose on her creamy skin. "I will give you as many orgasms as you can take."

"I don't want to sound naïve, but what's in a Screaming Orgasm?" she whispered.

"Me."

Her eyes widened. They were the color and clarity of priceless emeralds. She had the eyes reported of Venus, the Roman goddess of love and beauty. He had a moment of indecision. While it was in his nature to be bold, he wondered if he'd taken things too far. "Vodka, Irish cream, and Kahlua."

"I'm not much of a coffee fan, more of a tea drinker." She eyed the drink as it was set down in front of her.

"Try it." The dare was implied by his tone.

"I'm not going to give you my phone number," she blurted out as if needing to create boundaries.

"I didn't ask for it." But by the end of the day, she'd give him everything he would ask of her.

"Well...good." She picked up her cocktail and took a sip, her mouth twisting with distaste. "Yeah, not a fan." She set the drink aside. "I should have gone with a simple wine."

"Trade me."

"What is it?"

"Cardinal Sin." He slid his glass toward her. "Four parts rum, amaretto, triple sec, lime juice, and grenadine."

She bit her lip again, and then something made her pick up his glass. Gingerly she took a sip, her eyes widening in surprise. "This I like."

"It's settled then. I'll take your Screaming Orgasm and you get my Cardinal Sin."

She took another deep draw from his drink.

"You might want to sip that slower," he warned. If wine was her drink, this was going to hit her hard. But it was too late. She drained and set the empty glass down on the table.

"If it's all right with you, I'd like to be taken in the woods." She waved her hand as if to discount her words and explained, "I mean, I enjoy nature, and it's a beautiful afternoon to have...an interlude...outdoors."

She was delightful. "This isn't some Blair Witch Project?" he halfheartedly joked, signaling for the bill.

"What witch?"

"Doesn't matter. Aren't you afraid to be alone with me in the woods? You know nothing about me."

"You know nothing about me," she countered. "It's kind of an even playing field."

And straightforward, which he found stimulating. His blood thickened. "True. We could start with each other's names."

"We could. But wouldn't that make assumptions that this was more than today?"

"You do have a point." There was another level of excited mystery not knowing who she was even though everything inside him begged that he find out. Now. This was the most turned on he'd been in...centuries. If ever.

⁂

TIERRA HADN'T STOPPED TREMBLING WITH SEXUAL excitement from the first moment of his touch. Never had she been more in tune with her own sexuality. Not even on the solstice. He made her feel dangerous and special and beyond desirable. Powerful.

He was not handsome. That was too tame a word for how he looked. More like mesmerizing.

His hair was pitch-dark and she wanted to bury her hands in it like she did the rich soil she cultivated to grow her herbs. It was cut short to avoid the curl that was still present in the thickness. A few days stubble outlined his chiseled jaw, and eyes the color of obsidian seemed to see right into her soul, as if he knew what she wanted, needed.

His snug, black t-shirt outlined the muscles in his upper torso and his dark jeans hugged his trunk-like thighs. There was even a leather jacket hanging off the back of his chair.

He made her...*thirsty*. She licked her lips and the

blackness of his eyes immediately scorched where they landed on her exposed skin.

Tierra shifted in her seat. Everything felt...swollen, wet, and hot. His nostrils flared again like he could smell her mounting desire. It was disconcerting and more of a turn on than she'd ever thought. He looked at her like he needed to know her inside and out. And would. Her clothes rubbed against her skin, making her want to tear them off.

He worried her a little, though. Less, now that she'd downed his drink. Maybe she should order another?

Loosening the wrap from around her shoulders, she thrilled at how his eyes dropped with the fabric. She didn't have on anything revealing, but suddenly she wished she'd worn something cutoff like Moira did. She wanted him to see her naked. Yearned for him to touch her, take her, brand her.

Holy Mother of Earth. What was she thinking? *Brand her, really?* No man branded her. But she knew on some level that he would. She'd never be the same if she slept with him.

She should pick someone else.

That nice businessman who'd caught her eye when she'd first entered *Sirens* would be a better, safer choice.

But not memorable.

Hell, even if she didn't sleep with the dark, mysterious man across from her, she doubted she'd be able to forget him.

"Shall we go?" he growled. He tensed, and her pulse raced.

This was it. Did she want to go through with it?

If she wanted to know what sex was all about, this man dressed in black was the one to initiate her. He'd teach her more in one coupling than she'd learn with a dozen or more men. Might even discover the sexual power that Claire had hung in front of her like a carrot. She already felt more powerful just in his presence.

"Yes," she said before she lost her nerve. She stood up too fast and wavered on her feet.

He was suddenly there to steady her. Tossing cash on the table, he grabbed his leather jacket and steered her out of the bar. "How far is this place in the woods that you spoke of?" His voice rumbled in her ear.

"Not far, but we'll need a vehicle." She didn't even think her feet touched the floor as he ushered her out of the bar and down the stairs to Water Street. They came to a stop at a motorcycle. Pale in color and powerful in size, it had her misgivings rising back to the surface.

"Uh..."

"Come." His voice thickened and went smoky as it slid over her. He held his hand out and without thinking she took it, surprised by the heat radiating off of him.

He straddled the huge motorcycle looking like some avenging god. He adjusted his seat, and she couldn't help but look at his zipper and wonder what lay behind it. What size of condom would he need? She hoped the box burning a hole in her purse had something that could accommodate him.

"Wait! I-I need to do something first." She inched closer, and his nostrils did that flaring thing again. Damn, she liked that reaction. "May I—we—kiss to see..."

"To see if we're compatible? Don't worry, my gazelle, we will be. Here." He took her hand and placed it over his groin. His body shuddered and a curse escaped him. "Tell me how you feel, right now, touching me like this, knowing what you do to me?"

"Ache." She said the first word that popped into her head. "I *ache* for you."

He cursed again. "Hike up your skirt and climb on behind me and I'll take care of that...ache."

Power coursed through her veins, and she slowly

gathered the material of her skirts, showing off enough leg to make her sisters proud. Steadying one hand on his shoulder, she swung a leg over the leather seat and settled in behind him.

"Hold on to me." He groaned when she wrapped her arms tight around him.

"Don't you have a helmet?"

"I don't fear dying. Do you?" He asked the question as if he really wanted to know her answer.

"No, I'm not afraid of death," she breathed. Never really thought about death until recently, with those surprise attacks that had made her think of her own mortality. Which are what landed her here strapping herself to a man she didn't know on a motorcycle that seemed to have a life of its own.

"Let's see if we can change that." He started the engine, and it purred against her already overheated nether region.

"Oh, wow."

He chuckled and the sound rumbled like the beast between her legs. Her inner muscles clenched in response as they took off downtown.

This should scare the crap out of her, but it didn't. If anything she felt more alive than she ever had. She held on to him tighter as they negotiated the streets in town, but once he opened up the horses on the highway, she couldn't stop herself from releasing him and holding her arms out to her sides, her wrap flying behind her as her hair whipped and teased around them both. It was her turn to laugh, the air catching the sound like a song as they thundered down the blacktop.

Sunny had the shop and Moira would show up soon to help. Aerin and Claire had the house under control—as well as Aunt Justine—she hoped. The Horsemen had been quiet, probably still licking their wounds. And she was free, for at least the afternoon. Free to do whatever she wanted. Whoever she wanted. Reality and strategies would return soon enough. Today she was tired of being the responsible one. All her sisters were wild, which meant their mother had to have some of that in her as well, which meant so did Tierra.

Well, she was about to find out.

She directed him where to go—and started referring to him as *The Man* in her head. She had to call him something and *God* didn't seem somehow accurate.

They headed out of town, following Highway 20. Once they'd traveled a short distance into the hills that overlooked Puget Sound, she sent an appeal to the trees that hid a secret path. They were actually quite close to her home, but he didn't know that. The Sitka spruce, western hemlock, and bristlecone pines covertly pulled their branches back to reveal a dirt path. Silently she thanked them as they granted her request for passage.

Tierra pointed and he slowed to take the turn he hadn't noticed before now. About a quarter of a mile up the path ended at a secluded meadow. Wildflowers bloomed in a rebellion of color brighter and more fragrant as they mingled with the salty sea-air wafting up the hillside from the ocean below.

Suddenly she was no longer nervous. This was her element, her special place. The forest surrounding the clearing was old and stately and understood that she wished no harm and protected her as she cast and experimented. This is where she'd summoned her sisters. She jumped off the motorcycle, bent and unbuckled her golden, goddess sandals, tossed them aside, and let her bare feet connect with the earth. She sighed with pleasure.

She'd missed her time here. It had been too long since she'd been in touch with the rich soil, the deep-rooted trees, and flamboyant flowers. She spun around in a lazy circle as the sun shone down and the earth called out in welcome and enfolded her. The flora swayed in greeting, the butterflies and hummingbirds fluttered their wings, and seedlings broke through volcanic soil rejoicing in her presence.

"God, you are beautiful. Like Eve," he said. He reached out and grabbed the ends of her wrap and deliberately pulled her toward him. "All these soft fabrics, I want to—"

"Kiss me now?" she teased, knowing that wasn't what he was going to say.

He dropped the end of the wrap and cupped her face. His palms were warm and calloused against her cheeks. "I'm going to do more than kiss you, my gazelle. So much more." His eyes searched hers, for what she had no clue. Then his mouth—that gloriously carved mouth, which looked hard and merciless yet, wasn't—finally descended on hers.

Everything inside her unfurled like a budding flower, revealing its nectar as it was touched by the sun's shimmering rays. She'd been kissed before, but never like this. Tierra went completely still, doubting that if she'd struggled it would have made a difference. His kiss was the most amazing thing she'd ever felt, experienced.

His lips were confident and questioning, soft and tender, a strange mix for a man so dominant. She'd expected to be kissed, consumed, and then tossed to the ground and set upon. Had kind of hoped for that after the glorious ride on the motorcycle that had her ready and more than willing, but now that they were here, in her special place, she rejoiced in his exploration.

His big fist twisted in her hair and he pulled her head back. "Let me in," he growled against her mouth. Then he groaned deep in his throat as she eagerly parted her lips, and he kissed her deeper than she'd ever been kissed before.

Her wrap was tossed, forgotten to the ground, and his leather jacket followed.

"How does this release?" he asked, tugging at the waistband of her skirt.

"No, don't tear it. The fabric is very fragile...and precious to me." One of the reasons she loved the vintage clothes was because she hoped they'd belonged to one of her family members. Maybe even her mother. She strained to be free of his hold and put her hand up when he tried to pull her back. His eyes were impossibly dark now like a night with no moon, the kind of evening where nightshade bloomed in her witch's garden.

"Take off your clothes," he said. "I don't trust myself not to rip them." His fingers clenched into fists as though he couldn't keep them off her for long.

She took a few more steps back. He held his body barely in check, and all because of her. Because of his desire for her. It calmed her fears of the unknown and increased her excitement for what was to come.

She fumbled with the hook and eye closure at the back of her lace top, swinging her hair to the side. Once it released, she slowly gathered the fabric and drew it over her head, shaking out her hair, liking how his gaze heated as he watched her. This was heady stuff.

"More," he commanded, grabbing the back of his t-shirt and yanking it off, throwing it to the ground.

Oh, good goddess, he was magnificent. She reached out a hand to trace the contours of his pectoral muscles.

"No." He shook his head. "The rest first."

Quickly she freed the waistband of her skirt. Letting it pool at her feet, she stepped out of her clothes. She only wore a bra and panties in stark white. Virginal white. The irony wasn't lost on her, but she didn't consider the humor of it for long. Not when he growled, the sound sending shivers over her exposed skin. This time she shook her head when he reached for her. "You now."

He toed off his boots, popped the button on his jeans, and slid down the zipper.

She swallowed as he dropped his pants, taking his boxers along with them. He was glorious. There wasn't a soft place on him. He was made entirely of muscle like a man who had to physically work hard for his survival every day of his life. A Spartan warrior.

Maybe referring to him as a God was correct after all.

She unclasped her bra, and let it fall to the ground. He didn't move for several moments. His eyes roamed over her, touching on her bracelets at her wrist, his lips lifting into a smile at the tiny bells fastened around her ankle. Slowly, he reached out and traced the chain over her clavicle and down her chest to the medallion that lay between her breasts.

"You are so very lovely," he said, his voice raw as he outlined the curvature of her breast, hefting the weight, and molding it in his palm. He bent his head and his mouth closed over her nipple.

Her eyes shut on a moan and her head fell back. His arm snaked around her back and he pulled her lower body into his as he flicked his tongue over the tip, teasing, until finally he took her fully into his mouth, and sucked hard.

"Oh!" she gasped. Ripples of pleasure started in her core and traveled to her limbs and out to her fingertips. If he kept this up she might orgasm just from his sucking on her breast.

He paid her other nipple equal attention seeming to enjoy the strained sounds that flew from her mouth. The back of his fingers skimmed her stomach, pausing at the emerald suspended from her pierced bellybutton. "You are full of surprises."

"Don't want to be boring." Her voice hitched as his hand moved lower, caressing her hips, teasing as he bypassed her sex and brushed her inner thighs. She had to grab onto his shoulders in order to stay upright.

"That's right, hold onto me, my gazelle, I won't let you fall."

"Why? Why do you call me that?" She gasped as he ventured closer to her heat.

"It originates from the Arabic word, *ghazal*. Legends say that men can die of love-sickness after a single glance from a woman as beautiful as you." He looked deeply into her eyes as though he wanted to drown in them. "You made me feel like that when I saw you from across the room. You remind me of one with your graceful moves and haunting doe-eyes. Even though they are green instead of brown, which in itself is a depiction of all that is womanly and seductive. If I could die, I would like to die of such a thing as love-sickness."

"That's...like poetry."

"Like you, I am more than the motorcycle and leather jacket."

"But you're still a bad boy."

"Most definitely." As if to prove his point, he twisted the waistband of her panties in his fingers. "*These* I have to tear." He ripped through her silk underwear as if parting water and bared her to him completely. Words fled as he picked her up in his arms and laid her gently upon the soft, plush grasses, covering her with his body. "I'm about to show you just how much of a bad boy I am."

Her body trembled and even though she wanted to lock her legs, she spread them instead, creating a cradle for him that he settled into with a groan.

"You are so wet." He rubbed his shaft along her slick folds.

"Please." She braced herself and forced her legs to fall open farther to accommodate his size.

He grabbed one of her legs and draped it over his hip.

"Please," she whispered again. *Let this finally be it. With him.*

He positioned himself at her opening and plunged. Her back arched into a bow as he impaled her in one thrust and her breath strangled in her throat as pain swept through her.

He froze and muttered a curse "You're...*are you*...you haven't...*ever?*"

"No, but it's okay." *Oh dear goddess it hurt.* She closed her eyes and focused on the calming stillness around her, the steadiness of the slowly growing grasses, taking from the balm of the things growing around her to help ease the pain.

"Why didn't you tell me?" he demanded, still seated deeply inside her. He was so deep she couldn't breathe. He raised himself up on his elbows as if to help her.

"Is that a problem?" she asked. He wouldn't *stop* now, would he? "Are you going to be able to finish?"

"Does it *feel* like a problem?" he growled.

"Uh...no." *That* was definitely *not* a problem.

"I just wish you had told me. I could have made it easier for you."

"I-I was worried you wouldn't—"

"Oh, yes, I would. I will. I have." He dragged air into his lungs, the action pushing him farther into her, and pressure started to build as pain receded. "Why have you waited so long?" "I'm not that old," she defended.

"That isn't what I meant. You are a beautiful, enchanting woman. You could have had any number of men to rid you of your virginity, if you so wished it gone."

"I didn't want to...with just anyone." She let the rest of the sentence hang and arched up into him, enjoying the feel, the fullness of him inside her so much more than a few seconds ago. "Can we—"

"*Yes,*" he hissed and started to slowly thrust into her. One hand held her hip, preventing her from arching into him like she wanted to. The other lightly caressed the nub at the top of her sex. "Let me…"

Her blood heated, thickened and her vision went violet as a rush of pleasure bloomed inside her, expanding until it was everything. He was everything. With gentle firmness and teasing, coaxing circles applied with the rough pad of his finger, he slowly and evenly continued with shallow thrusts until she easily accepted all of him. Then he drove harder, heavier, until her gasps were pants and she begged, cried, and convulsed around him. Her stomach muscles cramped almost painfully as she ascended the crest. He held her there suspended for a moment, and then tumbled her over into the abyss.

He went rigid and strained above her, grunting with a mix of surprised thrill and torment. Then he followed helplessly after her, his hot seed pumping into her.

❋ 43 ❧

He gave her a moment to recover. It wasn't enough. For when he rolled her hips toward him and ground into her as though he couldn't hold himself back, it triggered another orgasm. Her cry rose to the tree tops and they curved to cover and seclude them as flowers burst into a riot of blooms around them.

He watched her come apart in his arms, his dark eyes wild on her as though he couldn't look away. When she calmed enough to focus and remember her name he smiled a wickedly naughty smile.

"I thought you were a screaming orgasm kind of woman, and I was right." His tone attempted to lighten the emotionally charged moment.

Gratefully, she followed his lead so she didn't do something stupid like ask for his hand in marriage and offer to bear his children. "You promised me as many as I could take."

"That I did." He flipped over onto his back taking her with him. "Since you are new to this, it would be easier on you if you drove."

He made her scream in orgasm over and over again, but then she made him shout out his pleasure too. The afternoon was spent in leisured exploration of each other. She found that she really enjoyed it when he bit her neck, and rumbled his pet name for her against her lips. But then she also really liked how he moved inside her as though he couldn't get enough. She doubted she'd ever have enough of him.

The sun was kissing the horizon as they lay in each other's arms. She was once again in the driver's seat, draped over his chest. Far off, she thought she heard her name whispered in the wind.

"What time is it?" she asked.

"I don't wear a watch," his voice rumbled under her where she nestled on his chest. "Time is relative anyway."

Relative. Relatives, family, *sisters*. That was Aerin whispering her name. Tierra listened closer hearing Moira's call over the ocean. They were searching for her. "I have to go." She didn't want today to end.

"It seems that all great things in life never last long."

"Can we do this—never mind, forget I asked that."

He sat up with her still straddled over him and cupped her face in his hands. Her hair curtained around them. "I wish we could, but my...business here is brief and I can't take you with me."

"I'm sorry, I shouldn't have—"

He kissed her, telling her with his body what their words couldn't. He released her. "Come on. I'll get you back to town." He lifted her like she was nothing and set her on her feet. He reached for his clothes, and she saw his back for the first time.

A full tattoo that seemed as ancient as time, covered his back. A black figure draped in a robe with a massive feathered wingspan, depicted a fallen angel holding a scythe. Fire and brimstone were layered behind him, and the River Styx flowed at his feet. A haunting skull looked at her from under the hooded robe.

No. Oh goddess, no. Not him.

He couldn't be, but that was the only thing that explained the Grim Reaper tattoo that stirred across his back like it had a life of its own.

He was the Fourth Horseman of the Apocalypse.

Death.

He yanked on his t-shirt, effectively covering the tattoo and breaking her out of the trance. He slipped on his pants and turned back toward her, buttoning his jeans. His smile faded when he caught a look at her face.

"What's your name?" she whispered.

"*Now* you want to know my name?"

Had he known all this time? Had he played her for a fool? Got her alone so he could dispose of her? She'd done *all* that with him, and had basically *begged* him to take her virginity. Gods. How freaking naïve could she be? Apparently more than she'd ever believed.

"Don't joke. Not now," she said. "Do you know who I am?"

An inhuman growl escaped him as he caught on. The sound caused the hair on the back of her neck to rise.

"Don't tell me," he said.

Okay, she wouldn't.

"*Tierra de Moray,*" he rasped out through clenched teeth.

Oh good goddess, her name sounded terrifying coming from lips that were swollen from kissing her.

"Does Death have a name?" she asked.

"Bane. Killian Bane." His lips twisted into a dangerous smile that didn't hold any humor.

"How...appropriate."

"My mother thought so."

He had a mother? Death had a mother? That thought went around and around in her head making her dizzy.

"What happens now?" she asked, afraid she already knew the answer.

"What should have happened before."

She swallowed to try and relieve the lump that had suddenly appeared in her throat. Turns out she was afraid of Death, er dying.

What the hell? Weren't they one and the same? "I don't want to die."

"One of you has to. Pick and it will be done."

Pick? She couldn't pick. "They are my *sisters*." Her family.

"Pick, gazelle," he growled.

"My name is Tierra de Moray and if you touch my sisters I will put you in the ground."

"Do you realize who you are talking to?" He reached for her, and she reacted without thinking, her hands rising up and deflecting him with a simple reflection spell.

He laughed at her attempts. "I've been around for millennia, *my gazelle*. You think that will keep me from you now that I've tasted you?"

Holy shit.

Her heart pounded in her chest and she quickly backed away from him as he stalked toward her. Commanding the willows, roots, and vines from the forest, she beseeched them to come to her aid. They locked around his wrists and ankles holding him in place. He smiled that wicked smile like he knew all her secrets, and she was worried he might.

Just as quickly as the branches and roots had ensnared him, they withered, died, and turned to dust. Breath escaped her body in grief for the plants he'd so easily, thoughtlessly destroyed. Anger and fear merged within her, and the earth trembled under him in response.

His dark-winged brows rose in surprise.

Well if that surprised him, he was going to be freaking amazed by this.

She split open the earth under him and he fell into the crevice she'd created. Swiftly, she buried him and sealed Death in the ground.

❋ 44 ❋

O h shit, she was in trouble.
The world around Tierra went still, not even the breeze stirred. She needed to get out of here.

Who knew if the ground would hold him?

Of course it wouldn't hold him! He was Death. He probably looked at a fresh grave as the ideal vacationing spot.

Ha. I've put Death in a grave.

Grabbing her clothes, she rushed and dressed, tearing the delicate fabric of her skirt. *Now*, she tore her clothes?

She'd been so careful all her life and the one time she'd given in and done something wild and impulsive all hell broke loose.

A hysterical bubble rose in her throat and she felt as though she'd suffocate. That is if she didn't hyperventilate first. She couldn't lose it now. She had to get to her sisters. Had to warn them.

Here, she'd so thoughtlessly believed she could have an afternoon free, and she'd just made everything a lot worse.

Stuffing her torn panties in her purse, her fingers connected with the box of condoms. Condoms she hadn't used.

She froze. How could she have not *used* them?

Think. We're talking Death here, the Grim Reaper, The Destroyer, the Ancient Greek Thanatos—oh good grief—it didn't matter what he was called.

Killian Bane. His name was Killian.

Be rational, Tierra.

He was Death so there was no way anything lived around him for long. That probably covered what she needed to be worried about better than a condom. Unless having sex with him had brought death to her doorstep.

Could losing her virginity have killed her?

Life so wasn't fair.

One last look at the mound of fresh dirt, and she fled on bare feet over the meadow and through the forest toward home, saying a quick blessing and asking for help in guiding her safely and keeping the ground undisturbed for as long as possible.

❧

TIERRA TORE UP THE PORCH AND THE DOOR SWUNG open. Moira took in her wild hair and torn shirt with wide aquamarine eyes.

"Where the hell have you been? And what have you done to yourself? Do you have any idea how worried we've been? You could have called, or picked up *our* call?"

"Gather everyone. Even Aunt Justine. We might need the coven."

"That ain't goin' to happen until you explain yourself, missy." Who was mothering who now?

"Justine isn't here," Aerin said moving to stand beside Moira. Claire stood right behind them in the entryway. "She went to meet with Gwen and said she'd be back later tonight. She wanted to consult with the coven on how to better protect the house against the Horsemen."

"Yeah, about that. We need to talk." Tierra turned, shut the door and locked the deadbolt, adding a ward, and briefly wondered if they should paint lamb's blood above the windows and doors. "Is that a hickey on your neck?" Claire asked. "Have you—"

"—had sex?" Aerin finished.

Tierra's hand flew and covered her neck where Killian had nibbled and bit. He'd marked her. Did that mean something? Her knees trembled and her vision swam.

"You did not!" Moira exclaimed, putting her hands on her hips.

"After all the preaching you did this mornin'?"

"I didn't preach." She never preached. Lectured too much maybe.

"You'd better sit down and tell us what happened." Claire took her arm and directed her to the sofa in the front parlor and sat beside her.

"I slept with Death," she blurted out.

Even though it wasn't late enough for crickets, she swore she could hear them.

"Come again?" Aerin slowly perched on the edge of a blue paisley-printed Queen Anne chair. She reached for her phone that she used like an umbilical cord to her empire, and shut it off. "Are you being literal?"

She nodded, the action jerky. "Please don't make me say it again."

"Did he force you?" Claire asked. "Your skirt is ripped and what happened to your shoes?"

"I'll kill that lowdown, dirty sumbitch!" Moira exclaimed standing in front of the fireplace her legs spread, ready to go to war. "No one touches my sister."

It was too much. Tierra burst into tears, dropping her face into her hands, hiding behind her tangled mane. She'd probably never get a brush through it and would have to cut it off. She didn't want to cut her hair. Like that was the least of her worries.

"There, there, sugar. It ain't that bad, really. I'm sure there are worse...men you could have rolled over for." Moira patted her shoulder.

"I can't think of any," Aerin snarked, then winced at the dirty looks Moira and Claire shot her.

"Let me get you a drink," Claire offered.

"No. No more drinks." One Cardinal Sin was more than enough. Tierra lifted her head, wiped at her tears, and tried to get herself under control.

"Tea, I can make you some tea," Moira suggested, her expression worried. "No angel blossoms, I swear."

Tierra could feel Moira's overwhelming need to help fix her and attempted to reassure her, but the tears flowed faster with the concern and love her sisters directed her way. They'd fought a lot since they'd been reunited, adjusting to their new reality, but they cared for her. Tierra turned into a puddle as sobs escaped her and her shoulders shook.

"Well, shit, that didn't work," Moira said. "One of you two *do* something. Make her stop all that weepin'." Her voice hitched like she was going to join Tierra at any moment if she didn't end her blubbering.

"What happened?" Aerin asked, finding and handing Tierra a box of tissues. "Start from the beginning and tell us everything."

Tierra did through her tears. She told them everything. Well, almost everything. There were some things she wouldn't be able to share even with her sisters. They were too personal.

Silence descended like a heavy blanket when she finished.

Moira was the first to speak. "I'll give you this, when you go for somethin', you do it with gusto."

"I know this is morbid and all—sorry, that was a slip

—but how was your first time?" Claire asked. "Are you... physically okay?"

Remembered pleasure flashed in her mind and regret that she'd never feel like that again settled in like a stone in her stomach. "I'm fine." She would be. A long soak in the tub was definitely in order. She'd be sore from her activities tomorrow as she was feeling them now. "Forget that, how was *he*? Did you have *la petite mort*?" Aerin asked, and then snickered. "Sorry, totally out of line, but *really* this shit doesn't happen every day."

Tierra snorted and grabbed at the steadying bits of humor Aerin offered. Tears were getting her nowhere. "I died over and over again in his arms," she admitted.

They all dissolved into a fit of giggles.

"You had an orgasm your first time?" Moira exclaimed. "I sure as hell didn't. But I guess it wasn't like anyone was fixin' to get their rocks off with Skunk Hurley—"

"*Wait*," Tierra interrupted. "You lost your virginity to a guy named Skunk?"

"Please tell me this wasn't because of a hygiene issue," Aerin said.

"Hell, no. They called him Skunk on account of his tail, but I didn't know that 'til he got up to get a beer."

"You slept with a guy with a tail?" Claire asked. "Is that like a bayou thing?"

"More like a his-ancestors-slept-with-one-too-many-cousins kind of thing," Aerin joked.

"No, it ain't a bayou thing." Moira ignored Aerin, addressing Claire. "What about you, Miss fire-in-your-pants? Did you give it away or make him work for it?"

"I waited. I know, big surprise with all my talk this morning. Tierra, I really hope what I said didn't push you to do something you weren't ready for."

"Honestly, you might have lit a fire under me, so to speak, mainly because with everything happening

around here—" she indicated the house in disrepair "—
I didn't want to die a virgin, and then you went and
mentioned the sexual power thing and I got curious.
Kind of a problem for me, in case you haven't figured
out that about me yet. And then I saw him in *Sirens*. He
was so daring, dangerous, and bold." He'd awakened her
sexuality. "Believe me," she continued. "I was ready for
him, just not ready for, you know...*him*." She had to take
a moment.

"I thought Death would be...less sexy somehow,"
Claire said.

"The rest of the Horsemen are smoking hot, why
wouldn't he be?" Aerin pointed out.

They all nodded in agreement.

Tierra changed the subject. "Tell us, Claire, who was
your first and how was it?" She'd never shared like this
before. Never had close friends. She had Sunny, and
Sunny would give her the moon if she asked her to, but
there was also the employer/employee relationship she
had to consider. Though that didn't seem to bother
Sunny in the slightest.

"Like I said," Claire started. "I waited, held out for
love. But he couldn't handle my fire and my love ended
up destroying him. Like literally destroying him. I
didn't realize what I'd done to him until it was too late.
I thought he was sick, but he started wanting sex all the
time, even though he was wasting away. I couldn't do it,
and then he died. His death certificate said he died
from pancreatic cancer, but I know it was me. I burned
him up from the inside."

Tierra laid her hand over Claire's.

"Well," Aerin said. "Given the choice, I would have
slept with the tail."

"Hey, it could have been worse." Moira knelt down
and sat cross-legged in front of the coffee table.
"Skunk's cousin had three balls."

"I guess if you sleep with enough cousins you're

bound to find your share of tail and testicles." Aerin laughed.

"How'd you lose yours?" Claire asked. "We've all shared. It's your turn."

"I auctioned it off to the highest bidder. What? Don't look at me like that."

"*You* were a prostitute?" Moira asked.

"More like a venture capitalist. You can't call me a prostitute if I only sold it once."

"You sold your ass for money. So technically..." Moira left the sentence hanging.

"Oh, come on, it's a valued commodity," Aerin said. "Why not sell it instead of giving it away?"

"How was it?" Tierra couldn't help asking, finding the conversation fascinating and more eye-opening into the life her sisters had led.

"Eh, okay." Aerin shrugged. "We were both nineteen. He was a geek, adorable actually with his horn-rimmed glasses and pocket protector. Still a turn on for me. Yes, he was the walking stereotype. It was MIT. Now he's a smarter, sexier geek with a wife and three kids. We still exchange Christmas cards and he went on to immortalize me in firmware."

"Don't tell me you're the Aer-in-port?" Claire asked.

"Cool right? Insert slot A into port B and you get O. You know, I miss him every now and then. I was his first, too, so there was a lot of fumbling though we'd both read up on the subject. He was sweet and extremely willing to please. I probably would have stayed with him longer except for the Dr. Who thing. You can only pillow talk that shit for so long."

"So what's the going rate for virginity?" Claire asked. "I feel like I missed the boat."

"I made enough to start my company." Aerin smiled. "You could say it was mutually satisfying for both parties."

"All I got was a chicken," Moira muttered. "She did

supply us with eggs every mornin' until we fried her up for dinner one night. Them was some good eats."

"Tierra, I think you can take something from our experiences," Aerin said. "There is no perfect first time. So you slept with Death. Given the chance I would have fucked the brains out of Pestilence."

"I thought I'd shared something special with Dru." Claire tightened her lips and suddenly flames flared in the fireplace. "It really pisses me off that it was all a carefully created illusion."

"Came close with Nick," Moira said. "And I have to tell you, it was the most satisfying almost-sex I've ever had. I'd like to play with him some more." Her look narrowed to calculating.

Claire shook her head. "We need to get back on track. There's a point we've missed in all of this. Tierra just had sex with Death and that means that all Four Horsemen of the Apocalypso are here in Port Townsend." Claire turned to Tierra. "Where did you leave him?"

"Buried six feet under."

"*What?*" Claire leaned closer. "What did you do?"

"I don't know how I did it." Tierra swallowed the lump that had returned. "I've been able to shake things up before, but when he demanded I pick which one of you to—"

"That motherfucker," Aerin spat.

"—and I just needed him gone, and then he was."

"That'll fix his little red wagon," Moira said.

Aerin nodded her approval. "Well, done, Tierra."

"Let's hope that keeps him for a while." Claire stood. "I suggest we get the book and figure out a way to fortify our defenses. They'll be coming for us and now they are four strong."

"And so are we," Aerin said with a glint in her eye.

$\mathscr{H}$ 45 $\mathscr{H}$

B ane entered the house located deep in the woods.
"You're late." Dru met him at the door and showed him the way to where the other Horsemen were holed up.

"Something came up," Bane growled. He wasn't surprised to enter a fully functioning headquarters/library. Dru had his way about setting up a base, and there was Julian to consider as he always traveled with trunks of books, while Nick needed all his computers and such.

"What have you been doing? Rolling around in the dirt?" Nick brushed Killian's shoulder and bits of soil fell to the Persian rug.

Something like that.

He had to give it to Tierra de Moray. The woman knew how to make a lasting impression. In all his years, he'd never had to dig himself out of the ground before.

"And what's up with meeting here instead of *Sirens?*" Nick continued. "The service here sucks."

"Get your own fucking drink then," Dru said. He handed the glass of scotch meant for Nick to Bane.

He took it and tossed it back, relishing the burn, but not the woodsy aftertaste. He needed something... else...to bury his day.

Bad choice of words.

He headed to the fully stocked bar near the wide windows that looked out over the evergreen forest that were the color of Tierra's eyes. Shit. He reached under the cabinet for the bottle of Patrón. Sharp and bitter. That's what he wanted. Hopefully, the tequila would burn the sweet, earthy, floral taste that Tierra had left in his mouth. Taking the bottle with him, along with a tumbler, he dropped into a seat not giving a shit that he was filthy and probably ruining the fabric.

"Let's hurry this along." He needed a shower and then he would to track Tierra de Moray down. He didn't know what he'd do when he got a hold of her, but it would be epic.

She'd buried him.

Him.

"What happened?" Julian murmured, from where he sat in the large corner chair. He saw more than the others, which was his way. He studied, analyzed, dissected, while Nick and Dru were all about formatting a plan and seeing it through to the bloody end.

The first shot of tequila burned a hole in his gut. "I slept with Tierra de Moray," he ground out through clenched teeth. And he would again if given the opportunity. Somehow, someway, he had to devise a plan for that to happen.

Soon.

"You've been in town *how* long?" Julian asked dryly.

"Apparently long enough," Dru added. "Son of a bitch."

"They are witches, seductresses. We warned you, and yet you *fucked* one of them!" Nick exploded. "*We* can't sleep with them—just have to *kill* one of them—but *you* can?" Nick swore a length of curse words that would make a sailor cringe.

"He's sexually frustrated." Dru took a swig of his fresh Johnny Walker Red. "Moira hung him out to dry."

"And who got his sword stolen?" Nick sneered, lacing fingers over his chest as he stretched and crossed his ankles.

"How long has this been going on?" Bane slid a glance toward Julian who regally sipped his vintage wine.

"The bickering? A while. We all have something we...want...in regard to the witches. They each have a flavor, if you will, that appeals to the man in each of us." He cocked a brow. "Which it seems, is also true for you, brother."

Bane downed another shot of tequila and refilled his glass. At this rate, he'd need more than one bottle to dull his senses, forget this afternoon and how she moved, smelled, came for him. He feared Tierra was etched into his memory forever. "I didn't know who she was," he admitted.

"Like that makes it okay," Nick said.

"Hey, I'm sure he's sorry." The sarcasm was heavy in Dru's tone.

"He looks sorry. Pathetic really. Ever going to explain the dirt?"

"No."

"Let me take a stab at it." Nick leaned forward in his chair. "Tierra de Moray meets Death in a bar. Yeah, the whole town is talking about her leaving on a pale motorcycle that looked like it just arrived from the depths of Hell with some strange, dark man. I'm thinking the two of you got down to *nature*. So did the dirt come after the sex or before?"

"Fuck you," Bane growled.

"Don't you understand what is happening here?" Julian tried to add a voice of reason. "Four of them, four of us, and an attraction that we find nearly impossible to resist. We are being tried by the powers that be. Tested, perhaps."

"Gods, haven't we been tried enough?" Nick fell back in his chair.

Julian slowly gained his feet, elegantly dressed in a suit even though it was the end of the day. Was he wearing an ascot? It did go great with the smoking jacket. The man could have walked out of a London men's club from the eighteen-hundreds. Bane wondered if he owned a pair of jeans.

Julian uncorked another bottle of wine. "It doesn't matter what we feel, humanity is at stake."

"Fuck humanity," Nick grumbled. "Or at least let me fuck Moira. She owes me."

"You really think you can ask to fuck her and get permission?" Dru asked. "Just how much have you had to drink?"

"Not enough. And *he* didn't ask." Nick pointed at Bane. "Next time that witch gets me wet, it won't be with a tidal wave." He paused, looking into the amber liquid of his glass. "*My* witch."

"She isn't your witch," Dru said.

"Like you don't think of Claire as yours," he fired back.

"Leave her out of this," Dru growled and jumped to his feet, his fists clenched at his sides.

"That's just it, you asshole, she's in it, as well as the rest of them. We're all fucked."

"Welcome, brother," Julian murmured to Bane. "Your presence has been in dire need." He indicated the other two with his full glass of wine before retaking his seat. "Did you at least learn anything during this passionate rendezvous with the enemy?"

She's a bewitching woman and a fucking powerful witch.

"We need to find out everything there is to know about them," Bane said. "From where they've been all this time, their strengths and weakness down to what kind of—"

"—panties they wear?" Nick drawled. "In Moira's case that would be none. What'd Tierra have on?"

Virginal white. His heart, which rarely quickened anymore, did so at the memory. He poured another shot of tequila.

"Enough," Julian said. "Bane's right. We need as much information as we can gather."

"On it," Dru said. "I'm already connected with one of the witches in the local coven."

"Keep your distance for now. Don't go off half-cocked or this might be over before it gets started." Bane downed another drink, finally feeling the effects. "I can't see into her soul," he admitted, though it pained him to do so.

Julian nodded as though he wasn't surprised, but then not much surprised his brother. "Aerin is immune to my touch. Moira bested Conquest, and War was out-maneuvered by Claire. So not being able to see Tierra's final destination isn't surprising in the least."

"This whole mess seems out of the realm of possibility." They were four women. Babes really in the continuum of time. How had they opened three of the Seals? They didn't even seem to know what they were doing.

"It will be interesting—when you meet the others—to see if you can ascertain their terminus," Julian mused.

"Or maybe it isn't decided yet if they are going to Heaven or Hell," Nick suggested.

"If we dispose of them before they do irreparable damage, it might be like saving their souls," Julian said, though the sentiment didn't seem to sit well with him. Or maybe his wine had gone to vinegar.

"You *would* be the one to put a heroic touch on killing them." Dru set down his whiskey as though he couldn't stomach the flavor anymore.

"We've all tried to dispatch one or more of them to no avail," Julian said. "They are stronger than even they realize, and we are...divided. Our desire for them is going to drive a wedge between us, and that would be disastrous. Not just for us, but for the entire world."

"What are you saying?" Nick asked.

"They all have to die," Bane finished, seeing the picture so clearly it blinded.

❧ 46 ❧

"According to the Grimoire," Aerin said, "this protection spell requires blueberries, er wait... maybe it says blueberry leaves?" She'd been pouring over the tome since dawn. It was now late afternoon.

"What do you think, Moira?"

Moira had shown a talent for figuring out the scroll pattern of the letters and deciphering the funky spelling. "Blueberry leaves would be my guess." She scratched Cheeto behind his pink ears. "How in the everlovin' hell are blueberries gonna protect anythin'? Are we fixin' to distract them with pie?"

For the ten days, they'd all been cramming, crash studying for a test that would most likely come before they were ready.

Tierra feared they'd never be ready since they had no idea what they were up against or how much to prepare for. She returned to the brew reducing on the stove. It smelled amazing. Cinnamon and apples, pears and ginger. If it wasn't for the bloodroot, it would probably taste as great as it smelled. She made a mental note to rework the protection potion as a fall tonic for the shop. That is...if they were still alive come Halloween.

"Hey, I'm just reading the book." Aerin sat back and

rubbed at her neck. "I don't comprehend this shit any more than you do."

"Blueberry plants are known for their neutralizing benefits," Tierra informed as she stirred the massive pot simmering on the gas stove. "They're great for strengthening the eyes, especially in helping with night blindness. There's documentation that the British fed blueberries to their pilots in World War II. Also they're beneficial for bladder, kidney infections, and acne."

Tierra diced some deeply clefted peaches to represent the female genitalia. The life-affirming powers of the female sex would hopefully counteract the forces of death, which probably wouldn't help all that much now that she'd flashed her genitalia at Death herself. She had to stop thinking of him.

"So what?" Claire said, sharping a knife at the table. She'd given up on the book and had started going more traditional in her choice of weapons. "Blueberries will help us see the Horsemen if they come for us in the dark, and we'll be able to bewitch them with our flawless skin?"

"Don't forget the bladder infections," Moira smirked. "Those burn like the Devil's ass cheeks."

"You grind and powder the dried leaves and sprinkle them around the perimeter of the property." Tierra tried not to take it personally and kept her tone neutral as she tried and explain.

"We don't have time to dry blueberry leaves," Moira said.

"In this heat, they'll dry in hours," Aerin said. "If not, we'll have Claire breathe on them. Will that AC go any higher?"

It was a hot summer's day and the sun shone over the Quimper Peninsula, making it glow like sapphires and emeralds outside the newly replaced windows.

And they were stuck inside, brewing protection spells and heating up an old house that didn't have reliable air conditioning. Tierra vaguely wondered if it wasn't Claire who was heating everything up.

Three of them had their hair restrained. Aerin's was perfectly kept back with a lacquered finish in a top bun that wouldn't dare move. Moira's bounced in a messy ponytail, and Tierra had done everything she could to keep hers in place. Pencils, chopsticks, clips. But the wavy mess continued to work its way free to brush and bother her bare shoulders.

Barefoot in the kitchen, she wore a thin, pink tank top, having disposed of her confining bra hours ago. She was taking pointers from Moira, and instead of her long flowing skirts, she wore a much shorter one that flirted above her knees. Not that it cooled her off any.

Claire's hair fell in shimmering flames around her shoulders, and Tierra's internal thermometer rose just looking at her.

"I'm still for makin' pie," Moira said. "Besides, I thought witches used salt for casting a circle of protection. Ain't that what the chick in Hocus Pocus did? Always did like that movie."

"Me too," Tierra agreed.

"This isn't Disney," Claire pointed out. "No man will come to our rescue. In fact, the men we're attracted to are the bad guys trying to kill us."

"I was more a fan of Witches of Eastwick anyway," Aerin said.

"You would be," Moira said. "Practical Magic is the best, plus it's all about sisters."

They all smiled and nodded in agreement.

"There's like a dozen or more pages dedicated to just protection spells." Aerin stood and rolled her head on her shoulders. "I need a break from this. What do we have to drink? Anything cold."

"I made some raspberry mint tea." Moira set Cheeto down, and he scooted away looking for a shaded spot. She opened the fridge and hung there for a minute in the cool air before pulling out the pitcher and filling four glasses.

Tierra picked up hers and held it to her forehead first, before drinking half of it down. "I don't have any blueberry plants in the garden. They're more wild than domesticated, but there's a patch not far from here."

"In the forest? You can't leave," Claire said, lining up the just sharpened knife with the others she'd honed. "You know that's how the girl always gets it in the movies. Those...men are out there waiting for us to do something stupid like that."

"We've been cooped up in this house for a week and a half now."

Aerin refilled her empty glass. "Nothing has happened."

"Yeah, until you walk out that front door," Claire mumbled.

"I know," Moira suggested. "Have Aunt Justine pick some up on the way home from Ambrosia's."

"She'll be too tired and it will be getting dark. Plus, I'm worried about how much she's filling in at the shop."

"Gwen's helping, along with Sunny." Claire said. "They got this."

"Yeah, but she's getting on in age."

"The old bat is ornery enough to outlive us all," Moira grumbled.

Tierra ignored her while she tended to her brew. "I miss my shop. I miss my customers." But more than anything she missed the freedom of going where she wanted, when she wanted.

Yeah, and the last time you did something you wanted, you slept with Death. Don't forget that.

How could she when all he did was haunt her thoughts? She felt like he watched her now. Glancing out the kitchen window, she spied a raven on a tree branch in the yard. She swore his black, beady eye was trained on her, and shivered.

"I hear that," Aerin said. "What I wouldn't give for a hostile corporate takeover. I need to kick some ass. We can't stay locked up in this house forever. We won't have to worry about the Horsemen killing us. We'll kill each other."

"What if we all go get the blueberry plants?" Moira asked.

"Not really much of a nature girl," Aerin muttered.

"Contact the coven and ask them to bring us some," Claire suggested. "Most likely they'll have some on hand."

"I'd really rather not bring in the coven any more into this than we have to." Tierra turned away from the window, but that didn't stop the sensation of being watched.

"Why not?" Claire asked. "We need all the help we can get."

"Well, I've been thinking." Tierra couldn't believe she was saying this aloud. "I believe there are members in the coven that might have been involved in taking you away."

"And I bet they were instructed to kill us." Claire shrugged and took over researching the Grimoire for Aerin. "Makes sense."

"See, and Aunt Just-for-now was a part of all that," Moira said. "I know she's up to no good."

"Well, shit." Aerin said. "It never stops, does it?"

Shadows started to fall outside, but not the temperature.

"Moira, can you make it rain?" Tierra turned off the flame from under the pot. "Or rain on Claire? It's just too dang hot."

"Sorry, I don't mean to heat things up. I'm ovulating and it seems to...be a side effect."

"You literally go into heat?" Aerin scoffed.

"Something like that. Don't you guys have something like that happen to you?"

"Not that I've noticed, but I'm pretty sure I'm too busy to ovulate," Aerin said.

"Wish I could make it rain on command." Moira leaned toward the book. "My powers seem to be tied to my emotions. Unless there's a recipe in there for storms too?"

"Haven't seen anything yet," Claire said.

"No, shit." Aerin sat and helped Moira with the apples.

To anyone stopping by, the kitchen looked like they were canning fruit. Aerin cut apples in half to expose their seeds in a star shape, which was supposed to deflect evil. Moira then took them from there and pierced the fruit with a darning needle and fishing twine so they could later hang them outside in the yard around the house.

"Whoever that Malcolm de Moray was, he liked his prose."

"Wish the damn thing had a table of contents," Claire said. Suddenly a gust of wind blew through the kitchen and the pages of the book shuffled back and forth, settling with a flourish on a page.

"Whoa." Claire sat back.

"That beats the shit out of Google." Aerin stood and leaned over Claire's shoulder along with Moira. Tierra wiped her hands on a towel and joined them.

"This is interesting." Claire followed the text with her finger. "I think this is a scrying spell."

"Let me see that." Tierra leaned in closer. "I think I've seen that crystal before." She traced the drawing of a crystal.

"Huh, here's an idea." Aerin's gray eyes lit from within. "With this, we might be able to find out where the Horsemen are holed up. The best defense is a good offense. Let's take this to their gates. If anything, it will save us on replacing windows again."

"I don't know if that is a good idea," Tierra hedged. "Isn't there a way we could make peace with them?"

"You put Death in the ground," Aerin pointed out. "Doubt he's going to be reasonable."

"But if we could come to an agreement of some kind?"

"Julian was pretty adamant about it being our fate to destroy each other." Aerin deflated, sitting in her seat and picking up an apple.

"I just don't understand why it's us or them," Tierra continued. It went against her nature to destroy.

"Because they want to kill us," Claire said.

"I don't want to kill anyone." Depression washed over Tierra.

"Just protect us with apples and blueberries," Aerin muttered, popping a slice of apple into her mouth and crunching.

"It sounds stupid when you say it like that," Tierra said.

"I can't lie, all this herb lore seems sketchy," Claire agreed with Aerin. "I'd feel better with more traditional weapons. Dru—War has a sword, and Conquest has a wicked bow and arrow. I want a freaking Smith & Wesson."

"At least a sawed-off shotgun," Moira added. "Someone needs their ass filled with buckshot."

"I can afford to pay for security. I know you think this 'magic' stuff is all good and stuff." Aerin said to Tierra. "But I highly doubt blueberries and whatever it is you're cooking, are going to keep them away." She held up an apple for emphasis. "They are men. Some modern weapons might be a good way to go."

"They aren't ordinary men," Tierra said. "I don't see a bullet doing any damage."

"Yeah, well...fruit probably isn't either," Aerin

pointed out. "So weapons might not kill them, but show me an immortal who isn't slowed down by a flame thrower."

"Y'all quit your bitching and let's find somethin' in that there book to use," Moira said. "Claire, can you toss fireballs? There has to be somethin' in there about using our powers and not just potions and spells."

"Sorry," Tierra said. "I guess, I'm feeling emotional."

"You droppin' an egg into the chute?" Moira asked. "But if Claire heats up, I'd figure flowers would bloom around you."

"Well, I'm bloomed out." She wiped at her brow. "I'm going to go look for that scrying crystal while the potion cools."

She turned and left the room, hearing Moira say to Aerin behind her, "I think you hurt her feelings."

"It's the fucking Apocalypse. If we don't figure a way to tap into our powers when we want to and not when we are pressured, feelings are going to be the least of our worries."

Tierra knew Aerin was right, but she couldn't help these churning emotions.

Nature was all she knew. She didn't know what to do. Maybe her blood sugar was low? Either way, if she didn't cool off and get ahold of herself, she was going to cry.

And she'd cried too much lately.

The attic was even hotter than the kitchen. The air was stale and roasted her lungs as she dragged it in. She knew right where to go, as if the crystal called to her. A copper-metal box huddled beneath some old whatnots in a trunk that had been tucked in the corner. Tierra had seen it years ago, and something had made her return it to the bottom, hiding it under sweaters and old clothes. Her hand went right to the box, and she opened it. The crystal glowed in welcome, and her mood lifted at the beauty of the prism on a long golden chain. Clutching the crystal in her hand, she ran back down the four flights of stairs.

"Here!" she exclaimed. "I knew I'd seen it." She set the crystal in the middle of the table.

"Wow," Moira said, reaching for it. "That's purty, all right."

"It feels really old," Aerin said. "Like ancient. Where was it?"

"In the attic."

"And you just found it?" Claire asked, her brows furling into a frown.

"I suddenly remembered seeing it years ago when I was, you know, shopping for clothes up in the trunks. It, like, called to me."

"Let me see that." Claire held out her hand for the crystal and placed the stone next to the picture with the scrying spell. "This has to be the same crystal used by this Malcolm de Moray. Eerie."

"Seems like we've entered another dimension. Every day is freaky," Moira said.

"And exciting," Claire said. "You have to admit, you feel alive."

"Sure, until we're all dead." Aerin nodded.

"Get me a map." Claire motioned for Tierra. "I'm dying to try this."

Tierra produced a map of the state of Washington, and they cleared off the table. "For some reason, I think you need some mugwort, cinnamon, nutmeg, and yarrow." She gathered the items and sprinkled them over the map. "Okay, go."

"Stand back, in case...well, you know, just in case." The three of them stepped back and Claire repeated the words of the scrying spell. She let the crystal drop from the chain as she held it loosely in her hand.

"Wait!" Moira called, scaring them all into jumping. "Sorry, but what do we do once we find them? And what if they *feel* us find them?"

"There's been no indication that our magic alarms them if they're not in our vicinity," Aerin said, but she didn't look as certain as her tone.

"We don't know that," Moira fired back. "Hell, we don't know anything."

"Well, what do you suggest?" Aerin asked. "Sitting around with our thumbs up our asses and waiting for Death to show on our doorstep looking for revenge?"

"I agree," Claire said. "I'm sick of waiting." Tierra wasn't afraid. She was just plain sick.

"Who do we look for first?" Moira asked.

Aerin pointed to Tierra. "Death. It's all she's thinking about, and he was the last one we came into contact with, so there might be some residual essence or something."

"Hey! That's...well, true, I guess." Tierra rubbed at the butterflies in her stomach. "Go ahead."

"Okay, here goes nothing." Claire held the crystal absolutely still.

"Show us Death."

Moira whispered, "Am I the only one who feels like we should be chanting or somethin'?"

The crystal started in a slow circle over the state of Washington, getting larger and speeding up. Its trajectory closed into a tight, fast spiral, then stabbed its sharp point into the map.

"Never mind," Moira said.

"Where is the bastard?" Aerin asked.

Tierra's stomach churned and her heart thudded in her chest.

"Here. He's here."

❧ 47 ❧

"Wait," Aerin said. "Don't panic. He can't enter the house. We made sure of that with the last spell we did. None of them can."

"He's not in the house," Tierra said. "But we have to get the potion around the perimeter before he destroys my gardens. We need my plants." She had to protect them and couldn't forget how Killian had destroyed the vines and willows she'd tried to restrain him with. No way was he touching her gardens. "Divide the mixture into pitchers," Tierra instructed as she got her wits about her. "Aerin, you and Claire take the front, Moira and I will take the back. Start at the same points, about a hundred yards from the house, and move outward, circling around. We'll meet in the middle. Pour slowly and steady in a thin stream. We only have so much and each drop is precious."

"I think we should—" Aerin started.

"Just do what I said, and don't argue with me. We must protect the gardens."

"And keep Death at the gate." Claire shrugged "What? Someone had to say it."

They distributed the potion in fours and Claire and Aerin went out the front while Moira and Tierra exited through the kitchen beyond the gardens.

It was dark for a summer evening. The sun had set fast, or time had gotten away from them. Tierra glanced around as she and Moira separated from each other, pouring the mixture onto the earth.

She could feel Killian—Death—looming, but she didn't know how and from where. She wished she'd paid more attention to the premonition she'd felt earlier. Could he have been watching her—*them*— all day?

What was he waiting for?

Moving quickly, she poured the concoction as steady as she could with hands that shook. A slight mist rose from the ground and she welcomed power from the earth seeping through her bare feet into her core.

A raven dove from out of nowhere, its black wings flapping in front of her. She gasped, jumped back and dropped the pitcher, spilling the contents at her feet.

Killian Bane manifested from the mist like the Prince of Darkness.

The massive blue-black of his wings spread to the sides and sent dread shooting straight to her bones. This was more of the image she thought of when picturing the Fourth Horsemen of the Apocalypse. Instead of the hooded, silent, scythe-carrying skeleton, he was a fallen angel from Heaven come to carry her off.

"Hello, my gazelle." His raspy voice washed over her in sensual waves, taking her right back to his lovemaking and how he'd called her that in the throes of passion.

Regardless of the heat still simmering in the night, she shivered.

"Your heart is racing. I can hear it."

Yeah, she bet he could. That was probably something Death was really good at, since he would be there to collect when her heart stilled.

"Why are you here?" She struggled to speak, struggled to move, but he held her bewitched. She'd never seen anything like him. He was frightening, yet, so sexy he stole the breath from her body. She wanted to reach out and touch him, trace her fingers through the soft blue-black feathers of his wings, and feel again what it was like to be held by him.

"We know of the preparations you've been making to try and thwart us. They won't work."

"Then why spy on us like a peeping Tom?"

"We are enemies." He raised devilish brows. "Enemies can still want each other. How are you feeling after our—"

"No, don't go there. It didn't happen."

"Want me to remind you of what we did together?"

"Why are you doing this?"

"You haven't been able to stop thinking of me, have you?"

"How am I supposed to do that when you're trying to kill us?"

"I'm not referring to that. I'm referring to you and me, when I took your virginity, when you gave yourself to me."

"Oh, you mean, when I buried you?"

His lips twisted into a smile as though he didn't want to find her fascinating but did in spite of himself.

"Fate might have us destined to destroy each other, but that doesn't mean I want you any less."

"I don't believe in fate," she whispered, her heart quickening at his admission. "You need to leave."

"Do you have any idea what the sight of you does to me? Watching you today, the moisture of your sweat making your clothes cling to your body?" His tone turned dark and dangerous. "I can see your nipples through your top right now. I know how they taste, how they hardened for me, only me. How my tongue can make you scream my name. I can smell your arousal. You want me now."

"No, I don't." She swallowed the lie.

"It wasn't easy climbing out of the grave you put me in," he admitted.

"If you don't leave now, you'll find yourself at the bottom of another one."

Quick as a snake, he reached for her. His hands clamped over her upper arms and he lifted her off the ground. Suspended, she lost her valuable connection to the earth.

"I wondered if that might limit you." His wings wrapped around her, encasing her within his deadly embrace. "How far would I have to fly for you to completely lose your powers?"

"Let me go." She hated the plea in her voice. She'd never been a fan of heights, and maybe this was why.

He groaned as she struggled in his arms. "Don't do that."

Another problem arose and pressed against her belly, and his mouth swooped down and took hers.

The kiss wasn't soft and exploring like the first time he'd kissed her. This one bruised and punished. Yet she softened under the pressure as another darker awareness welcomed him back.

The combination was her undoing.

He held her imprisoned and took her mouth, his tongue diving deep, his hands molding her to his flesh. Just as quickly as he'd kissed her, he tore free, breathing hard.

"Fuck."

Yes, please. *No.* No, she didn't want to sleep with him again. Couldn't. Tears threatened.

"Get your grubby paws off of my sister or I'll pluck you like a chicken!" Moira yelled.

"*Pick*," he snarled. "Just pick one of them and we can be together. This will be over. Not all of you have to die."

He tempted her like the serpent had Eve.

Aerin and Claire ran toward her too. Her sisters

coming to her rescue, yet she could be the reason one of them died. Panic filled her and iced any desire that remained.

"Let her go, you cock-sucking bastard!" Aerin screamed.

He raised his head and glared at her sisters. Then he threw his head back in pain as Claire sprayed him with the potion. Smoke and the smell of burnt flesh billowed up from where the liquid hit him. He released her.

Tierra fell to the ground and immediately linked with Mother Earth.

The rush of power was heady as it swept through her.

"Bury him, Tierra," Moira growled.

Tierra shook the ground under his feet.

"Don't you even think about it," he gritted out through his teeth.

"Then leave."

A black, inky cat suddenly appeared between her and Death. The cat hissed, and Death retreated a step.

"This is not over yet, *gazelle*."

The cat hissed again, arching its back. Its rumbled growl resonated over the still evening. On a curse, Killian Bane reverted back into raven form and flew away.

The four of them stood there in the dark.

Not even the light of the moon helped illuminate the night. She couldn't be the only one questioning what they'd just witnessed.

"What the shit is in this *stuff*?" Claire asked, breaking the quiet. "Forget Smith & Wesson. We need this potion loaded into water pistols."

"No kidding," Aerin said. "If we bottled this we could make a freaking fortune. We could call it, *Death Repellant*."

"A fortune ain't gonna help us in our present situation." Moira helped Tierra stand. "You okay?"

"Yeah, thanks for showing up when you did." She let

out a deep breath. "That was close." Closer than her sisters knew.

"Let's get you inside," Moira said. "We need to cook up some more of this kickass potion."

"I spilled mine," Tierra admitted still stunned. "Sorry."

"You're lucky that's all that happened," Aerin said.

"Hey!" Claire stumbled over the black cat. "Where the hell did this cat come from?"

"I think I conjured it." Tierra held her hand out for the cat.

"Don't touch *it*," Aerin said.

"It scared—well, maybe not *scared* Killian—Death— but he reacted negatively to the cat." The feline in question jumped into Tierra's arms and climbed up to her shoulders where it lay like a stole, purring like a well-tuned machine.

"Huh," Claire said. "Would you look at that?"

"I say we get our asses inside and start another caldron of that shit." Aerin looked around the back yard as if another Horseman might appear at any second. "The sooner the better."

Plus, they needed to find out why her powers reduced when she left the earth. Death knew, which meant the other Horsemen would soon know too. That was a handicap they needed to prevent from happening again.

❧ 48 ❧

"What did you find out?" Julian glanced up from his book-covered desk when Bane entered the library. "What in damnation happened to you?" He stood, his chair scraping back from the large walnut desk.

"You were not supposed to *engage* them."

"I didn't." Well, not *them*. He couldn't stop thinking about *her*.

Julian cursed. "She's bewitched you, hasn't she?"

Bane glanced around, glad to find the room empty besides the two of them.

"Drustan and Nicholas are still out. It's just us, brother. So tell me what happened? You know you can confide in me."

Bane strode to the bar and grabbed the Patrón. They'd have to get more if he kept drinking it like a babe with a bottle.

Julian hissed when he saw Bane's back.

He hadn't looked at it yet, but the wounds hurt like a son of a bitch. He'd dived into the salt water of the Sound to try and neutralize the burning. It had helped, after a fashion. At the first contact of seawater, he'd felt like he'd poured acid on a festering wound.

"What did they do to you?"

"They're witches. They've been *brewing*."

"Not—"

"Worse. Tierra has talent for concocting nasty potions. I don't even think she knows what she's doing or how talented she is. If we don't find a weakness soon and strike, their defenses will be too strong."

"What the fuck happened to you?" Dru said entering the library, Nick following closely behind him.

"Let me guess," Nick said. "Your dick got in the way."

"Doesn't it always?" Dru muttered.

"The witches are getting stronger," Bane admitted, but he didn't share that Tierra was weakened when separated from the earth. It was on the tip of his tongue to impart the information, but he couldn't seem to form the words. He swallowed more Patrón. "They've fortified the perimeter of the house. We won't be able to cross."

"Not even in winged form?" Julian asked.

Bane shook his head.

"There's a cat."

"Ah, shit I hate cats," Nick said.

"Yeah, well this one is a guardian. An old guardian."

Nick cursed again. "Moira with her fire-breathing pig, now there's a cat. Any of the rest of them have a familiar?" He looked at Julian and Dru.

"I didn't see one around Aerin, but that doesn't mean she doesn't have one," Julian said. "You?"

"No." Dru's mouth tightened.

"Well, that's good," Nick said. "They each get their familiars, and their defenses will increase."

"Did you two find out anything?" Bane changed the subject. He took another swallow and welcomed the numbing effects of the tequila as his skin began the painful process of knitting back together. He'd been burned down through the layers of the dermis to the muscle. In a normal man, it would have been crippling and would leave a scar he'd wear to the end of his days. Guess there was something to be thankful for that he wasn't a normal man. It would still take him days to re-generate. Maybe a week for a full recovery.

"They've learned to scry." Silence followed his words.

"They'd need something of ours in order to find us," Julian said.

"I don't think so. They found me, and they didn't have anything of mine."

"Don't tell me all they have to do is *envision* one of us?" Dru asked.

"I'm not sure."

"Well, I couldn't find anything about Moira," Nick said. "Woman doesn't even have a birth certificate."

"Claire has a fire-trail of dead bodies, if you will," Dru said. "So far, I've turned up three who mysteriously died in her presence. But no charges were ever filed."

They looked at Julian. "I'm having issues locating anything about Aerin other than her considerable busi-ness holdings."

"What kind of issues?" Bane asked.

"I think—" Julian looked at Bane "—perhaps, we should focus on a different sister than the ones we've been studying. I found that my concentration is...com-promised."

Did Julian know Bane had a weakness for Tierra? That he wanted her right now more than he wanted to save the world?

Of course he knew. He might be into his books and staying out of the public eye, but the man was too damned observant.

"That's probably a good idea. It might save the world." Bane repeated Nick's line, "Our dicks are get-ting in the way,"

"All right, how do we choose which witch?" Dru asked.

"WHAT HAS BEEN GOING ON HERE?" AUNT JUSTINE strolled into the messy kitchen and dropped her purse on the buffet table. She regarded each of them with displeasure like they were a bunch of teenagers who'd been left alone all night and had thrown a party.

Moira, Claire, and Aerin sat at the table with drinks in front of them. Tierra stood in the kitchen waiting for water to boil for tea and held the cat that had settled into her arms and seemed content to stay there.

The kitchen was trashed from all the potion making, and there was still a lot of cleanup to do. Tierra wondered if there was a spell in the book that magically did house cleaning.

Aunt Justine suddenly gasped and looked as if she'd seen a ghost. Her hand covered her throat and pointed at Tierra. Her jade eyes went wide. "Where'd you get that *cat*?"

"I think I kind of conjured it," Tierra said, petting the black cat in her arms with long strokes. She looked at Claire. "Can we do stuff like that?"

"I don't know. Let's find out." Claire pulled the book toward her. "Grim—what do you think of that for a nickname?" she asked everyone. "Rolls off the tongue better than Grimoire, don't you think?"

"As long as the book doesn't care, call it whatever you want," Aerin said.

"Grim, show me how to conjure," Claire said. The book flipped its pages. "What do you know. 'How to conjure.'"

"Ask and you shall receive," Aerin murmured, picking up her glass of scotch and taking a long sip.

"You don't understand," Aunt Justine said, pointing at the cat in Tierra's arms. "That is no ordinary cat. It was your mother's." The cat in question hissed at Aunt Justine. "I hate that damn cat."

"Obviously, it don't care for you much either." Moira chuckled and weaved in her chair. She'd had a bit too much whiskey already. "That there's a cat with some downright good taste."

The altercation with Death had put them all in the mood for a drink, or four. Pissing off the Reaper of Souls didn't make for a relaxing evening.

"*Wait?*" Aerin asked. "Our mother's? How is that fucking possible? She's been dead twenty-six years. Cats don't live even remotely that long."

"Ask the book," Justine sneered, arching a brow in irritation.

They all looked at the book.

"The cat is in the Grimoire?" Moira asked, scooting her chair back from the table and looking at the kitty. "What kind of voodoo hoodoo is this any-how?" The cat narrowed its eyes at her as if to rein-force the edict. "I've never cared for cats. Too much like women, I tell you. Cuddles one minute and then claws the next." It hissed at her as if it understood what she'd said. "This one strikes me as needing a se-rious attitude adjustment by the way of a squirt bottle."

"She's just protective. She seems to like me fine." Tierra rubbed behind the cat's ear and a loud purr echoed in the room. "See?"

"Legend has it—" Justine started.

"It ain't enough that we got to deal with Four Horsemen and the end of the world." Moira threw up her hands. "Now we have a legendary *feline?*"

"We have a prophecy," Claire said. "Why can't there be a legend about the cat?"

"Next the dead are gonna rise and the seas will boil with blood." Moira huffed. A sudden breeze stirred through the kitchen. "I didn't *mean* for that to happen or *nothin'*," Moira spoke to the ceiling. "I didn't cast no spell, in case anyone's keepin' track."

"You think?" Aerin lifted an artfully sculpted brow, much in the same manner as Aunt Justine.

"Would you like to hear what I have to say?" Justine continued, her lips pursed in a disapproving line. "No discipline. Witches need discipline."

"Fine, whatever," Aerin said. "Just tell us without the lecture." She looked at Tierra. "I see where you get it now."

"Hey!"

"Cats are the guardians of the underworld," Justine said taking the fourth chair around the table.

"I remember watching that in *The Mummy*," Moira said.

"This isn't a *movie*," Aerin said.

"So I've *heard*," Moira returned.

"Would you like to hear this or not?" Justine asked.

"Please, Aunt Justine, continue," Tierra said. "I'd like to know what we are dealing with."

"Pour me a glass of the rose wine?" Justine waited until Claire got up and filled a wine glass from the carafe in the refrigerator. She took a sip, let it sit in her mouth before swallowing, and then began. "It originates with the Celtic lore that cats were the guardians to the gates of the underworld."

"Might come in handy for your deadly boyfriend," Claire pointed out.

"What happened here tonight?" Justine asked.

Aerin caught her up to date with a few sentences, only hitting the high points.

"Obviously, that is why the cat has appeared once again." Justine drained her glass of wine and held it out to Claire for a refill. Claire returned to the fridge and this time brought the wine carafe with her, setting it in front of Justine.

"In Norse mythology, cats are sacred to Freya," Aunt Justine said. "They represent love and peace, and were the original fertility goddesses."

"What's all the crap about cats being the sign of the devil and witchcraft then?" Tierra asked.

"The Christians are responsible for that one. When they tried to establish Christianity as the only religion, they needed to break the pagan cultures. So the Church instigated what resulted in a thousand years of killing cats."

"Oh, poor kitty." Moira reached over to pet the cat, and yanked her hand back as it hissed at her. Moira raised an eyebrow and leaned in, just beyond paw reach. "That hissin' is cute and all, but Cheeto breathes fire, where I come from, cousins are free game."

"Interesting enough," Justine continued as if Moira hadn't spoken. "What brought about the appreciation for cats was the plague. The killing of cats stopped, but after they took care of the mice and the plague was obliterated, the Catholic Church once again began its persecution."

"So you're saying Julian—Pestilence—can be stopped by an ordinary house cat?" Aerin looked skeptical.

"Not stopped. But hindered, yes, as you no doubt witnessed with Death tonight."

"No help for War or Conquest?" Claire asked.

"As far as I've studied, I'm afraid not. I would go out onto a limb and say that the other two men sound more like dog people to me."

"They aren't the only ones." Aerin sneezed.

"Does the cat have a name?" Tierra asked.

"I'm not sure what its first name was," Justine said. "But legend has it that after the third time it came back from the dead the ancestors started viewing the cat as a curse. From there on it was referred to as Jinx. This will be that damn cat's ninth life, the time with your mother being the eighth."

"If the cat—Jinx—is a familiar, I figure since we're witches and all," Claire said, "wouldn't that make it sort of a protector?" At Justine's reluctant nod, she asked, "Then why didn't it protect our mother?"

"Because someone killed the cat first, right?" Aerin answered first.

"Yes. That is what I assumed happened," Justine was quick to add.

"Either that or the cat died because your mother did."

❧ 49 ❧

"You know they're planning something," Claire said looking out the newly fixed windows.

It had been a quiet two weeks. Too quiet. No sign of the Horsemen in town, no attacks, no weird shit. It was...normal, and the longer time went on without anything happening, the more anxious they became.

Tierra made another cup of lavender mint tea.

They'd been brewing potion after potion, and she was exhausted. Claire had ordered squirt guns from the internet, along with water cannons that Tierra didn't know how they were going to utilize. But Claire was in Amazon Warrior mode and if anyone could find a way it would be her.

Aerin was antsy, and Moira was sneaking treats to Jinx. Moira had changed in her thinking toward Jinx once Cheeto took one look at the furry seductress and immediately fell in love. It wasn't often they saw one without the other. Justine avoided both and her four nieces. She'd dived into running the shop, and Sunny had reported that things were going surprisingly well.

The next step in their defense would be to secure Ambrosia's, not only from Nick's farce of a takeover, but from evil entering too. So far, that had been a bit of a problem because it was a public place. To narrow down the evil was difficult. There were many evils in the world.

If they protected against them all, she'd soon go out of business.

After all, there was good and bad in everyone.

Tierra's stomach bubbled, and she feared the stress was getting to her. Slowly she sipped tea, hoping she didn't get sick, but the smells in the kitchen were too strong as Moira cooked lunch.

"What are you cooking?" Tierra asked, needing to know what the vile smell was so she could avoid it in the future.

"Chitlins. Shh... don't let Cheeto know."

"Chit—what?"

"Pig innards. Ain't much to look at, but once you clean them out and fry 'em up—"

"Stop talking." Tierra covered her mouth with her hand.

"Feelin' green at the gills? You've been picky for a while now..." Moira trailed off, her eyes going squinty as she examined Tierra. "I'll be a gator's granny!"

"What?"

"This ain't possible."

"What ain't—isn't—possible?"

"Aerin, Claire! Get your asses in here!" Moira hollered. "You," she said to Tierra, "sit down."

"Gladly." She dropped into a chair near the open window.

Moira turned off the stove and took the pan of what she'd been cooking outside, and returned in hurry.

"What's all the hollering about?" Aerin asked, entering the room wearing a velour track suit that looked way too expensive to work out in.

"We're not under attack again are we?" Claire slid into the kitchen with a water pistol in her hand and one cocked and loaded on her belt. She looked ready for, well, war.

"Y'all better pop a squat," Moira said. "We might have ourselves one helluva big-ass problem."

"What the hell are you talking about?" Aerin asked though she pulled out a chair and sat. Claire did the same, setting her water gun on the table in front of her.

"Now, Tierra." Moira took her hand in both of hers, slowly sitting in the last chair.

"You're scaring me, Moira."

"You're about to get scareder still." She looked deep in Tierra's eyes. "When was the last time you had your monthlies?"

Tierra went dizzy and the vision of her sisters swam in front of her.

"Sorry, I think I'm going be—" She ran to the sink and threw up.

"Oh, fuck," Aerin said.

"No, I *can't* be. *How* can I be?" Tierra's voice went high and shrill.

"It was *one* time," she rasped out. "It was my *first* time."

"All it takes is once," Moira said. "Didn't you ever take sex ed?"

"Didn't you use—"Aerin started.

"No." Tierra moaned. She splashed water on her face and rinsed out her mouth. "Sunny gave me condoms, but things got out of hand and we didn't..."

"I'll say," Aerin muttered.

"Not helpin'," Moira said.

"I think we're jumping to conclusions." Claire stood, gesturing with her hands. "She didn't sleep with a normal man. This is Death we're talking about. He doesn't create life. He takes it, right? So let's all calm down and work this out."

"But she's Earth," Moira pointed out. "The symbol of fertility and life. Maybe that's why the cat really showed up. Didn't Aunt Justine say somethin' about cats being a sign of fertility?"

"Stop, just stop." Tierra motioned with her hands. "I am not pregnant." There she said the word. "I can't be."

"Easy enough to find out," Claire said. "We'll have Aunt Justine bring home a pregnancy test."

"NO!" Tierra yelled. Oh goddess, please no. "*She* can't know...any of this."

"Is that one of the reasons you stayed a virgin for so long?" Aerin asked. "Because of her antiquated ways?"

"Wow, when you rebel, sister, you rebel," Moira said.

"Grim must have a way of telling us if you are pregnant or not." Claire reached for the book.

"First," Aerin said, "are you late?"

Mentally Tierra went through the calendar. "Y-yes." Fear slid up her spine. She went hot and then flashed cold.

"How long?" Claire asked.

"A-about ten days, maybe t-two weeks. I didn't even think." Her hand covered her flat belly.

"Don't *do* that!" Aerin pointed at her, sliding her chair back and getting to her feet. "Don't get attached. We don't even know for sure if you are...you know...and if you are, what are you *pregnant with?*" she finished with.

Tierra blanched.

"That is a valid concern." Claire nodded.

Suddenly Tierra felt too much, everything was too loud, too bright. She crumpled to the floor in a dead faint.

❧

TIERRA WOKE UP OUTSIDE ON THE GRASS. THERE WAS a cold compress over her forehead and her feet were propped up on pillows from the couch in the front parlor.

"She's coming around," Claire said from far off. "Tierra, look at me. That's right, focus."

"What happened?" she asked.

"You keeled over in the kitchen like a board," Moira said. "You're lucky you didn't bust your noggin'."

Jinx jumped up on the porch rail as though to oversee what was going on, her black tail curling along the railing. Cheeto plopped his butt down next to Moira, and a black bat hung from the corner of the eves above Aerin.

All eyes were on Tierra.

"We think we found something," Aerin said, the book laid open on her lap. "You are an earth witch, and therefore you are tied to reproduction—blech—you need to look inside yourself, connect to your uterus—gross—and therefore to the earth."

"I don't want to do this," Tierra said, panic rising.

"We have to know," Claire said. "*You* have to know."

She was right.

Tierra took a deep breath and lifted her feet from the pillows. She set them flat on the ground, doing the same with the palms of her hands. Closing her eyes, she opened her third eye, connecting to the earth.

Bees buzzed and birds sang, leaves rustled, and amongst it all a fragile quickening of life fluttered. Tears gathered and fell from her closed lids. Joy also flooded in. There was life inside her.

"Well, shit," Aerin said.

Tierra opened her eyes. The sun seemed brighter in the azure sky, the green of the trees greener. Everything smelled sweeter.

Moira sat cross-legged on the grass and gathered Cheeto into her arms, kissing his little pink head. "What are we going to do now?"

"Get rid of it!" Aunt Justine yelled, suddenly appearing on the back porch.

Tierra sat up, her head swimming from the action. Moving slower, she covered her belly with her hands. "No."

"I warned you. You spread your legs, and you'll get knocked-up."

"Wow, you grew up listenin' to this tripe," Moira said. "No wonder you were still a virgin."

"You slept with that *man*, didn't you?" Justine screeched, ignoring Moira. "The one you left *Sirens* with. He has friends and they've been asking questions." Her eyes slid to the Grimoire. "They want the book."

"They can't have it." Aerin gathered the Grim to her chest as if that would keep it safe.

"It's just a matter of time now that you let his spawn infiltrate you."

"Again, *wow*," Moira said. "You sure you wasn't a preacher in another life? Cause you sure spread guilt with the best of 'em."

"Just like your mother," Justine continued. "Knocked up by the first man that got under her skirts."

"*What?*" All four of them said at once.

"You know who our *father* is?" Claire asked.

"He didn't stick around long once he knew she was pregnant. Like mother, like daughter," Justine spat.

"All right, let's take a minute," Claire said. "Aunt Justine, why don't you have some wine?" She gestured for Moira to get the wine and for Aerin to get Justine comfortable.

"Right." Aerin jumped up, depositing Grim on the patio chair. "Why don't you sit down before you burst an artery or something?" She hustled Justine into a chair. "We can only deal with one emergency at a time."

"You doing okay?" Claire asked Tierra.

Was she? "It's better being outside."

"I thought so." She smiled at her. "Don't worry, we'll figure this out."

Sure they would.

She was pregnant by a man who carried souls to the

afterworld and who could also change into a raven whenever he wanted. She had no clue what else he could do, or what he might pass on to his child.

Her child.

Moira returned with a tray loaded with iced raspberry mint tea for them and wine for Aunt Justine. Something swirled in the wine, and Moira smiled under her brows at Tierra.

Cheeto's spit.

Should she warn her? It was too late as Justine picked up the wine and drank down the whole glass, pouring herself another from the bottle Moira had brought.

"My, that is refreshing." Justine smiled.

"Attitude adjustment," Moira whispered, retaking her seat crossed-legged next to Tierra.

"How much did Cheeto donate?" Tierra asked.

"So much so, she'll probably go comatose." They shared a look and then giggled.

"Good to see you girls getting along so well," Aunt Justine said.

"What?" Aerin started and then clammed up when Moira shook her head. She cleared her throat. "You were going to tell us what you know about our father."

"That's right. Your mother was so in love with him. I only met him the one time. He left right after the earthquake in 1990."

"Was our mother sad?" Tierra asked.

"She always got a bittersweet look on her face when she talked about him, which she did often to her belly. Strange that, I always thought."

"What did she say about him?" Claire prompted.

"Impossible things, like she'd conjured him and he'd suddenly appeared, stepping through the Standing Stones."

"Standing Stones?" Aerin asked.

"Yes, it was where you were born, and where she

eventually died." Justine's tone turned sour at the memory.

"Have some more wine." Aerin poured her another glass.

"Thank you, dear. You're not nearly as bitchy as I first thought you were."

Moira laughed and quickly covered it with a cough.

"Where was I? Oh yes, the Standing Stones. They are a sacred place, but stay away from them. The magic that residence in the stones is very powerful. Too powerful for you four."

They slid glances at each other.

$$\maltese \quad 50 \quad \maltese$$

"Y‌ou know where we're headed, right?" Claire regarded the three of them with a wicked smile.

They'd poured Aunt Justine into bed and now sat huddled around the kitchen table. Evening had seeped silently in.

"Mom died there," Tierra said. "We were born there. Answers are hidden there in the ground. I can feel them, but we need to know more about these Standing Stones before we go off half-cocked." There had been too much of that lately. And low and behold, she was the worst offender. Her hand slid to her belly and hovered over what was quickening inside her right now.

More than ever, she needed answers.

"We don't leave the sanctuary of this house without a solid protection plan," Tierra continued. "Weapons, spells, potions, all of it. You know they're waiting for us to do something like this."

"Look at Miss Bossy pants takin' over," Moira said. "I like it, and I agree. No goin' off half-cock—"

"Always full-cocked," Aerin added. "That's my motto."

"And loaded." Claire snickered. "Hell, I need to get out of here and *do* something."

"So where do you think these Standing Stones are?" Aerin asked Tierra.

"I don't know. I think—"

"You mean to say you've lived here all your life," Aerin interrupted, "and you've never found huge magical rocks? The peninsula isn't that big."

"Apparently it is, because I don't have a clue where they are. I've hiked all over the peninsula, and I've never seen or heard of these Standing Stones. But...I think I can find them." She didn't know why, but she felt a certain pull and could only assume it was Mother Earth whispering to her. "I need the map."

Claire produced it and they spread it out over the table. Claire also provided the crystal. "Here, you scry."

Tierra took the crystal in her hand, feeling the warmth of it against her palm. "How?"

"I'm not sure," Claire said. "I have no idea how it worked the last time. Maybe just put the thought in your head and see what happens. We have nothing to lose." She shrugged. "At least on this."

Tierra closed her eyes and brought into mind the forests, the trees, the meadows. A vision of a place high on the cliffs that overlooked the ocean and butted up against trees came into focus. Stones as tall as she, some taller, stood as sentries in a circle and gleamed like bones in the moonlight. She dropped the crystal and let it hang from the chain that she lightly held between her fingertips. When it thunked on the map, she opened her eyes. "The west side of the peninsula at Siren's Cry."

"Siren's Cry?" Aerin asked.

"The constant mist shrouding the area appears to weep, and the wind whistles around the cliffs, making this haunting sound as if a woman is crying..."

"Our mother crying?" Claire said. They looked at her horrified. "You were all thinking it too."

"Damned if that ain't sadder than kickin' a three-legged puppy," Moira whispered.

"It's supposed to be haunted," Tierra said. "No one goes there. The last teenagers who attempted came back with horror stories."

"You've never thought about investigating?" Aerin asked.

"Not until now. I always got this feeling of overwhelming sadness and pain. I-I just couldn't venture up there. But now..."

"We have to go," Aerin said.

"Yes." Tierra nodded.

"Tonight?" Claire asked. "Or should we wait until morning?"

"Tonight. Something, no, *someone* waits for us." Tierra's eyes widened as the words came out of her mouth.

Claire took her hand. "I feel it, too."

"It's decided then," Aerin said. "We go."

They all nodded.

"Let me get my shoes!" Moira hollered already turning and rushing out of the room.

"And the squirt guns." Claire left for the formal dining room that she'd turned into a weapons garage.

Aerin glanced down at her velour workout clothes. "I'd better change. Do you have any hiking boots or something without a high heel?"

"Come on." They went upstairs to Tierra's room.

"Wow, this is a lot of color," Aerin said as she entered.

"What's wrong with color?"

"Nothing. It's just a lot, that's all."

Tierra handed Aerin a well-worn pair of hiking boots. "Here. Try these, and maybe wear some jeans. Do you have jeans?"

"Sure I do. I bought this amazing pair in Italy."

"You attached to them?"

"No more than I am to any of my clothes. They can be replaced." Aerin turned to go, but stopped. "You okay with this?" She pointed to Tierra's middle.

"No."

"There are ways to—"

"No."

Aerin nodded. "Too early to talk about it and not the right time. Just know that we're here for you. I'm here for you."

"Thanks, Aerin."

"I'll see you downstairs." She closed the door behind her.

Tierra turned to the full-length mirror standing in the corner. Multihued scarves were draped forgotten over the frame. She gathered them up and tossed them on the bed in order to see her reflection better.

She looked pale, but then she'd had a shock, one she didn't know how to deal with. She unbuttoned the vintage lace vest and discarded the smoky blue camisole underneath. Cupping her breasts, she was surprised how sensitive and full they felt. She moved her hands down to her stomach. It was concave, flat with a hint of underlying muscle. Not ripped, but not bad. She traced the belly-button ring.

An emerald, the sacred stone of Aphrodite infused with the powers of healing, love and luck. She'd have to go with unlucky in love right now. The stone was also supposed to be a symbol of fertility and she'd gone ahead and pierced it over her heart chakra. Years ago she'd chosen it because she liked the color, as it reminded her of the forests she loved and the stone embodied the energy of nature. But could it have had a part in the child growing inside her?

How did one explain conceiving a child with Death?

What would he say? What would he *do*?

"*Tierra?*" Claire yelled up the stairs. "You ready?"

"Coming!" She couldn't deal with any of this now. She had time. Well, a little less than eight months thereabouts. She yanked her camisole back on and pulled over a long-sleeved sweater. Sliding her feet into another pair of hiking boots, she left on her cotton floral skirt knowing she'd move better in the loose comfortable fabric if she needed to. Jeans were just too restrictive for her.

She added bracelets of protection crystals against evil and black magic. Agate, garnet, and black tourmaline. Jinx meowed behind her where she'd curled up on the scarves. Tierra scooped up the cat's eye crystal, too, and then the jasper at the last minute. Jasper was protection during childbirth, but it should help while pregnant too, right? Wouldn't hurt.

She hurried and joined her sisters in the kitchen.

"Let's blow this crab shack," Moira said, antsy in her flip-flops.

"*Those* are what you're wearing to go hiking in the forest?" Aerin asked. "*At night?*"

"My thongs work fine for the bayou. Why would the forests 'round here be any more different? No gators."

"Fine." Aerin shook her head, but a smile teased her lips. "But grab a jacket, would you?"

"I got a hoodie." Moira held up the thin jersey.

"I need to take you shopping," Aerin mumbled.

"Why are you carryin' a broom? You plannin' on sweepin' some pine needles?"

"It's something I've been working on." Aerin smiled. "You'll see."

"All right, here we go," Claire came into the room loaded for bear. "I converted these military vests. It'll make the guns easier to carry and there's room for a back-up weapon, or three or four, maybe more." She pulled out a kitchen torch from the breast pocket of hers. "I'm still hit and miss on conjuring fire on command, but this way I have a flame to build on. Aerin you can blow my flame—"

"You got it."

"—and increase whatever storm Moira can stir up."

"Been workin' on that too." Moira slipped on the

vest, holstered her squirt gun, and picked up one of the water cannons and held it across her chest. "I feel like freakin' Rambo."

"What about Grim?" Tierra asked. "Should we take the book? We might need the spells if we get into trouble."

"We'd better leave it in case for that exact reason," Claire said. "If the book falls into the wrong hands—"

"It'll be grim?" Tierra said sheepishly. "Sorry, getting a little nervous."

"Grim's better protected here with the wards." Claire looked at them all. "We ready?"

"Ready," they said in unison.

Single-file they traipsed out of the kitchen. At the last minute, Tierra grabbed the scrying crystal, looped the chain over her neck, and tucked it under her sweater to rest between her breasts. She didn't take the map, and didn't question why she needed the crystal.

They ventured out into the night, the sky clear with a large solstice moon silhouetting the landscape.

51

"Let's ride," Dru said, his sword in hand. "Gwen from the coven called. The witches are on the move."

"Finally," Nick said. "Some action." He jumped up and grabbed his bow and quiver full of arrows.

"Where are they headed?" Julian asked, reaching for his trench coat and slipping it on.

"West of town, in a place she referred to as the Siren's Cry. Apparently Port Townsend has Standing Stones."

"Of course it does," Bane murmured. This place seemed as full of magic as the old country. Maybe even more.

"Horses then?" Nick said with relish.

"Yes, gather the horses." Julian shared Nick's smile. Julian hadn't adjusted well to motorized transportation and loved it when their spirit horses were called into service.

"We got a plan?" Nick asked.

"Yeah, stop them," Dru said.

"Good plan." Nick nodded. "I like it."

"Remember we need to stay focused," Julian said, looking at Bane.

"Humanity is at stake. We must do everything we

can to stop the Apocalypse from happening. No matter what the cost."

It wasn't like they hadn't done this before. They didn't need a freaking pep talk. "Would you shut the fuck up?"

"No need to be uncivilized, brother."

It wasn't lost on Bane that Julian left his gloves behind. Yeah, yeah, whatever. "There is nothing civilized about who we are," Bane growled.

"Enough bitching," Nick said. "Let's do this thing."

Their horses waited for them outside, prancing and nickering to run. War's steed was a rich, red chestnut with hooves that pounded the ground with excitement. While Conquest's, Magnus Rex, gleamed white in the moonlight and stood at the ready to be commanded. Archimedes, Julian's stallion, absorbed all the light around him, black as the deepest darkest place of hell, with a devilish attitude to match.

Death rode a pale horse.

Bane had never named him in all these years. Having seen so much death and sorrow, he hadn't wanted to get attached.

If he didn't care, there'd be no cause for grief.

The horse looked at Bane as though he understood. He welcomed him with a whinny that sounded much the same as his purr when in motorcycle form. Patiently he waited for Bane to mount.

Dru swung onto the back of his warhorse, brandishing his sword into the air. His horse arched up on his hind legs and led the charge.

"Such a fucking showoff," Nick said, as he reared his horse and spun Magnus in a tight circle before galloping off after Dru with a battle cry of his own.

"Shall we, brother?" Julian regarded him with concern, holding back an impatient Archimedes.

"This ends now," Bane said, giving the horse his head.

Tierra de Moray would no longer haunt him after tonight.

⁂

"You weren't kidding about the stones being haunted," Moira whispered. "I feel like I got ghosts usin' me for toilet paper."

"It's the mist," Aerin breathed.

"No, it isn't," Tierra said. "There's someone in there." Goose bumps rose on her skin as awareness of something—*someone*—made herself known.

"She's right," Claire said. "She's standing to the side of the tallest stone. Do you see her now?"

"Uh...I think so," Aerin said. "Holy Jesus."

"Uncle Sal told me never to talk to strangers," Moira said. "'Specially ones that might be dead. We ain't goin' in there, are we?"

"Yes, we are." Tierra stepped through the Standing Stones, her breath catching at the power that tingled and caressed her skin. It was almost painful, in an over sensory type of way, as the Stones allowed her entrance.

"*Tierra!*" Moira cautioned. "Well, shit. Here goes nothing."

"I can't believe I'm doing this," Aerin muttered, following Moira into the circle.

"Me, either," Claire said. "But what the hell? You only live once."

"I don't want that once to end tonight," Aerin said under her breath.

The four of them stood abreast of each other as an apparition glided over the glistening, mist-painted wildflowers. She was dressed in shimmering veils, her hair long and black flowing around her in shadowy waves. Her eyes were a startling sapphire blue.

"*Hello, my lovely daughters.*"

"Daughters?" Moira whispered.

"Listen to me, and heed my words."

"Wait," Aerin started.

Tierra grabbed her hand to silence her. "Shh, she isn't here. Now. She was when she left this message for us." She didn't know how she knew this, but she did.

Mirelle de Moray continued like an echo from the past that had lain dormant until the four of them had crossed over the threshold into the Standing Stone's shielded circle.

"I believe that life is made of choices and not dictated by fate. You came from me and your father. Created by a great love. A love like that doesn't produce evil no matter what anyone else says or what was prophesied a millennia ago.

"Know that you were wanted, that your father and I loved you all very much. We believe you will make the right choices. You are not the harbinger destined to bring about the end of the world. You come from a long line of powerful witches, and your father was one of the last Druids to walk the earth. The power is within you to destroy, but you don't have to choose to do so.

"Study the Grimoire, learn from it, and whatever you do, don't open the Seals.

Don't release the Horsemen—"

"Oops," Aerin said.

"Love and treasure each other as your father and I treasured you." Her eyes rested on each of them almost as if she really saw them in that moment and was not a missive from the past. A bittersweet smile appeared on her lips and she reached her hand out to them. *"Blessed be, my daughters."*

"No, don't go!" Tierra rushed forward, her hand outstretched to touch her, but she was gone.

Only the mist remained.

"*No!*" Tierra cried. She swiveled around the circle searching. Desperation and the need for a mother's embrace, for advice, choked her. She was alone but for her sisters.

Her wild gaze settled on the women before her. They were her mirror images. Part of her, her blood, her family. Elements of her mother.

"This isn't *fair*." The ground trembled under her feet.

"Tierra, this isn't the place to shake things up." Aerin looked around them to the Standing Stones. "Let's relax, and we'll talk this through. Whatever that was."

"I don't want to talk. I want my mother." Tears clogged her throat and flooded her eyes. "I'm going to be *one,* and I need *her*."

"You've got us, sugar," Moira said, reaching for her.

"No. Don't touch me." Tierra stepped back and wrapped her arms around her middle. "I just have to—"

She had to get herself under control. Everything was wrong. How they were taken from their mother, separated from each other, their mother killed all because of a goddamned prophecy?

"Damn it, she's right!" Aerin said, her voice breaking. "This *isn't* fair. We never asked for this." The air started to whip. "Since the moment I was born, I've had to fight for everything. Why do I need to battle some biblical Horsemen for my life?"

"We've all had to fight," Claire muttered, fire flaming in her eyes.

"And for what?" Moira added, the mist getting heavier, sharper as Aerin's wind swirled. "To spend the rest of our lives lookin' over our shoulders for Death to steal our souls and deliver them to Hell? Well, he can't have mine."

"No, he can't," Conquest said, riding forward into the stones on a white horse, an arrow notched in his bow. "Your soul belongs to me." He let the arrow fly.

Tierra reacted, didn't even think. The ground beneath them quaked in earnest, spooking the horse. He reared, causing the arrow to change its path.

Pain punched into her, and Tierra stumbled back.

Her sisters' screams spun around her in a dizzying vortex. Everything turned sluggish. Moira twisted toward Conquest and water rained down on him. Claire drew her weapons and shot at Dru while Aerin took her broom and twirled it, causing a wind tunnel that enveloped Julian.

Slowly Tierra looked down at her chest and the arrow that protruded from her sternum. She opened her mouth to shout, to cry, but only air escaped—the sound a death rattle as it bubbled out of her. She couldn't breathe. Everything hurt and it felt as though she was drowning.

Her knees buckled and she dropped to the ground. Crumbling backward, her hand covered her belly, and she silently conveyed an apology to her unborn baby.

A baby who never stood a chance.

Not with Death for a father and a witch for mother.

Darkness blurred the edges of her vision, and her gaze searched and connected with Death's. He'd take her now, and her sisters would be safe.

He observed her from atop his pale horse, his black eyes unblinking, his jaw set in a resolute line.

❧

BANE WATCHED TIERRA DIE.

He could see her soul now, and it was the most complicated, beautiful, dangerous thing he'd ever viewed. It stole his breath. He still couldn't perceive where she was to be delivered, but that would come once he had her.

Chaos erupted around him. One sister was engaged in battle with Nick, who was probably going to drown —someone should help him. Dru had been thrown from his horse, and had been smoked by Claire with what smelled like the same concoction they'd splashed him with weeks ago.

Aerin blew Julian somewhere and rushed to Tierra's side, her hands hovering above her body as though she didn't know where to touch, to help. Tears streamed down her face and orders for Tierra not to die came furiously from her mouth.

There was no help to give. She'd die tonight.

The threat of the Apocalypse would be over and humanity would be saved by the forfeit of one witch's soul.

Fuck.

Her emerald eyes stayed locked on his and he did her the honor of not looking away. He shouldn't care. He didn't care. It was just another day in an endless sea of days.

In time, he'd forget her.

Another much smaller soul joined with hers. Tiny, new, precious.

There were *two* souls, not one.

His heart thumped painfully in his chest.

How...could it be?

She was pregnant *with his child*.

He didn't question the facts. He knew the truth. Somehow he recognized the cherished soul of the unborn babe as his.

"*Stop!*" His voice thundered over the night and caused everyone to pause and look. He vaulted from his horse and ran flat out for Tierra.

"Save her!"

Save my child.

"What the shit?" Nick yelled, wiping water from his face.

"No, Bane!" Julian warned. "Let her die. Leave her be."

"*She's pregnant.*" He skidded to a stop at Tierra's side.

"How?" Aerin beseeched him with wet eyes. "Tell me how to save her."

"I don't know how! You're the *witch*. But so help me God, you don't save her and I will kill you myself and the place I deliver your soul to will leave you writhing in pain for eternity."

"Bane, don't do this," Julian said.

He stole a look at Julian, letting him see how unwavering he was.

Julian's fist clenched as though he wanted to reach out and touch Tierra. Nick notched another arrow, and Dru raised his sword.

"Did you not *hear* me?" Death roared through clenched teeth, his rage and fear releasing his beast. "She's with child. *My child*."

"Well, fuck," Dru muttered, lowering his sword.

Nick put away his bow and arrow. "Yeah, that's a serious game changer."

The other two witches knelt on each side of Aerin. Moira smoothed Tierra's brow, and Claire clutched the hand not covering protectively over her abdomen.

Moira closed her eyes. "Her lung is punctured. She's drownin' in her own blood. Maybe I can reroute it?"

"Blood!" Claire exclaimed. "That's it! That's the answer." She grabbed the arrow where it protruded from Tierra's chest. "I hope you forgive me for this someday." She yanked the arrow free. Tierra's body arched from the action, but nothing more than a wet gurgle escaped her. Her eyelids slid closed.

"*Oh, God, what did you do?*" Aerin covered the wound that bubbled over with blood, compressing her chest.

"You have to hurry. She's almost..." They were ready. Both souls— one precious, one enchanting—hovered, waiting for him. He couldn't look, once he'd connected with them, they'd be his to deliver.

"Let her blood spill into the earth." Claire took the arrow and cut her palm. "Here, now you."

"Do you know what you're doing?" Aerin paused.

"I think so. I hope so."

"You'd better," Bane growled. He'd kill every last one of them if they let her die.

Aerin looked at Julian, who slowly shook his head. She glanced back down at Tierra, and then took the arrow from Claire, slicing open her palm.

Julian turned and strode out of the Standing Stones, and Aerin passed the arrow to Moira who copied their actions.

"*Hurry*," Bane snarled.

Claire started to chant, mixing their blood in with Tierra's and the earth's rich fertile soil. The sisters repeated each word until they were all in unison, their voices lyrical as midnight lingered longer on this summer solstice.

Christ, they were learning fast.

> *"Goddess of souls, hear our plea*
> *Do not forsake this beloved sister—who beckons*
> *Set this mother and child free*
> *As payment for blood spilt today and for what was stolen,*
> *By earth, air, fire, and sea..."*

THEY REPEATED THE CHANT UNTIL THE AIR WHIPPED, fire burned, and the sea crashed against the cliffs in her fury.

And Earth released her hold of the dead.

In the Standing Stones, where the sisters' tragedy and a mother's sacrifice had already been taken, the four born of one opened Death's Seal.

❧ 52 ❧

S he'd died.

Tierra closed her eyes and let the water from the shower wash over her and hopefully rinse the memories away as easily as it had the blood.

Her soul—and that of her unborn child—had stood beside Killian as he'd barked at her sisters to save her.

Why didn't he take my soul?

The repercussions of his actions had to be dire. The actions of her sisters had epic consequences.

Why would he allow that?

She wished she could ask him, but there had been no sign of any of the Horsemen once the Fourth Seal had been opened and the spell had ejected the men from the stones.

Four of the Seven Seals were now open. Each of the Four Horsemen of the Apocalypse now called into service.

"You doin' okay in there?" Moira asked from the other side of the door.

"Fine," Tierra lied. Would she ever be fine again?

"Give a holler if you need anything. I'm right outside the door."

Moira had shadowed Tierra since she'd risen from the ground and gasped her first breath.

Tierra shut off the water and stepped out of the shower. Vapor covered the mirror, and she took a towel and wiped it off. Bracing herself, she looked at the scar that bisected her breasts.

There was nothing there but pink flesh, which looked a little irritated, but would clear up in a day if not hours. She moved aside the crystal she hadn't taken off and touched the area with her fingertips, feeling for a puncture wound or indentation in her sternum. The remembered pain of the arrow piercing her would probably remain until she died.

Maybe not the best analogy.

The area was sore, but that was all. There was nothing that marred her skin. No evidence that she'd been shot by Conquest's arrow.

Nothing.

Picking up the crystal, Tierra examined it. There was a fracture along the two-inch length that hadn't been there before. She knew the arrow had hit it, deflecting the deadly point from piercing her heart and allowing her sisters precious time to save her.

"Thank you," she whispered, hoping the man who'd fashioned this crystal might have known how important it was to her now.

Dressing in a soft, white cotton shift, she brushed her teeth, and did the normal things people do before heading to bed. But everything was different now, and the preparations seemed weird with the reality of what they'd done tonight replaying in her mind.

She opened the bathroom door and entered her bedroom. Aerin and Claire were reclined against the pillows on her bed. Claire stroked a purring Jinx, while Moira stood in the middle of the room, ringing her hands.

She rushed toward Tierra. "You're sure you're okay, sugar? Here, sit awhile." She guided her to the antique makeup desk with the oval mirror above.

"I'm fine, Moira, really."

"You sit still and hush." She pushed Tierra into the chair. "You lost more blood than a sow in the slaughterhouse."

"You kept most of it in my body." Tierra covered Moira's hand where it rested on her shoulder. "Thank you for saving my life."

"You took Conquest's arrow that was meant for me." Her eyes stormed for a second and then she tried to shrug it off. "And hey, it's nice knowin' I don't have to sleep with someone in order to help in healin' them."

Tierra gave a short laugh.

"You really feel okay?" Aerin asked.

"Good as new."

"The baby?" Claire asked.

"Fine." As far as she knew.

Moira picked up a brush and started to untangle Tierra's wet hair. "Wow, it's like a—"

"Don't say miracle," Aerin interrupted. "That word always makes me nervous. *That* wasn't a miracle. That was something...more." She looked at Claire. "By the way, wicked-ass spell. How did you come up with that?"

Claire gave a slight shake of her head, and the three of them shared a look.

"What?" Tierra asked, watching their reflections in the mirror.

"You've been through a lot," Claire started. "We can talk about it tomorrow."

"It is tomorrow," Tierra said. Morning had yet to steal over the blood moon that had appeared after the spell, but it was only a few hours off.

"Grim," Aerin admitted. "He's missing."

"Someone stole the book?" Moira pushed her back onto the chair and continued to brush her hair.

"Yeah, and before you ask, we checked on Aunt Justine," Claire said. "She's sleeping like the dead—sorry—

not the dead, but rather like someone who had too much to drink."

"Sawin' logs like a lumberjack." Moira said. "I thought for sure she'd done it."

"How'd they get past the wards?"

"We don't know yet," Claire said. "But we have to pick our battles. We won a huge one tonight."

"No, we didn't." Tierra shook her head, her hair pulling in Moira's hands. "We did what our mother told us *not* to do."

"We saved you," Aerin said. "No one died tonight. That's a win. The other stuff will be dealt with."

"I have a question." Moira brushed long strokes through Tierra's wet hair, the action more soothing than she'd imagined.

Tierra never had anyone brush her hair. Couldn't remember Aunt Justine doing it when she was a child. Aunt Justine had kept Tierra's hair short so that she didn't have to unknot the tangles. It wasn't until Tierra was in elementary school that she'd refused Aunt Justine's wicked scissors.

"Conquest has his arrows," Moira continued. "War has his sword."

"I still want that back," Claire said. "You should have felt how honed and balanced the blade was. Never have I held such a weapon."

"Ha, I bet," Aerin tried to lighten the subject matter with a joke. It didn't work.

"Pestilence has his weights and measures," Moira continued. "But what does Death have?"

"According to Revelations—yes, I've been reading the Bible," Aerin said, "he brings Hell, and there is something about beasts of the earth that I don't get. I wish we still had the Grimoire to look over the prophecy more clearly."

Tierra caught a flash of blue-black wings outside her

window. A raven was perched on the pine branch just outside of the circle, watching her.

"I think we're going to need something stronger than potions," Tierra said, her gaze connecting with Death's raven-black eyes.

"I agree," Aerin said.

Claire stretched and yawned. "Yeah, well, we'd better get some sleep, because if what Aerin said is true, tomorrow is going to be Hell." She had no idea how right she was.

ABOUT CYNTHIA

Cynthia St. Aubin wrote her first play at age eight and made her brothers perform it for the admission price of gum wrappers. A steal, considering she provided the wrappers in advance. Though her early work debuted to mixed reviews, she never quite gave up on the writing thing, even while earning a mostly useless master's degree in art history and taking her turn as a cube monkey in the corporate warren.

Because the voices in her head kept talking to her, and they discourage drinking at work, she started writing instead. When she's not standing in front of the fridge eating cheese, she's hard at work figuring out which mythological, art historical, or paranormal friends to play with next. She lives in Colorado with the love of her life and three surly cats.

Cynthia loves to hear from readers.

Visit her: http://www.cynthiastaubin.com/
Email her: cynthiastaubin@gmail.com

ABOUT CINDY

Amazon bestselling author Cindy Stark lives in a small town shadowed by the Rocky Mountains with a kindle of kitties, working her way toward official Cat Lady status. She writes fun, witch cozy mysteries, emotional romantic suspense, and sexy contemporary romance. She loves to hear from readers!

Cindy loves to hear from readers.
Visit her: www.CindyStark.com
Email her: CindyStark19@gmail.com

ABOUT KERRIGAN

Kerrigan Byrne is the USA Today Bestselling and award winning author of several novels in both the romance and mystery genre.

She lives on the Olympic Peninsula in Washington with her wonderful husband and Willow the Writer Dog. When she's not writing and researching, you'll find her on the beach, kayaking, or on land eating, drinking, shopping, and attending live comedy, ballet, or too many movies.

Kerrigan loves to hear from her readers! To contact her or learn more about her books, please visit her sites:

Kerrigan loves to hear from readers.
Visit her: www.kerriganbyrne.com

ABOUT TIFFINIE

USA Today Bestselling Author Tiffinie Helmer is always up for a gripping adventure. Raised in Alaska, she was dragged "Outside" by her husband, but escapes the lower forty-eight and returns to her beloved Alaska every chance she gets.

A mother of four, Tiffinie divides her time between enjoying her family, throwing her acclaimed pottery, and writing of flawed characters in unique and severe situations.

Tiffinie loves to hear from readers.
Visit her: http://tiffiniehelmer.com/
Email her: Tiffinie@TiffinieHelmer.com